NEVERLAND

Also by Shari Arnold

KATE TRIUMPH

NEVERLAND

Shari Arnold

ISBN 9781508846482
Published by CreateSpace

To my very own Nana and her little brother, Emerson. I love you both dearly.

PART ONE

Odd things happen to all of us on our way through life without our noticing for a time that they have happened.
-— J.M. Barrie
Peter and Wendy

CHAPTER ONE

It's just before dinnertime at the Seattle Children's Hospital. Beef Stroganoff tonight. My sister's favorite. I'm almost to the best part of *Peter Pan* — you know, where Wendy has just walked the plank and everyone on the ship is freaking out because there was no splash.

I pause for a moment and smile down at the newest addition to story hour. She smiles back. She's still clutching her mother's hand like it's her lifeline, but she's no longer hiding behind her. So that's something. Her light-colored eyebrows and pale skin make me think she was a blonde before they shaved her head and injected her with poison. And the light in her mother's eyes tells me there's still hope.

"Where's Wendy?" Jilly calls out even though she's heard this story countless times before. The way the children are watching me you'd think it was the first time I'd read it to them. Jilly claps loudly and the IV attached to her right hand sways back and forth as if it shares her excitement.

"Well," I say, drawing out the word. "What do you think happened to her?"

"Peter Pan!" the children chorus, all except Gerald. He's sitting in his mom's lap, eyeing me as if I'm foolish for asking this question.

1

"She's dead. Drowned in the water," he says, before his mom shushes him. Lately Gerald has developed a fascination with death. From what I hear some of the other parents find it off-putting.

"No! She's not dead!" Jilly says in her most authoritative voice. "It's Peter Pan. He's saved her."

And I laugh. Of course it is. Who else would it be?

I turn the book around to show them the illustrations and they collectively lean in close. A handful of the kids are sitting on the floor near my feet while the few who are too sick to leave their beds create a perimeter around us. But every last one of them is locked on, waiting for the happy ending. Even Gerald. Their eyes are wide and curious, and I love that. If I focus on their eyes I can forget the disease each one carries around like a nametag. I can forget that statistics rule their lives. I used to do this with my sister, Jenna, and near the end she would put her face right up to mine so that our noses were touching and say, "Can you see me, Livy?" and I'd say, "Always."

Sometimes when I close my eyes I still see her: honey and peach-colored and never without a half-eaten candy necklace hanging around her neck. At least that's how she used to be. But most of the time I have to pull out a photograph and remind myself of what her smile looked like, how her mouth was a mix of permanent and baby teeth. And how she had this funny little birthmark near her right temple that was shaped like an elephant, and when asked about it she would claim it was a tattoo because it would make my mother cringe and my father chuckle. After only four months of her being gone I have to rely on a photograph to remember how her eyebrows were so blonde you couldn't see them unless you looked really close. And how her laughter was so loud and freeing that it would usually catch the attention of perfect strangers on the street.

"Livy? What happened to Wendy?" Jilly says, bringing me back to the present. I turn the book around and flip to the next page.

2

"Tick, tock. Tick tock," I read and the children squeal: "It's the crocodile!"

I stop reading long enough to glance up. I wish I could capture their joy and hold it in my pocket, bringing it out on those days when even the promise of a new toy can't drudge up a smile. "This is what happiness sounds like," I'd tell them as if a simple reminder is all they need to feel better.

"What happens next?" Gerald calls out, and then thinking better of it he rolls his eyes and says, "not that I'm interested."

I'm about to answer when I notice him. That same boy. The one I occasionally see when no one else is paying attention. He's standing just inside the doorway wearing dark jeans and a hoodie. His arms are folded, his ankles crossed. He's lounging while standing up. And when our eyes meet he grins. *Who is he?* I know he doesn't belong to any of the children here because I've asked. In fact, no one on this floor seems to claim him at all. But nevertheless, there he is. Watching me.

"Are you going to finish, Livy?" Gerald asks with his sandpaper voice. "You know, some of us aren't going to live forever."

The boy in the doorway raises an eyebrow as if he too is wondering if I'm going to finish. But he isn't a boy. He's perhaps a year or two older than me, which would make him more adult than boy. But there's something about his smile that makes him appear younger. More youthful.

"Of course I'm going to finish," I answer, except now I'm nervous. My hand shakes when I turn the page and even though I will myself not to, I clear my throat.

"The sound of ticking is coming from the water down below. Tick. Tick. Tick." I take a breath while the children continue to hold theirs. And he's watching me. Still watching me.

I finish the story just as Nurse Maria strolls in to announce that it's time for dinner. But the children don't want food. They want

Peter Pan. The few who entered the playroom on their own two feet are now flying about with their arms extended and their pajamas flapping. I smile while I watch them. They look so free, so happy. For a moment I forget their troubles, just like they have.

"Again! Again!" they cry. "Read it again!" Even little Sammy, who rarely makes any noise at all, has joined in. Sometimes I don't even hear his footsteps before he tugs on my shirt to get my attention.

"Please, Livy!" Jilly begs from her hospital bed and I can't look at her when I explain that story hour is over. I never want to be the one to tell her no. She hears it enough.

Nurse Maria makes airplane noises as she pushes Jilly's bed toward the doorway.

"Don't leave without saying goodbye," Jilly calls out, her head arched back so she can see me.

"Never," I say. Just like I always do.

"See you tomorrow, Livy," Gerald squeaks out and his skinny arms wrap around me. He blushes when I kiss his cheek and it makes me want to hold him tighter, longer. "Try not to die tonight," he says. "It's dangerous out there."

"I'll be careful," I say and playfully swat at his hair.

When I glance toward the doorway the mysterious boy is gone.

Jilly is sitting up in her hospital bed, her small body only half filling it, when I stroll in. She's eating chocolate pudding and applesauce — her bites small and staggered — and drinking from her favorite Princess Jasmine cup. No Stroganoff for her tonight.

"Livy!" she calls out and pats the side of her bed.

I tuck myself in next to her and she turns her face on the pillow so that our eyes are aligned.

"I miss Jenna," she says and I nod. Jilly is one of the few people who still want to talk about my sister. Most don't bring her up at all or change the subject if she slips into a conversation. I've found that

4

death makes people uncomfortable, while the death of a child clears the room altogether. And that's okay. To be honest, it's not something I want to talk about either. But when I'm at the hospital with the kids everything is different. I'm different. I'm strong Livy, unshakable Livy. I talk about pain and death and how it feels to lose someone you care about, someone you didn't have enough time to get to know. Because the people I meet in the hospital are still living it; they're weeks or months away from being me. They come here with hope and if they're one of the lucky ones they'll leave with it. They're not like the rest of the world: too afraid to hear the truth when they ask, "how are you doing, Livy?"

"What do you miss?" I whisper to Jilly now. We're close to the end of visiting hours and even though there isn't a doctor or a nurse in this section of the hospital that would reprimand her for being awake — for being alive — I don't want to keep any of the other children up.

"I miss playing dolls with her and the stories she used to tell." Jilly's eyes take on a pleading look and I know what she's about to ask. She is never satisfied with just one story. She always wants more. More cake, more ice cream. More time with me.

"Which one do you want to hear?"

"*The Twelve Dancing Princesses*," she replies and I smile. Of course she'd pick that one. It was Jenna's favorite. "Will you tell me the story, Livy? Just until Grandma gets here?"

Jilly's grandma, Eliza, rarely makes it to the hospital before bedtime on Wednesday nights. She works clear across town and has to skip lunch just to leave a few minutes early in hopes of making it here before Jilly has fallen asleep.

"Please?" Jilly begs and I take a deep breath.

"Sure," I say, even though each time I tell this story it feels like I'm losing my sister all over again.

5

"Don't forget the dancing scenes," Jilly says. "Jenna used to stop and act them out."

Of course she did. My sister danced everywhere she went up until the end when her little body just couldn't do it any longer. That's when it really hits you. When your six-year-old sister, the one who would barge into your room first thing every morning to jump on your bed, can't hold herself up.

Jilly pulls the blanket up around her chin. All I can see are her wide brown eyes.

"I'm ready," she says, her voice muffled.

"There was a king who had twelve beautiful daughters," I begin and those brown eyes of hers crinkle in the corners just like Jenna's used to each time she'd smile.

I'm halfway through the story when Jilly's grandma rushes into the room. And I'm surprised, just like I always am, how fast she moves for a woman in her seventies. It's funny how love will do that to you.

"Did I make it?" she says out of breath.

One look at Jilly and she has her answer. Jilly's eyes fluttered shut about five minutes ago, just before the soldier arrived at the palace.

"When did they give her the medicine?" Eliza asks. She pulls off her coat and tosses it onto a chair in the corner, along with her purse.

"With dinner," I say sliding off the bed to make room for Jilly's grandmother.

"Any improvements today?" she asks, her eyes hopeful.

I look away. "Not much."

"Goodnight, Jilly," I whisper, but she can't hear me. She's been dragged down into the dark and dreamless world of undisturbed sleep, the kind that only heavy painkillers can produce.

"Goodnight Eliza," I say and Jilly's grandma takes her eyes off Jilly just long enough to give me a smile.

"See you tomorrow," she says and I nod, even though it wasn't a question.

I make my way down the hallway toward the stairs. Near the end of the hallway I can hear Sammy's parents beginning their nightly prayer from inside his room. With their hands they form a circle that includes Sammy and Sammy's favorite stuffed bear, Brown. I bow my head and join in even though I'm pretty sure it won't help. God doesn't save children around here. Sometimes it feels as if he's collecting them.

Sammy's parents murmur, "Amen," and I catch a flash of movement out of the corner of my eye. Someone in a dark hoodie has slipped inside the stairwell. And since I'm going that way anyway, I follow him.

CHAPTER TWO

I pull open the door that leads to the stairwell and catch a flicker of jeans right before they hop the railing, landing on the steps below. I'm not sure what I'm doing, or what I'll do if I catch up with him. But I want to know who he is. For weeks now I've noticed him; he shows up out of nowhere and sticks around to listen to the stories I tell. And he's always alone.

I sprint down the first flight, not brave enough to jump the railing like he did — show-off. But when I make it to the bottom floor I find I'm the only person in the lobby wearing jeans and a hoodie. I pause for a minute, looking around, but the boy with the smile is gone. He's managed to disappear again.

Outside the night is silent and wet. Typical. When I was younger, I asked my parents why it's always raining here. My mom answered, "Seattle is so beautiful even the clouds can't bear to leave it," while my father said, "After a while you don't notice it, Livy. Just you wait."

I'm seventeen now, and still waiting.

I pull the hood of my raincoat up and over my strawberry-blonde hair, the hair I inherited from my father, who inherited it from his mother who brought it to the US from Ireland where there are many strawberry-blonde relatives running about. I've never actually been there, but I imagine they're also cursed with pale skin and a dusting of freckles on the bridge of their noses. My father used to describe it as being sun-kissed until the day Jenna overheard and got upset, wondering why the sun hadn't kissed her too. The only way I got her to stop crying was to promise that the next time the sun came out we would go and ask it for a kiss. Thankfully when the sun finally did come out (three weeks later) she'd forgotten all about it.

I dodge the puddles in the parking lot even though I'm wearing rain boots. I hate being wet. I hate how you still feel wet long after you've come inside from the rain, as if the moisture has moved past your skin and into your bones. Some days it's like I'll never feel dry again.

There's a large puddle next to the driver's side door of my car and I think about what Jenna would do if she were here. Splash, of course. Stomp that puddle until the both of us were covered in it. Jenna never shared in my distaste for being cold and wet.

I'm reminded of one of our many visits to Alki Beach. I was standing on the boardwalk and Jenna was holding my hand. She was almost five. Each step I took she jumped, nearly pulling my arm from its socket. Even when there weren't any puddles on the ground she stomped. "I'm practicing," she'd explain.

"Chocolate and rainbow and mint," she sang. "And bubblegum."

She jumped again just as I was about to step off the curb and I stumbled slightly.

"Four scoops?" I said. "Do you really think mom will let you have four scoops?"

"But I can't decide!" Her grip on my hand tightened and I squeezed back.

"I like bubblegum," I said. "And I like rainbow."

"They're your favorite!" Her blue eyes turned up to me, her smile displaying the gap left behind from the two bottom teeth she'd recently lost.

"My favorite and my best," I said quoting her all-time favorite show, *Charlie and Lola*.

Jenna giggled and just like that it was decided. We'd be sharing ice cream that night.

Sometimes the memories crash against me like a tidal wave and sometimes they arrive as a feeling that hangs about all day. And even though I know it's good to remember Jenna, sometimes I wish I could forget, slip the memories into a large box and bury them in the ground for someone else to find. "Here lie my memories of Jenna Cloud. May you love her as much as I did, without the pain of having lost her."

My parents and I live in an apartment building, which isn't so unusual in Seattle. What is unusual is that we live on the entire top floor of a building my father designed. Marty, the doorman asks me how my night was and how Jilly is doing and I tell him she's strong and determined while he nods his head and forces a smile. We both know what I'm not saying: if Jilly doesn't find a match for her bone marrow transplant she probably won't make it to her seventh birthday. In my mind seven is the lucky number. Jenna never made it to seven. I'm convinced that if Jilly can she'll be fine. She'll begin to collect birthdays the way she and Jenna used to collect sea glass. Her birthdays will all knock around inside a Ziploc bag that gets heavier each time we visit the Sound.

With a soft *ping* the elevator opens. My mother's back is to me but when she hears the elevator doors she turns around and greets me with a close-lipped smile. This smile paired with her narrowed blue eyes is her working face, the one she wears pretty much always lately. It's the same look she gives me every time she asks if I'd like to visit with Dr. Roberts again. "He can help you work through it," she says, as if sadness is a math equation, as if instead of a prescription he can write out a simple formula that will help me when I'm as gray as the Seattle skyline.

But the truth is I don't need to see a doctor. I cried. I still cry. Crying is normal. I'm normal, unlike my mother who controls her emotions as if they're an outfit she can slip on and off.

"There's lasagna in the oven and garlic bread in the toaster," she says now, while the many people who help manage her career continue to talk around her. Most days I feel as if I've been dumped right onto another page from my mother's unwritten biography, entitled, *Mary Cloud, Washington State Senator.* Not that I'd even make it as a supporting character. If anything I'd be forever italicized in the footnotes as Olivia Cloud, first born. Even though for the rest of my life I'll be an only child.

"Where's dad?" I ask and she points down the hallway. The look on her face tells me I should already know the answer to that question, and then her attention is diverted back to the TV suspended above the kitchen cabinets.

"Mary, have you spoken with Bill yet?" Roger, her campaign manager asks. My mother nods, but she doesn't turn away from the TV. C-SPAN is the soundtrack to my mother's life right now with only six weeks until voting day.

Her dark blue eyes, so similar to my sister's, used to gleam, but now they're always serious. Serious is her camouflage. "No one wants to see a grown woman cry," I heard her tell Roger a few weeks after Jenna died. But I've noticed there are new lines around her eyes and a crease, dead center on her forehead. It must be her body's way of mourning my sister, even if she refuses to.

"Turn this up," she says to the person nearest the remote. I think his name is Tim or Bill. They're all the same to me with their suits and ties and firm handshakes — they all "yes, ma'am" my mother while barely tolerating me.

11

I hate these people in her life, how they fill her head with faux confidence and orbit around her like she's the sun. But if she loses the re-election they'll drop out of sight, leaving her burnt up and empty.

My father's office is the second to last room down the hall, and as I approach it I can hear the familiar sounds of Simon & Garfunkel escaping through the walls. Not a good sign. My father is listening to his music in the dark again.

I knock softly and then turn the handle. For a moment I let my eyes adjust to the darkness, even though I know where to find him. He's stretched out on his back on the brown leather couch he used to tell Jenna and me not to climb on. His rain-soaked boots are hanging over the side, which means he managed to make it outside at some point today. Where he went, I don't know. I doubt my mother does either.

My father's hand is draped over his eyes as if the world he lives in isn't dark enough, but I can tell from his shallow breathing he's not asleep. He doesn't sleep anymore, he prowls. Sometimes I wake in the night and listen to his footsteps moving along the hallway as if he's searching for something. He'll stop once in front of my door, move on to my sister's room and then linger for so long I end up falling back to sleep before I can determine his next stop.

"Hi, Daddy," I say. "I just got home." But he doesn't hear me. "Mom made dinner." Still no response.

I step back out into the hallway and with the close of the door Art Garfunkel's voice is muffled.

My father used to sing this song to Jenna to get her to fall asleep. Now he just plays it over and over again in the dark. I wonder if his memories are on repeat, just like the song. And I wonder if he'll ever stop punishing himself for losing a child.

Since Jenna passed away he doesn't work. He rarely leaves the house and if he eats, he eats alone. Sometimes he'll show up early in the morning while I'm having breakfast and startle me. Once I dropped an entire carton of eggs on the floor. I stared at him, my hands shaking and my feet dripping with egg yolk. He just moved on down the hall.

My father has become a ghost.

I take my dinner up to the roof. It's the place I go when I need to get away and be outside without actually being outside. Seattle has a lot of these places. Windowed rooms built into office or apartment buildings where you get the sense that you're out in open air when you're actually just enclosed in glass. The real outdoors would be preferred, but I hate always being wet.

I've just taken a bite of lasagna when my phone buzzes. It's a text from my best friend, Sheila. The only friend I've retained from my days in public school.

Where you at? she asks.

The roof, I respond.

I'm coming up, she texts back, and I take another bite of my dinner.

Sheila lives on the next block over with her dad and his new wife, while her mother lives in Bellevue with Sheila's younger brother and their two cats. It's not that she doesn't like her mother or brother — or the cats — she just didn't want to change schools. When she gave me this reason last year I nodded as if I understood, but ever since my sister died I'm not sure I do. Even though my family isn't what they once were, I need them near me. Every day. I guess when you've never lost someone you take it for granted that they'll always be around.

Sheila and I have very little in common, or so my mom thinks. But when Jenna was diagnosed with leukemia almost two years ago, the rest of my friends got all weird and distant. It was like I'd gone away for the summer and come back a different person, someone they barely recognized. And when my sister died they stopped calling altogether. Maybe they figured I was too busy mourning to need a friend. Or maybe it's just that death makes everything awkward. It was different with Sheila though. She held my hand at the funeral and it feels like she still hasn't let go.

The elevator opens and out comes all six feet of Sheila. Her platform boots click clack across the tile in the lobby and then shuffle toward me once she hits the carpet. She doesn't need her boots to be tall, but nevertheless she is rarely without them. I think she likes towering over people. It used to bother me always looking up. I've gotten over it.

"How's Jilly?" she asks once she's plopped down on the ground beside me. She's never met Jilly — she says the day she visits the Children's Hospital is the day she pops two of her mother's Prozacs — but she's one of the few people in my life who doesn't give me a hard time about always visiting the kids there.

"Not good," I answer, pushing the rest of my lasagna around my plate.

"Give me that," she says and takes the plate from me. "Wife-of-the-Moment is still in her cooking phase. Tonight I swear she cooked up our neighbor's dog. It smelled that gross." She shovels a large bite of my dinner into her mouth and then closes her eyes with enjoyment. "I love your mother's lasagna. Seriously. She could box it up and sell it like crack."

I watch her finish the last two bites and then pass her the rest of my milk. She thanks me and then guzzles it down.

She wipes her milk mustache off with the back of her hand. " So have you told your parents yet?"

"No."

"When are you going to?"

"I don't know. Before Friday?" I offer with a shrug.

"So... tomorrow, then?" Sheila pulls out her cell phone — an iPhone that used to resemble mine before she bedazzled it — and begins texting at rapid speed.

"Maybe," I say, watching as Sheila manages to carry on multiple conversations at one time.

Her fingers stop and she looks up at me.

"Don't you think they should know, Livy? I mean, this test is kind of a big deal, right? What happens if you're a match? What happens if the doctors say you're in?"

"In?" I pull my knees up and rest my chin on top of my knee.

"Yeah... like, in the donor club? What happens if they say, Olivia Cloud, you've just won the opportunity to save a young girl's life, and all that shit. Is that when you tell them?"

"Maybe." My eyes are focused on the elevator doors where I can see our reflections in the glass. "Probably," I whisper. I don't want to talk about this right now. I'm not ready. I mean I'm ready to give Jilly anything I can to help her make it to another birthday, but I'm not ready to explain it to my parents. It's my decision. At least it should be. And right now it's just a blood test. There's no point in telling my parents, getting them all worked up about the idea, if I'm not even a match, right? If I tell them now and they say no I'll never know if I could have saved her. And how can I live knowing I could have saved her?

"Huh. Alrighty then," Sheila says as she types something into her phone. "So we won't talk about it until we have something to talk about?"

"Let's do that," I say, and she smiles at me in the elevator doors.

Outside the windows and to the left the Space Needle is watching us. All my life this landmark has been my companion. It's comforting, like a neighbor you know will never up and leave.

"Hey Livy," Sheila says, grabbing my attention.

"Hey what?" I say back.

She smiles at me, her eyes dancing with laughter. "Do you remember that night we snuck out?"

"Which time?" I say, and thus begins another game of "Do you remember."

This has always been our way of dragging each other back from those dark moments that seep in periodically — although, it feels like it's always Sheila initiating the game lately.

"I remember," she says leaning her head against mine, "when we used to be much more fun."

"You're still fun," I whisper.

"That's right," she says, smacking my leg. "I keep forgetting that part."

And I laugh, which is exactly what she wants me to do.

"You'll get there, Livy," she tells me, and then immediately changes the subject to something safer — something lighter — while I'm left wondering if it's true.

With all the heaviness surrounding me, will I ever be fun again?

CHAPTER THREE

I don't go to high school like other kids my age. I haven't since my sister's health deteriorated last spring. My parents pulled her out of kindergarten and then agreed to pull me out as well. When someone important to you is about to die, normal life no longer applies to you. You aren't expected to act normal or do normal things. It's as if you have a pass on life, the my-sister-is-dying-so-I-can-do-what-I-want pass. Sheila said I should take advantage of the situation.

"Get a tattoo or pierce your bellybutton!" she told me.

But I figured I was in enough pain without having to worry about possible infection.

And now, four months after my sister passed away, I still don't attend public school. I have a tutor who comes to my house three days a week, who sits at my dining room table and teaches me what I should be learning in high school, minus the real-life stuff — I guess I've had enough of that lately. Sheila calls him Vladimir after the guy who wrote *Lolita*, but his real name is Steve. He shows up on time, rarely speaks of things outside of my school subjects and always carries tissues in the front pocket of his tan raincoat. After my sister died he brought me a handful of tiny daisies that I placed in a water glass because they were too small to fit inside one of my mother's crystal vases. They sat in the center of the dining room table for a week before my mother finally convinced me to throw them out. They were no longer standing up straight and their tiny petals had just begun to speckle the dark wood of the table. But I liked looking at them. They reminded me of my sister. Even though she was small, she had a way of making a room look lived in. She would have liked those daisies.

Today Steve and I are studying calculus, reproductive organs and Spanish. It has been a very long three hours.

"Next week we're on to the conjugations of to live, to eat and to speak," he says. "Viva la vida." He pushes his thin, gold-rimmed glasses back up on his nose and clears his throat. "So practice," he continues. "Remember to roll your r's." And then he demonstrates while I copy him. "I won't be here but I'll send a substitute."

"You're going to Florida," I say, because that's pretty much all I know about it.

"Yes. To visit my mother." He slips his books back into a shoulder bag that has a large wolf, the University of Washington's logo, on the front. "She's having surgery."

"Right. Well. Um, tell her I wish her luck." I've never met his mother, but it feels like the appropriate thing to say.

"Thank you, Olivia." He always calls me Olivia, never Livy or Liv. He likes to keep things formal, even though he's seen me cry, or perhaps because of it. "I'm sure she'll be fine. It's nothing major, just minor surgery."

I walk him to the door, as I always do. "See you when you get back," I say, and he pulls out his car keys, jingling them in his hand. The elevator ride down to the parking garage is a long one, but I guess he likes to be prepared.

"You're doing great, Olivia," he says just before the door closes. "You're a great student." He gives me a half-smile, which is pretty much what I always get from him, and what I always give back. I don't mind it. Half-smiles aren't as much work.

Sheila has sent me at least a dozen texts since she got out of school fifteen minutes ago. I know not to be alarmed. When Sheila wants to talk and she can't reach you she takes it as a personal challenge until she tracks you down.

"How's Vladimir?" she says instead of hello when I return her call. "Did he ask about me? He did, didn't he? You can tell me." Sheila has a crush on my tutor, even though he's more than twice her age. Or rather she has a crush on the idea of him. If she ever sat through one of our lessons (which she begs to do on a regular basis) she'd get over her obsession and realize he's just a grown man who teaches high school to kids who don't go to high school. He's not Jeremy Irons, Cary Elwes or any other male actor who has played a role in a *Lolita*-esque movie. He's just Steve the man whose left eye twitches every time he says the words fallopian tubes.

"What's up?" I say staring at the solar system mobile stapled to my ceiling. Jenna's room has a matching model. We made them together about five months before she died. I remember she wanted me to help her make a real-life example of outer space using tennis balls and marbles. "Because when you die," she said, "you float around with the stars. You don't become worm-food!" Which is what the kids in Cancer Camp, told her. "When I die I'm going to heaven," she explained. And because neither my parents nor I could describe what heaven was like she decided it looked like outer space, except with pink puffy clouds shaped like marshmallows. And those marshmallows are what I'm staring at when Sheila says, "You're coming out tonight."

She hisses at the yipping dog I can hear in the background and yells, "This is my bed. Stay off it." And then I hear the clipping sound of tiny nails on the hardwood floor just before her bedroom door slams.

Sheila's more of a cat person.

"I have Spanish homework," I say and she laughs.

"Well, he's not Spanish but he does have these incredibly sexy eyes."

"No," I say. "I appreciate the invite — "

"No you don't," she interrupts. "But you're coming out anyway."

"Sheila—"

"Livy! Listen. You had your blood test today, right? And you could potentially be getting your bones scraped, what, like any day after that… so I think you should come out with Grant and me tonight. He's bringing a friend, a friend I approved, by the way." When I stay silent she adds, "You don't even have to say anything to him. Just sit at the table, eat your bubblegum ice cream and look gorgeous. He'll love you, I promise."

Grant is Sheila's sometimes-boyfriend, which means that sometimes, when she wants a boyfriend, they go out. And when she doesn't want one, she sees other guys. Somehow she gets guys to agree to this. I think it's because she's so pretty and fun, but my mother has her own theory, one she doesn't share with me. Instead she purses her lips whenever I mention Sheila's name. She's a firm believer in: "If you don't have anything nice to say, don't say anything at all." What she doesn't realize is that when her eyes get all tiny and her nostrils flare I know she's holding back the not nice things. And all those not nice things make it so that we never talk about Sheila.

"Did you hear me, Livy?" Sheila says to me. "I mentioned ice cream."

"We're going to Molly's?" I ask.

"Who loves you?" she answers back. Just before she hangs up she adds, "I'll pick you up in thirty."

An hour later I'm sitting in a booth at Molly Moon's. The ice cream shop is crowded, but it always is. You'd think in a place this cold and wet the locals would stick to the coffee houses. I've ordered a large cup, which made Ryan, Grant's friend from hockey, raise his eyebrows and smile. But now that it's sitting in front of me, I don't want it.

"Hey Livy," Shannon, the owner of Molly's, calls out to me in between helping other customers. "How's Bubblegum Jenna taste today? We added more bubblegum, can you tell?"

"It's great," I say and then force another bite down, even though it's so sweet it makes my stomach churn. I should have ordered chocolate.

Sheila grabs the ice cream cup out of my hand and takes a big bite. "Yours is better," she says around a mouthful of bubblegum and then she slides her pistachio nut toward me. I give her a grateful smile because Sheila hates bubblegum ice cream.

Molly Moon's was my sister's favorite place. They even named a flavor after her, which means in the world of Molly Moon's, Bubblegum Jenna is now immortal.

I take a bite of pistachio nut and it slides down my throat, cold and tasteless.

"So you must come here a lot," Ryan says and Sheila bursts out laughing.

"Why don't you ask her her sign, Ry? Or perhaps, where she's been all your life?"

"What? I..." Ryan's face fills with confusion, which only makes Sheila laugh louder.

"I do come here a lot," I say, turning my back so that I can block out Sheila's smug expression. "Ice cream is my favorite." *And my best.* The words pop into my head but I somehow manage to keep smiling. "What flavor did you get?" I ask, even though I know just by looking into his cup he got banana chunk.

"Do you wanna try a bite?" He holds his spoon out toward me, and then blushes. "I mean, you can use your own spoon if you want."

"That's alright," I say, shying away from his spoon. If I've learned anything from the kids at the hospital it's how to keep my germs to myself. "It's making me kind of cold, actually. I think I ate too much." Ryan takes that as a personal invitation to move closer to me and pretty soon his leg is pressed up against mine.

"Sheila says you used to go to school together. Did you switch schools or something?" he asks and I glance away, not wanting to talk about this, or talk at all now actually, because every path eventually leads to my sister dying and I know from experience that is the quickest way to bring our conversation to a halt.

"Something like that."

I zero in on my melting ice cream, stirring it around and around until it resembles soup, while Sheila — who must sense I'm in no mood for talking — moves the conversation on without me. She appears to be feigning interest in hockey lingo, which we both know means I owe her big time. But I just can't bring myself to be a part of it all.

There's this feeling I get sometimes, that I'm displaced, like I've fallen and no one has noticed yet. If I stay real still they'll avoid me, put up pylons around me like I'm a large pothole in the ground. Yes. That's what I am. I'm a pothole. And until someone comes along and fixes me, I am dangerous. I am broken. I am not a part of this life and yet I'm still here. I know I'm supposed to get over losing my sister. I know that's what everyone expects. I'm just not ready yet.

Pearl Jam is playing in the background and Sheila hates Pearl Jam. She rolls her eyes at me because the universe has obviously done this intentionally, an elaborate ploy to ruin her night, and I realize this is my cue. I clear my throat and push my ice cream cup away, about to excuse myself from the booth —and this night. Then I see him. Right outside the window a group of teenagers is passing by, paired up in twos and threes, yet all together. Directly in the middle of them is the boy from the hospital. He's standing there looking at me while his crowd shifts and moves on around him. I sit up in my seat while he smiles at me through the glass. He's wearing a dark green hoodie that matches his eyes. And unlike the previous times I saw him his hood is down, revealing chestnut colored hair that is tousled from the wind and spiky with moisture from the light rain outside. It's odd to see him somewhere other than the hospital.

His gaze is locked on mine and in this moment we are connected. If he were to move back I would fall forward, and not even the glass window between us could keep us apart.

"Who's that?" Sheila asks, and just like that her voice cuts the string pulled taut between us. I fall back in my seat. She can see him! Up until this moment I was still pretty sure I'd imagined him.

"Who?" I ask and he smiles as if he's following our conversation and realizes we're talking about him.

"Green hoodie? Sexy hair? You know, the one who's staring at you as if the two of you share a secret? Go on, Livy. Spill."

"I don't know him," I say, which is the truth, even though I suddenly don't want it to be.

"Well, we're going to have to change that." Sheila pushes against me, sliding my body toward the opening in the booth.

"Sheila!" I push back, but she's stronger than me. I nearly topple out onto the floor.

"What's going on?" Grant asks, looking from Sheila to me and then out the window. "You know that kid?"

"Settle down." Sheila bats her eyelashes at him. "This one's Livy's."

But he's not mine. And that thought immediately makes me sad.

"Livy! Go get him!" Sheila says like it's something I do, run after boys. And then because she knows better she climbs over me to do it herself.

23

But it's too late. The boy has moved on. Sheila halts mid-step, staring after the crowd as they disappear down the street. And then she slowly turns back toward me. In her eyes is disappointment. But it is nothing compared to mine.

CHAPTER FOUR

"I won't be around for dinner tonight," my mom tells me, peeking into my bedroom. "So you're on your own." It's funny how my father doesn't even factor into our plans anymore. He's his own lost island, one that occasionally passes me in the hallway, holding onto his silence even when the edges of us touch. "And I won't be back until late. I have a meeting with the budget committee, and you know how that goes."

"I'll be fine." It's the only assurance she needs.

Jilly has been begging me to come and watch *Tangled* with her so my plans are set for the evening.

Tangled is Jilly's latest Disney obsession. "I want to have long hair when I grow up," she tells me, snuggling up next to my side so that she can borrow some of my warmth. She pulls on her thin hair that has yet to make it past her ears. "Long enough to braid."

I don't bother to remind Jilly what the peer counselor is always telling her, how she's supposed to make short goals, goals that she can accomplish over the next few days or weeks. Instead I pull out my iPhone and start Googling wig shops.

We're halfway through the flying lantern scene, a scene that's so sweet and magical it always makes me cry, when Jilly takes a sip of her water and starts coughing.

"I swallowed wrong," she manages to get out before her coughs turn into gags.

I get up and race toward the bathroom in search of the large pink, plastic tub she always uses when she's sick, but it's too late. Jilly loses what little she had for dinner, and more than likely most of the pain medicine she'd just swallowed, all down the side of her bed. Her body is bent almost in half. She's taking tiny breaths as if even the air is out to get her.

She looks up at me as the nurse rushes in and her eyes are wide and wet, but mostly frightened.

"I'm sorry, Livy," she says, as if this is her fault, like she can control the weakness of her stomach anymore than she can keep the cancer from spreading.

Nurse Maria strips her out of her pajamas and into some clean ones while I continue to hold up the doorway. I grip the doorframe so hard that my fingernails are practically embedded into the hard wood.

"It's okay, Jilly," I tell her over and over again, but when Nurse Maria's attention shifts from Jilly to me I figure maybe I've said it one too many times.

"All better?" she asks and Jilly nods. But Nurse Maria is still looking at me.

"I didn't feel sick," Jilly whispers, leaning back against her pillows. "I don't know what happened." Her face is pale and her little hands are shaking as she draws her blankets up close to her chin.

"It's the radiation, Jilly Baby," Nurse Maria explains. "Once you've been through it, your stomach is far more sensitive." She refills her water cup and adds, "Just take small sips. We don't want you to overdo it."

Jilly's hand slips out from her cocoon of blankets and reaches for her Princess Jasmine cup. Her voice is tiny, like she's buried under sand, when she says, "okay."

Suddenly the room feels like it's closing in on me. It isn't Jilly I see in that bed but my sister. Jenna's arms are thin and reaching for me. It's Jenna's eyes that are tearing up, blue not brown. Blonde eyelashes not black.

"Help me, Livy," Jenna whispers. "Save me."

"Livy?" Nurse Maria is calling my name but I can't open my mouth to answer. My jaw feels like it's wired shut. My chest tightens. "Livy," she says again, standing in front of me now.

"She's not going to die," I whisper. "I won't let her." But it's too late. Jenna's already gone.

Nurse Maria doesn't say anything for a moment and then she nods. She squeezes my hand as if to snap me out of this, but I'm too far gone. Too deep. Her voice is low enough for only me to hear. "Be strong for her, Livy. It's the only thing you can do."

"I know." My words sound shaky even though I've put everything I have behind them. "But I can save her." *I will save her.*

Nurse Maria simply smiles the smile of someone who's used to empty promises. "Why don't you go get some air? I've got this."

"Right," I manage to get out, and then my legs are carrying me, slow then fast, into the hallway. I lean against the wall just outside her room and close my eyes. I can hear Jilly calling out to me. "Li-vy," she says, stretching out my name so that each syllable grips my heart that much tighter. In and out I breathe while Nurse Maria explains that I'll be right back. Which I'm not so sure is true. All this time I thought I was so brave, spending time with these kids as if death no longer affects me. But I don't think I can watch another child die. Especially not Jilly.

I stumble down the hallway. I feel as if I might be sick. But unlike Jilly, the only things churning in my stomach right now are fear and sorrow. I pull open the door to the staircase even though I have nowhere to go. I don't want to leave and I definitely don't want to go home, but I can't stay here. Eliza should be arriving any minute and she can give Jilly the comfort I don't have for her tonight. She can cuddle up and tell her everything's going to be all right and for a fleeting moment that thought gives me peace. It doesn't take long before the panic I felt when Jilly started throwing up is back. It's like hunger, easily soothed — but it always returns.

I can fix her, I think to myself. *I can do this.* But no matter how many times I had said those words out loud, Jenna still died.

I sit down on the cold cement stairs, my head in my hands, and I don't even notice I have company until someone sits down beside me.

"I'm okay," I say, expecting it to be Nurse Maria or someone else she's coerced into checking on me.

"Are you now?" comes an unfamiliar voice.

I look up and there he is, the boy with the hoodie, except tonight his hoodie has been replaced with a black raincoat. His eyes, however, are still the same breathtaking green.

"Hello," he says and I catch the hint of an accent, one I don't recognize. "It's about time we properly met, don't you think?" His smile is lopsided, his right eyebrow raised. Together they convey a look of mischief.

"I'm Meyer." He holds out his hand and I take it. His hands are large; they swallow mine up with just the right amount of pressure.

Meyer. I practice it a few times in my mind; roll it around until it comes naturally. *Meyer.* Yes. It definitely suits him. He looks like a Meyer, even though I've never met one before.

"And you are…?" he says and I realize I'm just staring at him.

"Livy," I say with a sniffle, dashing away the remnants of my tears.

"Nice to meet you, Livy," he says and then after a slight squeeze he lets go of my hand. "Is there a reason you're hiding out in the stairway? Was I not supposed to find you?" There's a faint lilt in his voice that kind of makes me breathless.

"I..." I shake my head, unsure how to answer. "I just needed to be alone, I guess."

"Is that something you prefer, being alone?"

"Lately, yeah." I force a laugh and glance down at my hands. But it's not funny. The truth rarely is.

He shifts as though he's going to leave. "So, you'd rather I left you to it, then?"

"No! I mean, please don't." I clear my throat and start again. "I'd like you to stay."

Meyer sits back with a smile and I feel my dark mood lighten a bit.

"Let's play a game then, shall we? I believe you call it Truth or Dare, while I've always known it as Pain and Suffering."

When I just blink back at him he starts to explain. "Suffering, because a dare usually leads you to do something you're uncomfortable with, and pain because the truth always hurts."

"You want to play a game?" It's too much for me, seeing this boy — Meyer — here, while I'm worrying that life is about to repeat itself on me. Now, after weeks of wondering who he is, and what he's all about, he's here. And he wants to play a game?

"You first," he says, pointing his finger. "What do you prefer, Livy? Pain or suffering?"

"Neither, actually," I say, and he laughs.

"Truth, then." He leans his elbow up on his knee and pins me with an intense expression. He has ridiculously long eyelashes, which seems unnecessary considering the beautiful color of his eyes.

"What has you so sad?" he asks me. "Here, now. And every time I see you."

His question hits me directly in the chest, where my breathing is still too shallow to answer.

"You can tell me," he says, "I'm actually a pretty great listener."

But I can't talk about it. Any of it.

"Suffering," I say, daring him to contradict me. I'm not one for pouring my heart out to a boy I've just met. Or anyone, really. "I'd rather take suffering if you don't mind."

"Alright then." He jumps to his feet. "Let's be off." He holds out his hand to help me up and I take it, because I have nowhere else to go. Meyer is taller than I expected, but it isn't his size that makes me feel small. There is a heat coming off of him, an energy that seems to bounce around us, hitting the walls of the stairwell and turning the fluorescent lights on the ceiling a warm glittery gold.

"We're leaving?" I ask, stalling. Can I really leave? With him? Won't Jilly miss me? She's probably asleep by now, but shouldn't I stop in to tell her goodbye?

"Is that alright?" he asks softly. His eyes are heavy as though he didn't anticipate me saying no.

If you don't leave now, you never will. The thought comes out of nowhere, and because I know it's the truth, I nod okay.

I follow him down the stairs and out into the lobby. For some reason it doesn't seem strange to be leaving with this boy, it feels like a jailbreak. He doesn't tell me where we're going until we're on a bus heading downtown. "It's time for an adventure," is all he says. He's sitting next to me, our legs brushing against each other each time the bus turns a corner. "Are you up for a little adventure, Livy?"

I'm thinking an adventure is just what I need, even though my "yes" is nearly silent. And I don't think twice about it. Well, maybe I think twice. I definitely think about how I'm not exactly dressed for an adventure. I'm wearing jeans, a red sweater and my dark blue raincoat. It's not the most exciting thing I could have on, but it will have to do.

There are a few other people on the bus with us; an older man who has been glaring down at his hands since we got on, a group of girls around our age — who can't take their eyes off Meyer — and a young mother and child. The child, I would guess, is about Jilly's age. Her gaze is also on Meyer — her expression rather apprehensive, but when he smiles at her she grins back.

"Where are we going?" I ask after a few more stops, because I should really know this.

"The Sculpture Gardens," he says and the sparkle in his eyes tells me that's all the information I'll get.

I stare out the window as we cut across town, focused on the reflection of a girl whose eyes are still slightly red but bright and the boy sitting next to her who occasionally glances in her direction. I don't know this girl. She looks like me — she has the same hazel eyes and strawberry blonde hair — but she definitely doesn't act like me. I would never get on a bus with a strange boy. I would never go out into the night in pursuit of an adventure. No. I don't recognize this girl, but I want to be her. I like the way I feel right now, how each and every breath I take is spreading throughout my body like a wildfire, not trapped, as it usually is, below the heavy feeling in my chest. It's been a while since I felt like I could breathe freely.

At the next stop he jumps up and I follow him off the bus and then down the path toward the seawall. I'm nearly jogging to keep up with him but once he notices, he slows down. Soon our steps are in sync. After a few minutes he glances over at me and I figure he's going to say something, but he doesn't, instead he starts whistling. The tune is playful and unfamiliar. It carries over the grounds of the Sculpture Gardens and out over Puget Sound.

"What is it we're doing, by the way?" I ask. "Shouldn't I know, considering it's my dare? Or rather, my Suffering?"

Meyer smirks but he doesn't stop whistling. He doesn't answer my question either.

So far I've only noticed a handful of people since we got off the bus and they were all back near the road. The grounds, from what I can tell, are empty. "You're not going to ask me to jump in the Sound, are you?" I stare out at the cold water and a shiver moves through my bones.

"Just up here." He pauses briefly on the sidewalk but I'm not expecting it and nearly collide into him. "Just remember," he says, "it's a game. It's supposed to be fun." His hands are on my shoulders, steadying me. He's really quite tall, so tall I have to look up, standing this close to him. "Never forget that." And then he's off again, moving down the path with a purpose. I hurry to catch up.

"Are you from around here?" I ask and the look he gives me is as vague as his answer.

"Sometimes."

"Are you in town because you know someone at the hospital? Is that why you're always there?"

"Yes," he answers, and I realize this could continue all night.

"I don't like mysteries," I tell him and my voice carries out over the grounds. "I want to know more about you," I add softly. Especially considering it's just the two of us alone out here in the dark.

"But you like adventures and romance and heroes who risk it all for the woman they love and heroines who save themselves, is that right?"

"You mean like the stories I read to the kids?"

He tilts his head, studying me and I realize we've stopped walking again. "Are you as brave as the stories you tell? I wonder would you risk it all like the girls in your stories?"

"Risk? Risk what? What are you *talking* about?" But he doesn't answer. He's back to walking.

"Why do you always leave before the story ends?" I call out to him. I'm hurrying to catch up when he stops suddenly and I'm

32

forced to catch myself before I crash into him again. His dark auburn hair hangs just slightly in his eyes and my hand itches to brush it away. His shoulders are wide, wider than I realized, and I wonder why I thought of him as a boy before. Now that he's standing so close, I'm pretty sure I'll never think that again.

"Maybe I don't like endings," he says, his eyes laughing at me. "Or maybe you've been telling them wrong."

"That's ridiculous. I just read them the way they're written."

"They aren't just stories, they're adventures." He leans close and it's so cold I can see his breath. "And a true adventure never ends."

"O-kay," I mutter, but he's already moving on without me.

I follow him across the lawn toward an assortment of sculptures. There's a group of about twenty or so kids, standing in an open area up ahead. Some are skateboarding while others are paired up in clusters of twos and threes. Some are on their phones, their faces illuminated in the dark each time their fingers fly over their tiny keyboards. They resemble giant fireflies, flashing here and there, lighting up the night as if they're afraid of the dark.

"This is Livy," Meyer calls out to them. "And since it's her first night she'll be hiding with me."

"What?" *Hiding? Who said I was hiding?* I grab his arm and turn him toward me. But once I realize I'm touching him, I let go. "I don't understand. What are we doing here? What does any of this have to do with my dare?"

"I dare you," he says with a low bow, "to have fun. And if you can't have fun," he waggles his eyebrows at me, "you will suffer the consequences."

"Is this part of the game?" I'm still confused. Did he plan this? Did he know before we met up tonight that this was all going to happen? Or did he just take pity on the girl crying in the stairwell and I got sucked into his plans?

"It's up to you. Do you take the dare or not?" he challenges.

33

I glance around at the faceless shapes around me. It's too dark for me to make out more than that. What I do know is that we are not supposed to be here at this time of night. At any moment a security guard could catch us and kick us off the grounds. Or worse, call our parents.

"Livy?" Meyer is smiling, his white teeth a flash in his otherwise shadowed face.

"I'm in," I say and a tiny thrill of excitement rushes through me. What other choice do I have? Do I go home? Leave Meyer to think I'm afraid and sad and pathetic? It's too soon for him to know this about me.

"We'll keep the boundaries close tonight," he calls out to the group. "Consider the walkway off limits." He points in the direction we've just come, where just past the path I can see the Sound fidgeting in the moonlight.

No one objects to Meyer's amendment. Instead, a dark-haired girl steps forward and begins to explain the rules, even though it appears I'm the only one who's never done this before.

"Have you ever played hide-and-seek?" Meyer's voice is soft beside me.

"Of course. Who hasn't?"

I tuck my hands into the pockets of my raincoat. The night is cold and wet, my least favorite combination, but I try not to dwell on it. *Warm and dry is safe and boring*, I think, and then wonder where that thought came from.

"Good then," Meyer says. "They have a lot of rules you see, but the only thing you need to remember is: don't get caught."

"Alright." *Don't get caught. Getting caught is bad.* I can remember that.

Meyer leans close. "But you needn't worry about that, Livy. Not tonight." His smile is mischievous. "I never get caught."

I clamp my teeth together, covering the chill that has set them chattering. I'm cold, yes, but the weather never sets my stomach fluttering. Not like this.

He claps his hands and the noise around us stops. Everyone is on alert. I can feel it, like we're all waiting for a race to begin.

"Have you got a cell phone, then?"

"Yes."

"Give us the number."

Us. Not me, but us.

"You'll get a text once each person is found, that way you know who's still in the game."

"Okay. Makes sense." I call out my number to the twenty or so people standing around me, the twenty or so people I don't even know. I mean, it's just a cell phone number, right? It's not like it's anything personal. And yet it feels personal. But again, I don't care.

Someone calls out, "Let's do this!" Suddenly everyone is moving, running in all directions and Meyer and I are the only ones left.

He holds out his hand to me and I stare down at it. It's not that I don't want to hold it; it just feels so intimate, holding hands.

He must sense my hesitation but instead of pulling back from me his eyes soften. "I'm not someone you should fear, Livy." It seems like such a funny thing to say considering we're standing all alone in a dark field, but it makes me feel better. I have to admit, between the way he looks at me and the inflection in his voice, fear is the last thing I feel right now. It's something else. There's something… exciting about him. He's different and different feels very good right now.

Despite the fact that everyone else has scampered off, Meyer doesn't seem to be in a hurry. His hand is still reaching for mine. I get the feeling we'll stand here all night until I take it. Even if it means we're the first to get caught.

"Shall we go then?" he says, and I nod.

His hand is warm, which I like, and soft. When his fingers close around mine I realize I don't want mine back. I feel brave with my hand in his.

"This way." His grip tightens as though he worries I'm about to let go. He tugs on my hand not once but twice, until I follow him down the path toward the trees. We move quickly up a hill that leads to a large staircase.

"I've never been here before," I say

"It's even prettier in the day."

And then we're silent; the only sound is our footsteps trudging up the cement stairs.

We move toward an open area where just ahead I can make out an assortment of sculptures all staggered and yet together. From my viewpoint there are five, five willowy walls as tall as the trees. I can't make out what they are exactly, just that they appear to be blowing in the wind even though they are solid and unmoving.

"This is where we wait," he says, pulling me back behind one of them. And I don't question it. He seems to know what he's doing. However, there are tiny pebbles under my feet that make it difficult to move without making noise.

"These pebbles don't seem to help our cause."

"It's better that way. We'll be able to hear their approach."

He's leaning against one of the wall sculptures while I stand a few feet away, not quite sure what to do with my body. Do I stand next to him? Do I hide nearby? He reaches out and then pulls me up next to him as though he's noticed my hesitation.

"It's important that you hide in this game," he whispers in my ear, and I feel myself flush with embarrassment. Thankfully it's too dark for him to notice.

I open my mouth to respond, but find he's just too close for words to move between us. I don't even realize I'm staring at his mouth until he smirks, and then I'm not looking at him at all. My eyes drop to the ground, only returning when the sound of his soft laughter mocks me.

"I get that we're supposed to be hiding," I whisper, "but aren't we also supposed to be quiet?"

Meyer lifts an eyebrow and then tips his head as if to say, "touché."

And of course now that I've shut him up all I can do is think of the questions I'd love to ask him, like, How often do you do this? And, do you live in Seattle? Anything to find out more about him. But it really isn't the best time for a chat. We are hiding after all.

"So when is it your turn?" I whisper when I can't take the silence any longer. "And what will you choose, pain or suffering?"

Meyer grins and my stomach flutters again. "I prefer suffering to pain," he says. "Always."

"So you're a risk taker." I could have called that seeing as he's avoided every personal question so far this evening.

"What is life without risk?"

"Long," I answer, even though I'm sure he didn't mean it as a question. "And safe."

Meyer's eyes narrow. "Is that what you want? Safety? Predictability?"

"I just want to know that everything's going to work out. I don't like surprises."

He's quiet, as if he's taking this in. His gaze is upon my face as though it's a touch. All at once I'm very aware of the fact that I'm all alone out here with Meyer, someone I just met. I should feel uncomfortable, or awkward, or something, but I don't.

"Wasn't tonight a surprise?" he says softly. His lashes lower, mesmerizing me. "And me? Would you rather I left you in that stairwell?"

I'm saved from answering when off in the distance we hear footsteps. Meyer presses up against me.

"If they get any closer we're going to run," he whispers. I can feel the smooth texture of his raincoat against my cheek and his heartbeat is quick and steady, just like mine. "Follow me and stay close."

I nod and the zipper of his coat scratches against my chin. We're so close it's like we're sharing heat. And I like it. It's been awhile since I've stood this close to someone.

The footsteps stop a short distance away and then move off in the opposite direction. "Are you ready?"

"Y-yes," I say and take a step back from him. I reach up to brush the hair out of my eyes and realize it's damp. I hadn't even noticed the rain.

Meyer creeps to the end of the wall, and begins searching the grounds down below us. He turns back to me, his eyes lit with excitement. "How do you feel about heights?"

"Heights?"

"Are you afraid of heights?" he asks me impatiently. "The next spot is rather high."

"Um. I don't think so…"

"Good. Let's go then." He takes my hand and pulls me closer.

The sound of pebbles rustling underfoot startles me and I tense up with anticipation. Meyer tugs on my hand and I follow him. We move through the wall sculptures slowly at first and then we're running. We hop over bushes and fly past trees as he leads me around the grounds like he can see in the dark. Back behind us I can hear our pursuer's footsteps quicken on the grass, heavy and determined. This whole thing starts to feel like more than a game. We are running — fast now — as though our pursuer is something to fear, something life-threatening. I like that I'm a tiny bit scared. I like that every shadow feels like a threat. But mostly I like running with Meyer's hand in mine.

After a few more minutes the footsteps fall off and disappear completely.

We stop to catch our breath — even though I'm not sure I'll ever get mine back. Meyer, however, doesn't even seem winded.

A drop of moisture rolls down my face. I'm surprised when it feels refreshing. I even contemplate taking off my raincoat, anything to cool me down.

"What is it?" Meyer asks, and I realize I'm smiling. I'm soaked to the bone, my hair is hanging limply against my back, but I don't mind.

"This is fun," I say, even though that doesn't nearly cover it. The air smells like a mix of evergreens and salt water and I swear the next time I go to the beach I will smell the sea and remember this night. And Meyer. Mostly I will think of Meyer.

He is grinning at me and I can almost hear the words he's not saying, *I told you so.* When he doesn't say them, I like him even more.

My phone buzzes in my pocket. I pull it out to see three new texts. All read the very same thing: *out.*

Meyer glances over my shoulder. "That leaves us, and two other groups." He takes my hand and we're off again. Across a giant lawn and then up a flight of stairs until I'm so out of breath my lungs hurt. I'm not stopping though. I don't even want to slow down. I stop paying attention to how high we've climbed until he leads me across a cement walkway that overlooks the entire garden. On either side of me it's a straight drop down into darkness. How did we even get here?

I can see the Sound off in the distance. The moon is still bouncing along on the choppy water. And it's all so beautiful. Everything in this moment is perfect.

Meyer appears in front of me, his eyes serious. "If it bothers you, don't look down," he says, but the way I'm feeling has nothing to do with heights.

Down below us I can make out a few voices and then once again my phone is buzzing. Meyer's hands are warm on my shoulders — his knees touching mine — and the look in his eyes is like a burst of adrenaline. I feel like I'm lit from the inside. For the last few months I've had countless eyes watching over me, making sure I'm okay, that I'm not going to lose to the battle of sadness. But when Meyer stares down at me I'm amazed that one person can make all the difference. With his attention clearly focused on me I feel as if I've been noticed for the very first time.

"Have you ever wanted to fly, Livy?" he asks. I don't tell him that, at the moment, I feel like I *am* flying. We're standing higher than the apartment building across the garden and higher than anyone should be allowed to stand without a guardrail protecting them from the ground below, and yet I'm not afraid. Meyer makes me unafraid.

"Always," I say, and I realize it's the truth.

"It's easy, you know," he says and squeezes my hand. "One day I'll show you."

The thing is, I believe him. I believe he could fly if he wanted to, because in the matter of a few hours he's made me feel weightless. So incredibly light that at any moment I could lift off. And that's really all you need to fly, isn't it?

"Meyer!" someone yells up at us. He doesn't respond. A few seconds later my phone begins to buzz.

Game over, the text reads. *You win.*

Back down on the ground Meyer keeps hold of my hand as we make our way toward home base. Another game is forming but he explains that we're done for the night, how we'll catch them another time. I can't help but feel disappointed. Funny thing is I don't know any of these kids, I wouldn't even recognize them if I saw them in the light of day, but I don't want to leave them. Especially if it means my time is up with Meyer as well.

He has hold of my hand and he's directing me across an intersection as the walk signal flashes a warning that we have five, four, three, two and then the light turns green.

"You did it," he says. "You had fun!" And I realize he's the only one of the two of us who doesn't appear surprised by this.

I did do it. Who would've thought, Livy Cloud was capable of having fun?

"That means it's your turn," I say, smiling up at him. That lightheaded feeling from before is still there, making me giddy.

"Next time," he says, making me feel like a child being told it's well past my bedtime.

There's a bus waiting on the corner. He leads me toward it and then helps me up the steps. His hands are strong against my back, his fingertips firm, as if I have no choice but to leave him.

"I know you miss her," he says from the street below, "but she wants you to be happy. Do you think you can be happy here?" Who is he talking about? He couldn't be talking about Jenna, could he? The door slides shut leaving Meyer standing on the street alone, and me on the bus headed back toward the hospital.

CHAPTER FIVE

I never wanted to be an only child. I sometimes wonder if my parents had Jenna just to shut me up. I wanted a little sister and I was pretty vocal about it. Every year at Christmas it was the same thing: me on Santa's lap pleading for a sister. I explained how if he gave me a sister he wouldn't have to give me anything more until the following Christmas. I figured that was fair.

I asked until I was too old to believe and then I went straight to the source and begged my parents. I was ten when Jenna was born, eleven when she took her first steps and twelve when she crawled up on my lap, wrapped her chubby arms around my neck and told me she loved me best. Most teenage girls would complain about their kid sister shadowing them around everywhere they went, but I liked her company. Jenna wasn't like other kid sisters. She was special. I realized it the very first day we met. While all the other babies were sleeping in their little incubators Jenna was screaming her head off. My dad called her his little fighter, because when Jenna wanted something she would do her best to get it, not in an annoying, bratty kind of way, more like when something was important to her, she did everything in her power to make it known.

She *was* a fighter. Stubborn and determined. I guess that's why when she took her last breath I didn't feel sad, I felt betrayed. Like she'd given up on me. If she'd really wanted to stay with us, with me, she would have fought through it. She would have beat cancer, and survived.

Over the next few days I almost tell Sheila about Meyer at least a dozen times, but something always stops me. How do I explain that night? Oh, by the way, the boy with the hoodie showed up, took me to the Sculpture Gardens where we ran around playing hide-and-seek and then disappeared again? Oh and his name is Meyer, but I don't know anything else about him other than I think I could spend the rest of my life holding his hand.

Because I really do think I could.

I'm not sure if it's his eyes that I like the best or his smile or the way he makes running around outside in the rain feel fun again. What I don't like is how little I know about him. How he asked me if I could be happy, as though it's an emotion I'm incapable of feeling. But I can be happy. I remember happy. I just don't feel it very often.

But most importantly… who is *she*? It only makes sense that he'd be speaking of Jenna, but how is that possible? Did he meet her at the hospital before she died? Did he visit her? The questions continue to breed as I think about that night. But the answers are as out of reach as Meyer himself.

Occasionally I scroll through the list of cell phone numbers that are still in my call log, the numbers that belong to Meyer's friends. How easy would it be to text one of them and say, *I lost Meyer's number, can you send it to me?* But I don't because I know I'll see him again. It's his turn next, and Meyer strikes me as the kind of person who doesn't like to miss his turn.

Meanwhile, I have bigger things to worry about like Jilly and my test results, and how to tell my parents I'm a match — if I *am* a match —and how I'm going to be a donor whether they want me to or not. I've spent the last few nights hanging out with Jilly, making sure she sees how I'm strong and confident and that everything is going to be okay. Because if she sees that I am calm, she sleeps. And when she sleeps, she is at peace.

The doorbell rings and my mother knocks on the door of my room looking for me.

"Your new tutor is here, Livy."

When I simply blink back at her she adds, "Mr. Hale."

"Oh crap," I mutter under my breath. The last thing on my mind is Spanish homework. I haven't even studied, which isn't normally a big deal with Steve, but I don't want to waste Mr. Hale's time. Nor do I want to come off as some kind of slacker.

"I didn't know he was coming today," I say to my mom.

"Well, he called yesterday to reschedule. I'm sure I left the message in your room."

Sure enough there it is, right next to my computer, a bright yellow Post-it note with my mother's perfect handwriting: *Mr. Hale. 1pm Tuesday.*

"Right," I say.

My footsteps are slow as I make my way to the dining room. I am anticipating another old professor or a teacher's assistant, someone who is looking to impress Steve by donating his time, but the man waiting for me is not old or stuffy looking. He is beautiful. Truly. His face is ageless, as if tiny fairies sweep away his wrinkles while he's sleeping, leaving his skin smooth, his eyes bright and his features chiseled. He's young enough to be a recent college grad, but with his tailored dark suit he must be older than he appears. College grads can't usually afford such luxury.

"You must be Livy," he says and even his voice is attractive. He reaches his hand out to me and I take it. Hesitantly. "I'm Mr. Hale, but you can call me James."

I clear my throat and say, "It's nice to meet you, Mr. Hale. James."

He smiles and gestures for me to take a seat, as though this is his apartment, not mine. I hesitate a moment and then do as he says, my hands clenched nervously in my lap.

My mother is somewhere nearby — the kitchen perhaps — but in the dining room it is very much just the two of us. I am aware of James the way I've never been aware of Steve. He makes me nervous, almost jittery. Not in a romantic, teacher-crush sort of way. I don't get off on that like Sheila. However, between his beauty and his poise I find him… dangerous. That word comes out of nowhere and then retreats because it doesn't make sense. Why would my substitute teacher be a threat to me? Steve is probably one of the most intelligent teachers I've ever had, and yet he doesn't intimidate me.

James' blue eyes are so pale they're almost silver, which is a stark contrast to his jet-black hair. He sits across the table, carefully studying me as if there is a secret message to be found in my expression. It's unnerving to be examined so thoroughly, especially by someone so appealing. I wish I could hold his glance and return the favor, but it's too much, those eyes.

"I'm afraid your Mr. uh… Steve, has been held up with his mother a bit longer than expected," he says. "So I will be taking over his position until he can find his way back."

"Is everything alright?" I'm immediately worried about Steve, but most of the anxiety centers around the possibility that he won't return and I'll be forced to concentrate in a room with James for the next ten months.

"Everything's fine, Livy." He reaches out his hand as if to pat mine, but my hands are still buried in my lap so instead he touches my shoulder. "You know how it is when someone you love needs you. You'd do anything for them, right?"

"Of course," I say. His hand moves off my shoulder and returns to rest on the table in front of him.

"So. Instead of a lesson today I thought we might just get to know each other."

"Okay." I don't know why this upsets me, but it does. I mean, it sounds like a normal request. We will be spending a lot of time together, especially if Steve decides to stay away. But I'm not sure I want James to get to know me.

James must sense my unease because he sits back in his chair, his light blue eyes on me, and gives me a soft, comforting smile.

"Tell me, Livy. What was your sister like?"

"J-Jenna?" I stutter. As if I have another.

"Yes. From the photos on the wall I see she looked a lot like your mother, didn't she?"

"Yes, she did." Why is he bringing up Jenna?

"I'm sure you miss her." His mouth is turned down in an apparent attempt to mirror my sorrow.

Oh no. Not this again. I sit forward in my chair, my hands flat against the table. "You're not really a tutor, are you?"

James shifts in his seat, his eyes piercing mine. "What do you mean? Of course I am."

I narrow my eyes at him. "My mother arranged this, didn't she? She thinks if she can fix me she'll fix herself, but I won't do it." I stand up and move behind my chair. "I don't need to see a shrink. I'm sad. I'm allowed to feel sad! My sister is dead!" My hands are gesturing at nothing and then they come to land on my hips. "Just because she can pretend she didn't lose a child doesn't mean the rest of us can't mourn her!"

"Livy." James reaches out to me again, but I'm using the chair as a shield. His hand lingers a moment in the air and then falls flat against the table.

"No. I'm sorry. This was a mistake. I don't need a shrink, she does."

"Livy?" I look up and find my mother standing in the doorway. Her face is as white as the blouse she's wearing. "Livy, this is Mr. Hale, he comes highly recommended—"

"I don't care how *highly recommended* he is! I don't need a shrink!"

"—by Steve," my mother finishes. "It was *Steve* who sent him here for the time being."

The room is silent while I look from my mom to James and then back again.

"He's a *tutor*," my mother says, enunciating each word clearly and deliberately, the way I've seen her do countless times before when she's explaining something simple to her campaign team. Her color has returned but her mouth is pinched like she's just tasted something sour. "His specialty is language arts. Steve thought he might be able to help improve your Spanish while he's away."

"Oh," is all I can muster. *Crap.*

"What's going on?" My father materializes just behind my mother in the doorway. It appears the only way to get him out of his study in the middle of the day is to start screaming at strangers. He's wearing the same clothes I saw him in two days ago. His red-rimmed eyes narrow on James just as James comes to his feet.

"Hi Daddy," I whisper and his attention shifts to me.

"Livy? What's wrong?" he asks.

I wish I had the time to tell him. I wish I could lay it all out on the dining room table with flow charts and spread sheets, but I'm not prepared for the moment, so instead I say, "Everything's fine, Daddy. I'm fine."

The look he gives me nearly breaks my heart altogether, because in my father's world there is no fine. There is only heartache.

It is my mother's responsibility to smooth everything over. That's what she does best, clean up and make pretty. In a matter of minutes my father is tucked safely back in his study, and after giving me a look that can only be interpreted as annoyance, she leaves James and I alone at the table.

"I'm sorry," I say. "That was kind of awkward for your first day. I apologize. We're usually less dramatic than that." At least, I am. I force myself to look at him even though I'd rather keep looking down at my hands.

"There's no need to apologize, Livy," he says, and I'm surprised to find that his expression is sincere. "I'm quite used to drama."

"I'm sorry," I repeat. My mother didn't make it to State Senator without some grooming and that grooming has been instilled in me as well. "So." I clear my throat. "Perhaps we could start again?" I reach my hand out to James and he slips his over mine. "I'm Livy," I say. "Nice to meet you."

"James," he says, his smile as bold as the twinkle in his eye. "And the pleasure's all mine."

CHAPTER SIX

The next night Sheila and I are at the movies. It's some end-of-world thing where aliens or zombies — I lost track about a half hour ago — are trying to take over the world, but it's difficult to follow along with Sheila and Grant playing find-the-tongue-who's-got-the-tongue right next to me. Sheila doesn't usually get into the whole PDA thing but Grant's been out of town on some hockey tour. I guess when the cat's away the heart grows fonder? Or something to that effect. Ryan was supposed to come but changed his mind at the last minute, and now here I am rolling with it like the third-wheel I am. I pull out my phone to check the time, wondering if I could sneak out without them noticing, when someone plops down in the seat next to mine.

"They all die in the end," Meyer says and I let out a little gasp that sounds a bit like, "Oh!" I'm not sure if my heart is beating faster because it's him or because he's startled me. Either way I'm happy to see him.

"What are you doing here?" I whisper, failing to hold back a smile.

"I figured if I spoiled the ending you wouldn't want to stick around."

"Do you have something else in mind?" I ask, sounding so flirtatious I barely recognize myself.

"Do you like fish?" He gives me this lopsided grin, the kind of grin you know is trouble, and I feel as if the happy switch has been turned on inside of me.

"That depends. Are we talking on a plate or in a tank?"

"The smell, actually."

"Um...?"

Meyer doesn't give me another second to think about it. He grabs my hand and drags me — albeit willingly — from the theater.

"Should you...?" He nods toward Sheila who hasn't even looked up, and I shrug.

"I'll text her," I say without hesitation. Now that Meyer has appeared I just want to get out of here.

I follow him outside where the rain is still falling but once we take off in a run I barely notice it. It's like we're moving too fast for it to touch us. Meyer leads me down one street and then another until we arrive at the entrance to Pike Place Market. I love Pike Place. Jenna and I used to come here every Saturday. Her favorite thing was walking around the flower market, smelling all of the different kinds of flowers, especially the ones you don't see every day like gerbera daisies and peonies. Even though I haven't been here in a while the familiar smells hit me like it was just yesterday, and the sadness that follows rests heavy upon my shoulders.

"I'm sure you're wondering what we're doing here," Meyer says. But I'm not, actually. I'm too busy dodging memories of Jenna to notice that we've stopped dead center in the middle of the fish market. To my left is the hot chocolate cart where we always began our shopping trip. Jenna would remove her lid so that after her first sip she could smile at me with a whipped-cream moustache. Next we'd wander over to her favorite fish thrower, Blaine, who'd always break into a song about *Jenna, Jenna, the beautiful Jenna who smells like flowers while he smells of fish.* Then he'd threaten to throw a large salmon at her while she'd scream and hide behind me. I realize with horror that I haven't been back since Jenna died. What will I do if Blaine asks about her? What will I tell him? It's not like I can yell, "She's dead!" across a line of customers. Should I pretend she's at home and then never come here again? I'm working this out in my head when Meyer's face materializes in front of me, blocking out the flower market, Jenna's favorite spot of all. How many hours had we spent wandering those aisles, reading each flower label as if she hadn't already memorized them?

"Livy?" Meyer says and his look of concern snaps me back to the present. "Livy? What's wrong?"

But I can't tell him. My throat is so tight I can barely speak.

I shake my head and force out a smile. *Not now. I can't think about this now.*

"Your next dare is awaiting, my lady." He holds his hand out and bows dramatically. For a moment I think he might just get down on one knee, and how silly would that be, in the center of Pike Place Market? His smile is wistful, and beautiful. With the soft light of the Market falling upon his features he could be a lost soul who traveled here from another time period. Not just a boy who lives to play games.

"Wait, that's not right," I say slowly, attempting to drag myself out from under my memory-induced misery. He lifts an eyebrow and I explain, "It's my turn to ask. Not yours."

He nods in consent and without me even asking, throws out, "Suffering."

"Alright." I glance around the market, wishing I'd been better prepared for this moment. Had I known I'd see Meyer today I would have made a list of dares and truths. "Just give me a second…"

"If you can't come up with a dare, you forfeit your turn and you'll be faced with a dare or truth by yours truly." Meyer is circling me now as if he is the lion and I am the gazelle. You have only a few seconds," he says dramatically, "before the tables are turned."

"Hold on." In a panic I look around for inspiration, taking in the crowd and everything I have to work with, but nothing is coming to me.

"10, 9, 8, 7 —"

"Just let me think a second," I say, covering my ears to keep his countdown from distracting me, but silly me, it's not the numbers that distract me, it's him. His challenging stare is almost threatening as he continues to circle me.

"6, 5, 4, 3 —"

"Sing!" I yell and he comes to a stop. "I want you to sing in front of all these people."

"Is that all!" he scoffs. He seems disappointed by my lack of creativity.

I hold up a hand. I'm not finished yet. "I want you to sing as loud as you can — an entire song, not just a note or two — right here, in front of everyone." I'm smiling as I finish because I know this is a dare that would make almost anyone uncomfortable, especially me, and if he fails to do it he must answer a question of my choice. At least that's how I think the rules go.

Meyer is watching me. He is so cocky in his casualness. He tips his head in acceptance of my dare and then he begins to whistle.

The market is crowded for a Wednesday night. Most of the shoppers appear to have just gotten out of work and are looking to throw together a late dinner before they retire in front of the TV. The last thing they are expecting is Meyer belting out a tune. And the last thing I'm expecting is his voice when he does. He starts out slow, struggling to fit each word to its note. I wonder if he's making it up as he goes, but just before the second verse his voice grows louder.

Stronger. He sings about a boy lost at sea with only his heart to steer him home to the girl who is waiting for him. As engaging as his song is it's his voice that captures my attention.

That melodic lilt to his voice is thicker now, as if it's part of the melody. The crowd shuffles past, their footsteps slowing, until they form a circle around us. Meyer sings on until he reaches the chorus, where the boy calls out to his lover in the dead of night, and his eyes lock onto mine. *She is mine*, he sings. *And I am lost.*

I don't notice when he closes the distance between us because once he started singing it felt like I was being drawn toward him anyway. But it's still a shock when he takes my hand and bows over it with a dramatic finish. The crowd breaks into applause.

"I do believe it's your turn," he says. Then he winks at me, a slow rakish wink that in the aftermath of his performance makes me dizzy. *I'm* the one on stage now, and I'm so caught up in the moment I just might fall off.

Meyer knows he has won when I remain silent. He's unnerved me. The smile that soon follows leaves me without breath. It's not fair this power he has over me. Not fair at all.

"Well done," I tell him. His body is so close we cast one shadow.

"Are you ready?" he says, and there's no need for me to answer. We both know my curiosity is piqued.

He takes my hand, leading me back toward the hidden shops behind the market.

We enter a shop I've never been in before; truth is I've never even noticed it. In the window is an assortment of costumes, some looking very renaissance while others are as cliché as a simple white dress with angel wings. Inside the store it feels crowded until I realize that the only other patrons are Meyer's friends, the kids from the Sculpture Gardens. They greet him and even wave to me. Not one questions my being here.

"Pick something, Livy," Meyer says. "But keep in mind, whichever costume you choose, you are that character for the rest of the night."

"Are you serious? We're playing dress-up?" I'm shocked, but it doesn't last long. My hands are already reaching out and touching the row of ball gowns hanging to my left.

"I dare you," Meyer says, leaning in so that I can hear him over the loud chatter inside the shop, "to be someone else tonight. Someone you've always wanted to be."

"You mean like a princess?" I point to the blue and gold gown one of his friends is carrying into the dressing room. "I *have* always wanted to be a princess…"

"Have you?" He shuffles back a few steps, bouncing on his heels, even though his words are anything but playful. "Or was that someone else, I wonder?"

"What do you mean?" I say, but even if he's heard me, he doesn't answer. He disappears behind a wall of hats.

There is an odd odor to the air, like time and dust have all gotten lost here. The costumes are all hung up or displayed on mannequins, not folded and crushed into a plastic bag like you'd find in some run-of-the-mill Halloween store. As I walk through the aisles I notice most of Meyer's female friends have chosen to be maidens or princesses. There's even the occasional fairy. I know that Jenna and Jilly would have gone straight for either the sparkling princess dresses or the whimsical fairies. But tonight my disguise is up to me, and me alone. This new adventure seems silly, so childish. Who plays dress-up at our age? In fact I'm surprised everyone is going along with it. The kids I know wouldn't. But Meyer isn't like most kids, and apparently neither are his friends. I know Sheila would be appalled if she knew what I was up to. Which makes me glad I left her back at the theater.

Hanging on the wall in front of me is a long sword with a golden hilt. Fake rubies and emeralds speckle the bottom of the hilt leading me to believe that this sword is meant for a pirate, not a knight. No knight would flaunt such a gaudy weapon. Carefully I slip the sword off the wall to test its weight. It's lighter than it looks.

"I saw something near the back that would be perfect with that," a blonde princess tells me. She smiles and gestures for me to follow her. From behind I notice her hair is multicolored, at least until she tucks her dark braid up and under her long, blonde wig.

Yes, I will definitely have to remember this place so that I can bring Jilly here some day. She could spend hours playing dress-up, conjuring a story for each style of costume. What an adventure she'd have here.

The princess leads me to a back corner where one lonely rack of clothing has been pushed to the side.

"Here," she says, pulling out an outfit that perfectly complements the sword. "I think it would look great on you," she adds and then she flits away with a light rustle of silk.

I stare down at the costume, taking in the black pants that might just fit me, and the flouncy green shirt that would match Meyer's eyes perfectly. But it's the pirate hat, strapped to the hanger that captures my attention. It's gold and silver and littered with jewels, something more Captain Hook than Livy Cloud.

When I try it on, I'm surprised by how well it fits, jutting out just over my left eye, as if I'm eternally challenging someone. This is it, I think. This is who I want to be tonight. Not a princess, but a rebel — a character that fights and survives, and never depends on others to save her.

I gather up the costume, head into the dressing room, and emerge a pirate.

"You look great!" The princess is back and this time she's brought her entourage, which includes one prince and three damsels. "Just wait until Meyer sees you!"

And then he's here, standing in front of me with his sword at his side and his hat held to his chest, as one does when they've encountered a lady. The only bit of him out of character is his feet. He's still wearing his black Chuck Taylor's.

"What's this?" he says, his eyes on me. "Do I spy the pirate queen?"

I catch a glimpse of my reflection in the standing mirror and then tilt this way and that until I've seen all of me.

"Why, yes, I do believe it suits you," Meyer says, sizing me up as if I am his opponent. "The question is, are we united or are we adversaries?" His hand moves to the hilt of his own sword like he senses danger and he's ready to fight. But his eyes are sparkling.

I tip my hat, and with my best imitation of his strange accent, say, "Let's see how the night plays out, shall we?"

CHAPTER SEVEN

There are twelve of us now; I counted as we stood at the cash register. One by one we hand the girl behind the counter our credit cards, that is, everyone but Meyer. When it comes time for him to pay he winks at the sales girl who blushes and waves him on by.

We are dressed like it's Halloween, even though it's a few weeks away, and we make quite a scene as we walk through the market. A few people call out to us, "Where's the party?"

Apparently wherever we are tonight.

"Where are we going?" I ask Cecily, the blonde princess, once we leave Pike Place Market behind. She introduced herself back at the costume shop while we were waiting in line and then made sure to point out her boyfriend, Will, who is now dressed like Zorro.

"There's an old amusement park up ahead." She grabs my hand and drags us to the front of our crowd where Meyer and Will lead the way.

"Isn't it closed?" I ask, but she just smiles.

We shuffle on down the street, taking alleys when they present themselves and avoiding the main roads. We are loud in our appearance, but nearly silent in our steps. To look at us, it is as though we are walking through time. Or rather we've escaped it. Right now I am not Livy Cloud, nor should I think like her. I am fearless. I am brave. I am a pirate. I am smiling, thoroughly caught up in the moment, when my cell phone rings.

When I pull it out of my pocket all I see is Sheila's face flashing on the screen. In the screenshot she's sticking her tongue out at me, her tongue ring proudly displayed.

I should answer it, but I don't. Instead I text her back: *I'm okay. Call you later.*

And her response is: *Yes you will.*

Meyer is only a person or two ahead of me but every once in a while he turns, perhaps making sure I'm still here. When I catch him, he winks at me, and even though it's just a little thing, this wink, it still manages to trigger a flutter inside my stomach.

"He's never brought anyone with him before," Cecily says. "He's always alone." She's watching me closely and I look away before she notices the sudden blush staining my cheeks.

"How do you know him?" I don't know why I'm whispering — he couldn't possibly hear me.

"I don't." Her half-covered shoulders rise with a shrug. "No one does, really. We just know where he'll be."

"What do you mean? I thought maybe you all went to the same school or something."

"No. I'm not even sure Meyer's from around here. Sometimes he disappears for weeks on end. We figure he's gone for good and then he shows up again, out of the blue."

I open my mouth to ask another question but Will pops up in front of us and grabs Cecily around her waist, causing her to shriek with glee. "Come along, Princess. These streets aren't safe." He wraps his cape around her and as they move on up ahead all I hear is giggling.

I continue along with the crowd as we make our way toward the old Seattle Center. My attention strays back to Meyer and it's as if he senses it. He raises an eyebrow like he knows we were discussing him and he finds my curiosity amusing.

"You're a mystery," I mumble under my breath, and he tips his hat, his smile spreading.

The old amusement park is in a part of town that used to be alive with activity — when the nearest pier was in its heyday — but now it stands forgotten. The old factories that border it are boarded up and even though they hold the promise of one day becoming renovated and artsy, tonight they are simply abandoned.

There's a large fence around the park and the chain that keeps it closed off is rusty, but solid. A few of Meyer's friends try to climb the fence and then give up when it buckles under their weight.

"How do we get in?" a green fairy asks. She's rubbing her arms to keep warm and her teeth are chattering. At any moment I expect to see her shiver herself into a pile of pixie dust.

"How did we get in last time, Meyer?" Will asks, looking around as if he's lost something. "Meyer?" He glances over at me. "Where is he?"

This is a good question, one I don't have an answer for, and soon we're all looking around. But Meyer is nowhere to be found.

Suddenly the amusement park comes to life with a loud whir. I jump back as if I'm under attack, but the only thing assaulting me is the out-of-tune organ music coming from the broken-down rides. A chill ripples over my skin and for a brief moment I wonder if this park is haunted.

"Over here!" Meyer calls out. He's standing on top of a large ceramic whale at the entrance to the park. He waves his hat in the air and I notice he's made a new friend. A night security officer is standing next to him on the ground, his ring of keys a welcoming, if not curious, sight.

"Tom, here, is giving us the run of the place tonight, as long as we're good." Meyer takes a moment to study each one of us, and then he calls out, "What say you, my friends. Will we be good?"

A roar of agreement breaks out around me and then we're running toward the opening in the fence. The guard doesn't exactly seem happy to see us. He looks confused, as though he knows what he's doing is wrong but can't remember why. When I pass him I call out, "thank you!" But he just nods, his eyes locked on the ground.

"Livy." Meyer takes my arm and pulls me into his side. "It's time for our next adventure," he says. But I'm pretty sure it has already started.

As we head toward the rides I realize there is something off about this park, something missing. It's not long before I realize what's missing is the scent. Amusement parks should be fragranced with cotton candy and fried food, the aroma so strong you're not sure if it's the aftermath of riding a rollercoaster that has you dizzy, or if it's just the sugar high. But here it doesn't smell sweet; it smells like rusting metal and burning oil, which contributes to the park's creepy atmosphere. With nearly half the lights shattered or broken, and most of the adornment on the rides faded and corroded from years of wet weather, it's like something out of a horror movie. It certainly doesn't help that we're the only ones here. I keep looking over my shoulder, expecting at any moment an evil clown with a half-melted-off smile to pop out from the funhouse holding a scythe.

"Do you do this a lot?" I ask. "Break into old amusement parks while dressed in costume?" When Meyer doesn't answer I add, "I mean, it's cool and all. Just different."

"But we're not in costume," he scoffs, "we're in character." He grabs my hand and leads me toward the largest ride in the park: the Ferris wheel.

"Your ship awaits," he says, gesturing grandly to the spinning ride towering over us.

"You want me to ride that?" I stare up at the rickety ride, surprised it's even working. Of all the rides in the park, this one appears to be the oldest and most neglected.

When Meyer nudges me forward I say, "You first."

"As you wish, my lady." With a low bow he steps into the nearest bucket seat.

"Who's going to operate the ride?" I ask, stalling for more time.

"Why, Tom, of course." Meyer is leaning back against the seat, his arms folded behind his head like he's resting on a couch not a broken-down death machine. He nods toward the control box and I see Tom hovering over the controls.

"Are you sure this is safe?" I ask Tom, and he shrugs.

"They haven't torn it down yet," Tom tells me.

"Well that makes me feel better," I mutter to myself.

"Come on, Livy. What are you afraid of?"

"Everything," I answer instinctively, and even though it's said under my breath, I'm pretty sure he hears me.

"I told you, there's nothing to fear. You're safe with me." He's leaning forward now as he waits for me to make up my mind. "It's all part of the adventure."

Ah, yes. The adventure. That's what this is. How could I forget? This isn't everyday life where I spend my hours watching the people I care about die, or that large part of my day-to-day routine where my parents are so caught up in their own worlds they don't notice I'm still around. This is my adventure, the one where I get to pretend I'm okay with how things are, at least for a little while.

"Alright," I say, hopping into the bucket seat. "Let's do this." The smile on Meyer's face tells me I've made the right decision.

Before I sit down I remove my sword and pirate hat and place them near my feet next to Meyer's sword.

"How do pirates sit with those things attached to their hips?" I mumble. Walking with one was difficult enough.

Once I'm seated I try not to notice how the chair tips slightly to the left and how my seat strap doesn't click into place. After fumbling with it for another minute or so Meyer reaches over and ties the two straps together into a knot, securing me to the seat in a rather makeshift way. He's looking quite satisfied with himself, as if he considers the problem solved, while I, on the other hand, take a deep breath and try not to think about what could happen if this bucket seat spins around and tips us upside-down. Or how without a working seat strap, we really shouldn't be on this ride at all.

With a loud creak and a jolt the ride starts up. I don't realize I've got hold of Meyer's hand in a death grip until one by one he peels my fingers back. "I thought you weren't afraid of heights," he says.

"I'm not. I guess I'm just afraid of dying."

Meyer gives me a funny look, one I can't even begin to decipher, and then he turns away.

"Or perhaps just broken-down Ferris wheels," I mutter under my breath.

"It's a beautiful night," Meyer says gazing out over the park. His feet are crossed and stretched out in front of him. When he leans back I notice he hasn't even bothered with *his* seat strap.

"It is beautiful," I say but my voice is so high-pitched and nervous it comes off as a question.

I take a breath and then another, forcing them to be something they're not — slow and steady — while Meyer continues to turn lounging into an art form. He's so relaxed he appears sleepy. Is he doing this just to annoy me? If so, it's kind of working.

"How do you know these kids?" I ask, gazing out over the park.

"Hmm. I don't, really."

We're both watching as a small group of princes stage an impromptu sword fight on one of the old stages. You can hear their voices rise each time one of them lunges at another.

"If you don't know them, how did you hook up with them?" I ask.

"I guess you could say, they found me."

"What do you mean they *found* you?" I snort. "Were you lost?"

Meyer tips his pirate hat forward as if he's looking to take a nap and crosses his arms. "You sure do ask a lot of questions."

We're nearing the top of the Ferris wheel now, and spread out below us is a full view of the park. I can make out Cecily and Will swirling around on the carousel, while three longhaired princesses attempt to ride sidesaddle behind them. Over on the swings the green fairy is kicking her feet, her arm reaching out to the blue and gold princess beside her as they sway back and forth, occasionally grasping hands. When the ride starts up the green fairy shrieks with joy and I watch as her wings fly out behind her. There is a prince and a princess running just below us. Their hands tie them together as they hurry to the next ride. They come to a sudden stop and the prince spins the princess in an elaborate circle that makes her dress spin out around her.

"Unbelievable," I whisper. It's like a living fairytale, like *The Twelve Dancing Princesses*, but instead of gold-and silver-tipped trees our paths are littered with neon lit carnival rides and old, broken-down food carts. And instead of going dancing we're breaking and entering.

"I'm glad you came, Livy."

I glance over at Meyer and find he's watching me. His hat is still low over his forehead but he's cocked it so that he can spy me with one very green eye.

"I'm glad too," I say and then realize I'm not nervous anymore. My stomach isn't filled with knots and I'm actually leaning forward in my seat.

"I knew you had it in you." He tilts his hat back down as if he's done talking, but the smile remains on his lips.

"How did you know?" I ask. "When I didn't."

Meyer's mouth turns down into a frown. It's the only sign he's even heard me.

"You're really sticking with this whole mysterious thing aren't you?"

Much to my annoyance, Meyer simply shrugs.

"Well, thank you," I whisper. "Even if I never find out anything more about you, I really needed this." I'm staring out toward the Seattle skyline, not expecting a reply, but he gives me one anyway.

"You're welcome, Livy."

We're almost halfway down when our ride comes to a jerky stop. I remember this part of the ride from past carnivals, where one by one the riders get off while others climb on. But we're the only ones who appear to be brave enough to ride this thing. Down below I can make out an empty platform and when I look back toward the swings I see Tom still manning the controls.

In other words, there's no reason for us to have stopped.

"Meyer?" I squeak out. But he's already sitting up. He leans over the side to get a good look down and the chair tips forward. "Please! Don't do that." My eyes are squeezed shut and I'm leaning so far back in my seat I'm nearly arching.

"I think the ride has stopped," he says.

"You caught on to that, did you?" Without opening my eyes I know when he's returned to his seat, mostly because the chair stops swaying.

"Livy." Meyer touches my face and I open one eye. "Do you trust me?" These are the last words I want to hear. Had he said we're all going to die I think I would have handled it better, but *do you trust me* can only mean he wants me to do something I don't want to do.

"We're not that far off the ground," he explains.

But he's wrong. We're at least three stories high.

"And Tom won't be able to hear us all the way over there." He points back toward the swings where it appears Tom has decided to take a nap. He's slumped over the controls while the swings continue to spin around and around. "What say we climb down?"

My eyes widen at his suggestion and I shake my head. "What say we don't," I hiss. "What say we stay up here until someone saves us or the cops come or... Yes! I can call the police!" I pull my phone out of my pocket but my hands are shaking so badly it slips through my fingers and clatters to the floor. "NO!" I scream as it takes a sharp bounce off the side of the seat and plummets to the ground as if in slow motion. "No," I say again, my voice soft with defeat this time.

"It's okay, Livy." Meyer takes hold of my hands. He keeps tugging on them to get my attention, but I don't want to look at him. If I look at him he's only going to try to get me to follow him over the side.

He squeezes my hands. "I won't let you fall." The next thing I know he's untying the straps holding me in my seat.

"I can't do it." I shake my head and try to push his hands away, but he's quick. He has the straps free before I can stop him.

"You *can*," he says. "Just watch. It's easy." And then he's climbing over the side of the chair, holding onto the metal beams — the ones you're never supposed to touch — as though it's perfectly normal to exit a ride this way. "Follow me." His hand is reaching for mine. "Just don't look down."

Which is the first thing I do. I lean over just slightly to get a good view of the ground, but it's enough movement that the chair tilts forward.

Meyer loses his footing and drops back into the chair. The force of his landing jerks something free and our chair shifts violently to the right. I scream and grab onto Meyer, while Meyer latches onto the side of the chair. Now we're dangling. My feet are reaching for the ground but it's too far away. A rush of air surges up and around me. It moves along my body and across my face and then my teeth start chattering. I know I'm no longer tucked, safe inside the chair, but I know nothing more. I can't look, I won't.

My arms are wrapped around Meyer's waist; the side of my face pressed into his stomach. He is holding us in place, his strength the only thing keeping us from instant death. I can hear his heart beating, slow and steady, unlike mine. And when something clatters to the ground below us I can't help it, I flinch.

"Was that my sword?" I gasp. It took awhile to hit the ground. Too long. *Are we higher up than I realized?* With that thought my shivering grows worse.

"I'm going to die," I whimper. "Before I can save Jilly." Before I can save myself. I take a shaky breath, but it's not enough. I'm squeezing Meyer so tight my arms are aching.

"Do you trust me?"

There are those words again. I really wish he would stop using them. I jerk my head, no, and then grip him tighter.

"I'm going to get us down," he says, and I should probably ask how, but I'm too afraid to find out.

He shifts above me, like he's changing up his hold and then his arms wrap around me.

"Wait! What's happening?" I cry, my eyes popping open. But everything is black. I'm pressed up against his chest so tightly I can't see anything.

And then I swear I feel my feet touch the ground.

It's a light landing, a mere brush with the earth, but even though I should feel safe, or at the very least relieved, I can't let go of Meyer.

He tilts my chin up so that I'm looking into his eyes. His mouth so close to mine I can feel his breath. "We're down now. Back on the ground." But I don't believe him. It's not possible.

His hands are on my shoulders. He's not pushing me away nor is he keeping me close, just holding onto me. I stare up at the ride where our broken chair is still dangling sideways, so far above us.

"What happened?" I squeak out. "Did we jump?" *Please tell me we jumped.*

"I told you it was easy," Meyer says, and the flashing lights of the Ferris wheel illuminate his triumphant smile. But he's the only one smiling. Me? I'm crying. Tears are sliding down my face and I can't stop them no matter how hard I try. I'm terrified. Even though I'm safe and back on the ground, I'm still trembling. I open my mouth to say something and then quickly close it when a tiny sob slips free. Meyer tries to collect me as my knees buckle and I go down, but instead I take him with me. He hovers over me as I press myself into the cracked sidewalk. It's everything I can do not to kiss the ground.

"Livy, I'm so sorry," he says. His smile is gone, and his bright eyes are now filled with remorse. It's a new look on him, one I barely recognize. He pulls me to my feet and then cups my face in his hands. The way he's looking at me is so intense I stop breathing. "You have nothing to fear, Livy. *Nothing.*" I nod my head so that he knows I've heard him.

But the moment he drops his hands, I take off running.

CHAPTER EIGHT

I leave Meyer and his friends at the amusement park. I don't bother to say my goodbyes. I just run. Meyer doesn't try to stop me. He just watches me go. Those words he said follow me home. They're still with me when I step off the elevator, back into my real life.

Nothing to fear.

His words swim around inside my mind, searching for a new way to come to shore.

Nothing to fear. Nothing to fear.

But I have *everything* to fear. I'm afraid of what happened tonight and what didn't. And most importantly I'm afraid of how I act with Meyer. I seem to forget who I am. That first night I loved it, I loved escaping from me, but tonight it became abundantly clear that his version of escape comes with too high a price. And my sanity is not currency. I have very little of it left these days, and he's not going to rob me of it.

Isn't that what happened tonight? I lost my mind a little? Otherwise I wouldn't believe that Meyer could fly. It just doesn't make sense. I think back to that first night at the Sculpture Gardens, how he asked me if I ever wanted to fly, and how I said yes even though I didn't think it was possible. Because it's not possible. Yet somehow he got us safely back down on the ground. Somehow he saved us. Me. And with no one else around to witness it I'm forced to believe this explanation because I'm still alive when I shouldn't be.

I should be dead.

This is what I'm thinking when I come face to face with my mother. Luckily I had the presence of mind to change out of my pirate costume downstairs in the lobby restroom. I'm not sure what she would have done if I'd walked in still dressed like a pirate queen. On most nights I could probably slink by with a backhanded wave and a "goodnight," leaving her to whatever she was doing. However, tonight she's sitting at the kitchen table, a large mug of steaming tea in her hands, and she doesn't look happy to see me.

"Hi Mom," I say, continuing down the hallway.

"Olivia," she calls after me. "Would you mind taking a seat for a minute?"

"Of course." I backtrack to the kitchen and plop down into one of the kitchen chairs. My legs and hands are still shaking. I hide them under the table where my mother's narrowed eyes can't find them.

"What is it?" I ask, already eager to get to bed and be alone with my thoughts. I keep my face blank and my breathing slow. All I really want to do is bury my head under my covers and block out the feeling of falling to my death.

"Dr. Lerner's office called today," she says, and that's all it takes to break free of this evening's spell over me.

"Dr. Lerner?" I say with forced casualness, but inside I'm choking.

"Yes, Olivia. Dr. Lerner. His nurse called, actually. She asked to speak with you and since I wasn't sure why she would be calling here, I asked for more information."

"I see." I clear my throat but it doesn't help. The tightness moves into my chest and then takes hold of my heart. "Did she tell you why she was calling?"

"She did." The tone of her voice is so calm and yet the look in her eyes is anything but. "She wanted to let you know that they'd like you to come in for some additional tests."

"Oh." This one little word is all I can manage.

"Yes. And because I didn't know anything about the first test, I figured she should fill me in on what exactly you were being tested for."

"Right." I clear my throat again and then get up to get a glass of water. "So she must have told you." I'm staring into the cupboard for what; I'm no longer sure.

"Yes, she did." My mom's hand moves past me to grab a glass and I jump back. I didn't even hear her get up. She fills the glass with water and then hands it to me. I take it, but I can't think what to do with it.

"I'm going through with this," I say. "I'm going to do whatever they ask me to and you can't stop me."

"You know that's not true, Olivia." Her mouth is a single tight line. Without its usual red lipstick, it appears even more threatening.

"I have to do this, Mom," I whisper. My hands are shaking so badly that water spills over the side of the glass and sloshes to the floor.

My mother doesn't react. She just stares at me like she doesn't recognize me, as though I'm someone else's child.

"She's dying. Jilly is dying." I take a breath and try to squeak out the rest of my explanation, all the words I've been rehearsing since the day I decided to do this. But the only word that makes it out is, "please."

For a moment I think I've convinced my mother to care. Her eyes are blurry and wet, like she's on the verge of tears, but perhaps she's just tired. One can never really tell with my mother. She raises her chin as if she's been caught with her guard down before finally turning away from me.

"No," she says, and if that word wasn't damaging enough, she adds, "and I told them the same thing, Olivia, so don't bother going back down there."

And that's what finally gets me. My mother has spoken, and as far as she's concerned this discussion is over. She's walking away, leaving the kitchen. Her blonde ponytail is swinging back and forth as if it's sweeping up the remnants of this conversation.

"This isn't your choice!" I yell. "You have no right to stop me." I raise my hands as if they alone can keep her from leaving, but my words already have.

"Don't you dare tell me what rights I have!" She spins back around, her blue eyes blazing. "This isn't your battle, Olivia. When are you going to realize that? You can't save that little girl any more than we could have saved Jenna!"

Jenna. My sister's name bounces around the walls and ceiling as if our apartment has been craving the sound of it and is now making up for the loss. Even my mom is taken aback. Her eyes widen and the stiffness in her posture slips. Like she's crumbling in front of me. It's a little thing, really, but the sound of Jenna's name falling from her lips has nearly broken her.

I don't want to yell anymore. Truth is, I've never been much of a yeller. My mother knows this because neither has she.

"If I don't try, I'll never know." My words are like a slap to her already stricken face.

She shakes her head violently. "No more hospitals," she spits out. "No more worrying. No more, Livy. I can't."

"It's just a procedure, Mom. Nothing serious." *Nothing to fear.*

"You can't keep getting attached to these kids," she continues. "When will you learn?"

"But it's Jilly," I cry. "She's not just some child I latched onto at the hospital. She was Jenna's best friend."

"Please, mom," I beg when she remains silent. "Please. Just think about it before you say no. I promise, I'll be fine."

My mother looks at me, really looks at me, as if I can make this promise. As if she needs me to.

"Please!" I say. "Don't say no."

And when she turns around and leaves the kitchen she doesn't say no. But she also doesn't say yes.

I barely sleep that night. Each time my eyes close I'm back to falling, and then I jerk awake only to find that I'm not at the amusement park, I'm in bed. But my mind refuses to accept it.

The next morning I slip out early to return my pirate costume. I come prepared to pay for the missing sword and hat, left behind with my hasty getaway, but to my surprise I find that someone has already returned them, that and my cell phone. It's not broken and lost, like I'd originally thought. It actually looks as good as new. I almost ask who it was who returned everything, but then I stop myself. What does it matter, anyway? After last night I don't think I'll ever see Meyer again. Whether or not he seeks me out, I think it's better this way. Better for me.

I take the long way around Pike Place, avoiding the fish market that will now forever remind me of Meyer and his song about the lost boy at sea. I realize he has stolen one of my Jenna places, and that's nearly unforgivable. There's a part of me that wants to resent him for that. Yet I can't. It's too good a memory, that song of his. When I think back on our last adventure it's the one part of last night that doesn't kickstart a panic attack.

By the time I make it back to the apartment I'm wet and cold and miserable. I'm in such a funk I don't even notice James is waiting for me in the lobby until he calls out to me.

"Good morning, Livy," he says. When I glance in his direction I'm once again caught off guard by his beauty. He's wearing a dark gray suit today, which normally would come off stuffy like the suits my father wears, but on James it appears casual yet polished. Or to sum it up in one word: smooth. And his pale-colored eyes are darker today, almost stormy. Just like the weather outside.

"Do we have class today?" I blink up at him in a stupor, desperately trying to remember what day it is. Thursday? Yes, it's Thursday, which means we don't have class.

I should only be subjected to James on Tuesdays, Wednesdays and Sundays. Not Thursdays.

"I'm sorry. I thought your mom gave you my message. We're going on a field trip today."

"A field trip?" I couldn't sound any less excited, but James doesn't seem to care.

"Yes. A field trip." He reaches for the long dark raincoat resting next to him on the chair and slips it on.

I'm thinking about how to get out of this when my cell phone buzzes. It's a text from my mom. *Forgot to tell you,* she says. *You're going on a field trip with Mr. Hale. He should be here soon. Have fun.*

"Interesting," I mumble.

"Isn't it?" says James.

I slip my phone back in my pocket, my eyes narrowed on him. This all feels too coincidental, the timing especially. That could be my newfound paranoia talking — which settled in after last night's brush with death — or it could be that I'm always going to feel trepidatious when I'm around James.

"Do you need anything from upstairs before we go?" He gestures toward the elevator and for a moment I consider making a run for it.

"I guess not."

"Alright then." James walks ahead of me, opens the door and waits for me to exit first. "Shall we?"

"May I ask where we're going?" My legs feel heavy as I make my way back outside. I pull my hood up and over my hair, keeping out the early morning rain. "I didn't pack a lunch or anything," I mumble.

Back in public school, field trips to the Seattle Aquarium or the Space Needle would have kept me up half the night before, riddled with excitement, much different from how I'm feeling now. The idea of spending time with James greatly disturbs me, even more so when it's just the two of us.

"Does my mother know where we're going?" I hate that I ask this. I sound suspicious, and if I were truly suspicious I wouldn't be going. Would I? I mean I have a text from my mom telling me to go and James is my teacher after all... but still.

"Steve and I never did field trips," I mumble.

"Your mother and I planned this yesterday." James pauses on the sidewalk to open his black golf umbrella. When his hands wrap around the handle I notice how his fingernails are perfectly manicured, not bitten to the quick like mine. When he catches me studying him he asks, "What's wrong, Livy? Do I make you nervous?"

"No," I say far too quickly.

"Well that's a relief." He smiles and offers me his arm. "Stay close, now. This rain can dampen any adventure."

Adventure?

That word immediately sounds an alarm inside my mind. I tilt my head up to look at him and a raindrop hits me right in the eye. Before I can wipe it away James is holding out a handkerchief, and then dabbing it against my cheek. His touch is gentle, much more so than I would have imagined. And I should move away, tell him I'm fine, but suddenly I'm a statue, molded in place by his gesture. All I can do is wait as he wipes the moisture away.

"All better." He hands me the handkerchief and I take it, noticing the initials, JH, stitched into the fragile fabric. "Keep it. You never know when you might need it." And then he's off, moving down the street, while I'm left to trail after him.

CHAPTER NINE

"Is there something on your mind? You looked upset back in the lobby." We're walking down Virginia Street. I'm still not sure where he's taking me; only that we're headed downtown. After a few more beats of silence James adds, "Anything you'd like to talk about?"

We pause at the stoplight. I watch as the red hand flashes its warning to stay where I am, wondering if it's trying to tell me something other than now is not the time to cross the street.

"Nothing important," I say. Just thinking about a boy who may or may not be able to fly.

"Boyfriend stuff, eh?"

I glance at him quickly, wondering if I'd said the thought aloud, even though I'm sure I didn't.

"I don't have a boyfriend."

"Well," he says with that look that adults get when they're on the cusp of being patronizing "I'm sure it's only a matter of time."

When the light turns green he leads me to a restaurant just a few blocks away. I'm glad we haven't gone far, relieved actually. However, once we step inside the restaurant it's as though we've traveled to a foreign land. Spain to be specific.

"Estrellas is known for its amazing tapas and inviting atmosphere," he tells me.

I follow him to a table near the back where we're partially hidden by a dark black curtain draped from the ceiling.

"Let me guess, you're a Yelp reviewer in your spare time?" I say while pulling out my seat.

He lifts a brow, but doesn't give me the satisfaction of a comment.

"Today you order in Spanish," he explains. "And you eat what you order, of course." His smile is wide and playful and I know this is all part of the teach-Livy-Spanish program but there's something about James that makes me think he's not one to play games. Or if he did, his games would all end with him stuffing small children into a large brick oven.

"What if I can't pronounce the words?" I ask once I'm seated.

"Then the waitress and I will have a good laugh, and the next time we come you'll be the wiser."

The wiser? Who talks like that? I roll my eyes while he removes his coat.

An attractive older woman stops by our table and does the kiss-each-cheek thing to James. Agata is her name and she says it so quickly it's like she's clicking her tongue. She swishes her long brown hair back and forth over her shoulders while she speaks, her movements so graceful she could be dancing. And while her voice is lovely, her Spanish is rapid-fire fast. The only words I can make out are beautiful and friend. When she turns to me I figure I don't need to understand Spanish to translate the color of jealousy in her brown eyes.

"She is my student," James explains in English. "Today we learn the flavor of Spanish cuisine."

"And tomorrow you learn the pleasures of love?" Her accent is thick when she switches to English, but not thick enough. My face erupts in flames.

"Tomorrow," James purrs, "is a question without an answer." He glances up at Agata as if he has more to say, but his lips don't move. Even the air in the room is still.

"Perdón," Agata stammers. Her face has lost its color; even her full mouth appears bloodless. She drops two menus on the table and hurries away.

There is something dark and powerful about James. It hovers around him like smoke. If I could bring myself to move I would leave this restaurant and go home, but I've made the mistake of meeting his eyes, his pale blue eyes, so unusually clear they're like staring through water. If I look close I can see myself, almost as if he wants me to. And I don't like what I see. I don't like the girl who frowns so deeply her shoulders can't hold the weight of it. I don't like how vulnerable she looks, and I definitely don't like how small she appears. Soon my discomfort breeds anger, but the glare I toss at him is squandered away. He's too busy studying the menu to notice it.

"The chorizo-crusted cod is quite good here," he says, and I realize he has given me an out. The sooner we order the sooner I can leave this place. I lean down and focus on the menu.

A young waitress approaches our table. She doesn't make eye contact with James but listens closely when he speaks. When it comes time for me to order I somehow manage to sound less like an American than I anticipated. I even remember to roll my r's.

"Well done, Livy." He tilts his head curiously. "Do you actually know what you've ordered?"

"Pig, potatoes and spice." I mirror his challenging stare. "And if I don't like it, *you'll* have to finish it."

Much to my surprise James laughs. His eyes gleam in the low light of the restaurant and I find I'm jealous of his beauty. Those eyelashes are wasted on him. And his skin, it's far too clear and smooth to belong to a teacher. It would be better suited to a movie star.

He catches me watching him and I drag my gaze away, wishing the waitress hadn't left with our menus. I have nothing to hide behind now.

"I used to bring my wife here." He sits back in his chair. "She loved Spanish food. She said it was just what the heart craved."

"Your wife?" It seems odd to think of him as married, perhaps because he appears too perfect to travel life like the rest of us. "What does your wife do?"

"Anything she wants now. She passed away over four years ago."

"I'm so sorry," I say, because that's what you're supposed to say. But I am sorry. Suddenly I'm so sorry I feel sorrow bubble up inside my throat, threatening to spill out. "What happened to her?" I ask, even though I know better. How many times have I flinched when someone asked me how my sister died?

"She died in her sleep." James smiles this beautiful, peaceful smile that no one should wear when speaking of the dead. "She died the way she wanted, at peace with herself and all she'd accomplished."

I'm waiting for his calm façade to crack, an eye to twitch or his smile to tremble and slip down in one corner. But it seems James is full of surprises.

"Don't you miss her?" I lean forward, my attention completely focused on him. Normally this is not a path I would travel, but I have to know. How is he so calm about this? How can he be so unfeeling? Is this what I can expect to be like in four years? Will I talk about Jenna as if it's a good thing she's dead?

"She has only passed, Livy. She is not gone. She is all around me."

"Oh." I sit back and release the slight shiver that has been building since James first mentioned his wife. "So you're one of those, then."

"One of those? I'm sorry. I don't follow."

"You're one of those people who believe that the dead dwell among us." I shake my head and slouch further down in my seat. "Sheila's stepmother gives people like you half her husband's salary, trying to figure out what her future holds." I hold out my hands even though they're still shaking. "Are you going to read my fortune now? Study my lifeline?"

When James stays silent I drop my hands. "Or maybe you're religious? Is this the part where you tell me how I'll see Jenna one day? How she's happier where she is. How she's better off away from this evil place. Away from me."

"Is that what you believe, Livy? Do you believe this place is evil? That God is taking children one by one, tearing them from their loved ones simply out of spite?"

"So you *are* religious then."

"That's not an answer," he fires back.

"I don't know what I believe." My voice is soft but I know he hears every word. "I used to beg Him to save her. I used to make deals, promises, anything to keep her here." I shrug as if this subtle movement can lessen the pain that has filled my chest. "I guess He didn't hear me. Or you."

James sits back in his seat. His arm is draped over the back of his chair as if this is a casual conversation we're having, but I know better. I wish I didn't sound like this. I wish I didn't sound so bitter. This person I hear, sure she sounds like me, but this isn't who I am. I'm better than this, right? There has to be some hope left inside of me otherwise I wouldn't still be fighting for Jilly.

James is studying me as if he can see something buried beneath my skin. "I never asked for more time with her. Nor did I plead for her life."

"So then you didn't love her." The second I've said it, I know I've made a mistake. James doesn't move but I feel his tension all around me. It closes in on me and nearly steals my breath.

"You have a lot to learn about love, Livy. Love isn't selfish. It may be unkind and it will definitely humble you, but never will it demand what it can't give back."

"So then it's my fault? Are you suggesting I didn't love her enough?" I don't realize I'm yelling until everyone else in the restaurant falls silent.

"It's never anyone's fault." James sits forward in his seat, his hands pressed into the table. "Even though I do find most people like to blame themselves."

"I blame her!" I hate that I've said it, but it's how I feel. And once those words are out there, they shatter the pressure I've been carrying around with me since the day she died. "I wish I didn't," I whisper, my throat so tight I can barely finish my thought. "But I do."

That's when our food arrives. The waitress slinks up to our table as if she wishes she didn't have to. I stare down at each item she places in front of us. We've ordered a feast, but I'm not hungry.

"I've changed my mind," James says once the waitress scampers off. Neither of us has made a move to start eating. This conversation is our first course. "There *is* someone to blame here. Your fault lies in that you didn't let her go. Until you do, you'll never be free."

"Free?" I laugh, but it is without humor. "Is that the goal? I'm supposed to feel free?"

"You're supposed to be happy."

"Oh, well that's easy enough. I *am* happy." I smile at him, my lips stretched across my teeth to prove my case. I don't need to see myself to know I must look crazy. I definitely feel crazy. My smile slips from the weight of his stare, and the words tumble out. "I just miss her."

James reaches across the table and places his hand over mine. I want to pull away, but I don't. His skin feels warm when he gives my hand a squeeze. His touch is gentle.

"We seek out other people to fight off the loneliness but it's like we're children playing at pretend. We are alone in everything we do, Livy. Alone but not without company."

"I don't want to be alone. I want to be the one who goes off to college knowing that Jenna's at home searching through my stuff and trying on my clothes." I hate that I'm telling him this; I hate it so much I'm glaring at him. But I can't stop talking.

"She used to go to camp. Cancer camp." I stare down at my fingernails, noticing how they don't look like my hands anymore. Jenna used to paint them all different shades of pink, but she's been gone so long now they're bare.

"It was only for a weekend. They would leave Friday afternoon and come back Sunday morning and it was too much. Too much for me, having her gone, even then. I used to wander around her bedroom, lifting her toys, sitting on her bed like I was the younger sister."

"Would it make you feel better to know that she's happy?"

I hear James say these words, but it's Meyer's face I see.

"How…?" I begin, but then stop. It doesn't make sense that they've both asked this question.

"Think about it, Livy," he whispers.

But that's just what I'm doing.

"Imagine it. Imagine her happy."

I close my eyes, lulled by the softness of his voice. *Would* I feel better if I knew she was happy? Would I sleep better knowing she's still out there somewhere? Her energy or soul — or whatever it is you become once your body has given up on you — floating around in a place that's peaceful and beautiful like they say heaven is. Would that make me feel better?

"No."

I pick up my napkin, place it over my lap and force myself to take my first bite of fish. James is still focused on me; I know this without looking up. I take another bite and then two more, chewing but not tasting the food in my mouth. I won't look at him. If I do he'll see that I'm lying. He'll see that I'm just a child acting out, and I can't have that. I've always wanted Jenna to be happy. I did everything I could to make her that way. But I wanted her happy *here*. I want to see her happy. Without that reality she's just gone.

Eventually James joins me in the meal. The subject is abandoned for now. Hopefully for good. He steers the conversation to the places he's visited in Spain and Morocco, and I'm grateful for the distraction. His stories are entertaining and exotic, though I do wonder how much of it is true. He tells me of the pirates he encountered off the coast of Morocco the summer he worked aboard a cargo ship and the food in front of me is forgotten as I take in every last word. I imagine those weeks were terrifying for him until James calls the pirates "mere amateurs."

"It was always about the money with that crew," he says. "They never appreciated the joy of the open sea the way I did."

I have to smile when I think about James hanging out with pirates. I imagine him dressed in a flouncy shirt like the one I wore just yesterday. The image sticks with me and soon I'm laughing out loud.

"What is it?" He's in the middle of explaining the difference between storms in the Atlantic Ocean compared to the Mediterranean Sea when he realizes I'm no longer paying attention.

"I'm sorry," I say, holding back my laughter. "I'm just envisioning you with a pirate hat and an eye patch."

"Don't believe everything you read, Livy," he says, giving me a condescending look. "We weren't nearly that theatrical."

It's late afternoon when we leave the restaurant. The air feels colder, and the stormy sky is almost black. Even though our lunch ended on a far more conciliatory note than it began, I still can't stop thinking about James' question and why it upset me so much.

We are standing at the corner directly across from my apartment building, waiting for the light to change, and when it does I step off the curb. I don't see the bus, nor do I hear it. I'm too wrapped up in my own thoughts. The sound of screeching tires wakes me from my stupor. The next thing I see is James. His face is hovering over mine, his hands gripping my shoulders. I don't know how I made it back on the sidewalk or how I managed to avoid getting hit by the bus, but I'm pretty sure James had something to do with it.

"Not yet, Livy," James whispers. "Not yet." He's holding onto me as if I might try to slip away, but I'm shaking so badly I'm not sure I could walk if I wanted to.

I hear the squeak of a door sliding open and then the bus driver steps down to the street. His hands are trembling when he gestures to the street and then he turns back to me. I can't make out what he's saying; all I hear is a loud buzzing in my ears.

When I don't answer he moves closer, as close as James will allow. Even though James is a makeshift barricade between us with his back to the bus driver, I sense he's aware of every move the bus driver makes.

"Are you okay?" The bus driver stops. I notice his face is an odd shade of green. "I thought…I thought I hit you."

"She's fine," James says. "Thank you for your concern."

"Concern?" The bus driver stutters over a few choice words and then tries to move closer again.

James holds up his hand. "We're fine here. Move along."

For a minute I think the bus driver is going to protest but then he shakes his head and climbs back onto the bus.

James takes me by the elbow and half-drags me over to an empty bench. "Are you alright?" he asks once I'm sitting down. His arm is wrapped around my shoulders. I'm not sure if it's meant to comfort me or keep me in place.

"Thank you," I say. I can feel the shock moving through my body now, first dizziness, and then nausea until I feel a tight pulse behind my eyes. "You saved me. I don't know how, but you saved me."

James just nods.

"That's twice now," I whisper. "Twice someone has saved my life in the last two days."

"You should be more careful." James doesn't ask me about the other time my life was spared, which is odd because I would.

"Careful. Yes." I run my hands down my slightly damp jeans, brushing off the dirt on my knees.

We sit in silence a while longer. I'm busy rewinding the minutes leading up to my second near brush with death, and James; well James is sitting tall in his seat, his eyes focused ahead. He is so still it's as though he's not even here.

But the moment I speak his full attention snaps back to me.

"I wasn't there when she died," I tell him. "I had stepped out for a moment. I was thirsty. The room, it was so hot. I couldn't breathe. I never thought I wouldn't get a chance to say goodbye. Out of all the things that aren't fair when it comes to losing Jenna, that one's the worst."

"Everyone must have their goodbye," James says. "You can still have yours."

"In person," I spit out, frustrated. "Don't you get that?" I glare up at him, wishing I had it in me to lash out at him physically.

"I do," he tells me, his voice so soft I can barely make it out. His eyes are filled with understanding and something else: compassion. Normally these emotions would be the opposite of what I'd want from someone, but they look right on him. They look sincere.

And just like that I'm deflated. The anger and frustration I carry around with me slip away and I'm left feeling a bit vulnerable with James.

An hour ago I would have done anything to get away from this man but in the matter of a few minutes all of that has changed. I feel safe leaning into him. Comforted.

He could have left me back there, watched it happen without intervening. He could have, but he didn't.

"Thank you," I say. "Thank you for saving me today." I look up and meet his gaze.

"You're very welcome," he says with a smile.

The moment I smile back I feel it. Something has changed.

I think I might have to trust him.

CHAPTER TEN

There is nothing more boring than a ballroom full of politicians on a Friday night. I'm wearing a light blue dress that hits me right above the knees while my mom's dress is the same shade as her dark red lipstick. Together we represent a well-adjusted American family. My mom hasn't stopped smiling since she left the parking garage; the only time it falters is when she looks directly at me. She knows I'm not fooled. She didn't want to come to this benefit tonight any more than I wanted to, but as they say in theatre, "the show must go on."

Ever since our little chat the other night she has barely spoken to me. Apparently I've disappointed her. You wouldn't think that attempting to be a donor is such a horrible thing, but I guess in my mother's world it is.

When I returned home from my field trip with James yesterday she didn't bother asking me how it went. She hasn't initiated any conversations with me lately as though she's afraid I'll bring up Jilly. She'd be right, of course. I won't let this drop. It isn't like I'm asking her permission to take the car across town to see some boy she doesn't approve of. This is a little girl's life. If I can help her, I should. Of all people, my mother, who has spent the last few years of her life donating her time to a dozen different causes, should understand that. She knows what it feels like to lose someone. She shouldn't want anyone else to feel that loss if she could help it.

Halfway through dinner I realize I'm the only one left at our table. My mom is off somewhere with her publicist, practicing her speech, and where she goes her team of supporters follows.

No one notices when I make my way toward the exit, which is lucky since everyone here knows me. Just like they knew Jenna. They're too polite to mention her tonight, however, even though just last year she created a paparazzi spectacle when she began to spin in circles on the dance floor. She even made it on the front page of the events section of the *Seattle Times*.

There was a time I used to enjoy these events, look forward to them, actually. My mom would take us girls to the salon early in the morning. I felt so important — like I was a grown-up — with my fancy clothes and shoes and hair. Now she goes alone. I guess she'd rather not stare at the empty chair reserved for Jenna, and since I'm not enough to distract her she leaves me at home to fix my own hair.

Outside of the Grand Hyatt it's no longer raining. The sun went down a couple hours ago but luckily it doesn't feel as cold as I'd expected. There's really no place to stand outside where I won't be noticed by people coming or going from the banquet so I decide to take a walk. Downtown is beginning to arise from its day-slumber. The restaurants are spilling out onto the street with music and people. Everywhere I look the culture of nightlife is calling. At the busy intersection across from the hotel I pause and take it all in. It feels nice to be on the street for once instead of looking down on it.

Once I'm a safe distance from the hotel I slow my pace. It doesn't take long for him to join me. Somehow I knew he would.

"How was the fish?" Meyer asks, falling into step beside me.

"Greasy," I answer. "It's always greasy."

I steal a quick look his direction and find him smiling at me. I'm not sure what I expected after our last encounter, but I'm a little shocked by his outward confidence. You'd think he'd appear a bit awkward seeing as I ran from him the last time we were together. Or perhaps that's just me.

My foot catches on the uneven curb and I stumble. "Are you stalking me? You know stalking isn't in anymore, right? It's just plain creepy now."

Meyer ignores me and keeps smiling. "You didn't want to stay for the dancing?"

I turn away and focus on the street in front of me. "I felt like taking a walk."

"So I see," he says, and then nothing. He doesn't speak again until we stop at the next intersection.

"Blue's a good color for you," he tells me. "It brings out your eyes."

"My eyes aren't blue, they're hazel."

"I know." His mouth curves into a smile and for a moment I can't look away.

"I have questions, Meyer. If you're not hear to answer them, then go away." I pull my gaze from his and begin to cross the street.

"I wouldn't expect anything less from you, Livy," he chuckles.

"So then answer my question."

"You haven't asked one. Well, that is, not in the last few minutes."

I roll my eyes and sigh dramatically. He just smiles.

"I want to know what happened that night— "

"Do you?" he interrupts.

We've come to the end of the intersection. I feel Meyer's hand grip my arm as I step up on the curb. He pulls me to a stop as the other pedestrians move on without us.

His hand is warm against my skin. I hate that I like his touch so much, and because of that I try to pull away. But he doesn't release me.

"There are certain things you will never truly understand," he tells me. His expression is dark with intent, his eyebrows furrowed. "I promise one day I will explain it all to you."

His words are so cryptic — so much like James — it sets me back a minute. When he notices the look of surprise on my face he smiles as though what he's said isn't nearly as serious as it sounded.

"Just not tonight."

"Not tonight?" I repeat, staring up at him.

"Nope." He takes my hand and urges me forward.

"But, why?" I ask, refusing to budge.

"Tonight is about ice cream."

"Ice cream?" I repeat again, stupidly.

"Yes. Ice cream. We must relieve your tongue of that greasy fish."

"I don't want ice cream," I say stubbornly.

Meyer's eyes narrow. "How could you not want ice cream? Everyone likes ice cream."

"Meyer—"

"Livy." He crosses his arms as though this is the end of the discussion. Our showdown lasts about as long as it takes for him to break his concentration and smile.

"Have I promised you?" he asks just loud enough that I hear him over the street noise. "Have I promised that I will explain it all one day?"

I think back to a few moments ago. "Yes..."

"And I will," he tells me. "Just not now." His hand slides down my arm and soon my fingers are captured in his. He gives a slight tug and my feet begin to move. But then I stop.

"Wait," I call out. "One question."

His mouth sets into a thin line, and I hurry to explain.

"I just need to know one thing. One thing or you'll be eating ice cream alone."

He raises an eyebrow inquisitively and I take that as a green light.

"How did you know where to find me tonight?"

His eyes darken for a moment and then he quickly smiles. "Your mother is famous, right? A politician?"

"Senator," I say slowly.

"Right." His smile grows. "Shouldn't be that difficult for someone to find you, even if they aren't me."

I can't help laughing at his impish grin. "I guess..."

"Shall we, then?" he tugs on my hand once again and this time I follow. I can't help it. He's too alive for me not to. I think he must know this about me. It must be why he's always smiling.

"I thought girls liked the idea of a boy always knowing where to find them, no?" Meyer asks as we make our way down the street.

"Nope. Stalkers are only sexy in the movies," I tell him. "Real girls are a little easier to please."

"Yeah?" Meyer says.

"Yeah."

"So then tell me, Livy. What would it take for you?"

"Me?" I glance up at him so quickly I nearly trip.

He raises an eyebrow in reply and my heart skips around a bit.

"Hmm," I say staring back down at the ground. "Could it be you're inquiring about how a boy would go about turning *my* head?"

Meyer laughs softly under his breath. "I might be, Livy. I just might be."

"Well, then," I say with a smile. "There is one thing that gets me every time."

We walk a few more feet before Meyer takes the bait.

"And what might that be?" His voice is soft, his footsteps much slower.

I smile up at him, nearly catching my breath at the serious gleam in his eyes.

"A straight answer," I tell him.

His eyes widen for a moment and then he bursts out laughing. And that full-belly laugh of his is like a gift I never knew I wanted, until now.

"You present quite a challenge, Livy," he says, still smiling.

"Apparently," I mumble, and he laughs again.

Meyer takes me to an ice cream place I've never been to before where they mix up your selections right in front of you on a cold stone and then scoop it into a large cup. It is delicious. Better than I was expecting. When I don't finish mine (because they gave me enough for two Livy's) he takes my spoon from my hand and finishes it himself. He nearly licks the cup clean. I am hypnotized watching him. There are moments when he can be so youthful, like a child who is experiencing something for the first time. And then other times he seems like an old soul trapped inside a teenage boy's body.

Meyer's eyes crinkle in the corners as I continue to study him. I should look away, but I don't. He doesn't seem bothered by my curiosity. It's almost as though he enjoys it. He likes being noticed by me.

My phone buzzes and Sheila's face appears on my screen. When I don't answer she immediately calls back. She knows I'm keeping something from her. I turn my phone off before she begins a text-assault, and slip it back into my pocket.

"You know, ice cream is my favorite," I tell Meyer before I can stop myself. I'm so comfortable in this moment, comfortable and yet slightly exhilarated. It only makes sense that something would slip past my Jenna-guard.

"What about me, Livy? Am I your favorite?"

I blink up at him, and all thoughts of Jenna fade away.

"I wouldn't mind being your favorite, you know," he tells me. "I think it would be rather… interesting, actually."

When I continue to look at him without speaking, he laughs softly under his breath.

"Perhaps one day you'll answer *my* question, Livy."

"Maybe," I whisper, but I doubt he hears me. He's halfway to the trashcan with our ice cream cups in his hand.

Meyer walks me home soon after that. My mom has already texted me twice. The first time was to find out where I was hiding. After I told her I'd stepped out to take a walk, she asked if I would need a ride home. I didn't mention I'd been gone for hours, or how I'd missed her speech. What she doesn't know generally keeps me from irritating her.

In front of my apartment Meyer and I stand facing each other, like it's the end of a date. And I wish it were a date because then I could lean in, and he could lean in, and this thing I'm feeling would stop simmering in my stomach and instead take flight like the rest of me.

Just kiss him, I tell myself. Who needs words when a kiss says so much more? My last boyfriend used to kiss me all the time, even when the mood wasn't quite right, like when I'd have just returned from taking Jenna to one of her treatments. I know it was his way of showing support, but to me it was just another thing keeping me from breathing.

I can't help but wonder what would happen if I kissed Meyer? He's so different from other guys I've known. I imagine every other kiss I've experienced will feel like a rehearsal.

"Goodnight, Livy," Meyer says before our silence stretches on any longer. His eyes are dark, his lashes lowered, and that stirring in my chest returns with a vengeance.

In that moment I realize I want him. The feeling comes out of nowhere. It must have been hovering just off in the background waiting for the right moment to make its presence known. I want Meyer. I want him close. All at once I am dizzy with it, the need for something of my own.

"When will I see you again?" I flinch at how desperate I sound, but I can't just let him walk away.

"I promised you," he says while walking backward. "You *will* see me again. I owe you answers, remember?" His face is lit with mischief and I smile back at him before he sprints off down the street.

And even though I'm left feeling kiss-less, I carry his promise with me as I enter my building. It's more than anyone has given me in a very long time.

CHAPTER ELEVEN

The elevator doors slip open and I step out into a dimly lit apartment. I don't expect my mother to be waiting up for me, but she's usually still roaming the halls when I arrive home. Tonight, however, everything is still and quiet, only the faint smell of my mother's nightly cup of jasmine tea remains.

"Mom?"

It's funny how the sound of your own voice in a silent room can startle you and set your heart racing.

"I'm here, Livy," my mother calls out, her voice slightly muffled, coming from deep inside her bedroom.

I find her sitting on the floor in her closet. Her arms are resting lightly on the tops of her knees and her head is leaning against the back wall. She's sitting amongst her racks of shoes, the bottoms of her dresses nuzzling the top of her head. It wouldn't be unusual for my mother to randomly decide to organize her closet, but that's not what she's doing. If anything it looks like she's playing hide and seek, and the sad expression on her face is a clear sign that nobody has come to find her.

The last time I found my mom looking this lost was the day the doctor started using words like "terminal" to describe my sister.

"Mom?" There's an edge of panic in my voice. I can hear it so I'm sure she can too, but she doesn't react to it.

"Did you know there are five white bath towels in my bathroom that have never been used?" Her eyes are closed, her voice soft. "Five beautiful, fluffy, brand new bath towels. I bought them last December, just before the Mayor's ball."

"Okay."

She lifts her head and looks at me — her eyes so blue, and so like Jenna's, I nearly tear up staring into them. "Have you seen them? Have you seen these towels?"

"I didn't take them," I quickly point out. Is that what she's been up to? Is she on a mission to find her missing bath towels? "Maybe Dad—" I begin, but her laughter stops me.

"They aren't missing, Livy." She wipes her eyes and her laughter comes to a halt. "They've never been used!"

"Yes. You mentioned that."

"And do you know why?" She brushes her blonde hair back off her face but it isn't her hair that's battling for her attention, it's the dress she wore to her last inauguration hanging directly above her head. Red and black, like a ladybug. The bottom swings back and forth as if taunting her, but after a couple of pitiful swipes, she just ignores it.

"Do you, Livy?" she asks when I don't respond fast enough. "Do you know why my bath towels were never used?"

"Why?" Suddenly I feel very tired. I slip to the floor across from her.

"They're too nice!" She pushes her hands through her hair and then leans her head against the back wall again. "Your crazy mother bought the most expensive Ralph Lauren bath towels she could find, brought them home and hung them up so that the bathroom looked just right and then I never used them!"

"Why?" Only now do I realize my mother's eyes are red and puffy with dark smudges underneath.

"Because…" She takes a deep breath and then rubs her eyes, which makes the dark smudges worse. "Because I was saving them. They are too special for every day. I called them my Special Occasion Towels. Just like I save the best part, the best bites of every meal, for last." She breaks out into this sad mix of laughter and tears and says, "But of course I never get to take those best bites because by the time I get to them I'm already too full!"

I think I already knew this about my mother, although I've never really thought about it until now. I've watched her eat for years, her fork always hovering around the pieces of lettuce with just the right amount of salad dressing and cheese, but then she'll move on to those pieces that remind you you're eating rabbit food. She avoids the shrimp in her favorite dish, Shrimp Scampi, forcing herself to eat the pasta first and rarely having a big enough appetite for the rest. It's almost as if she's punishing herself.

"And who has time for leftovers," she mutters, carrying on the conversation with herself.

"And the bath towels?"

She lifts her head up, her expression as far away as her thoughts.

"They're still as fluffy as the day I bought them," she tells me. "That is, they look fluffy."

"Mom—"

"No. It's my turn to talk." She scoots forward so that she's perched on her knees. Her hands reach out for me and yet we're not close enough to touch. "You were with me when I bought those towels, Livy." Her eyes well up making mine sting a little. "You used to always want to be with me."

She shakes her head when I attempt to speak.

"I'm going to let you do it, Livy." She takes a deep breath and pushes her shoulders back. She tries to look at me but it's as though her head is too heavy to hold up. "I'm going to let you help Jilly." Her lips quiver when she says her name. "I don't like it, but I get it. You can take those tests."

My breath catches in my chest and I'm not sure if it's fear or excitement that settles in my gut.

"You always believed there was a way to save her. Both you and your father." Her unfocused eyes stare off above my head. "We did everything we could. *Everything*."

"Mom?"

Her eyes snap to me, and just like that she's back. She clears her throat and wipes at her eyes. Her features tighten back into her fighting-face, and my heart squeezes.

"I can't keep you from doing something good just because I'm—" She stops and shakes her head. "I only ask that you keep me informed of every little detail. And I plan on coming with you to your appointments." She reaches up to smooth her hair again and I notice her hand is trembling. "I have a lot of questions."

"Of course. Whatever you want." I'll do anything to keep her yes from turning back into a no.

"What I *want* is for none of this to be happening!" She takes a deep breath and then runs her hands down the sides of her pants as if she can smooth out her outburst. "Not you. Not Jilly," she says calmly. *Not Jenna.*

"But it is," I tell her.

"Yes. It is," she whispers back, each word more difficult than the last.

She goes on to explain how she's already made an appointment for me to go tomorrow morning for more tests. My heart skips a beat when I hear the word "tests." I wish it would stop doing that. I want to do this. I have to. Now is not the time to think about needles and anesthesia. Or hospitals where *I'm* the patient. I must think about Jilly. Only Jilly. But what happens if I still can't save her?

Before that thought paralyzes me completely I push it right out of my mind. My mom said yes! I must focus on that. I'm one step closer to saving Jilly. One stop closer than I was yesterday. So that's something.

It's too late to call the hospital and talk to Jilly and I wouldn't tell her anyway, not until we know more. But it's not too late to text Sheila, and that's exactly what I do. Sheila immediately texts back filling the screen with exclamation points. No words are needed, apparently.

Tomorrow. You. Me. Celebratory snacks. Yes?

I text back: *Yes*

I stand up, noticing how my legs are back to feeling slightly shaky. The hug I throw at my mom catches her by surprise and instead of pulling away quickly, the way I normally would, I linger a bit longer.

"I miss you, Mom," I say, surprising her as much as myself. Her arms tighten around me, nearly stealing my breath.

"Promise me you'll be fine, Livy," she whispers against my hair.

And I say it, those words that people say even though they shouldn't.

"I promise."

The morning of my blood tests I awake to a smell that is so familiar and yet strangely out of place. I haven't smelled the rich and delicious aroma of German pancakes in so long it immediately floods me with memories. I can almost hear Jenna's bare feet padding down the hallway toward my bedroom, her excitement reaching out to me through the walls. My heart clenches as I await the sound of my door opening. But when it comes it's my mother standing in the doorway, not Jenna.

"I made us breakfast," she says. "But then I remembered the nurse mentioned you shouldn't eat before the blood work." Her hands are fidgeting with her dress, then with her hair until she crosses them against her chest. "We can reheat them when we get home."

"That sounds great." I make a move to pull my blankets back but then stop myself. My purple and yellow plaid bedspread is just what I need to protect myself from the anxiety in my mother's eyes.

"You're sure you want to do this?" She pauses. "Of course. Of course you do. Well, we should get moving then. There's sure to be traffic."

Twenty minutes later I'm showered and dressed and on my way to the front door when I catch sight of my father in the kitchen. He's wearing his dark blue bathrobe and his hair is wet from a shower. What strikes me as odd is that he's not slumped over his bowl of cold cereal, and is instead setting the table. He has the nice placemats out — the ones my mother saves for Christmas morning, not the usual blue and white-checkered cotton ones that loiter on our table everyday. As I stand in the doorway, unnoticed, I watch him move about the kitchen as if everything is normal, like he hasn't spent the last four months living in his own misery-induced hell. I force myself to stay still. I don't want to startle him. I'm afraid he might scamper away like a startled rabbit. But I also can't believe my eyes. He's clean and upright, someone who pays attention to the day instead of avoiding it.

And then it hits me. There are four places set at our table. Four, not three.

"Daddy?" I whisper. When he doesn't hear me I try again. "Daddy?"

"Oh, there you are," he turns to me with a smile and that smile is a punch to the gut. I know exactly how long it's been since I've seen that smile. I know the very last time we all wore them. In celebration of Jenna finishing her chemo treatments we went on a vacation.

"To the mountains!" my father had exclaimed, because as far as he was concerned that's where you go when success is at your fingertips. We packed up our car and drove all night and when I awoke ten hours later we were in a snow-covered paradise, where everything was blue and white and frozen and the mountains were bigger than I ever could have imagined. Even though it was cold and the snow was wet when it touched my skin, I didn't care because I couldn't stop smiling. All four of us, we just couldn't stop smiling. In that moment we had hope and hope smelled like maple syrup and German pancakes, apparently, which is what we ate each morning for breakfast and sometimes late at night when we weren't quite ready for the day to end.

But now that smell is making my stomach churn. It doesn't smell like hope. It smells of disappointment and sadness, and the look in my father's eyes is a touch mad because of it.

"You'd better sit and eat while it's hot," he says now. He places his hand on my back and leads me to the table. "You don't want your sister to eat it all, now do you? It's her favorite." He winks and then scurries off toward the silverware drawer.

"Daddy?" I say again, but it comes out so strangled it sounds more like a cough. "Daddy, what are you doing?" I grab hold of the top of the chair. I need to feel something solid before I lose myself completely.

"I'm setting the table, Livy. What do you think I'm doing?" He turns back around, his hands filled with forks and knives, his eyes lit up like a Christmas tree. "What could be keeping your mother? And where's Jenna? You'd think she'd be out here by now."

My father moves back toward the table but when he catches the look on my face he stops completely, and I get to see him lose Jenna all over again. His hands go limp, and all the silverware he's holding

101

goes clattering to the floor. For a second I think he might soon follow, but instead he takes a wobbly step backward, reaching out to grip the kitchen counter.

"I thought... I smelled German pancakes and I thought." He shakes his head, his eyes still wide like he's seen a ghost. "I dreamt about her, Livy. I swear she was alive."

"Daddy, don't!" Tears stream down my face but I don't have the strength to brush them away. My hands are too heavy. This moment weighs too much.

"But she was right there." He points to the spot at the table where Jenna always ate, the place next to mine. "She was right there. And she asked me to make her breakfast." He shakes his head again as if what he's seeing now isn't real. He should be seeing Jenna, not just me. "And I smelled breakfast..."

"Mom made pancakes," I say, the words so useless I wish they would disappear. My father just looks at me. "Dad?" My voice is wobbly, a reminder that I'm not as strong as I'm trying to be. "I can make you a plate."

My mother chooses this moment to reappear. She walks in clutching her purse and her car keys, and then comes to an abrupt stop when she notices my father.

"Peter?" she calls out to him. But he doesn't answer. I can see the darkness closing in on him. His eyes are hollow, he's staring right though us. And then he walks away.

CHAPTER TWELVE

"So let me get this straight… you just filled nine vials of blood for the hell of it?" Sheila is staring at me while a large ranch dressing-dipped French fry hovers near her mouth. She shakes her head — her long brown hair spilling around her shoulders — before she folds the entire fry into her mouth.

"I had to Sheila. It's how they determine if I'm a match or not."

Sheila's dark brown eyes are unconvinced.

"I'm serious about this."

"Serious and crazy-pants ride a fine line, Livy," she says around her food.

I roll my eyes. I don't expect her to understand.

"Well, whatever." She takes a long sip of her drink and places it down in front of her. "I know how much you want to help Jilly, but I'm with your mom on this one. It kind of freaks me out this whole bone-scraping thing. Not that I don't want you to do it," she adds, holding up her hand before I can interject. "I just don't like thinking about it."

"It's not scary and it's not dangerous. I promise."

"Then why all the tests? Why do they have to make sure *you're* okay?"

"Because it's surgery. But believe me, my recovery is nothing compared to Jilly's."

"What does that mean?" Sheila asks. "Are you telling me that after all of this Jilly could still die?"

"She won't die," I say, twirling my straw around and around my tall glass of lemonade. We're sitting at Sheila's favorite sandwich shop, Donnelly's. I have to lean forward to catch most of Sheila's comments due to the loud lunch rush. But if I'm being honest with myself I'm not even sure I want to continue this conversation.

"But she could."

"She won't." I take a bite of my B.L.T. mostly to avoid her stare. I'm no longer hungry. The bread tastes like sandpaper, making it difficult to swallow.

"Alright. No more. I'm done with the hospital talk." She brushes her hands off and pushes the sleeves up on her dark purple sweater. "So. Are you going to tell me why you've been avoiding me lately, or do I have to start stalking you?"

"I haven't been—"

"Who is he? And don't lie. I know it's a he because your texts get all shifty every time I ask where you've been."

"I'm not shifty," I say, not that I even know what would constitute a shifty text.

"AH HA!" Sheila exclaims. "You didn't deny the boy part!"

Sigh.

I take another bite of my sandwich. I've never kept anything from Sheila, and I never thought I would. But how do I explain Meyer? There are moments when I still wonder if I'm imagining him.

"So? When do I get to meet him?" Sheila asks, and I realize I should have predicted that one.

"I'm not really sure. He's not from around here. He only visits once in a while." Yes, that works. This is the vague truth I know abut Meyer — which only proves that I don't know nearly enough about the boy I've been avoiding my best friend for.

"So where is he from?" she asks.

"Well, we've only been hanging out a short time. Honestly, the bio is still a bit thin."

"But you like him." She's grinning at me with a look that tells me I never should have let this conversation begin. Or better yet, I should have lied. She isn't going to let this go until she knows every last detail. "I can't believe you like a boy and you're just telling me now!"

"I'm sorry," I say. "It's just that I barely know him and... it's weird when you're first starting to get to know someone, you know that." Especially when the boy you like isn't quite like everybody else.

"So then I'll help you." She stands up and grabs my hands, dragging me to my feet. "This will be great," she says. "Friday night we'll all go to my friend Kenny's party. By the end of the night — with my help, of course — you'll know him so well that all that awkwardness will be gone and you'll be ready to get to the fun part of the relationship."

"No, definitely not!" I shake my head. I should have known better than to have even mentioned him. This is Meyer we're talking about here. Not some friend of Grant's. Not some boy from school. Meyer is different. I can't just take him to a party, can I? And even if I wanted to, how would I even make it happen? I don't exactly know how to get a hold of him. I mean, it's not like I have a special signal.

The thought of seeing him again makes my stomach flutter. It's easier when he just appears. I don't have to get all worked up about seeing him; he's just there.

Sheila's smile is large, like the Cheshire Cat. "Wait," she says, her eyes growing huge in her face. "You really like this one, don't you?"

"Sheila, don't—"

"You do, don't you? Otherwise you wouldn't be all squirmy."

"Squirmy. Shifty. Geez, Sheila. It must be love." I roll my eyes and scoot away from her, hoping she'll take the hint and leave this be.

"Nice try, Livy. I know you better than that." She follows after me. "Is he hot? He must kiss better than Scott, right? I mean, from what you said, anyone would."

"Sheila!" I whip around dodging the curious glances turning our way. "I never said Scott was a bad kisser." At least, not out loud. Scott, my ex, was nice to a fault. Always worried that I was happy. I really liked Scott. He's one of those people you can't help but like. But I didn't have time for fun or happiness while my sister was dying. So I let him go. I let everything go.

"So?" Sheila sidles up next to me and tucks her arm in mine. "What's he like? I need all the steamy details."

"It's not like that. At least, not yet."

"You mean, you haven't done anything yet? No kissing? Nothing?" The look on Sheila's face goes beyond disbelief. She almost looks disgusted.

I sigh deeply, wishing I was somewhere else, but in the end I know I won't get out of answering. "No. Not yet. Like I said, we just started hanging out."

"But you want to." She leans her face in mine, batting her long eyelashes at me. "Admit it, you want him." When I stay silent she adds, "Come on. I'm your best friend. It's either me you tell, or your doorman Marty. And if you spill to Marty before me I'm not sure our friendship could survive that. Sure, Marty has those sexy, understanding eyes and all — hell, I've told him things too — and it's nice because he doesn't really say much. But you're parents help pay his rent, Livy. Which is weird, you know, like he's your shrink or something. So... tell *me*." She crosses her arms in front of her chest, blocking my escape from the restaurant. "You want him, don't you?"

"I want..." I look away, not sure I can say it. "*Something.*"

Sheila opens her mouth, obviously unsatisfied with my answer, but then she shakes her head and says nothing. Just waits.

"I do like him," I whisper. And that's all I have to say about that right now.

Sheila is silent a moment longer, just studying me. "Alright. I get it." She brushes my hair back off my face. Her touch feels protective, her expression a bit wary. "The two of you are new so you're playing it safe. Understandable. Very like you."

Very like me. Right. In other worlds, very *not* like Sheila.

"That's it then," she says once we're back outside. "Friday night we'll all go out and you'll wear that dress you're always too afraid to actually wear, and he won't be able to resist you. Especially with this new pouty thing you've got going right now. Seriously, Livy. You're like a young, vulnerable Nicole Kidman in like every TV interview from the last ten years. You were hot before, but now, well, let's just say, if Grant goes anywhere near you..." Sheila winks to let me know she's kidding but then her eyes grow serious. "You know it's okay to have fun still, right? Jenna would want that." We've come to a stop in front of her car and Sheila pretends to dig around inside her purse for her keys, avoiding my eyes.

I stare up at her in shock. She never says my sister's name. It's like she knows the rules without me having to explain them. Finally she looks up and gives me a smile. There is so much concern in her expression. How have I never noticed this before? Sheila is worried about me.

"This is going to be awesome," she says. "Seriously. Like, you know. Before." She squeezes my hands and does this little dance-step-thing that nearly pushes us into oncoming traffic.

"Yes," I answer, still wishing I had lied about Meyer.

"Awesome." I don't want to go to a party, and I definitely don't want to bring Meyer to one. But I can't bear to tell Sheila no. Not now. Even though I'd rather spend another night hanging out with Meyer and Meyer alone, and even though I'm convinced that everyone else would just be noise and interference, I can't ruin her fun.

"Livy?" Sheila is watching me closely. "You're coming, right?" When I don't answer immediately she adds, "You need this. We *both* need this."

Her brown eyes are lit with excitement and I realize it's been a long time since I've seen this look on her. Too long, actually.

"I'll ask him," I say. How or when, I don't know. He's found me before; let's hope he finds me again before the weekend.

Sheila grabs me and squeezes me so tight I start laughing. For the first time in a long while I realize I'm looking forward to something.

CHAPTER THIRTEEN

By Wednesday night I'm getting nervous. It's been five days since I last saw Meyer. For all I know it could be weeks before he reappears. Sheila keeps checking in — desperate to know if he's said yes — and I'm running out of reasons for why I haven't asked him yet. I don't want to admit that I don't have any contact information for the boy I'm supposedly seeing. Truth is she wouldn't believe me. In Sheila's world if you don't have a cell phone you may as well be dead.

I leave the hospital right around dinnertime. Jilly's grandma took the day off so I leave them to their soup and crackers and make my way home.

My mom won't be around until later but she texted me earlier to let me know where to find the leftovers and how to make them edible. She's good like that. Since I got tested she's not quite hovering but seems to be checking in more often.

Marty the doorman gives me a rare smile as I walk through the swivel-door.

"Interesting kid," he says as he pushes the up button on the elevator.

"Excuse me?" I'm not sure why he's in such a good mood. Wednesdays are his double-shift days.

"Is he your boyfriend, then? Now that Scott is out of the picture?"

"Who?" I stare at him blankly as we wait for the elevator to arrive.

"You know, tall kid, brownish hair. Smiles a lot."

"Marty, I don't—"

"He said he was here to see you. Sent him up even though I knew your dad was the only one home." Marty shakes his head the way he always does when my father is mentioned. "He said his name was Meyer. That ring any bells?" Marty continues.

Meyer.

"Are you telling me he's upstairs?" I race into the elevator as soon as it arrives and hit the penthouse button before Marty can reach it.

"Yep. Sent him up myself." He's watching me curiously from outside the elevator.

"He's up there now? With my *father*?"

"Yep." I catch one last glimpse of Marty shaking his head before the elevator doors close.

Thirty seconds later I've arrived. I step into my apartment —my senses on high alert. I'm greeted with silence. I move to the hallway, my footsteps light. Still nothing.

"Livy?" my father calls out. "Is that you?"

It's been days since I've heard my father's voice. I barely recognize it.

"It's me," I say, continuing down the hallway.

My father's office door is open and his drafting table light is staining the carpet out in the hall.

"We're in here," he tells me. But I don't believe it, even when I see it.

My father is leaning against the wall near his drafting table while Meyer stands nearby poring over my father's designs.

"I've… uh, been talking to Meyer here," my father stumbles. "I wasn't sure when you… would be home." He looks away with embarrassment and pushes himself off the wall. He's dressed in his usual day attire: plaid-striped pajama pants and a purple *Go Huskies* sweatshirt.

I open my mouth to smooth over the awkwardness, but Meyer beats me to it.

"Your dad was kind enough to let me stay and wait." His attention has barely left my father's sketches. "Did you know he designed one of my favorite buildings?"

My father's hands are pushed down in his pockets and he's staring at the ground, but there's a hint of a smile upon his lips. "Which one?" I ask softly. "He's designed many buildings around here."

My father looks up at me when he catches the trace of pride in my voice.

"That box-looking building down in Capitol Hill." Meyer finally glances in my direction, his eyes sparkling. "You know the one that's mostly made of glass? What is it, Mr. Cloud? Some kind of residence or something?"

My father's face fills with a smile the moment Meyer addresses him. "It is a residence, yes. One of the first completely energy-efficient homes in the area."

"I can't tell you how many times I've stood outside that building just studying the lines," Meyer tells him. "The people who live inside must feel like I'm watching them, like they're some kind of reality show or something." He laughs and my father laughs. I remain speechless.

"It was never the people inside who fascinated me though," he tells us. He crosses his arms and leans his hip against the side of the drafting table.

"What was it then?" my father asks. He's studying Meyer so intently, it's as though he's desperate for Meyer's answer.

Meyer smiles at me and then turns and shares it with my father. He's drawing out this moment. Keeping my father engaged for as long as he can.

"Well," he says softly. "It's always reminded me of a large treehouse. I used to imagine it would be the kind of place I'd like to live in. You know, when I get older."

"Yes," my father says, grinning. "Me too." He's standing up a bit straighter, leaning in toward Meyer. "My daughter, Jenna, used to beg me to build her one of her very own. She made me promise—" he stops with a jolt, his smile dropping completely. "Well, yes," he stutters. "Anyway." He rubs his hand against his jawline and then up toward his eyes.

"Daddy?"

My father glances over at me with surprise as though he's just noticed I'm here. "Your friend shouldn't stay too long, Livy," he says. "Right?" He appears confused as though he knows he's supposed to say something else but he's not quite sure what.

"Of course, Mr. Cloud," Meyer pipes in. "I'll only visit for a moment. I wouldn't want to keep Livy too long."

I glance at Meyer in time for him to wink at me.

My father moves toward the doorway and waits, ushering us out of his office.

"It was nice to meet you, Mr. Cloud," Meyer says once we're in the hallway.

"Yes." My father smiles at him for a minute, a hint of life still in his eyes. "It was nice to meet you too, Meyer. I hope— " He clears his throat and starts again. "I hope one day you get your treehouse."

Meyer grins at him and reaches out to shake his hand. "Perhaps one day you'll build it for me, yeah?"

My father's eyes widen as though he's taken back by Meyer's suggestion, but then he nods. "Perhaps I will." His gaze falls on me and I blink up at him. If I move too quickly I might ruin this moment. I might scare his smile back into the place where it has been held captive these last few months.

"We'll have to see, then, Livy. Won't we?"

"Y-yes," I stutter.

My father reaches out like he's going to ruffle my hair but then his hand drops and falls back to his side. The next moment he's back inside his office with the door closed and Meyer and I are left standing out in the hall.

"Well that was interesting," I tell Meyer once we're in the living room. I take a seat on the couch while Meyer continues to stand. My legs are so shaky they might just give out on me.

"Really? How so?"

"I mean my father and you talking? My father *talking*?" I shake my head, unsure how to put into words the feelings I'm feeling right now.

"He doesn't speak normally?" Meyer's eyebrow rises in confusion.

"No, I mean he speaks, he's just…" I stop. "It's just…" I shrug my shoulders. "He seemed to like you."

"Well, who doesn't?" Meyer chuckles. "I'm a likable guy. Right, Livy?"

I can't help but laugh. "Yeah, I guess you're likable."

Meyer smiles.

"Hello," he says.

"Hi." I'm still smiling.

"So this is where you live, huh? Nice place." He looks around the room, taking in my mother's perfectly selected artwork hanging on the walls.

"Um. Thanks."

"Your father is very talented."

"Yes."

"Can I see your room?"

"My room?" My eyes widen at his request.

"Yes. Your room. You know, the place where you sleep and spend your time when you're not with me." Meyer winks again, his smile a bit mischievous.

"Oh. Right." I stare down the hallway to where I can now hear Simon and Garfunkel spilling out from under my father's office door.

I hesitate for a moment and then slowly rise from the couch. Showing Meyer my bedroom feels so personal, like in a small way I'm opening myself up to him. I could tell him no, but I don't want to. He got my father to talk. To smile. I feel as though I owe him the entire world right now — or, at the very least, a tour of my room.

Meyer follows me down the hallway— past Jenna's closed door — and waits as I open mine.

Thankfully my mother has trained me to always make my bed first thing in the morning and put my dirty clothes in the laundry. My room is generally tidy and neat, but that doesn't mean I don't give it a quick once over, worried that something could be out of place.

Meyer pauses in the doorway, and then moves to my dresser where there is an arrangement of photographs attached to my mirror. They're all faces he wouldn't recognize but he studies them as though they mean something. Directly at the top of my mirror is a photo of me and Jenna holding hands and laughing. Meyer pauses on this one the longest but he doesn't ask me about it. My hands start to shake as I prepare myself for the dead-sister conversation but the moment never arrives. Instead he moves on to my desk, leaving the photo and my stories behind.

He picks up a book or two off my desk — two rather boring classics James has me reading — and then puts them down.

I watch him move about my room, feeling more and more insecure by the minute. There is a line people cross once they're allowed to enter your domain. They go from a general acquaintance — someone you've only shared a few random encounters with — straight to someone who now knows the color of your bedspread and what you see before you close your eyes every night. These things may seem insignificant but at this moment they feel rather intimate to me. Truth is, I kind of like that Meyer knows these things about me now.

Meyer walks over to my bed and throws himself down on it, crossing his arms behind his head. "This is comfortable. I like where you sleep."

"It's alright." I haven't moved from my spot near the window. I figure it's safer over here. One thing is for sure, I will never get the image of Meyer lounging on my bed out of my head. Not now. Not ever.

He raises an eyebrow, daring me to come closer, but I hold my place. This is completely new territory for me. Scott was never allowed in my bedroom, not that I really wanted him there.

When the silence stretches on a bit too long, I say, "I don't really sleep a lot actually."

"Nightmares, huh?" Meyer asks. His shirt has ridden up a bit, exposing his stomach. I try not to stare at it, but it's right there. On my bed.

"No," I whisper, meeting his eyes. "Worse."

Meyer sits up, focused on me. "What is worse than a nightmare?"

I shrug my shoulders. I'm not sure why I've allowed myself to head down this path. I've never told anyone this before. "Too many nights I dream that my sister is still alive." I shrug again, as though it's that easy to brush it off. "I prefer not to sleep. It's easier that way."

Meyer is silent for a moment, holding my gaze, and then he pats the spot next to him on the bed.

"What?" I say, pretending I don't understand.

"Come here, Livy."

I stare at him, not quite registering what he's saying to me. "Why?" I ask, hating how my voice squeaks. "What do you want?" It's difficult not to notice that Meyer hasn't asked me about my sister. Most people would at this moment. But Meyer isn't most people. Part of me wonders if he already knows about Jenna.

He reaches out his hand, urging me forward. "Come here."

I hold my spot, choosing to defy him. Man, I'm such a coward.

Meyer raises an eyebrow. He must think the same thing.

"Livy, just come here."

I obey, reluctantly.

"Which side of the bed do you sleep on?" He's sitting up cross-legged in the middle of my bed.

"Um. I don't know. The right side, I guess?" I'm not really sure I sleep on a side. Usually I just flail around until I've no choice but to sleep.

"Alright." He scoots over, freeing up the right side of my bed, and then lies back against the mattress. "Come on," he says when I continue to just stand here. "Don't tell me you're afraid of me." He waggles his eyebrows and even though I don't want to, I laugh. But it's a nervous sounding laugh. I notice, and I'm absolutely sure he does too. He gives me a cocky smile. He is enjoying this moment far too much, I think.

"Lie down the way you would at night," he says once I've managed to get myself on the bed.

"Like this?" I ask resting on my back. My arms are straight and stiff next to my sides. I must look like a corpse.

Meyer laughs and I turn my head to look at him. He's so close, his lips so close, I just stare at him, forgetting my question.

"What makes you think *I'd* know? Do you think I watch you when you sleep?"

I glare at him and he laughs.

"Turn on your side and face me, Livy."

I follow his instructions even though it brings us closer to together.

"Is this how you sleep at night? On your side?"

"Yes," I whisper, and he smiles. He's lying on his side as well, one hand resting between us while the other rests under my pillow.

"Alright." He tucks his arm under his head so that he's hovering just slightly over me. "So now, when you're having trouble sleeping," he says, "just imagine I'm right here, like this, and talk to me until you fall asleep." When I just blink at him his mouth loses his smile. "Unless there's someone else you'd rather imagine yourself talking to?"

"No," I say, smiling. "You'll do."

He laughs softly, his breath tickling my skin. "I'll do, huh?" He reaches up, brushing back a loose strand of hair against my cheek, and I fight the urge to close my eyes.

I'm not sure how this is supposed to help me sleep. I'm pretty sure for the rest of my life I'm going to envision him lying next to me like this and sleeping is the last thing I'll have on my mind.

My eyes drop to his mouth just in time to see his wicked grin. "Who knows," he says. "Maybe it'll work so well you'll dream about me."

I feel heat rise to my cheeks and I know the minute he notices. His eyes darken and drop to my lips. And suddenly my breathing has decreased significantly.

"Unless you do already." His lips turn up in one corner. "Is that it, Livy? Am I what's keeping you up at night?"

"You wish," I say, holding back a laugh. But my face is still on fire.

I close my eyes, trying to gain some composure. When I open them again, Meyer is watching me, his dark green eyes heavy and rather intense.

Ask him! Do it now! Here's your opportunity, Livy! But I can't. It feels too intimate a moment to be asking him out. What if he says no and this moment is forever ruined because of it?

"Are you afraid of anything, Meyer?" I whisper instead, and the sound of my hushed voice adds a whole new level of intimacy to this moment.

His eyes narrow, studying me, and then slowly he nods his head.

"What is it?" I ask, not quite believing him, but completely intrigued nonetheless.

He hesitates, perhaps debating whether or not to tell me, and then his smile returns. "Butterflies, for one."

"Butterflies?"

"Butterflies," he says with an affirming nod.

I choke out a laugh. "You're kidding, right?"

"No. Why would I joke about that?" When I give him my most disbelieving look he says, "I'm completely serious, Livy. Everyone thinks they're so beautiful and magical but have you ever seen one up close? Have you ever really looked into their scary little faces?"

I burst out laughing, and then realize he's being straight with me. Or at least, trying to. You never know with Meyer. "I can't say I've spent a lot of time studying butterflies."

"Yeah, well don't," he says, shifting a bit closer. "Trust me."

"Okay." I smile at him, nuzzling deeper into my pillow.

Meyer's eyes are bright. He has that look he gets when he's been issued a challenge, one he's determined to win.

"Let's go," he says all at once. He sits up, pulling me with him.

"What? Where are we going?" I'm immediately resentful of the distance between us. I liked lying next to him. A bit too much, actually.

"Take me somewhere special to you." He's already across my room, his hand reaching back for me to follow.

"Special to me?"

"Somewhere you go when you want to be alone."

I look around my room, wondering how he knows this isn't it.

"Um…" I stare out over Seattle. "You mean like my roof?"

"Your roof?" Meyer's eyes light up. "Is that your special place?"

I nod once, not trusting myself to speak. The only other person I've allowed up there with me is Sheila.

"Let's go," he says, opening my bedroom door.

My father's music is still playing. There's a faint light slipping out from under the door. Tonight may have started off as different but it always ends up feeling the same as far as my dad is concerned. I don't bother telling him I'm leaving. Instead I leave him to his solitude.

Meyer follows me into the elevator and watches as I push the button for the roof.

"Are there any other ways to get to the roof?" he asks me.

"The stairs," I tell him. "But you need a special key."

"Hmm," he says, not looking away from me.

I clear my throat, and with a casualness I don't feel, say, "Where are your friends tonight?"

The elevator comes to a stop and the doors open.

"My friends?" he asks after following me out of the elevator.

"Yes. The ones I met. Cecily and Will and everyone else."

"Right. My friends."

Meyer moves about the roof, taking in the view of Downtown Seattle.

"This is nice," he tells me. "I can see why you like it."

"Thanks," I say, looking around as well. I try to see it from his perspective, but find it's nearly impossible. Maybe if I knew more about him.

"You know, I have friends," I say, when I realize he's not going to give me anything more.

"You do?" His eyes follow me as I walk toward him. "And who are these friends of yours?"

"Well, there's Sheila." I slow my pace once I'm a few feet away. "She's the only other person I've ever brought up here."

Meyer smiles at this, his eyes speculative.

"And there's her boyfriend, Grant," I hurry to add.

"Nice people, I presume?"

"Sure." I pull my trembling hands into the sleeves of my sweater. It's really not that cold but pretending it is gives me a way to hide the evidence of my nerves. Why is asking him to a stupid party so difficult, anyway? The worst that could happen is he says no, right? That's not so bad, really, I tell myself, even though the possibility feels pretty horrible.

"They want to meet you," I say eventually. I fumble with the loose thread along the sleeve of my sweater until the silence begins to feel painful. And he's waiting for me, just waiting for me, to look up at him.

"Do they now," he drawls, a gleam of amusement in his eyes. "So you've told them about me then?"

"Just Sheila. She's my best friend," I answer as though that explains everything, which it totally does not. But that's all he gets.

The lights are pretty faint up on the roof and the way Meyer is facing me leaves his face in shadow.

"Are you cold, Livy?" he asks. Before I can answer he reaches behind his head and pulls off his dark green sweatshirt — the way that only boys do. The motion causes his T-shirt to ride up in the front, exposing his stomach, and that hint of skin is again all I can focus on.

Meyer slips his sweatshirt over my head, pulling me close at the same time. With my arms trapped he pauses for a moment, staring at me from under his long eyelashes.

"You were saying…" His smile lifts, displaying his amusement.

"I was?"

I step back a bit, pulling my arms through the sleeves. It hangs long on my arms — and everywhere else really — but it's warm. I breathe in the smell of burning leaves and crisp night air, feeling as though I am bathed in Meyer.

"Your friends?" he says, with an arch of an eyebrow.

"Oh! Right. They, um. They're getting together Friday night and well…"

"Yes?" He closes the space between us with one step.

"It's nothing really. Just a small get-together. I mean if you're not busy…"

"I'm not."

"Oh," I exhale.

"Where should I meet you?"

"Meet?"

"How about downstairs?" he suggests.

"Downstairs?" *Stop it, Livy! Stop turning everything into a question!*

"So is this like a date?" he asks and my knees nearly give out on me.

"Um, well—"

"Because I should probably know if it's a date or not."

"Right." I reach up to untuck my hair from behind my ear, hoping to hide my flushed face, but then I remember it's still back in a ponytail. *Just say it's a date. That's what it is, anyway. Isn't it?*

"Perhaps I should probably ask you." Meyer tilts his forehead toward mine, and I look up. We are nearly touching. "Livy, would you like to go out with me Friday night to meet your friends?" When I continue to stare at him he adds, "Isn't that how it's done?"

And then he grins, that wicked grin of his that always makes me want to smile back.

"Say yes," he whispers, the heavy look in his eyes urging me to do exactly that. "Because whether or not it's a date, I'd still love to come."

"Yes," I say, and then before I can stop myself — before I can even think — I lean up and brush my lips against his. I couldn't *not* do it.

The kiss is a barely-there kiss. A promise kiss. Meyer pulls away and I let him go.

"Oh," I whisper, needing to fill the gap between us with something. "I'm sorry... I'm..."

Meyer is just watching me, his eyes wide and full of confusion as though he's not quite sure what happened.

"I'm sorry," I stammer out again. "I shouldn't have—"

"Yes," he says quickly, interrupting the rest of my confession, and I don't know if he's agreeing or accusing. Either way that one little word fills me with shame.

"Well, then," I begin, shoving my hands in my pockets. "I should—"

And then he's kissing me. His hands are on either side of my face while my hands stay trapped in my pockets. I can't think to move them. I can't think at all. This time the kiss is longer. Deeper. I feel the warmth of it throughout my body. I need to take a breath, but I don't dare pull away. Not when it feels this good.

Meyer's hands move down my face to the back of my neck. I press against him as though he is the ground I need beneath me, and he pulls me closer, deepening the kiss. I feel warm all over, the kind of warmth I didn't believe was possible, not here in Seattle. I hear the rain falling against the glass windows and the sound usually makes me feel cold. But there isn't anything that could ruin this moment. Not the rain. Or anything else.

"Your mom," Meyer says against my lips.

Okay. Only that.

I break away and look around, expecting to see her on the roof.

"We need to go," he tells me, pulling at my hand. "She's looking for you."

"What?" I say, staring up at him completely confused.

"You should go," he tells me. "*I* should go."

"O-kay…" I watch him move toward the elevator.

"Friday," he says, like that one word explains everything. No mention of the kiss we shared, or if there will be another. Just *Friday*.

He smiles at me one last time and then the elevator swallows him up. And he's gone.

My phone buzzes in my pocket and I jump with surprise.

I'm home. Where are you?? reads the text from my mom.

I stare at the words on my screen until she texts again, this time in all caps.

WHERE ARE YOU?

On the roof, I reply. *Coming down now.*

I stare at my phone a minute longer and then slowly make my way to the elevator.

Maybe I was right to think that Meyer knows about Jenna. He seems to know more than he should. About everything.

CHAPTER FOURTEEN

Friday afternoon finds me sitting at the dining room table with James. It isn't our usual study day but James called early in the morning, letting me know he felt it was necessary to add a day this week.

"I would hate to see her fall behind," he told my mother. And that's all he needed to say to convince her that I needed to be subjected to another James tutor session.

I'm supposed to be listening and following along while he reads to me from *Meditations on Quixote* by Spanish liberal philosopher, José Ortega y Gasset, but my thoughts keep drifting to Meyer.

James tells me it's impossible to understand the Spanish language without first understanding the people, which makes sense and all, but there's no room in my thoughts for new people today. I can't stop thinking about Meyer. About how he kissed me, how it felt like not just *a* kiss, but the first kiss of many. I thought about it all night, reliving it like I was afraid it was too perfect to have happened. And it was perfect. Well, not at first. Not when he was pushing me away while I was pushing myself on him. Every time I think about that moment I want to hide my face in embarrassment. Did I startle him with my kiss? It felt like the right moment, and then it didn't. But then it did again. Maybe Meyer is simply old-fashioned. Maybe he prefers to be the instigator of these kinds of things. I mean, if that's the case, that's cool, I guess. But I'm not so sure that is the case. So... then. What happened? When I see him tonight, will he be the Meyer who wants to push me away or will he take the initiative and make something happen? I definitely know which one I want him to be. It is a date after all.

Suddenly James throws his arms into the air and exclaims, "Yo soy yo y mi circunstancia."

I gape at him as if he's gone insane and he gestures at me impatiently. "Translate!"

"Oh, um... I am... that is... I am I and—"

"I am I and my circumstance!" he finishes impatiently. "What do you think that means, Livy?"

"Well... I think it means—"

"Nothing. You think nothing because you haven't been concentrating."

For a moment I just stare at him, wondering when he morphed into my fourth grade teacher, Mr. Wells, who used to get off on embarrassing his students. I hated Mr. Wells. We all did.

"I'm sorry," I begin. "I didn't realize—"

"—that you were miles away from here? No. I can see that."

My mouth is left hanging open and then with a *snap* I close it. I've never seen James this intense, I mean he's always intense in a stare-through-you kind of way, but this is different. It's like he's genuinely angry with me.

"I'm sorry," I say again and sit up in my chair, giving him my complete attention.

His stern expression hovers there for a minute and then eventually smoothes out into a smile. "It is obvious you are not with me today, Livy. May I ask where you've been? Or what has your attention?"

My face flushes at how close his guess is and of course he catches it. He misses nothing. There's a curious look in his eyes as he waits for me to answer his question.

"You're right. My mind was somewhere else, but I'm back. And I'm sorry."

James nods his head and sits back in his chair. "Perhaps you'll share with me what has your thoughts today? Or should I say, who?"

"It's nothing," I answer quickly, but he doesn't buy it. Thankfully, he lets it slide.

"Shall we continue then?"

"Of course."

He shifts in his seat and ponders the painting on the dining room wall. It's a bunch of lines and squiggles (the composition is kind of nice, though) from some local artist my dad knows. But I doubt James is actually taking it in, let alone appreciating it. He seems to be deep in thought. His fingers are tap tap tapping the table and I'm watching them, absolutely captivated, until he says, "What do you think happened to Jenna?"

My breathing shudders to a stop. It's crazy how my sister's name can do that to me. One minute I feel light and — dare I even think it — happy, and the next I'm back to feeling lost.

"I don't know what you're asking. Do you mean, why did she get sick?"

"No." James leans forward so that his arms are resting on the table. "What do you believe happens to us when we die?"

"Oh, like do I believe in God?" I squeak out a nervous sounding laugh. "Are we back to religion again?" For a tutor he sure does bring this up a lot.

James shrugs. "Some people believe that philosophy and religion are one and the same. But I want to know what you think."

"Well, I've never really thought about it before." Which is a lie. I think about it all the time. Mostly I think about it when I visit Jenna's grave. It's so quiet and soothing there, with a view of the Sound and the Seattle skyline, and there's even a little bench next to her grave so that you can sit and visit with her — my parents picked it for that very reason. I don't like to think about her body buried underneath the ground. If I think about it too long I'll end up digging her back up. I imagine her down there as she used to be, not how she is now. And she wants out. She doesn't want to be left alone in the dark, cold ground. She wants to be with me. This is why I don't visit her very often. I just end up hyperventilating, staring down at the ground wishing I could save her all over again.

"But if we don't bury her, then what?" my mother asked me when I refused the idea of a burial. "I know you're sad, Livy, but I can't take this right now."

Well, neither could I. But the other options were worse. Burned? Incinerated? No. Never. Especially since Jenna was always afraid of fire.

James is still waiting for me to say something more, but I don't want to talk about this. I'd rather go back to hearing about Ortega y Gasset. Of course what I really want is to get back to thinking about Meyer. He's the only one who keeps me from sinking. But James is still waiting, his expression as patient as it is stubborn.

"What do *you* believe?" I ask, because that's what I do when I don't have the answers. I turn the focus away me.

James pauses for a minute, even though his answer is sure to be on the tip of his tongue. His hand begins to tap again, two quick taps and then a third.

"Death does not exist," he says, "not the death the world imagines."

"Okay." He hasn't said much, but I'm intrigued nonetheless.

"Nothing is lost forever, Livy."

"But if I can no longer see it or feel it, then it's gone."

James smiles at me and I can't tell if it's the triumphant smile of a teacher who has finally gotten his pupil to engage or if it's the smile of a hunter who has finally caught his prey in his carefully prepared verbal-trap. Either way I find it annoying. "What of love, then?" he says. "You can feel it, see it, taste it." He leans forward and I am ensnared within his gaze. "Does love ever disappear?"

"Sometimes." I think of my parents and how they barely communicate. I think of Sheila's parents and how her dad fell out of love and moved on to someone new. And I think of myself and how sometimes I worry that the love I feel for Jenna is already less than what it used to be when she was alive. Can people fall out of love just because the physical reminder of it is gone? They say absence makes the heart grow fonder but does it eventually lead to forgetfulness?

"You told me I don't know anything about love, remember?" I say.

"And I must have been right since you've thrown my words back in my face." James is smirking at me and I hate him for it, but mostly I hate him because he could be right. What do I know of it? Everyone who is close to me is slipping away.

I glare at James. I don't want to talk about love or death. I miss my old tutor. If Steve were here we would be conjugating verbs, and I'd be counting how many times his eyes blink during a single sentence, but instead I'm stuck dueling with James.

"William Shakespeare wrote, 'Love looks not with the eyes, but with the mind.'"

"Yeah, well, what does he know about it? He killed off the two most romantic characters that ever lived."

James laughs. "Again with the death. I think you focus on death far too much for a girl your age."

"You brought it up," I remind him.

"Yes, you're right," he murmurs. "I did."

I take a deep breath and relish in the moment. It feels good to hear James concede a point. But he's far from defeated. Clearly this is no ordinary lesson. He's still leaning toward me. He's so focused it's uncomfortable.

"What if there was no death? Not death like you imagine it. What if there was something more, or rather, something else?"

"What do you mean? Like immortality?"

"Immortality!" James scoffs. "Immortality is the selfish dream of a stupid man. I'm not talking about Gods or vampires, Livy."

"Are those my only two options?"

"Not everything is black and white," James says, ignoring my sarcasm. "The existence of life doesn't have to have a conclusion."

"So then you're saying…" I pause and try to put my thoughts into words. "I'm sorry, what are you saying?" Somewhere in this conversation I obviously slipped off the path.

James reaches across the table and takes my hand. Once he has a hold of it, I worry he will never give it back; his grip is that strong.

"She isn't gone, Livy. There is no death."

"What do you mean?" I shift closer in my seat. Even though what he's saying is ridiculous, there's a part of me that wants to believe he's right, that he knows something the rest of us don't.

He's silent for a moment, but his eyes are burning into mine. I still don't understand what he's trying to tell me, but I feel it. It moves through our hands like a ripple of energy, starting with the touch of his fingertips against the palm of my hand, and then it travels like a slow-building wave down my arm and toward my heart.

"What is this?" I ask him, my words a hiss against the silence. "What are you doing to me?"

"What do you *feel*? Tell me." Everything about him demands an answer; his eyes, his voice, and most of all his touch against my skin.

"I don't know. I don't understand what's happening." I want to pull away; it's frightening this feeling. It's not painful exactly but it's like nothing I've ever felt before. I imagine this is how it feels to touch the tail end of a lightning bolt, but without the mess of electrocution. I know I should pull away from him, but I can't. The fire spreading down my arm is filling me throughout, wrapping around the tightness in my chest and then reaching out. It's only a matter of time before I begin to sweat.

"You are alive," James whispers. "Do you feel it?"

"Yes," I answer. My chest is so full it feels like it's going to burst. One moment I'm not sure if I can breathe and then the next my lungs are brimming over. It's like the energy he's giving me is doing the work for me. I don't have to think about my next breath, I don't have to fight through the heaviness surrounding my heart, my body has replaced it with… what exactly?

And then it's gone. Just like that. James drops my hand on the table with such force it bounces against the polished wood and falls into my lap.

"Livy." My mother peeks her head around the corner. "I'm sorry to interrupt, but there is a young man waiting for you downstairs. He says his name is Meyer?"

Meyer! He's here? My heart starts to beat frantically and I'm not sure if it's the remnants of whatever James did to me, or nervous energy, but I'm too dizzy to think straight.

"Should I tell him to wait?" my mother asks. "Or have him come up?" I can tell she's doing her best to sound casual but she can't hide her curiosity. Not from me. When I look at James I find he's just as curious. But he's also smiling. Why is he smiling?

"Who is he, Livy?" my mother asks. "Have I met him?"

"He's a friend." I scoot my chair back. The further from James I get the cooler the air in the room feels. It soothes my heated face and body, all the way down to my trembling fingertips. "Um. I actually have to go. I'm meeting Sheila." I get up from the table and carefully slide my chair back in place. "I'm sorry," I say to James. "I mean, we were done, right?"

"For now." He has begun to gather his things, but doesn't appear to be in any kind of a hurry. Not like me.

"Um. Good then." I turn to my mother. "Can you tell him I'll be down in a minute?"

"Of course," my mother says, "but who is he, Livy? And what are your plans?"

"There are a few of us going — it's a get-together with a friend of Grant's. Sheila planned it. I shouldn't be out long." Why do I sound so sketchy? It would be so much easier if I could just get my mouth and mind to form a complete sentence. How easy would it be if I could just say, "I have a date with a boy. And I really like him."

And then she would say, "Have fun! If you decide to stay out late give me a call!"

But this is the real world, not make-believe. So instead my mom gives me her best scowl and says, "Is Sheila driving?"

"No."

"Are you driving?"

"Yes."

"And you won't be out past eleven?"

"No."

"Alright then." She touches my shoulder as I move by her. I pause, hoping for a hug, but it doesn't come.

"I'll wait and ride down with you," James says and I hate that he witnessed another episode from *Livy's Awkward Moment Diaries*. I hate when anyone does.

"You don't have to wait," I tell him. "There's no need—"

"This way we can finish our lesson on the ride down," he interrupts.

"You mean you weren't finished for the day?" my mother asks. Her face is back to looking pinched.

131

"I only need a minute," James assures her and then he turns to me. "Isn't that right, Livy?"

"Uh, right." I stand there, hovering in the hallway. I hate being tricked almost as much as I hate being hurried. "I just have to get something quick." I point toward my bedroom and then I take off down the hall, desperate to get one last look at myself before I have to meet Meyer.

In my room I glance in the mirror, applying lip gloss and checking my hair. I throw on my dark green shirt, the one I'd planned to wear — not the flirty little dress Sheila wants me to wear. This shirt is fitted where it needs to be and slightly low in the back, and it looks great with these jeans. It also brings out the green flecks in my hazel eyes. One last turn in the mirror and I'm convinced I look fine. Maybe even a little better than fine. My face is flushed and that's okay. Whatever James did to my hand has brightened my eyes, but I can't think about that right now, because if I do I just might hyperventilate. And a paper bag isn't quite the accessory I'd planned to bring with me tonight. Instead I slip on the diamond earrings my mother bought me two Christmases ago. I take a deep breath and let it out the way I learned to do in Yoga class and then I do it one more time.

"Soon," I tell the flustered girl in the mirror. "Soon I will take a moment to think about the weirdness that is my life right now. Soon I will confront all these things that aren't exactly normal. But not now. Not tonight." The girl in the mirror nods her head with acceptance — if not denial. "Go!" she tells me, because what I really need is to get myself downstairs before my mother decides she has to meet this boy, Meyer. The boy who has secrets of his own.

James is waiting for me at the elevator.

"Are you ready?" I say and he smiles.

"We'll continue our discussion another day," he tells me and the look in his eyes leaves no room for debate.

"Bye, mom!" I call out and then she's there, watching as I step into the elevator.

"No later than eleven," she says just before the doors shut and I'm left alone with James.

"I'm sure you have questions." James is standing next to me — not touching, but we might as well be. I'm more aware of him than I am my own breath.

"Always," I mutter. "But the real question is, will you answer?"

James is quiet, waiting for me to continue.

"I don't know what you want," I say.

"Are you sure that's really what has you concerned?"

"Can you stop talking in riddles, please? You're supposed to be my Spanish tutor, not my psychologist!"

The elevator becomes thick with silence. The kind that goes on far too long or maybe not long enough because suddenly the doors open and there's Meyer. He gives me a lopsided smile, his eyes heavy on mine. He opens his mouth to say something but the moment he catches sight of James his expression changes completely. His eyes widen with shock, or possibly recognition — it's hard to know for sure. He takes a step back as though he's desperate for more distance between us. For a second I'm afraid he'll bolt. But he doesn't. His feet ground him to the floor about ten paces from the elevator. His eyes have gone hard. So still is he that were I to touch him I might find that he's frozen.

"Meyer?" I call out. But he's ignoring me. His hard green eyes are locked on James, who steps off the elevator looking far more composed and relaxed than anyone should considering the bristling tension in the air.

"James Hale," he says to Meyer, extending his right hand. "I am Livy's tutor."

Meyer reacts as if he's been slapped. His body unfreezes, his lips curl and his eyes narrow into two tiny points of fire.

"Nice to meet you," he says, ignoring James' outstretched hand and brushing past him on his way toward me. "We should go, Livy. We mustn't keep them waiting."

"No," James says. "Never that."

I have just enough time to smooth my nervous hands along the side of my jeans before Meyer grabs my arm and tugs at me.

"Wait." I pull back from Meyer and his narrowed eyes move from James to me. For a minute I think he might force us to make a run for it, but then his grip on my arm loosens.

"We were just discussing Ortego y Gasset," James says, and I blink up at him until the familiar name strikes a memory.

"Yes. James is teaching me about Spanish philosophy." I tug on Meyer's hand, wishing he wouldn't pull me so hard, but it's like fighting with a wall.

"Is that right?" Meyer's hooded expression is difficult to read but the strength behind his grip tells me he's done here. I guess I'm not the only one uncomfortable around James.

"Ortega y Gasset believed that we cannot put off living until we are ready. That, as he put it, life is fired at us point-blank. In other words, you must live it, not *escape* it."

"Right," I say, studying James. There's more to this lesson, I think. A message just for me.

"No time like the present." Meyer's hand is against my back, directing me toward the doorway. When I glance at him in surprise, he smiles, but there's an edge to it.

"Have a good night, James," I call over my shoulder and he dips his head to us in farewell.

"And you as well, children," he says in return. "And you as well."

CHAPTER FIFTEEN

Meyer leads me down one flight of stairs to the parking garage and then waits while I search for my keys. The tension coming off him is as loud as an echo bouncing off the cement walls.

"We're meeting Sheila and Grant at the party," I explain once I pull out onto the street, but he just nods and stares out the window. "It's at some kid's house on Mercer Island," I add. "So, not too far." Pause. "Have you ever been to Mercer Island?" Again I'm met with silence. "It's really beautiful," I add softly, turning my attention back to the road.

The windshield wipers swish back and forth and I'm more aware of my driving than I have ever been before. My foot slips off the gas pedal twice causing the car to jerk slightly. *Get it together, Livy. He's just a boy,* I tell myself. But who am I kidding? He's not *just* anything.

If my GPS is correct we have another twenty minutes until we arrive at the party. But twenty minutes of silence could last a lifetime. An eternity.

"I forgot to bring your sweatshirt," I tell him. Or rather I didn't forget. I simply cannot bear to part with it. Especially when it still smells like him. But I'm not about to tell him that.

"Keep it," he says without turning away from the window. "I have others."

"Oh. Okay." I glance over at him, noticing how the sweatshirt he has on tonight is similar to the one he leant me, but darker.

"Is something wrong?" I ask with a grimace. I hate that barely ten minutes into our first date I have to ask this question.

Is he mad about the kiss? Does he wish he were somewhere else? *With* someone else? All of these questions and doubts are pushing their way into my thoughts. I can barely concentrate. I swear something happened back in the lobby between Meyer and James. Could that be what's bothering him? Could it be as simple as that? I got the distinct impression that either they know each other or recognized each other. Either way something's up. The problem is neither of these mysterious new men in my life is capable of answering questions, so the puzzle is mine to solve. Alone.

Meyer picks up my iPhone and starts scanning my collection of music. I pray that he'll put something on, anything — but then he sets it down and the painful silence stretches out past the dimensions of my car. I'm about ready to roll my window down and start talking to random people on the street when finally he speaks.

"James is… interesting," he says. "How long has he been your tutor?" He's looking at me, his face occasionally lit by the headlights of passing cars.

"Um. Not long… maybe a week or two? About as long as—" *As long as I've known Meyer.* But for some reason I stop myself before completing that thought "He's just temporarily filling in. My real tutor is out of town."

"Interesting," he says again, drawing out the word.

"Yeah." I sit up taller in my seat. "I know he comes off as pretty intense." I clear my throat, not exactly sure how else to describe him. "He's mainly helping me with my Spanish." Which is the truth, actually.

We pull up to a stoplight and I take the opportunity to study Meyer. His hand is resting on his leg, his finger tapping against his knee. He keeps frowning out the window as if he's attempting to work something out, and I know the feeling. If only we could work it out together.

"Did you, um, recognize James, or something? It kind of seemed like—"

"No." He shakes his head and then says it again, "No." And then as if to soften his response he smiles. "Just, you know, wasn't expecting your tutor to be so dashing."

"Dashing?" I say with a laugh.

"What? You have a better word to describe him?"

Intense? Intimidating? Sure, dashing also works.

"He makes me nervous," I say and Meyer's hand stops tapping on his leg.

"He should. He holds your fate in his hands."

"What?" I say, glancing over at him with surprise.

"Without him you'll never make it past high school, right?" Meyer gives me one of his trademark smirks, but I'm not buying it. Something in his voice tells me there's more to that statement.

"Right," I answer.

"I'm really looking forward to meeting your friends." He relaxes back into his seat and that light of excitement brightens his eyes. The dark electricity from before has fizzled out and settled down near my feet. It's not gone completely, just dormant for now.

"It should be fun," I say, even though I'm pretty sure it won't be. Parties really aren't my scene. A year or so ago Sheila and I were

desperate to be invited to a party like tonight's, but now it just feels…
I don't know, *different*.

"Fun," Meyer says, looking back out the window, "is just what
we need."

About twenty minutes later we pull up to a large log cabin-esque
house overlooking the water. I can't make out the number on the
mailbox but the sheer volume of teenagers going in and out of the
house tells me we're at the right place. Not to mention the loud bass
coming from the house.

"This must be it. We're here." I turn off the engine but remain in
my seat.

"So," Meyer says. "Shall we?"

He climbs out of the car and moves around to my side before
I've even had time to remove my seatbelt. He opens my door and
even takes my hand to help me to my feet.

"I like parties," he says. Of course he does. To him this is just
another adventure.

He tugs on my hand, dragging me toward the front door. He
must sense I don't really want to be here. But I follow him regardless.

"Heeeyyy!" says some guy I don't recognize as we step up to the
front door. "Welcome! Everyone is welcome!"

He slides up closer to me and I feel Meyer's grip on my hand
tighten.

"Especially you," he continues. His finger circles the perimeters
of my face as if he's trying to touch me, but he's so drunk he can't
figure out which one of me to touch. "I don't know you, but you can
come to my party." Then he aims his pointed finger at Meyer. "But
you, you I'm not so sure." He starts laughing. "I'm just messing with
you, man! Everyone is welcome!" He spreads his hands wide, nearly
knocking me sideways.

"You're too kind." Meyer steers me around the guy and we head into the house. The music we could hear from just outside is much louder now, far less like sound, more like pressure. My chest is pounding from the bass, and my ears are ringing.

I don't recognize anyone so far, not that I thought I would. This isn't my world anymore. A few years out of school and the people I grew up with have moved on to new friends and new surroundings. I'm the girl who may look slightly familiar, but without the constant reminder at school, I'm nobody.

I follow Meyer down the hallway, dodging people left and right. He has hold of my hand, which is a good thing. I don't want to lose him in the crowd.

We enter a large family room where about thirty or so kids are dancing. This is where I would normally find Sheila — dancing like the world is her stage — but I don't see her anywhere. Meyer turns and says something to me and I shake my head in confusion. Even if he screamed it in my ear, I doubt I'd hear him in here.

"Outside," he mouths, and then points to the back of the house where someone has just opened the sliding back door.

I nod with understanding and then follow him out onto the back deck.

Even though it's still lightly raining the party has spread outside. There are at least a couple dozen kids hanging out around a large fire pit, in their hands are the ever-present red plastic cups that always seem to accompany a party. I feel a flicker of apprehension when I realize I don't know much about Meyer, whether he drinks or, well, anything. More than likely he's not like me, the girl who doesn't mess with things that make her feel less in control. Truth is, not many are.

"Would you rather go back inside?" Meyer asks, as I stand frozen in the center of the deck. "You look cold."

"No, I'm fine," I say stiffly.

"Alright." He buries his hands in his pockets. "Do you want a drink?"

"It's really not my thing," I tell him.

"What is your thing then?"

"I have lots of things," I say, not exactly looking at him. "But getting drunk isn't one of them."

"Fair enough," he says with a shrug. "So no drinks."

Meyer is staring out at the trees and the darkness. Some of the tension from before still lingers around his eyes and mouth, but when he catches me studying him he forces it off.

"Don't let me stop you," I blurt out. "Just because I'm not into it—"

"Haven't you figured me out yet, Livy?" he says.

"Um. You're kidding, right?" I laugh, and he looks on in confusion. "Maybe I would if you'd give me a straight answer once in a while." I pull my coat tighter sealing in what little body heat I have left. It's so cold out here I can see my breath. When I look up Meyer is watching me, still waiting for an answer.

"Is this some kind of a test?" I joke.

Instead of answering, he crosses his arms in front of him.

"Alright," I say, drawing out the word. "So you don't drink."

His only response is a subtle nod.

"And you don't go to public school, at least nowhere in Seattle."

He lifts a brow as if he's curious how I came upon this knowledge since he never provided it, but he doesn't deny it either.

"You're more of an adrenaline junkie than anything else. Which is dangerous, but occasionally fun."

Meyer bursts out laughing.

"Occasionally!" I repeat. "And you have an accent that I can't quite trace, not that I'm some authority on accents. But sometimes it's so strong and then other times it's barely there."

Meyer tilts his head, obviously enjoying this, and gestures for me to continue.

"Um..." I tap my finger against my lip, thinking, but when I notice he's focused on the movement — on my mouth — I stop. Heat rises to my cheeks, and there's nothing I can do about it.

Meyer's lips curve with amusement, but I continue as though everything's normal.

"You hang out at the hospital a lot but I'm not sure why."

His eyes cloud over, but then he nods. "Keep going. What else?"

An image of us hanging from the Ferris wheel comes to mind and I feel my body tremble in reaction. "You have a lot of secrets," I whisper. "Things that I want to ask about, but I'm afraid to."

Meyer stiffens, his eyes piercing mine. "You should never be afraid of me."

I nod my head slowly. Truth is, I knew this already.

"What else?" he coaxes. "What else do you know about me?"

"Nothing," I answer with a frustrated sigh, but as soon as the word is out there I know it's a lie. I may not know the little details that make up Meyer, but I feel like I know him. Maybe even more than anyone else could claim. And judging by the look in his eyes, I'm not alone in this theory. He must feel it too.

"What about me?" I say. "What do you know about me?" Because if we're going to play this game I should also be given a turn.

A mysterious smile moves along his lips. "You, Livy," he says, "well, let's just say I thought I had you figured out." He lifts his hand up to my face and I catch my breath the moment he touches me. It's barely a touch at all, actually. He's merely brushing my hair back, but with his touch comes warmth. It colors my cheeks and slides down my neck, pooling in the pit of my stomach.

"I'm not all that complicated," I say, unable to look away from him.

"I didn't say you were complicated." He pauses. "Just different from what I was expecting."

What were you expecting? The words are right there, gathering together, ready to fly. I open my mouth. I narrow my eyes.

"I expected the sadness," he tells me, practically reading my mind. "I expected you to be mourning her."

Jenna. So I'm right. He does know about her.

"But there's more to you than that," he continues. "There's more to me as well."

And with these words I feel the truth is so close, closer even than the short distance between us.

"Tell me," I say, taking that last step that's been keeping us apart. "Tell me everything."

"You came!" Sheila appears from somewhere off in the darkness and wraps her arms around me, pulling me in for a tight hug. "I thought you'd chicken out," she whispers in my ear.

"I told you I'd be here," I say a little defensively, and she sticks her tongue out at me. I long to push her back into the darkness —at least until I can finish this moment with Meyer — but I don't.

"Where is he?" Sheila spins around, her short black skirt pirouetting with her. "I've got to see the guy who—" and then she stops. Her eyes widen and her mouth forms a little oh. "You didn't tell me it was sexy-hoodie guy!" She slaps my arm and I take a step back.

"He isn't… I mean … I'm not…" Sigh. "I'm sorry," I mutter to Meyer.

But he just smiles. "I've been called worse."

"So you're Livy's," Sheila says, grinning.

Meyer smiles at me and my face erupts into flames. I want nothing more than to duck my head and hurry past the tiki torches set up along the patio, out to where the darkness would welcome me with open arms and sealed lips. That's what I love about the shadows of life, they never ask questions. My face continues to burn with embarrassment as I contemplate just how to disappear. My eyes narrow, silently communicating to Sheila how little I'm appreciating this, but she ignores me.

Meyer holds out his hand for her to shake. "I'm Meyer. You must be Sheila." But she doesn't take it.

"Well, look at that. Livy's got herself a gentleman. With a cute accent too." She smiles at me and then rolls her eyes at my glare. "What? It's cute!" She sidles up next to him and adds, "*You're* cute."

"Glad to hear I meet your approval," Meyer drawls and Sheila giggles.

"Say approval again!"

"Uh…" Meyer's mouth lifts in a crooked smile, his eyes flashing in my direction. "Approval," he says and Sheila squeals with delight.

She sways a bit closer and I realize with a shock that she's drunk. She grips his shoulder while her body continues to sway slightly. I've never seen Sheila drunk. I didn't even know she drank. She never drank before. With me. And of all the nights to find out…

"Well done, Livy!" she says, her face far too close to Meyer's. "Where are you from? I've been asking, but Livy won't tell me." She frowns in my direction, her eyes seeking me out. "She used to tell me *everything*."

"Sheila." I take a step closer but she puts up a hand, stopping me.

"No, Livy. We're talking. Stay over there."

Meyer raises an eyebrow and I shrug, but I do as she says.

"I didn't even know about you," she tells him. "I had a su-spi…sus-pish…suspicion," she finally gets the word out and then she breaks into hysterical laughter. "That's such a silly word!"

"Sheila?" Grant walks up and joins our group, barely glancing my way in greeting. His eyes are on his girlfriend.

"There you are!" Sheila exclaims. "See that one," she stage-whispers to Meyer, pointing over her shoulder at Grant. "He's mine. Isn't he cute?"

Meyer gives Grant an apologetic smile. "He seems nice."

"He is nice," Sheila says with a dramatic sigh. "But he doesn't have a cute accent."

"Sheila," Grant says again, this time with feeling. "Would you mind letting go of Livy's date?"

"Would I mind?" Sheila is petting him now, her hand brushing over his shoulder as if he's a house cat. I can't blame her actually. He does have nice shoulders. And arms. "She used to tell me everything, you know," she continues. "She used to be my best friend."

Used to be? I take a step closer and her eyes flash in my direction.

"Now she's too wrapped up in saving the world, she can't be bothered with me."

"Sheila!" I gasp.

"What!" She's glaring at me now. Her brown eyes flashing a hurt she's never once directed at me before. Her hands are bunched up in Meyer's dark hoodie. "It's true and you know it." She aims her body in my direction while Meyer holds her up. "It's like we — *I'm* not enough for you," she mumbles. But I hear her. And so does Meyer. "I begged her to come tonight," she says to him. "Did she tell you that? I had to *beg* my supposed *best friend* to spend some time with me."

I flinch and that layer of guilt that surrounds me every time I think of my father or Jenna stretches taut as it welcomes Sheila to the fold.

"It's not like that—" I begin but Grant cuts me off.

"That's enough." He brushes past me and removes his girlfriend from Meyer's chest. "I'm sorry," he says to Meyer. "She isn't usually like this."

"No," Sheila giggles. "I'm usually much more fun."

"No worries," Meyer says, his eyes on me.

"I mean, I know you're sad, Livy." Sheila calls back over her shoulder. "And I know you think those kids need you." She's staring right at me as her words carry over the noise of the party. "But what about *me*?" She stops just shy of the trees, her voice cracking. "Did you ever think of that? That maybe *I* need you?"

I feel as if someone has punched me in the stomach. Does Sheila really believe that? And if so, how come she's never said anything? I know I haven't been around much lately, but I thought she understood.

Meyer walks up beside me, but he doesn't say a word. We watch in silence as Grant drags Sheila out of hearing range. Grant really isn't into scenes. But then again, neither am I.

"So. Those are your friends, eh?" Meyer says and I flinch.

"They aren't usually like this," I whisper. "I didn't know she ..." I stop and shake my head. "It doesn't matter."

"Doesn't it?"

My silence is his answer.

"She seems pretty upset about something."

"I didn't realize." And I hadn't. How could I have? I've been so caught up in my own sadness, I never gave a second thought to Sheila's feelings. "She always seems so strong. So put together. Even when her parents divorced she didn't seem to need anyone."

Then it hits me. She's just like my mother. She's brave and strong and solid to the rest of the world but inside she's weak like me.

"Livy?"

I turn at the familiar voice and find my ex-boyfriend, Scott, standing just behind me.

His smile is big, even for him. "I thought that was you."

"Hey, Scott," I say, not quite over the last scene with Sheila, and definitely not prepared to introduce Meyer to my ex.

"Hey," he says just standing there. He doesn't introduce me to the girl at his side. He just keeps on smiling at me. "I didn't expect to run into you."

"Yeah," I sigh. Likewise.

"It's so great to see you."

"I'm Livy," I say to his date when he still doesn't offer up her name and the pause in conversation goes beyond awkward. "And this is Meyer."

"Shay," she says smiling at Meyer, but not quite acknowledging me. She brushes her blonde hair off her shoulder, and leans a bit closer to Scott.

"Nice to meet you," Meyer says and Shay giggles.

"You have an accent," she says.

"So I've heard."

Shay giggles again.

"I'm so glad to see you," Scott says. "Wait. Did I say that already?" He laughs and I laugh. But neither Meyer nor Shay finds it amusing. Shay presses herself up against Scott, slipping her hand along his arm.

"Scotty," she coos. "I'm thirsty."

"Okay," Scott answers, but I'm not sure he actually heard her. He still hasn't taken his eyes off me. "You look good, Livy. I mean, it's good to see you out."

Out? Is that where I am? I thought maybe this place was my own personal party-hell.

"Yes," Meyer drawls. "We try to let her out of her cage at least once or twice a week. Don't we, Livy?"

Surprised, I turn to Meyer. He's smiling down at me, a heavy look in his eyes. He reaches up and tucks a strand of hair behind my ear, his touch lingering a bit longer than necessary along the side of my face.

I attempt to answer and then forget all about it when his eyes drop to my lips. Just like that I'm thinking about yesterday and how he kissed me. And judging from Meyer's smile, he knows it too.

"It was nice meeting you," Shay says, pulling at Scott. She's nearly moved him away when he stops and turns back.

"See you later, Livy," he adds, while his eyes say so much more.

"Well, he seemed nice," Meyer says once they've moved on.

"Yeah. Nice. Scott is… nice." That's pretty much the word I always used to describe him. To be honest he was nice to a fault. He took it as his personal mission to make me happy, to save me from myself, and my sadness. And I'm pretty sure he wouldn't have given up on me. Not like I did on him.

"Was that another friend of yours?"

Meyer is studying me closely, but I don't want to talk about Scott. Not at all.

"I want to talk about yesterday," I say before I can chicken out.

"Yesterday?"

"I want to talk about how I kissed you." There. It's out. I've said it.

Meyer is silent, his only reaction is a lone eyebrow-raise.

"I didn't, I mean, I wondered…"

"Yes?" He's smiling now, but not touching me. Which is what I really want, him touching me. Holding me. The two of us back on my roof, above the world. Alone, and yet together.

"I like you," I whisper. "A lot." Wow. I didn't see that one coming.

Meyer's smile slips off, dropping somewhere I can't find it.

"I… I thought you should know," I continue. Now that I've made the leap, I may as well keep talking. "I'm sorry if I've made things awkward."

Meyer takes a step back and I feel that space between us like a slap.

"You don't have to say anything. I mean, I wish you would, but you don't—"

"Livy."

Oh no. I close my eyes not wanting to see his face when he tells me he doesn't feel the same way.

I'm expecting the band-aid to tear at my skin when he rips it off. I'm expecting his words to pierce through my heart. What I'm not expecting is his hand against my face, so when I feel it, I jerk away as though he's hit me.

"Livy," he says again, softer this time. He reaches up slowly to touch me again, but then he changes his mind and his hand drops to his side.

"There's so much," he begins. "So much you don't know about me."

"So tell me!"

His expression is dark. He's battling with himself. I blink up at him, afraid to speak. For a moment I wonder if he's battling me.

"I can't, " he whispers. "It's just that—"

"Grant says I should apologize." Sheila has arrived with the worst possible timing. She's swaying less, but she's still grinning like a psychopath.

"Geez, Sheila!" Grant says coming up behind her. He's glaring as if she's hopeless, but he's still hanging around. He always is.

"What?" She spins around nearly knocking him over. "I'm getting there. Just settle." She latches herself onto me. "I love you, Livy. You know I love you. I'm just so freakin' happy to see you here! Out of your house! And with a boy!" She turns her face toward Meyer who takes a step back.

Their presence has erased whatever it was he was about to say.

"So don't be mad, Livy-poo. You can't be mad. *Please*."

Livy-poo?

Meyer lifts an eyebrow as if to ask the same question, and I blink at him, wishing, for the first time, my best friend had some idea when to leave it alone.

"I love parties," Sheila giggles.

"Who doesn't?" Meyer says, smiling as though we weren't just having a moment.

Me. I don't like parties. I'm sure of it now.

"You live here?" he says to Grant.

"Nah, that kid over there does. Kenny." Grant points to the kid who greeted us at the door, who at this moment is drinking out of two red cups at the same time, spilling nearly every last drop down the front of him.

"You been drinking?" Meyer asks.

"Nah." Grant gestures at Sheila. "I'm the DD."

"Right," Meyer says, nodding. "You feel like jumping?"

"Huh?" Grant says.

"Um, what?" I say.

Meyer points at the large rock jutting out over the water from the side lawn. "Off that."

"For real?" Grant says, but there's a gleam in his eyes that tells me he's already considering it.

"Wait, what?" Sheila says, sobering up. "You're going swimming? It's like freezing in that water!"

"It's not *like* freezing," I tell Meyer. "It *is* freezing." I shake my head at him, feeling like my mother. "You can't be serious about this, Meyer. It's not safe." And now I sound like her.

Meyer glances out over Lake Washington and the flickering flames coming off the tiki torches provide enough light to see just how serious he is.

My shoulders drop with a sigh. In my opinion what Meyer is planning is far more dangerous than anything in those red plastic cups.

"I think this party needs something. Don't you?" Meyer asks us.

"I don't know, I'm kind of enjoying myself," I answer, glaring at him, and he laughs. "Besides, I'm pretty sure drunk teenagers and water are a bad combination. Factor in heights and… well… you've got yourself a mass suicide."

Meyer rubs his hands together. That smile of his is back. "Don't worry, Livy. I won't let anyone try it unless they've got their wits about them."

"Well then," I tell him. "You may want to try a different party."

But Meyer isn't listening to me. He's already walking toward the large rock with Grant following close behind.

"You're crazy," I call out once he's reached the top.

"Not crazy," he yells back. "Just ready for some fun."

"If you don't want to stay at this lame party, we can go!" I tell him as he circles the top of the rock, searching for the best point of entrance. "All you had to do is ask!"

But again he just laughs.

"Why are you doing this?" I yell. For one moment I have his complete attention. He turns from the water, his gaze finding mine in the darkness.

"Live as if they're going to tell stories about you," he says. And even though I don't agree, even though I would never jump off a rock, completely dressed, in the middle of the night — I feel his excitement. I felt it the moment I acknowledged my feelings to him. I don't need to jump off a rock to feel some kind of an adrenaline rush. I simply had to fall in love with a boy.

"What he said," Grant laughs, breaking the connection between Meyer and myself. Meyer goes back to gazing down at the water, lost in his thoughts, while the cool night air rushes up around me, sending a shiver along my skin, reminding me why I hate the cold.

"And I thought I was crazy," Sheila says, staring up at him. "You sure you can handle this one, Livy?"

"Not sure," I say, but what I really mean is, I'm not sure I have a choice.

It doesn't take long for Meyer to gather up a posse of lemmings. They're grouped together at the top of the large rock, occasionally glancing down into the dark water, while Sheila and I huddle together not daring to look over the side, and yet needing to be a part of it.

"How deep is it down there?" some guy asks.

"Deeper than it needs to be. Just jump!" yells Kenny.

Normally I wouldn't believe anything Kenny said, but I've gone swimming in this lake. It's not the depth of the water that worries me, it's the temperature.

The cool breeze up on the rock is helping Sheila to sober up, or maybe it's the distance between her and those red plastic cups. "I'm so sorry," she whispers in my ear. "I'm sorry for the stupid things I said before. I won't blame you if you never talk to me again. I'm surprised Grant still is."

"It's alright," I say. "I'm sorry I've been such a horrible friend."

"Not horrible," Sheila says. "Just… I miss you."

Sheila leans her head on my shoulder and I welcome her warmth. "One day he's going to stop forgiving me. And one day you're going to realize I'm not worth it," she whispers.

We're both watching as Grant and Meyer begin to peel off their layers of clothing: first sweatshirts, then shoes, followed by their socks. Once they're barefoot and sleeveless my teeth begin to chatter.

"I don't believe in one day," I tell her and she sighs.

"I know you have to help Jilly," Sheila says. "I just wonder…"

"Wonder what?" I say. "Tell me." I'm so tired of people keeping things from me.

"I just wonder how far you'll go. How many kids you'll try to save before you realize she isn't coming back."

I close my eyes, blocking it all out: Meyer, Grant, the cold water, and drunk but brutally honest Sheila.

"You're so sad all the time, Livy. And I hate it! I keep hoping this thing with Jilly will fix you. I mean, not fix you. You know what I mean."

"Yeah. Sure." Of course I know what she means. She thinks I'm broken, which isn't far from the truth, actually.

She squeezes her arms tight around my shoulders. "You're coming back, right? This isn't what you're always going to be?"

What am I? I want to ask. What do I look like to the people who are supposed to know me best? All this time I thought I was fighting off the sadness, peeling it back so that no one can see how it surrounds me, but I guess I'm more transparent than I thought.

"I'm trying," I whisper back. And, man, it's the truth.

We stand like this a few minutes longer as the crowd beneath us continues to gather. The cold is battling its way through my raincoat but I refuse to go back inside. Not when Meyer's out here. I just wish this new stunt of his didn't feel like a ploy to avoid talking to me. I get that he's all about the adventure, but for a moment there… it felt like more than just a silly game.

"Is he really going to jump?" Sheila asks. "It seems a bit extreme, even for a party."

"He's really going to jump," I say. And then just as I'm gearing up for round two of the you-shouldn't-do-this-Meyer! debate, he does it. He takes a running start and throws himself off the side of the cliff, down into the dark water below.

"Holy shit," Sheila whispers, and I nod my head in agreement.

When Meyer breaks the surface I can't see him but I'm sure he's smiling. I can hear it in his voice. He yells up to the rest of us so that we know he's okay, but for me there was never any doubt. Meyer is invincible.

"That was awesome!" Kenny says. "I'm next!"

Everyone on the rock hurries to discourage him.

"You're drunk, Kenny!" some girl down on the ground yells up at him.

"I ain't rescuing you neither," someone else says.

Kenny shrugs it off and turns to watch the next kid hit the water. "I'm not that drunk," he mumbles.

It continues like this for the next twenty minutes or so, until at least a dozen kids have jumped and half the party has gathered outside to watch the madness.

Meyer joins us a few minutes later. I've lost track of how many times he's made it off the rock. He's soaking wet but doesn't appear to care.

"How about it, Livy? You going to give it a go?"

"Livy?" Sheila laughs. "She would never. Maybe before… but not now." She squeezes my hand to show me she means no harm and I squeeze back.

"Maybe next time," I say, not quite meeting Meyer's eyes.

But his silence is deafening. He doesn't move on, even though everyone keeps yelling at him to jump off again.

"Pain or suffering, Livy?" he says softly and I've no choice but to look at him.

"What?" I let go of Sheila and move closer to him. "It's not my turn, it's yours."

"Not true," he says, his eyes piercing mine. Now which is it?" He tilts his head toward the cliff where two girls are gearing up to jump, their hands clenched in solidarity.

"I'm not going in that water," I say defiantly and his smirk is nothing if not challenging.

He crosses his arms against his chest. "So I win, then?"

"What are you guys talking about?" Shelia's holding Grant's hand. She doesn't seem to care that he's dripping all over her.

But Meyer and I ignore her.

"Well?" Meyer's eyes refuse to leave mine. "Is the game over?" In other words, are we done here?

"No," I say, feeling a bit desperate. Is that what it means? If I don't jump, will Meyer win? And if Meyer wins, will he disappear from my life? Forever? "What you're doing is dangerous. It's too cold and too high and too scary!" I'm trembling now, my teeth chattering loudly.

"And yet we're all okay."

"Hell, yeah!" Grant says, and I roll my eyes.

"You didn't know that before you jumped. It was a risk. A silly risk." I can feel myself getting worked up. It was fun before, this game of pain and suffering, but I can't gamble with my life like this, even if it means losing Meyer. I've seen what death does to people. I've lived through the aftershocks.

"Please don't do this," I whisper. Don't make me choose.

"Livy?" Meyer is staring at me with confusion. "Why are you so upset? This is just for fun."

"But that's just it," I say. "It's not fun, it's dangerous. And I don't like dangerous. I don't like risk! Not like you." But I'm not really talking about the game anymore, and we both know it. This isn't about jumping. Not to me. This is about taking frivolous risks and gambling with something I'm not willing to gamble. And if I'm being completely honest with myself, it's also about the kiss. How it felt real. And right. But I guess to Meyer this is all just a game.

I glare at him and he glares back.

"Then pain it is." He shrugs, and just like that I'm trapped. We're both very much aware that sometimes the truth is a far greater risk than one silly jump into dark water.

"What is he talking about, Livy?" Sheila has moved away from Grant. She touches my arm to get my attention or maybe to show me that she's here. She's with me.

Meyer has to be cold; he's making me cold just looking at him with his dripping hair and his wet-like-a-second-skin clothing. "The choice is yours. Pain or suffering. That is, unless you're willing to admit defeat."

"Defeat?" I glare at him and he looks pointedly down at the water. He must know that defeat is not an option for me.

"Oh, I get it!" Sheila bursts out. "You guys are like playing truth or dare, right?"

"Alright. What do you want to know?" I'm desperate to find an exit from this conversation. But the only way out is down.

Meyer just smiles.

"Go ahead. Ask your question, already," I say in a huff. He already knows how I feel about him. Really, what's the worst he could ask? But in true Meyer fashion he simply lifts an eyebrow, dragging out the silence until I can bear it no longer.

"What? You want to know my greatest fear?" I gesture to the water. "Haven't you figured that one out yet? I throw my hands in the air with frustration only to discover my hands are visibly trembling. I grip them tightly, pulling them against my chest as though they could shield me from Meyer's question, but judging by the look in his eyes I need more than a shield to escape what's coming next.

Meyer continues to study me. He hasn't made a sound.

"Just ask it, already," I whisper. "Please. Cause if you think I'm going in that water—"

"Why do you do it?" he says finally. His voice sounds a bit ragged, like the words have been ripped from him. "Why do you spend so much time with those kids when you know they're only going to leave you?"

Sheila's laughing at something Grant is telling her and the repeated sound of splashing is loud, and all around us. But the look in Meyer's eyes is crippling. This question isn't just for me. I don't quite understand it, but I feel it. He's desperate to know the answer.

"I don't understand what you're talking about," I say, but that lifted eyebrow of his mocks me. He knows I'm lying. Damn it, he knows.

"They need me," I whisper. Once again my chest feels tight. With one little question Meyer has reached in and discovered the one area I keep closed off.

"Do they?"

I nod my head even though we both know it's the wrong answer.

"Answer the question, Livy." His arms are crossed in front of his chest. He isn't going anywhere. "The truth this time."

"What's the question?" Sheila pipes up. "What'd I miss?"

Meyer is waiting for me to answer.

Everyone around me has gone silent. Even the music that was pouring from the house has stopped, like they're changing the music or something. The kids are no longer jumping — all eyes are on us.

I curse under my breath and Sheila chokes back a laugh. I hate that this has become such a scene.

"I should have jumped," I mutter under my breath, and then Meyer is right up next to me, pulling me, dragging me closer until it's not just him that's soaking wet, but me as well.

"Why do you do it? Why do you spend so much time there?"

"I just want…"

"What, Livy? What do you want?"

I open my mouth to answer him, but I can't. What can I possibly say? The truth isn't an option. It's too embarrassing or humiliating. Mostly it's too personal. There's no way I'm willing to blurt out, "I just don't want to feel alone anymore!" Even though it's the horrifying truth. I want to feel something again. Something good. Something real. I want to know that when she died I didn't die with her.

"Livy?" Meyer whispers my name. "Just tell me." *Trust me.*

He's so close. His hands are pulling me, moving me so that everything around us is just background.

"I want…" I say and his gaze drops to my mouth. My eyes well up, my chest expands. I'm so close to losing it — at a party of all places — I really should have just jumped in the damn water.

"Geronimo!" Kenny yells, racing past us. His arms are wide, his steps determined as he runs toward the edge of the rock. Everyone jumps out of his way, including me and Meyer. But not Sheila. She's caught up in his momentum. Her feet swept out underneath her.

Sheila's head knocks against the rock and then her body spirals down into the dark water.

CHAPTER SIXTEEN

Meyer is the first to react. He dives off the side and I hear him splashing around in the water, trying to locate her.

"Sheila!" I scream, tearing at my clothes. I manage to get my coat off and then I'm jumping off the rock at the same moment as Grant. I don't think about the cold or the risks, I only think of Sheila. But as my jeans and shirt begin to absorb the water I realize I should have also removed my shoes. They weigh me down, and kicking becomes difficult. But I fight through it anyway. I have to.

"Sheila!" I keep screaming, diving under the water again and again. But I don't know where she is, or where she went in, or how deep she could be now. It's been a while since I've seen Meyer emerge but Grant is a short distance away and his arms are empty. So empty. And that emptiness terrifies me.

The water is quickly filling with buoyant teenagers, all of us searching for a girl who may or may not still be drunk. Or conscious. My head is pounding. Each splash crashing against my body feels like it's dragging me down. With every second that passes I imagine she's slipping deeper and deeper, down into the water, where none of us will ever reach her.

"Sheila, please," I cry.

Grant is freaking out, his voice high and shaky, as he continues his search. The more he freaks out the less hope I have.

It's happening. This can't be happening.

"Call 911!" someone yells but I know it's too late. It's been too long. I imagine her drowning in the dark water. My arms stop moving, my legs stop kicking — I'm sinking. And I don't care.

I'm not sure I can survive this. The words bounce around inside my mind and I know they're selfish words, desperate words, but that's what I am: selfish and desperate.

"She can't die," I whisper against the water. "She can't die," I say again, except this time I swallow them down with lake water as my mouth dips below the surface.

No. Not Sheila.

I close my eyes. *Please,* I beg. *Please. Not again.*

"I've got her!" Meyer yells. His head is bobbing about ten feet away from mine and in his arms is a very limp Sheila.

I can't tell if she's alive or dead, all I know is I have to get to her. I swim toward them slicing through the water with a strength I didn't have mere seconds ago, and then watch helplessly as someone pulls Sheila up and out of water. My breath fogs the dark night and then blows back toward me each time the wind moves along the water.

"She's breathing," Meyer says, climbing up next to them, and my body starts to shake. I don't feel cold, I don't feel anything, but I can't stop shivering.

I hear sirens in the distance and then the trees are lit with flashing lights. I keep swimming. I'm afraid to get out of the water, afraid of what I'll find.

"Livy? Where's Livy?" Meyer calls out and I should answer, but I don't.

"She was right next to me," Grant tells him but he doesn't look up from Sheila's prone figure on the ground.

"Livy!" Meyer is on his feet, his eyes scanning the darkness and then they come to rest on me. For a moment neither of us moves and then I'm pulling myself up onto the shore and he's right there helping me.

"She's okay, Livy. She's going to be okay," he says. But I won't look at him.

"Livy?" he says, rubbing his hands up and down my trembling arms. "Did you hear me?"

"You need to go," I tell him, and his hands stop. "You need to get away from me. And leave me alone." When he doesn't move I say, "Now, Meyer."

"Didn't you hear me? Sheila is going to be fine."

"You don't know that. You don't know anything." I start pushing at him, desperate to get some distance between the boy who thinks everything is a game, and me, the girl who is anchored by death.

"Livy—"

"I'm serious, Meyer. I need you to leave me alone. I need you to listen to me and go."

I push at him once more and this time he lets me. His hands drop from my arms and fall to his sides and for a moment he looks lost. But can you be lost when you never truly let yourself be a part of anything at all? He doesn't know Sheila. He barely knows me. How can you feel detached and empty inside when you've never opened yourself up to anyone?

In Meyer's world we're the lost ones, not him. Never him. Not until now.

"Just go," I tell him, and when he doesn't move I yell it. "GO!"

Sheila is perfectly still on the ground. I should get to her. I should push against her chest until she spits out water like the drowning victims always do in the movies. But I can't get my feet to move. I'm stuck. Frozen to the ground about ten feet away from her. I watch the EMT do what I should be doing. His hands press against her chest and then he breathes into her mouth. I watch him do it over and over again. Each time he takes a breath, I take one with him.

I don't want to watch her die.

"Please, Sheila," I beg. "Please."

"Livy." Meyer's hands reach for me, but they don't touch. "I don't understand."

"No," I tell him. "How could you? You're too caught up in your *adventures* to ever take anything serious. And this is serious, Meyer." I point to Sheila. "That's serious," I whisper. "*You* did that."

Sheila starts to cough and it's the most beautiful sound I've ever heard. I stare at her, wondering if I've imagined it, but when Grant wraps his arms around her I know she's alive.

"I told you she'd be okay," Meyer says, but he doesn't sound concerned, only defensive.

"You did this," I tell him. "You nearly took her away from me tonight and because of that I can't play your games anymore. I can't be with you." I don't care how I feel about him. I can't care. He nearly took away my best friend. This is better anyhow. Now I don't have to prepare myself for the day he leaves me.

Meyer reaches out again, but I pull away. I can't bear his touch.

"Grow up," I whisper, and it's as if I've slapped him. His eyes widen and he stumbles back a few steps.

I don't stick around to see what comes next. I just walk away. I won't look at him and I don't look back. I leave him to do what he will. Without me.

CHAPTER SEVENTEEN

I don't think about Meyer the entire way to the hospital, nor do I think about him while I'm walking the halls, waiting for Sheila's mom to come and tell me that everything is fine, that Sheila is going to be fine. The moment she hit the water I stopped caring about fun and adventure. And Meyer. Because there is nothing more serious than death, nothing quite like the possibility of losing something you need to survive. And Sheila is that something for me. I go days without seeing my father. I go for days without really talking to my mother. But I need Sheila to survive. I may not have realized this before, but I need her.

The waiting room chairs are not comfortable. Even if they were plush and reclined all the way back so that I could pretend to be sleeping instead of watching the hallway for the possibility of news, I still wouldn't be able to sit still. Pacing is how I spend the minutes. If I stop pacing I'll just see Sheila fall from the rock over and over again. I'll keep thinking about how she could be dying at this very moment just two doors down the hall.

Grant, however, doesn't seem to mind the hospital chairs. As soon as he arrived he fell into the first chair he could find, the one facing away from the large TV, and he continues to hold his head in his hands as if the weight of it — of everything — is too much for him to bear.

It's so quiet in here. Even with the TV turned up. The things we're not saying to each other, the morbid thoughts that assault our minds, are so loud they make everything else in the room feel hushed. The rest of the world is on mute while I wait for news. I can't talk to anyone — not even my mother — until I know whether or not I still have a best friend.

About an hour later Sheila's mom drags herself into the waiting room. She's wearing dark pajamas — the ones she was wearing when she got the phone call earlier tonight — and she looks like she's aged ten years since the last time I saw her, which was just a couple of weeks ago.

"She's going to be fine," she tells us before bursting into tears.

I want to comfort her, wrap my arms around her and celebrate the news, but it's difficult to believe someone who can't stop crying. I know what denial looks like. The average mature adult will behave more like a toddler when the news is bad, their tantrums loud and ugly. And it's heartbreaking, this transformation. To watch someone you care about grab a passing nurse and begin screaming in her face, begging her to fix his child.

It's far worse when the adult is your very own father.

"Livy?" Sheila's mother reaches out to me, a smile breaking across her tear-streaked face.

I know she wants me to come to her, share in the joy that is this miracle, but I can't just yet. I stand back and wait for her hands to start beating against Grant's back. I wait for the screaming to begin. But instead she's comforting her daughter's boyfriend. She's holding him tight and telling him everything's going to be okay, and I've been waiting so long for those words, I don't believe them now that they've arrived.

163

"Is she—" I choke out.

"She's okay, Livy. The doctor says she has quite the concussion but she's going to be just fine."

Grant makes a noise that is a cross between a sob and a laugh. "Can I see her?"

"Yes," she says, and then he's off, his wet shoes squeaking loudly down the hallway. I'm glad for that noise. It's a good noise, a noise that means that Sheila's mom is right. Everything is going to be okay, because no one hurries to see a dead body.

"The doctor doesn't want a lot of visitors," Sheila's mom tells me. "Would you mind waiting for Grant to come out before you go in?"

"Of course," I say, but I'm lying. I've never resented Grant in all the time he's been a part of Sheila's life. Until now. I'd give anything to switch places with him.

"Thank you, Livy," she says, wiping away tears. "You're such a good friend."

I look away because I have no answer to that. Especially when this is all my fault. I'm the one who invited Meyer.

About twenty minutes later Grant finally emerges. It's my turn to visit Sheila. The walk to her room takes longer than it should. My feet weigh about a thousand pounds. I take a seat in the chair that has been moved next to her bed and I stare at my sleeping friend. She looks younger, and so fragile. I've never seen Sheila look fragile before tonight, and it scares me. Even back at the party when she was drunk and confessing her true feelings about me she looked brave. She didn't care how it would affect me, she just wanted me to know she cared.

"I'm sorry," I whisper. "I'm sorry I'm such a horrible friend." The emotion I've been holding back for the last few hours threatens to spill down my cheeks, but I fight it off. I won't cry over her like she's dying. Because she's not.

"Your mother called," Sheila's mom says from the doorway. "I told her what happened."

"Thank you," I say without turning around. Sheila's mom doesn't ask why I wasn't the one to tell her in the first place. But I can tell from her expression, she does wonder. She remembers how close we used to be, even if it seems as though my mother has forgotten.

"I said you might be staying the night, which you're welcome to."

"That would be nice."

"Have you eaten?"

"No. Not for a while."

"The cafeteria is closed but there's a vending machine down the hall."

When I stand up she walks into the room, hovering over Sheila's bed.

"Do you want something?" I ask, and she shakes her head no. She continues to stare down at Sheila like she's never seen her before, probably noticing, like I am, how her eyelashes are dark against her pale skin and how the bandage wrapped around her forehead hides most of her beautiful blonde hair.

"She'll still be here tomorrow?" I whisper, still not quite believing it.

"Yes. They want to keep her a day or two for observation," she answers. But that wasn't what I was asking.

"She's lucky," I choke out.

"That's what the doctors say."

"Lucky and brave," I say.

Sheila's mom smiles. "That's funny," she tells me. "That's what she always says about you."

I have exactly three dollars on me, not much in the way of a vending machine meal, but it's something. After staring at my options for about five minutes through rather blurry eyes I decide on a bag of chocolate chip cookies and a Vitamin Water. I'm just taking a sip when someone emerges from the staircase down the hall. I wouldn't normally notice the comings and goings of the hospital staff but this person isn't staff, nor is he unfamiliar. He doesn't look at me, even though we are the only two people in the hallway. Instead he moves quickly in the opposite direction. But I don't need to see his face to know who he is.

"James," I call out.

"James," I say a bit louder. Still no response.

I cap my drink and decide to follow him, eating my cookies as I go. If he's looking for me he's certainly not doing a very good job. Visiting hours are long over so it doesn't make any sense for him to be wandering the halls, unless he has family here. Or a close friend. Yes, that would make sense. But what doesn't make sense is this tightness building inside my chest. I feel anxious as I follow him down the hall. The faster he moves the worse I feel. My heart is racing, but I'm not sure why. It might have something to do with the fact that I sense he knows I'm following him, and if that is true, where is he leading me?

"James!" I call out one last time, just before he moves through the double doors of the children's wing. I know he's heard me. There's no way he couldn't have. And yet he still doesn't turn around.

My hands are cold as they hold onto my Vitamin Water, the rest of my cookies forgotten at the bottom of the bag. My breathing is quick, uneven and unusually loud in my head as I hurry down the quiet hallway. I tell myself it's the residual shock from witnessing Sheila's fall earlier this evening. It's normal to feel nervous after you experience shock. I know this. Same goes with fear. But this desperate feeling in the pit of my stomach is something altogether different. It sickens me, nearly bringing up what I've just eaten.

The hallways are dark and quiet in the children's wing. The only sounds come from the nurse's station where three nurses are sitting at a long desk, talking in hushed tones. I slip past them with my head down and they don't stop me. This isn't the first time I've shown up in the middle of the night. But I am curious to know how James managed to slip by.

I lose him somewhere between the staircase and the nurse's station, and I panic, wondering if I'm too late and then wonder, *Too late for what?*

I quicken my pace to a run, not caring how loud I sound as I come to the end of the hallway — a hallway that seems to go on forever.

Just before I turn the corner my feet slide out from underneath me and I hit the ground. My Vitamin Water does too. It rolls down the hall and comes to a stop mere feet from James who is now standing directly outside of Sammy's room.

"James," I choke out, clamoring to my feet. But he doesn't even acknowledge me. His light-colored eyes stare into Sammy's room, and then slowly, he enters his room.

No! my mind screams as I hurry down the hallway. I'm still not sure why I'm so afraid. But whatever is happening can't be right. It definitely doesn't feel right. I peek into the room and find him sitting on the edge of Sammy's bed. His back is straight and his hands are in his lap. He is watching Sammy sleep. He's dressed all in black, from his pants to his raincoat, and he stands out in a room bathed in white.

"What are you doing here?" I whisper. "Why are you in Sammy's room?"

But it isn't James who answers.

"Livy?" Sammy calls out. His big dark eyes blink up at me, barely awake. He looks so small in his bed. It makes me want to crawl in beside him so that I can keep the bed from swallowing him up.

I fight the urge to run to his side. Even if James is menacing enough to smell fear, I don't want him to see it on me. I enter the room, slowly at first. My shoes squeak upon the floor.

"Visiting hours are over, Livy," James tells me without turning around. "You shouldn't be here." He reaches his hand out, brushing Sammy's hair back off his forehead and the gesture is so familiar, so comfortable, it's clear he's done it many times before. Sammy nuzzles back into his blankets, his face turned toward the wall. Is he sleeping? How can he be sleeping when I feel like I'm in the middle of a nightmare?

"Did you follow me here?"

"I don't have to follow you to know what you're up to." He tucks the blankets in close to Sammy and Sammy lets out a sigh.

"Goodnight, Livy," Sammy whispers. And then his breathing evens out as he slips back into sleep.

"What are you—"

"Shh," James says. His finger is pressed to his lips as he rises from the bed. His light eyes pin me to my spot on the floor. "Let him sleep." And then he brushes past me.

I pause long enough to drop a soft kiss on Sammy's forehead before I hurry after James.

"Wait," I call out once we're in the hallway. "I don't understand. How do you know him?"

James turns, giving me all but one second before he continues on his way toward the elevators.

"Go home, Livy," he tells me as he pushes the elevator button. "You spend too much time away from your family. And way too much time here."

We stare at each other until the elevator doors close between us. No *goodbye*, no *have a good night*. Just nothing.

I check on Sammy one more time before I make my way to Jilly's room. My eyes are so heavy, my body limp, for all I know this is just a bad dream. I curl up beside Jilly, breathing in the smell of her favorite strawberry scented shampoo, and she turns to me in her sleep. Her eyes open only long enough to see that it is me, and then her little hand reaches for my face.

"Love you, Livy," she says, leaning her forehead close to mine. Her fingertips barely brush against my cheek. She doesn't know what those words do to me. She doesn't see it in my tired expression.

"I love you too," I whisper, right as my eyes shut.

CHAPTER EIGHTEEN

The call comes the following Friday.

I'm home alone when Dr. Lerner's office reaches me. Everything changes the moment they say those three little words: "You're a match."

"How soon?" my mom asks when I call to tell her.

"They think they can make it happen next week," I answer.

My mother's response is silence.

"I'll tell your father," she says finally, her voice hushed as though she's afraid he could be listening nearby.

"Okay." She won't get any arguments from me. I'd pretty much agree to anything right about now.

"This is it, right Olivia?" she says before she ends the call. "After this… we're done, right? No more tests?"

I don't know why I hesitate.

"Olivia?"

"Yes, mom. Just Jilly."

But that night when I visit the hospital I'm not sure I can keep that promise. There are so many kids who need something. And I'm more than willing to give what I can, even if it means I read to them for the rest of my life. I have to do it. Do something. Jenna would want me to.

I don't usually read to the kids on Fridays but the girl who does called in sick and I was here visiting Jilly anyway, so why not? It's not like I have anything else going on. Sheila is hanging out with Grant tonight. When I told her my plans for the evening she rolled her eyes and said, "Typical." But she was easily appeased once I agreed to hang out with them tomorrow. She knows I'm trying, and that's something at least.

Jilly's actually out of bed and in the activity center playing with the collection of dolls Jenna left her. Every few minutes or so she checks on me as if she's afraid it's all a dream and she's going to wake up to find she's still waiting for the chance of a miracle. Her grandma has yet to stop crying.

I'm sitting in the middle of the floor with Sammy and Brown the Bear on my lap. Tonight's story is *Robin Hood*. When it's time to turn the page Sammy places Brown's paw against the book so it appears that the bear is the one turning the pages. The children laugh every time. Sammy's mother is the only one not smiling. She's watching Sammy with a look I recognize. I've seen it before. She is already mourning the loss of him. She's watching each smile, each laugh, memorizing each movement. Like she's preparing to give up.

Sammy's face is a bit thinner than the last time I saw him and it's harder for him to grip the pages — like he can't convince his hand to do what he wants. But he's still laughing. When he glances up at me his smile grows and I squeeze him a little tighter. He feels smaller in my arms, more fragile than normal. He still sounds like Sammy, his giggle more hiccup than laugh. And his eyes still shine. That has to be a good sign.

Once the story ends Sammy closes the book with a *snap* and struggles to his feet. I watch him make his way over to his mother, who kisses his head and holds him close, while Brown the Bear dangles, half in and half out of their embrace.

I hate this place sometimes. I hate that there is even a need for a children's hospital. There should be a rule universally accepted when it comes to kids, like an age restriction. Nothing and no one should harm a child during the time they are too young to fend for themselves. I get that life isn't fair. But it's far worse when you don't understand what is happening to you. When you're too young to even make sense of it. The death of a child goes beyond unfair. It feels like a punishment.

Over near the doorway a shadow emerges. It catches my eye, drawing my attention away from Sammy and his mother. I don't know how long Meyer has been standing there, but it seems as though he's waiting for me.

"Hey Livy," he whispers once I'm in front of him. "I was hoping you'd be here tonight. I've been looking for you."

It's been seven days since Sheila's accident — seven days since I last saw Meyer — and yet it feels like years. He's wearing a black sweater today and dark jeans that match my own. His hair is slightly mussed, enough that I want to smooth it down around his ears, but we're no longer on a touch-each-other basis. Not after that night.

Standing under the bright lights of the hospital's activity center I realize I've never seen him so well lit before. Because of this I catch myself studying his face, how his nose is sun-kissed like mine except his freckles are darker, like three beauty marks purposefully placed around the bridge of his nose. And then there's his impossibly long eyelashes. They make his eyes appear innocent when he wants, but dangerous as well. I turn away when he starts to smile, hating myself for wanting to look at him. How silly of me to think I'd be able to move on.

There is activity all around us as the nurses and parents hurry the kids off to bed. Their voices move down the hall, and then the hallways fall silent. I don't want to look at him again, and yet I'm not leaving. I'm waiting for something, and perhaps so is he. I finally give in and meet his eyes.

"I choose pain," he says, once he has my attention. His words strike like lightning.

Honestly I never imagined he'd give me this kind of opening. It feels like a gift or at the very least a step in the right direction.

"You mean... I get to ask you a question?" I ask in disbelief.

"And I must answer with honesty," he says, completely resolute.

So many questions spring to mind. I can't seem to hold onto just one. There's so much I want to know — like how he knew my mom was looking for me or how he always seems to know where I'll be before I do. There are so many details I'd pay to know about his life, but the question that seems to plague me the most is how he saved us that night on the Ferris wheel.

I clamp my lips together. If I ask my question I'm allowing the game to continue, and I don't want it to, right? This is over. *We're over.*

But if I don't ask now I'll always wonder.

"What happened that night? On the Ferris wheel? You told me you'd tell me one day. I want to know now."

"You mean, how did I save you?" His smile is wicked, his eyes bright. I've willingly walked into his trap, and we both know it. "If you really want your answer you have to come with me, Livy." He shifts closer and I catch a faint scent of burning leaves and autumn wind. Man, I love the fall. It's completely unfair that Meyer smells like my favorite season. When I hesitate he adds, "I promise you'll be safe."

"You can't make that promise, Meyer. Not to me."

Meyer's smile slips from his face, replaced by frustration.

"I'm not going anywhere with you tonight," I tell him. "Not until I have my answer."

"If truth is what you want from me, you have to take the risk." His eyes are lit with a challenge. He holds out his hand for me to grasp.

I cross my arms and wait. He won't bully me into it this time.

"Alright," he says, smiling as though I've pleased him somehow. "What are you asking me, exactly?"

"You know," I say, lowering my voice. I look past him down the hall. We're alone for now, but there are always people near. I peek down the hall again and then lean close. "I want to know if —"

"If I can fly?" His voice isn't nearly as soft as mine, which causes me to gasp out loud.

"Shush! Are you crazy?" I grab him by the arm and drag him back into the activity center. "What if someone hears you?"

Meyer shrugs as though this is no big deal. "Whether they hear me or not is none of my concern. Do you want your answer or are you too afraid to ask?"

"Of course I want my answer! I just don't want anyone to hear us. They'll think we're crazy. That *I'm* crazy."

"What if you are, Livy?" he says, staring at me with wide eyes. "What if you're just imagining all of this? What if you've imagined me?" He makes a face and then bursts out laughing. To him this is all a joke. Everything is, apparently.

"I've actually considered it," I tell him, completely serious.

"Well you're not," he says, moving so close his face is next to mine. "So go ahead, ask away."

I close my eyes for a second in an attempt to calm down. To return to the game.

We are completely alone in the activity center. With most of the lights off no one would think to come in. And yet when I ask him my question I lower my voice.

"Can you really fly, Meyer? And if so, how?"

"I don't know how." He answers as though we're talking about something trivial like walking or chewing gum. "I've always been able to fly." He shrugs his shoulders and shoves his hands into the front pockets of his jeans. "It's just something I've always been able to do."

I stare at him unbelieving. It isn't possible, right? No one can fly, and yet we did survive that night. Somehow he got us safely to the ground. And haven't I been carrying around the possibility? Thinking it's the only thing that makes sense?

"It's not possible," I whisper. I shake my head, completely in denial, while Meyer watches from behind hooded eyes.

"So you have your answer," he says, crossing his arms. He leans forward, his face so close I draw myself back. "It's your turn now."

"What? What do you want?" I know I've asked the wrong question when his smile turns up a bit more and he lets out a faint laugh.

He doesn't answer me right away, just continues to study me until I can't take it any longer. I squirm under those heavy green eyes —he has to realize what he does to me, right? Meyer's mouth turns up with amusement as though I've asked the question out loud. Yes, of course he does. But let's hope for my sake, it isn't part of the game.

Out in the hall I hear the nurses talking and the occasional ding when the elevator doors open or close. I should check in on Jilly and Sammy, grab my coat and go home. And yet here I stand. The two of us so close we're nearly touching in a large and empty room.

"Come with me," he whispers, his words like magic dusting the air.

"Where?" I answer, not quite sure why I feel the need to whisper back.

"Does it matter?"

I hate him for this question. I hate that he knows the answer, and has asked it anyway.

With his hand in mine I instantly feel a heat move through my body. His touch isn't as satisfying as a kiss, but it's something. More than what I had a mere moment ago.

Meyer tugs on my hand, leading me toward the hallway. For a moment I follow, walking slowly behind him. Then it hits me. I can't do this anymore. I have to think of Jilly. I could save her life. She is not a risk I can take.

"No," I say, pulling my hand from his.

Meyer turns back, his expression confused.

"I can't do it," I tell him. "Not now. Things are different. I can't go with you any longer."

"What do you mean?" He moves toward me, clearly anxious to change my mind.

"No." I walk backward toward the exit, holding out my hands to ward him off. "No, Meyer. I'm sorry. The game ends here." I turn toward the staircase, looking to make a quick escape, but his words stop me cold.

"I'm leaving, Livy. After tonight you won't see me for awhile."

"What?" I turn back hesitantly, worried this is some kind of trick.

"I came to tell you goodbye."

"Goodbye?" My hands are instantly shaking.

Meyer moves toward me until we're once again facing each other. "This is it, Livy. Our last adventure." He leans his forehead down, resting it against mine. "Won't you take it with me?"

"Where are you going?" I ask panicked. "When will you be back?" But the Q&A portion of the evening is over.

"You must decide," he tells me. *You must trust me.* The words are so clear in my thoughts I swear he said them out loud.

Meyer knows my decision the moment I make it. His smile is triumphant. I take his hand because I have to. My need to be with him is stronger than my need to protect myself. His grip tightens on my hand as though we are sealed, and I like the way it feels. He holds my hand like it's his hand now.

We travel down hallways and stairs, and through doorways. Once we hit the street we're running, leaving the hospital and everything I know behind. I feel free again, just like the first night I met him.

"Are you going to tell me where we're going?" I call out.

"You'll see."

We're sliding and stomping through puddles as we make our way across town. After a few more blocks we stop and I catch my breath while he ponders an old historical building directly in front of us. It is taller than the other buildings around. It nearly towers over the old church right next door. I don't remember what it's called and neither must anyone else because the sign went missing ages ago, and has yet to be replaced.

"We're not going in there, are we?" I ask, still rather breathless from our run.

"Not in. Up." Meyer points to the top of the building and says, "To the roof." His eyes are sparkling — truth is, I'm pretty sure they always are — and that mischievous smile he always seems to carry around with him flashes at me under the streetlight.

I follow him around the back where a rusted wrought iron fire escape is still anchored to the side of the building. He climbs on but then thinks twice about it and jumps down, gesturing for me to go first.

"This way I can catch you if you fall," he explains and just like that I'm worried I will.

I stare at the fire escape and the countless rungs that lead to the sky. "Are your friends up there?" I haven't moved any closer to the ladder. My feet are planted in the muddy grass.

"It's just you and me tonight, Livy," he says and I hate that his words make my heart beat faster. I hate that I like that we're alone. I am a traitor to my own self.

I wrap my arms around myself, fending off the cold. There's this funny feeling in the pit of my stomach. It tells me what I'm about to do is bigger than Meyer's other adventures. There is more at stake tonight. And yet I agree to it anyway. I move toward the ladder and begin my climb up to the roof. The iron is rough against my hands but I grip it like it's the only thing keeping me alive.

"All the way up," Meyer says from just below me.

I nod to let him know I heard him. If I lose my focus, I'll think about how high I'm climbing and that would end this adventure prematurely.

Why am I allowing myself to get caught up in his games again? And why do his games always test my comfort with heights? Why can't we play, you know, on the ground? There has to be something we can do without using gravity as our catalyst.

I'm so wrapped up in my thoughts I don't notice how far I've climbed until the rungs run out and I'm pulling myself up onto the roof.

"What do you think? Isn't it beautiful?" Meyer is just behind me. He vaults to his feet like a professional swimmer emerging from a swimming pool.

I take a moment to look around and get my bearings. He's right. It is beautiful. I feel like I'm back in my bedroom, staring out at the world, except this time I'm not trapped behind glass wondering what it feels like to be a part of the night. I have to admit this feels better.

"See that building?" Meyer points toward downtown Seattle where a large apartment building stands higher than any neighboring structures.

"Yes."

"That's our next destination." He brushes past me, moving toward the edge of the roof and then right before I think he's going over the side, he stops. "Are you with me, Livy?"

"What does that mean exactly?"

"Have you ever been roof jumping?" Meyer is gazing out over the city. "I think you'll love it. It's exhilarating."

"You mean like *jumping* jumping? Like…" I use my fingers to illustrate a person running and then jumping to the next building.

Meyer slowly shakes his head. His lashes are lowered, his gaze intense.

"So then…" I look out at all the roofs in the distance, zeroing in on the one he pointed to earlier. It is so far away, much further than one could reach with a jump. "So then we're going to run and…?" I point at him and then scrutinize the skyline. "We're not jumping, are we?"

"Yes, Livy." Meyer strolls over to me, moving so slowly he must be afraid I might startle and run away. "Remember when you asked if I could fly?"

I nod my head slowly.

He stops once he's in front of me. It's so cold outside each word he says comes with a puff of air. "I thought I might show you how it's done."

"Show me what?" I whisper.

Before I can stutter out my thought he tugs on my hand, pulling me flush up against his body. "Don't let go of me." His arms wrap around me, and the nervousness I'm feeling doubles the moment he says, "Whatever you do, don't let go."

"Wait! Stop!" I cry out and he freezes. "I can't do this. I can't fly with you. It's crazy!" My breath is coming fast now, tiny gulps of air that — this time — have nothing to do with how close we're standing.

"You already have, Livy. How else do you think I got us down from that ride?"

"No! I don't know!" I push at him, needing some distance and he gives it to me, albeit reluctantly. "It's not possible."

"What are you afraid of? Do you think I'll drop you?"

"Well there's that." I start to panic just thinking about it.

"'Cause I won't." He moves a bit closer and I almost step back, preferring my distance from him, but then decide against it. "You can trust me, you know," he continues. "I won't let you fall."

I shake my head, holding my hands up. "This is too much," I tell him. "People don't fly."

"Some people do." His eyes narrow upon my face. He appears offended.

I continue to shake my head. It helps to keep saying no. It makes me feel more in control, almost as though I'm willing the world back to normal.

"How about this." Meyer holds his hands out, showing me he means me no harm. "How about if I fly around for a bit so you can see how it's done, and then we'll try it together?"

"But I can't fly." Not sure why I have to spell that one out.

"You can!" His smile is so innocent, like a child's. "I'll show you!"

"Alright." I brush him off, gesturing with my hand. "Go on. Go fly about. Maybe that will make me feel better." Yeah, right. But I can't concentrate with him just standing there, staring at me.

He gives me one last flash of a grin and then he leaps up into the air. And sure enough, he is flying. Meyer is flying. His body is moving through the air like a bird just without the flapping of wings. His arms are at his side while he moves in a forward motion around the sky. It doesn't seem possible. Of course it's not possible. But there it is.

"Holy... Wow."

"See, Livy!" He calls down to me. "It's not scary at all! You should try it!"

"No, definitely not," I mutter to myself. "That is definitely not going to happen." But I can't stop watching him. He's so graceful, and confident in the air. His movements are smooth like he's gliding on ice. He does a little flip, showing off, and his laughter carries back down to me.

"Amazing," I whisper, no longer focused on my fear, but instead caught up in what I'm seeing.

"I don't understand how you do it," I tell him once he's back on the roof. His descent was so smooth and easy, it makes me wonder why airplane landings are always so abrupt. "It just doesn't make sense. People aren't supposed to be able to fly. It's not possible."

"Well, I'm not sure why you still believe that after watching me." He points to the sky, his eyebrows lifted in challenge. "Should I have a go again? Will that convince you?"

"No." There's actually only one thing that will convince me, I just have to get up the courage to say it.

"Well, Livy?" he says, reading my mind. "You ready to try?"

"I'm getting there." I cover my face with my hands and let out a nearly silent, little scream. "What are you thinking, Livy?" I ask myself. "How are you even considering this?"

"I won't drop you," Meyer says and without opening my eyes I can tell he's moved closer.

"Drop me? Please, let's not talk about that."

"Fair enough," he says and then he's pulling my hands away from my face. "Come on. Trust me." His eyes are pleading with me. He wants this so much I feel as though he's the one with the greater risk.

"You're going to wrap your arms around me like this." He takes my arms and places them around his neck. "And I'm going to hold you like this." He wraps his arms around my waist, pulling me close, and I close my eyes, pretending we're dancing. Yes. That's what we're doing. We're dancing. Not leaping to our death. Not thwarting gravity. I take another breath — desperate to relax — but he smells so good, and he's so damn close, I can't concentrate.

"All you have to do is say, *down*, Livy. That will be our safe word, alright?"

"Down," I repeat, trying it out on my lips. "Down." I nod my head, liking this idea. "Alright."

"But give it a chance," he begs. "Promise me you'll give it a moment before you freak out."

"I'm not going to freak out," I tell him. "I'm *already* freaking out. But I will promise to stay up longer than a second. How about that?"

Meyer laughs and it's a nice sound, rich and deep. I feel it lightly flutter my hair. "That's all I can hope for," he tells me softly. "At least for now."

I look up and his eyes meet mine.

"Why me?" I whisper suddenly.

"What do you mean?" His mouth is so close, his expression heavy like the feeling in my stomach.

I blink up at him. "This isn't part of the game, is it? This secret of yours, I can't imagine you go around telling everyone. So why me?"

His eyes narrow and I worry he's not going to answer. Without thinking about the consequences I lift my hand up and touch his face. Instantly he freezes. His arms are tight around my waist, his eyes on mine.

"This is too big a secret." My voice stays soft. "You can pretend this is just a part of the game, but I know better."

Meyer remains still as though he's barely breathing. His expression so dark he appears dangerous. "Is it that important to you, my answer?"

"Yes," I whisper.

A flicker of doubt crosses his face and then it's gone, hidden where I can't find it.

"I want—" He stops and then starts again. "It's just that …" He looks away, a heavy scowl marring his normally smooth complexion. I've never seen him so at war with himself. It's rather off-putting. And a little bit exciting. It's pretty clear that whatever he's feeling, he doesn't want me to know.

"You're right," he says, still scowling off at the night. "I've never done this before. I've never taken someone flying here."

"Here?" I whisper, not wanting to interrupt, but needing clarification.

"Just you." His scowl softens when he looks at me.

I can't stop the grin from erupting across my face. Apparently it's contagious because Meyer smiles back. It's a simple smile, not crooked or mischievous like his usual ones. This one is… sweet. Heartfelt. I like this one best.

I stop myself from asking anything more, even though I would love to dig around inside his feelings until I feel reassured and comfortable. But seeing how I actually got him close to answering one question, I really shouldn't press my luck.

"Thank you?" I say, and Meyer laughs.

He pulls me in close again and it's everything I can do to keep from sighing. With his hands around my waist I feel safe. Well, perhaps not safe, but protected. Less alone.

"I'm going to count to three and then you're going to feel us rise above the ground."

"Right now?" I jerk away, or at least I try to. Meyer's grip is steadfast.

"Right now."

My heart slams against my chest. I worry I might pass out.

"And then what?" I ask, squeezing my eyes shut.

"And then we'll be flying."

"But what if I start to slip or you can't hold onto me?"

"That's not going to happen, Livy." He sounds so calm, I wish I could borrow some of that composure.

"How do you know? I'm not the lightest thing you could carry while flying. What if I'm too heavy? What if you can't hold onto me?"

"Well, here's the thing," he tells me as my feet rise up off the ground.

"What? What is it?" My toes are dangling, not touching anything at all. I point my toes back toward the ground, stretching them as far as I can. But it's not enough. I'm still above the ground.

"I don't actually need to hold onto you like this."

My head snaps up and I stare at him. "You don't? What do you mean?" I'm not really following what he's telling me. I'm just waiting for the moment when he propels us into the sky and gravity takes us over.

"I can make you fly with just the touch of my hand." His warm breath brushes against my ear when he whispers, "I just thought it might be more fun if you held onto me."

With that we ascend into the air. I watch the roof that was, a mere moment ago, beneath my feet get further and further away.

"Holy crap!" I scream and squeeze my eyes shut. The air rushes around us, coming from every direction.

"Livy! Open your eyes!"

I take a breath and then I do it. I open my eyes. Meyer is still holding me around the waist while I cling to him, deathly afraid to let go. Our faces are so close we could be two lovers caught in an embrace, except that one of us is holding on out of sheer fright.

"How does it feel?" he asks me. "How does it feel to fly?"

I look down and see the roof about ten feet below me. "This is flying? Because it doesn't feel like flying. It feels like hovering. Why are we hovering?"

"I wanted to make sure you weren't going to panic on me." He studies me for a minute, his gaze more intense than normal. Then he smiles. "Do you want more?"

This question is so weighted. Yet the answer is suddenly clear. Do I want to believe he can fly, that such a thing is even possible? Do I want to accept that there could be something more than the simple life I lead? Do I want to rise above it all — with Meyer — and feel like this... forever?

"Yes."

His arms tighten around me and then we're moving again, flying through the air. I feel a scream bubble up inside my throat as I press closer to him, my face buried against his chest, and then with a light thud we're back down.

I hear the crunch of an old tar roof under my feet just before I open my eyes. In the matter of a few minutes we've traveled three blocks closer to downtown Seattle. I can hear the traffic near Pike Place Market. And we're still so high I can see it.

He drops his arms from around me, slowly taking a step back. "Well? That wasn't so bad, was it?"

I touch my hands to my heart, feeling it beat rapidly inside my chest. There's a look about Meyer right now. He seems unsure, hesitant.

"Well, Livy? What did you think?"

What did I think? Hmm. Good question. What *did* I think?

"Let's try it again," I say, and that trace of hesitance in his expression falls away.

"Really?" he says. "Are you serious?"

"I think so?" I start to laugh, and then realize I mean it. I do want to try again. "So, I really don't have to hold onto you?"

"No, you really don't." He looks a bit bashful all of a sudden and I like this look on him. It's not like his other looks. It makes him appear vulnerable.

"So then. why did you…? Why did we…?" I feel my cheeks grow warm. I can't bring myself to ask this question, but he gets it anyway.

"I've never tried that before," he says with a boyish grin. "It was nice though, right?"

I fight back a smile of my own, but it's too difficult. "It *was* nice." I glance away, not wanting him to read more into this than he should, but who am I kidding, with my pink cheeks and my downcast eyes, it's pretty damn obvious how I really feel. "I think… I think I'd still prefer it, if that's okay with you."

"Prefer what?"

I glare up at him, hating that he's playing dumb, but my glare has no effect on his playful grin. If anything it widens it.

"I'd feel safer if we, you know."

"If we what, Livy?"

Damn him. Damn his beautiful smile, and all of him, actually.

"If we…" I sigh loudly and throw my hands into the air. "I'd prefer if we, that is, if it's okay with you…" I tug him toward me, and his lashes lower, darkening his eyes. "Held onto each other again. Like we did before?"

"It's okay with me."

I nod my head, staring down at his chest, waiting for the moment when he takes hold of me and we leave the ground. But it doesn't come. We stand like this a moment longer, neither of us speaking, until, finally, I raise my eyes to his.

"Are you ready for this, Livy?" The laughter I expected to find isn't there. Instead he looks quite serious.

"Yes," I whisper, feeling sure that it's the truth.

"It's in your hands, you know. All of this."

"You mean—"

"How far. How high. You call the shots." When I remain silent he says, "I just thought you should know."

He reaches for me, wrapping his arms around my waist, and I settle against his chest.

"Ready?" he asks me.

"Yes."

Meyer wastes no time. We lift off the ground with a subtle jump. You'd think to get two people in the air it would take more work than this, but Meyer makes it look so easy. We're only in the air a moment when we touch down again.

"Let's try something different." He lets go of me, only keeping hold of my hand. My eyes spring open. "We're going to run and jump," he says.

"What?"

He's already poised and ready.

"Are you sure about this?" I say a bit panicky.

Meyer stops and leans close. His hand reaches up and touches the side of my face. And just like that I stop freaking out. His touch soothes me. "I want you to trust me. Do you trust me, Livy?"

"No. Definitely not." I shake my head, and try to pull away, but he won't let go.

"I think you do," he whispers in my ear, and just like that I have goosebumps.

"On three. Ready?"

"Wait! Just give me a second…"

"One."

"Meyer! I don't think I can do this! Maybe if you just hold onto me again."

"Two."

"But I don't know how to fly! I can't—"

"Three!"

Suddenly we're running. He's gripping my hand so tight I have no choice but to run alongside of him.

"This. Is. Crazy!" I scream.

"Jump!" he yells.

And I jump.

My feet lift off the ground and I know I'm coming down right in the space between the two buildings. Right where the grass is muddy and wet, fifty feet or so beneath me. But I'm wrong. Instead I launch into the air with Meyer at my side and when my feet hit solid ground it isn't with a tumble and a mess of broken bones, but rather lightly atop another roof just over from where we started.

"See!" Meyer shouts. "I told you it was easy!" His smile lights up the sky and I'm so happy to be alive that I smile back. He whoops into the air and then picks me up, spinning us so quickly I squeal and shut my eyes.

"Let's try it again," he says, once I'm back on the ground. "Come on!"

He tugs on my hand and even though my legs are shaking I start running.

Soon I'm soaring through the air again, touching down on rooftops, and the boy at my side is laughing. His face is breathtaking under the night sky. His hair is whipped back, his eyes clear. He is beautiful.

"You're flying, Livy! You're flying!"

Over and over again we jump, flinging our bodies into the night like we're invincible, the air catching us and lifting us ever so gently to the next building. Up ahead I can see the Space Needle, its lights a blurry mix of white and red as the fog rolls in from the Sound, shrouding my favorite landmark in mystery. But I see it. It stands where it always does, making me want to get closer.

"Over there!" I point and Meyer squeezes my hand in agreement.

As we head toward the Space Needle the buildings get shorter, and the rooftops further away. We're riding a roller coaster of our own making. I lose count of how many times I catch my breath, occasionally needing Meyer to remind me not to close my eyes, while one word continues to flutter across my thoughts. *How. How* are we doing this?

We touch down on the roof of the large apartment building he'd pointed out to me earlier, just shy of the Seattle Center.

"Let's stop here," he says.

He still has hold of my hand as he leads me to the edge of the roof, the side facing the Sound. We stay like this, together yet separate, gazing over the water as the fog continues to roll in. All around us people are safe behind their windows and doors, their nights centered around the television or a good book, while here I stand on the roof, holding the hand of a boy who can fly. I can see them, these people, secure in their nighttime worlds, but they don't see me. No one is looking outside their window. And even if they did see us, would they really see us, two roof jumpers out for a bit of an adventure? Or would they see our shadows and mistake us for birds soaring over the city.

Either way it doesn't matter because I know the truth. And, wow, do I like it.

"How can you do this?" I ask Meyer. "How can you fly?"

"I don't know. I've always been able to," he tells me again as though this is his standard answer, his rehearsed reply.

The word *always* gets stuck in my head. *Always*. Like I've always had hazel eyes or I've always been able to hold my breath underwater longer than anyone else.

"I just wanted you to feel it, you know?"

"Feel what exactly?" I say.

Meyer tilts his head as if he's not sure why this would be a question. "How it feels to be free."

"Oh," I say, realizing he's right. I did feel free. I still do. Everything below me weighs me down; the buildings, the streets, the people. Up here none of that can touch me. I am free of gravity.

"That feeling of being free. There's not much else to get excited about in this world of yours, is there, Livy?"

"World of *mine*?" The words snag my attention as though they are the missing piece to the puzzle that is Meyer. "As opposed to *your* world?" I laugh out loud, making it clear that I get the joke. You know, in case it is one.

Meyer smiles at something off in the distance, but he doesn't say anything more.

"You should know it's all going to be okay," he tells me. "You will get through this, Livy." He turns toward me, his eyes dark. "Do you believe me?"

"I want to," I whisper. There is a goodbye hidden in these words of his. I know it and I hate it.

"I wanted you to feel something," he says. "You deserve to feel something." He pauses a second, and I hold my breath. "I just…"

"What?" I ask him when he doesn't continue.

He's silent a moment, just studying me. "I just didn't expect to feel it too."

He gives me one of those smiles that is more mysterious than anything else and then we're moving, dropping toward the ground like two people standing in an elevator, except we're not in an elevator, we are simply drifting with nothing but air all around us.

"That's enough flying for one evening," Meyer says once my shoes sink into the grass. "Come on, I'll get you home."

We walk in silence all the way back to my apartment. I keep remembering how the air smelled while we were above the ground, salty and yet clean, and how it tasted fresh with a spicy hint like my mom's favorite tea, which doesn't make any sense at all, now that I think about it. But there it is. And how being out in the crisp night air should have made me feel cold, but instead it made me feel like I was lit from within.

"I have so many questions," I tell Meyer once we're standing in front of my apartment, but he just nods. He must expect that by now.

My smile is wide. I can't stop grinning. "Can we do that again?" I ask and then it hits me. This is it. This is the last time I'll see him.

"I promise I'll say goodbye," he tells me, once again reading my mind.

"How soon?" I ask, staring down at the ground.

"Soon," he answers.

Even though he's made a promise to say goodbye when it's time for him to go, tonight he leaves me without one. He leaps into the air and flies away, leaving me on the ground feeling more alone than ever.

PART TWO

They flew away to the Neverland, where the lost children are.

-— J.M. Barrie

Peter and Wendy

CHAPTER NINETEEN

One week later

"Are you ready for this?" my mother asks. She's sitting across from me while we wait for Dr. Lerner. He should be here any minute.

"I'm ready," I say, giving her a smile that is meant to show her how ready I am. I'm so nervous though I doubt I pull it off.

She opens her mouth to speak and I know what she wants to say, how I can still change my mind, how it's not too late, or perhaps, let's just walk away now, but she doesn't say any of that. Not this time. She's asked enough these last few weeks to know what the answer would be.

I'm doing this.

I've endured countless tests and exams and I've made too many promises to back out now. Today is the day I'm giving Jilly some of my bone marrow and after today she will be on her way to good health and birthday number seven and I will be slightly uncomfortable for a couple of weeks — at least that's what they tell me. And it will be worth it.

Jilly will get better.

It's cold in this room. I can't stop shivering. I pull the blue and white striped hospital gown around me. Not only is it thin, it barely covers my body. It's doing nothing to keep me warm.

"You know," my mother says from her metal folding chair across the room, "I waited until Jenna was three before I gave her peanut butter."

And just like always, the sound of my sister's name on her lips gets my attention.

"The doctor said two was fine but because of her allergy to strawberries I wanted to be safe." She smiles but I don't smile back. I'm too stiff and cold to smile. "I never let you eat grapes or hot dogs. Either of you. I figured I would wait until you were older."

She slides her hands down the sides of her wrinkle-free black pants, and I recognize this nervous habit because it's mine. It's the thing I do when I don't know how else to fix something. I grip my fingers together, refusing to let them mirror my mother's anxiety and watch as her hands find their way back into her lap. She is nervous, just like me. I know it. I can feel it. But you'd never know to look at her. Her hair is perfect, Her clothes are pressed. She's even wearing jewelry. Who thinks to wear jewelry to the hospital? Or to paint their nails to match their outfit? Apparently my mother does.

"Jenna never did try a hot dog," she continues. "Not once."

"Well she didn't miss much," I say, even though it's not true. I'm quite partial to turkey dogs with a thin strip of mustard on top. But my mother doesn't need to know this.

"I used to wash her hands every time we came home from the store. I used to carry around those bottles of anti-bacterial lotion. She hated it, always complained it hurt her hands."

"I remember."

"But I was militant," she continues. "Used to buy them in bulk."

"You can't wash away cancer," I tell her. I don't like where this is headed. I don't like the expression on her face. Her eyes are focused on the clock behind my head and even though she's talking to only me, not once has she really looked at me, just around me, as if I'm not really here.

"What I'm trying to tell you, Livy," she says, and then she stops and doesn't say anything more until the silence fills the corners of the room, making every sound out in the hallway seem loud in comparison.

I wrap my arms around myself. It's so cold in here! Why is it so damn cold?

My mother's shoulders flatten back against her chair as if there's a ribbon attached to the top of her head and someone is pulling it straight to the ceiling. She keeps taking these short breaths of air. It sounds like she's choking.

"You couldn't save her," I whisper into the cold room. "No one could."

"And yet you keep trying." Finally she looks at me, pinning me to my spot on the exam table. "That's why you're here, isn't it? To save her?"

"I'm here for Jilly," I say though tight lips. "Jenna's dead." Dead. Dead. Dead. The word weighs me down, tugging on my shoulders until I fold into myself.

"Well I hope you don't have a difficult time of it," she says with a clearing of her throat. "The recovery, I mean." She pulls out her iPhone and begins scrolling through it. "There are only two weeks left before Election Day," she tells me, as if I'm not already aware of this. As if I don't walk past the gigantic calendar hanging on the kitchen wall where every number is circled in red, leading up to that magic day when the country comes together to determine the fate of our world. And my mother's sanity.

"I won't need your help," I tell her. "I have Sheila." Sheila has already vowed to be at my side through all of this. She's even promised to stay the night if I need her to.

197

My mother's eyes lift off her iPhone just long enough to spill annoyance in my direction.

"I'm not saying I can't help you, Livy. I'm just saying—"

"You're busy. I know. I get it." I play with the loose string hanging from the bottom of my hospital gown. I'm afraid to tug on it. It might just unravel on me, and I have very little fabric covering my body as it is.

"If I could go back," my mother says, and I look up. "If I could go back—"

But she never gets the chance to finish her sentence. Dr. Lerner comes through the door with his nurse right behind him and then they're using words like, *it's time* and *we're ready for you,* and then I'm hugging my mother — who doesn't let go of me until I tell her to, and even after her arms drop from my shoulders she holds onto me with her eyes until that very last moment when she's forced to walk one way, and I another. Right before I turn the corner and she disappears behind a door, I call out, "Bye, Mom. See you soon."

What I actually wanted to do was ask her to finish her thought. What would she do if she could go back? How does that sentence end? I wish she'd tell me, because it feels really important right now. *If I could go back* has plagued my mind for months. I used to sit up at night thinking about the things I would have done with Jenna, the places we should have gone, the things I should have shared with her. I've strung together those should-have memories so often they're like cobwebs clouding up my mind. Sometimes I confuse them with the real memories and I have to remind myself how I never took her to that new park they were building just before she died. How she never got to play on it even though she watched it grow day by day.

"What would you have done?" I want to ask, but I don't say the words. They're too personal for a hallway. Too dramatic for this pre-surgery moment. Instead I lift my hand and wave. She waves back, and then she's gone. The door closes behind her with a click and that click echoes down the hallway and washes over me.

"Are you ready, Livy?" Dr. Lerner asks. I've answered this question so many times, in so many ways. This time I simply nod.

CHAPTER TWENTY

They lead me into an operating room that is bright and sterile and even colder than the waiting room.

"Lie down here," the nurse tells me and then covers my body with these white scratchy blankets that aren't the slightest bit comfortable, but I like how heavy they feel upon my skin.

"This will pinch a little," the nurse says, right before she sticks the IV into the top of my hand. It does pinch, but it's not that bad. I jump anyway.

"I'm sorry," I tell her. "I'm just nervous."

She squeezes my shoulder. "You're doing fine, Olivia."

"Livy," I correct her.

"Livy," she says with a smile. "You're doing just fine."

I decide I like her. She's nice. I feel safe here. But I still can't stop shaking.

"Relax and lie back," she tells me, even though I'm already lying down. "When you wake up you'll be in a different room. Your mother will be waiting there."

"Will you be there?" I ask.

Again she smiles. "Yes, Livy. I'll be there."

Dr. Lerner is moving about the room. He seems busy so I try not to pay too much attention to him. But then he turns, comes right up to me, and I realize this is it. This is the moment when everything will start to happen.

"How are you today, Livy?" he asks me.

"Good. Ready." Didn't he already ask me this?

"Great," he says.

"You're going to start to feel yourself relax," a new voice tells me. It's over to my right and it sounds deep and male, but I don't feel like turning my head to find him, so I close my eyes. The lights are so bright in here.

"Just relax," someone says and I nod my head. My movements are jerky and stiff as if someone else is controlling me.

"I'm cold," I say and once my mouth opens my teeth begin to chatter. I instantly feel embarrassed.

"Just relax," the voice says again and then warm hands press against my shoulders.

"I'm. Trying," I say around the chattering and someone chuckles just off to my right.

"You're doing just fine," the nurse says again, and I realize this must be what she tells everyone, which means I'm actually not doing fine. I'm freaking out.

"I want you to count back from 100," the voice tells me.

"Okay."

"Starting now, Livy," the nurse tells me.

"100, 99, 98, 97," I pause to lick my lips. I'm so thirsty, more thirsty than I've ever been. I haven't had anything to eat or drink since last night, just like they instructed me.

"Keep counting," the deep voice says.

"96, 95, 94."

It's getting darker, like someone is dimming the lights in the operating room. My eyes fly open and I find the nurse hovering over me with a smile. I try to smile back but I'm sure it just looks creepy. My teeth won't stop chattering.

"93, 92… 91."

And then I don't want to count anymore. My head is too fuzzy to count, like I'm falling backwards. My body is slightly warmer than it was before. I don't feel shaky. I just feel calm.

"Promise me I'll see you tomorrow," Jilly says. I can't see her but I hear her. I can't see anything. "Promise me you'll be fine."

"I promise," I tell her, just like I did last night before I left the hospital. "It's just a simple procedure. They take some of my marrow and give it to you. And then you'll be better. So much better that you'll leave this place."

"And go to the park!" she yelled.

"And go to the park."

"And go ice skating!" she yelled even louder.

"And go ice skating!" I yelled back.

And we continued listing all the things we'd do until Nurse Maria and her grandmother joined in. And then the four of us were yelling and laughing until the announcement came over the hospital speakers informing us that visiting hours were over.

"And you promise," Jilly asked me just before I left. She was holding onto my hand as if the strength of her weak grip could hold me here. "You promise you'll be back tomorrow. Promise, promise, promise!"

"Promise! Promise! Promise!" I said. "I will be here."

I *will* be here, whether I feel up to it or not. I will visit her so that she knows it's happening. She's getting better, just like I promised.

As I drift off in the operating room all I hear is Jilly's voice in my head and all I think about are the promises I've made. The promises I'll keep. They float around with me on a pink cloud that reminds me of Jenna's version of heaven as I sink into a place where dreams don't reach. It's so dark and soothing here I never want to leave. I want to float around like this until everything is fixed.

This isn't so scary, I think, relaxing back on my cloud. Not scary at all.

I awake with a gasp. The lights are far too bright — violently bright — and strangely colored. They aren't white like the operating room. They are blue and red and gold. And flashing. They stab at my eyes, the pain so intense I can barely breathe through it.

There are people talking above me but I can't make out their words. I just know that something is wrong. I should be sleeping. I should feel nothing. I want my pink cloud back and Jilly's voice in my head. Anything but this.

Something is terribly wrong.

I can't open my eyes, or maybe they are open but the lights are so bright I can't make anything out. It's hard to know for sure because of all the strobing colors. They blur everything together, creating a dizzying effect.

Make it stop! Please! Someone make it stop! My teeth are clenched together in pain and I don't know how to get anyone's attention.

Someone is shaking me, lifting me up off the table and thrashing me about. I try to yell at them to stop, but my voice is still buried deep inside of me, trapped behind my swelling tongue.

Pain is bubbling up from my stomach, reaching for a way out. And I want it out now. Please. NOW!

And then everything just disappears. The lights. The colors. The voices. Everything shuts off like a switch. I sense that I'm no longer in the operating room. I'm no longer in the hospital. I feel it. I'm somewhere else.

A feather-light breeze moves along my skin and I like it. It reminds me of warm days without rain. It is quiet wherever I am, not silent, just still. But I sense that I'm not alone.

I find my voice and ask, "Where am I? What happened?" I don't have to wait too long before a voice answers.

"You are here, Livy. You are safe."

"Where is here?" As I think it, I hear it, but I can't tell if it's in my mind or out loud.

"Look around and see if you can guess," the voice says, hushed this time, but closer.

I try to sit up, realizing that wherever I am, whatever I'm sitting on is soft, not hard like an operating room table, but also not cushioned like a bed. "What happened? I should be in the hospital. Why am I not in the hospital?" I ask the voice.

"Because you're here, with me," it tells me. As I start to come around I notice that the voice sounds funny. It's deep and melodic. And so familiar.

"Who are you?" I say. "Why can't I see you?"

"Because your eyes are closed," he says matter-of-factly. I am surprised to realize he's right. They are closed. I've yet to open them.

"Open your eyes, Livy," he says, and I've heard this before. He's said this before.

"I'm dreaming," I say aloud, because in this dream apparently I always say what's on my mind. "I have to be dreaming. That's why you're here." Because he shouldn't be.

"You may think of it as a dream," he tells me. "You may call it that."

"What do you call it?" I ask him, and then slowly, ever so carefully, I open my eyes.

It isn't the colors that surprise me at first but how they're all shaped, swirly and tall like a mountain, and then small with overlapping hills. All around are blues and greens of every possible shade like color-coded crayons lined up in a box. I want to ask who drew this picture because that's what it looks like at first. As my eyes focus and the fuzziness slips away, I realize this place isn't just colorful: it's art, or rather a child's version of art, pieced together with an exaggerated hand, bold yet imperfect.

"What is this?" I say out loud, hoping the voice will answer, hoping it's still close. And then, there he is — Meyer — sitting to the side of me with his legs crisscrossed underneath him and his hands resting lightly against his knees.

"Are you here to say goodbye?" I ask him. "I'm not ready. I don't want to. Not yet."

"Not goodbye." He's smiling at me, his eyes twinkling before the most beautifully drawn star-lit sky. "Things have changed. You're with me now."

"Where?" I ask, still looking around.

"There are subtle truths buried in every make-believe," he tells me. "You never know where you might find one." His voice comes at me loudly at first and then fades away as if he's off a far distance. But he hasn't actually moved.

"I don't understand. Where are we?" I can't focus on his response. I'm too distracted by the background and the fact that he's here, sharing it with me. I can't seem to wrap my head around anything else. Am I dreaming? Usually when I ask this question in my dreams I wake up. But I'm still here. The sky is still starry. I reach my hands out and discover I'm sitting on grass — rather vivid-green grass. It is soft and smooth. And undeniably real. I am not waking up. This dream may not actually be a dream. Wherever I am, I am here.

There are truths in every make-believe? What does that even mean?

His words are like a puzzle, incomplete but waiting to be put back together. I know there's something buried within them, but I'm going to have to come back to it. Maybe once I've stopped looking around.

Meyer rises to his feet with such grace and confidence that he captures my full attention. He sweeps his hands out from his body as if he's gathering everything up into his arms and I watch in wonder as the background begins to change. The dark colors are slowly becoming light and one by one the stars burn out in the sky. The most vibrant and colorful sunrise I've ever seen is cresting the strangely shaped mountains to the left and even though I could stand here forever, watching as it grows, I can't turn away from Meyer. He is electric in this moment. He is so alive.

"Not every place here has a name," he tells me, turning to see what I see. "But the whole of it," he adds, pausing, his eyes flashing with excitement, "we call Neverland."

CHAPTER TWENTY-ONE

"Neverland?" I repeat back to him, and he nods.

"Like Peter Pan and Tinker Bell?"

"No Tinker Bell," Meyer says with complete seriousness. "There was never any Tinker Bell. She must have come from some other story."

"You're joking."

"No, Livy. Really. There has never been a little blonde fairy with the voice of a bell here. I promise."

"Oh. Okay then." I nod as if it all makes sense now, waiting for the moment when he'll end the joke and laugh. And then I'll laugh. And I'll feel so much better because I didn't fall for it. But the laugh never comes.

Meyer just stands there looking like he is waiting for something from me, but I don't know what. His arms are crossed in front of his chest and his eyes are more serious than I've ever seen them.

"So you visit me in my dreams now? That's new."

"You're not dreaming, Livy. It's important that you know this."

"Of course I am!" I turn around, taking in the Crayola landscape around me. "Have you seen where we are? Are you trying to tell me that you managed to kidnap me in the middle of surgery and bring me to a place that is literally ripped from the pages of a children's story?"

"Would you like a tour?" Meyer is back to looking boyish. That gleam in his eyes is built on excitement, not humor.

"A tour?" I choke out.

"Right now we're in the waiting room. This isn't what I would have wanted you to see first, but I don't really get to control everything here." He pushes his hands into his front pockets and I notice how even in my dreams he dresses the same — dark jeans and a hoodie. It is slightly comforting. But not enough. I still don't believe anything he's telling me.

I glance down at myself and find I'm wearing the same clothes I wore to the hospital: my favorite blue sweater and my dark jeans. I'm not sure where my shoes and socks have gone, but it could be worse; at least I'm not naked in this dream.

"This is where everyone enters Neverland," Meyer explains.

"Right." I look around, taking in the sketchbook mountains and painted trees dotting the landscape. To tell you the truth it does kind of resemble the Neverland I've seen in books.

"Why Neverland?" I ask aloud, not really expecting an answer. "Why would I dream about Neverland?" I could have just stayed floating on that pink cloud.

"You're not dreaming, Livy." He looks like he's about to say something but then he gives up and shrugs instead. "We need to move on. I have work to do."

"Oh. So you work here?" I nod and then add, "Yeah, that makes sense."

Meyer chooses to ignore my sarcasm.

"This is what I do." He reaches down and grips my hand, pulling me to my feet, and his touch ripples through me like a wave of energy. I pull away, a little startled by the intensity of his touch. But then again, it's just a memory. I'm remembering how I used to feel when he'd touch me. This isn't real.

"Come on." Meyer's gaze is steady. "I'll show you." He reaches his hand out, waiting for me to grab hold, and I'm immediately reminded of that night in the Sculpture Gardens. Even then I felt the need to trust him. Even though I had no reason to.

"I would never lie to you," he tells me. "I've never given you a reason not to believe me."

"Right," I say reluctantly. I reach out my hand and he takes it, pausing for a moment.

"I've imagined you here," he whispers. His words are spoken so softly I almost can't make them out.

I lean a bit closer, hoping he'll say more, but instead he smiles. And that smile warms me far more than his touch. I love Meyer's smiles.

"So," he says, breaking through the moment. "I promised you a tour."

"Right," I answer, allowing myself to be pulled along. My legs are shaking but I force myself to fall in step with him.

Once we reach the top of the swirly hill I pause to catch my breath. Down below us is something — some place — not even I could conjure up in a dream.

No longer does the landscape resemble something drawn with a child's hand. No, those simple strokes have no place here. This new world is so unrealistic in its beauty it could only be created by computers. It's like something out of a movie. I look around expecting to see two moons or some strange alien-like creature walking toward me, because that would make more sense. Maybe all the movies Sheila has dragged me to have finally taken over my subconscious and that's why I'm dreaming in sci-fi. But there are no moons in the sky or creatures around — just one golden sun shyly peeking out from behind the mountain like it's afraid to leave its hiding spot. As it spreads its light, it leaves everything sparkling with a sort of pixie dust. The grass, the water, even Meyer and I, all have a glow about us that wasn't there before. I glance down at my hands, turning them palm side up. I am lit from inside as if by magic, or maybe not magic, but the strange energy I felt the moment Meyer touched me.

Straight ahead, reaching high into the sky, is the peak of a blue-green mountain. It should cast the valley down below in shadow, what with the sun just coming up and all, but it doesn't. Nothing in this world is dark. Every color, every detail, is vibrant. Almost as if each element of Neverland has a desire to be seen. They battle each other in their beauty like it's a competition. The water sparkles so brightly it takes me a moment before I can look at it. And the valley just off the hill is covered entirely with flowers — every possible flower you could imagine, some I've never even seen before. I want nothing more than to lie down in the velvety-looking grass and stare up at the ever-changing sky. But the rest of Neverland is calling me. And I want to see it all.

"Welcome to Neverland, Livy," Meyer says, and our feet begin to rise up like they've been waiting for just the right moment to leave the ground.

"Please tell me this is all real," I whisper. "Please don't let this be a dream."

"It's not a dream," he reassures me, and I want to believe him. More than anything. "Look around. How could any of this be a dream?"

"Because it's too beautiful," I whisper. But he's right. I don't think I could conjure up this place even with heavy anesthesia. I'm pretty sure no one could.

"I want you to try to believe, Livy," he tells me as we hover a few inches off the ground. "I know your first instinct is to not believe. I know that your world has made it so that you can't." He leans in closer, drawing me in. "But promise me you'll try."

Before I can answer he grips my hand and stretches toward the sky, and then we're flying, moving out over a place that is enchanted. It has to be. I can see our reflections in the crystal-clear water just below and I can't look away from them. When I'm close enough I dip my hand into the water, and even when I pull my wet hand back, I still don't believe. Maybe if I went swimming? Maybe if I rolled in the grass or smelled the flowers, then would I believe?

"Look! Over there!" Meyer says, tugging on my hand and pointing near the edge of the water where a large rock is cut deep into the side of a cliff. It juts out like a diving board.

"What?" I ask him, wanting nothing more than to dive below the surface of the water, just to see what it would feel like, but afraid it might jolt me from this dream.

"Mermaids," he tells me and there they are, lounging on the rocks, standing out against the cool tones of the water. I should have noticed them before, but I didn't. Not until I looked for them, almost as if Meyer telling me they were there made them appear.

"That can't be real," I whisper.

"Do you want me to pinch you?" he says with a wicked smile. "Isn't that usually what it takes for someone to wake up?"

"No," I tell him. I don't want that. If this is a dream, I'd like to stay a while longer. My dreams don't usually have mermaids. At least, not since I was a child.

Meyer steers us to the right toward a large island off in the distance. As we get closer I realize it isn't one island but many islands, so many different islands lined up one after the other, all nearly on top of each other. Some even overlapping.

"What are those?" I ask, but he shakes his head.

"Later. First things first," he tells me pointing to the left where the sun is fully formed in the sky. When I look at him there's no doubt he reads the disappointment in my eyes, how I want to keep exploring this place. Forever, actually.

Meyer's features soften, taking on a warm hue from the bright orange-yellow sun in the sky.

"Someone's waiting for me and I must never let them wait," he tells me, as if it's the number one rule in Neverland.

We head back toward the place where I first found Meyer, only now everything is covered in sunshine. Everything that was colored in shades of green and blue before is now orange and yellow. Even the trees are shaded in gold. How the sun was able to do this so quickly, I don't know. I wonder what shades of color the afternoon will be. Or if it ever rains here.

"Why are we back?" I ask, taking a seat in the grass, while he remains on his feet.

The color of Meyer's eyes is changing as the palette of Neverland morphs yet again. The lively green in his eyes takes on a hint of purple from the sky, and his cheeks are a shade of pink. It is unnecessary, this heightened color. He's so beautiful it seems unfair to add to his appeal.

"Neverland looks good on you," he tells me and I blush, realizing our thoughts are a mirror image. I wonder what he sees when he looks at me. Has my face gone all splotchy with embarrassment? Am I biting my lip too much? I know I'm short of breath, I can feel it, but that's his fault, not mine.

He kneels down in front of me in the grass. "What color is this?" he asks, holding up a strand of my hair and studying it closely.

"My father calls it strawberry-blonde." I say. "It's kind of a family trait."

"Not all of your family, though."

"No." I give him a funny look. He's never asked about my family before. "Just me and my dad."

"It looks more red than blonde here."

NEVERLAND | Shari Arnold

"Maybe it's the sky doing that," I finally say. I sound so breathless I don't recognize my voice. I keep looking at his lips, remembering what they taste like. It was a while ago, that kiss, but I remember the feel of it. Mostly it haunts me.

Meyer tucks the strand of hair behind my ear, and I feel his touch all the way down to my toes.

"He's almost here," he tells me, and I feel that flutter again, like something's about to happen. Something important.

"Who?" I ask.

"Come with me," Meyer says, pulling me to my feet.

Just past the three orange-yellow trees and out into the golden field of grass, we walk. Meyer is so sure in his footsteps while I am hesitant. Like every other dream I've had I'm unsure what to expect. Will this dream turn menacing and end with me waking up drenched in sweat, or will it fade into just another nonsense dream?

"Wait here," he tells me, dropping my hand. "It will be easier if I find him alone." And then he's gone, swallowed up in the tall grass.

"Okay," I say after his abrupt departure, looking around at a scene that continues to change right before my eyes. The sky is now cloudless and pale yellow. I can hear something moving about within the landscape, but I can't see it.

Suddenly a child's face pops out of the tall wheatgrass.

"Hello," the face says.

"Uh, hi," I answer, jumping back a few steps.

"Did I scare you?" the child asks with a smile full of tiny white teeth.

"You know you did," I tell him, and even though my words come off as harsh I can't help but return his smile.

The child bursts into giggles, his blue eyes so bright they stand out against the yellow sky. He takes a few steps toward me, emerging from the tall wheatgrass and I realize he is dressed just like Meyer, dark jeans and a hoodie. He's much smaller and rounder though, and looks to be about ten years old.

"I'm here to watch over you," he says pulling himself up to his full height, which is only slightly below my ribcage. "Meyer trusted me and no other."

"Now that ain't true," another voice says and I jump again, watching as the wheatgrass shifts around. But this time a girl emerges.

"Hello," she says to me, ignoring the glaring boy at my side. She is tall and willow-like, and a couple years older than the boy. Her long dark hair is pulled back off her face and loosely tied at her neck. "I'm Jane, Meyer's first in command. And this," she flickers her hand toward the boy, the move so graceful it's as if she's rehearsed it, "is Echo."

"Echo, Echo, Echo," the boy crows. And then his face is back to smiling.

"Yes," Jane says with a roll of her eyes. "And don't we know it."

"Um. Hello," I say, wondering if they actually need me here to continue this conversation. "Did you by chance see Meyer in that field?"

"He's coming," Jane says. "He's picking up the newbie. He'll be along soon."

Her dark features pinch together as she slowly sizes me up. With a definitive nod she crosses her arms in front of her chest. I'm guessing I passed her inspection.

"Newbie?" I ask, looking back and forth between the young boy and the girl. They look nothing like anyone I know, which is odd for sure. Shouldn't I recognize the people in my dreams?

"Newbies are visitors," Jane explains. She turns her head back toward the field and her dark ponytail swishes across her back. "This newbie's name is Jeremy."

"Right. Jeremy," I repeat.

"You look like her," Echo says, studying me.

"Who?" I ask, but all I get is his toothy grin.

"Did your journey hurt?" Jane asks me. She reaches behind her, plucking at the tall wheatgrass. Once she has a long strand she begins to tear it to pieces with her fingertips.

"Hurt?" *My journey?* Is anything these kids say supposed to make sense? "I don't understand. I'm just waiting for Meyer."

"He likes you, you know," Echo says.

"Well, we're friends," I say, holding back a blush, but I figure I'm not very successful when Jane gives me a rather disbelieving smirk.

"We didn't know you were coming. Neither did Meyer, I suspect."

"Yeah. Well, neither did I."

Jane shrugs it off and her attention returns to the wheatgrass in her hand as she twists the last tiny piece like a pinwheel. "It's alright. I knew you'd show up sooner or later. He couldn't seem to stay away from *you.*"

I don't have a moment to think about this new information. Echo slaps his hands to his sides as if he's been drawn to attention and then the field begins to move again. High above the gold-colored grass Meyer's dark hair can be seen as he makes his way toward us.

Echo and Jane greet him with a smile, but I'm the one he's focused on. He pulls his hand forward and a child emerges from behind his back. "Livy," he says, walking straight toward me. This is Jeremy."

"Jeremy," I say softly, smiling down at the child. "It's nice to meet you." His big dark eyes blink back.

"H-hello," he says, his attention flickering back and forth between Meyer, the sky above us, and me. "It's nice to meet you too."

"This is who we were waiting for," Meyer explains, but I'd already figured that part out. What I don't understand is why.

"I see you've met Echo and Jane," he says, and they immediately begin to glow under his inspection.

"Yes, they've been keeping me company."

"I'm glad," Meyer says, his eyes skimming over me. "I didn't want you to be alone."

"And *I* didn't want her to be alone," Echo says.

Jane just rolls her eyes.

"It's just like he told me," the boy whispers, once again capturing my attention. His head is thrown back as he takes it all in. The mountains. The sky. I realize he's seeing something different from what I first saw. His first glimpse of this world is an orangey-warm summer day where mine felt more like early dawn.

"Who?" I ask, but if he hears me, he doesn't answer.

His eyes widen and he begins to jump up and down. "I know exactly what my island will look like. I've been thinking about it, Meyer! I know just what I want!"

Meyer lets out a loud laugh, and it startles me, but no one else apparently. They all laugh right along with him.

"Are you thinking about it now?" he asks the boy. "Can you see it in your mind?"

"Yes!" the boy answers, nearly breathless in his excitement.

"Well, then." Meyer stands back, his arms crossed against his chest.

"Well then," Echo says, mirroring Meyer's stance.

"We should probably make our way to the Treasure Islands," Meyer finishes.

"To the Treasure Islands!" Echo repeats.

"To where?" I ask.

"Come along, Livy," Meyer says, his eyes burning into mine. "It's time for that tour I promised."

216

CHAPTER TWENTY-TWO

The five of us set out across the golden field. Meyer and Jeremy are in the front, their heads bent close as they talk in a low whisper. Echo is whistling a tune that reminds me of something Meyer would whistle, while Jane walks beside me, feigning an interest in the ground each time I catch her studying me.

"So you don't know then," she finally says the next time our eyes meet.

"Know what?"

"She still thinks it's all a dream," Meyer pipes up, not bothering to look back at us and therefore missing my glare. Instead he just continues his conversation with Jeremy as if he didn't say anything at all.

"Yeah," Jane says to me, "that's what I thought at first too. Except that my dreams were never so…" She looks around for a moment, struggling for just the right word.

"Beautiful?" I offer. "Vivid?" When she shakes her head I continue, "Creative?"

"Safe," Jane says, catching my eye one last time before she turns her attention back to the path in front of her.

"Jane has been here even longer than I have," Echo tells me. "And I've been here longer than most."

"I like it here," Jane says with a shrug. "I find it..."

"Safe?" I throw out with a lift of an eyebrow.

"Comforting," she says with an edge.

"Yes." I look out at the ever-changing landscape. "I can see that."

"And there's so much more to see!" Echo throws in. "I can't wait until you—"

"Not yet, Echo!" Jane interrupts, and Echo's mouth snaps shut.

"Right," he says. "It's a surprise."

"What is?" I ask him, but he just smiles.

We've reached the top of the hill now, the place where I caught my first glimpse of Neverland, and even though it wasn't very long ago, an hour tops, I still find it takes my breath away.

My father used to have this file in his office. He called it his wishing file. Inside was a large selection of photos of places he wanted to see before he died.

"It's important to want for things," he would tell my sister and me. "When you stop wanting, you stop living." And he was right. The day my sister died he stopped living, partly because he didn't get what he wanted, but mostly because once Jenna was gone he gave up wanting altogether.

But in that file there was this one photo of an island that I would take out and look at more than any of the other photos. The name of the island was something I could never pronounce, something with far too many vowels. To me it was so beautiful it didn't need a name, let alone a name I would always stumble over.

"Will you come with me, Livy?" Meyer says, interrupting my thoughts. He's standing in front of me now. I didn't even hear him approach. "There's something I want to show you."

"Is it the Treasure Islands?" I ask, feeling that energy build into a wave of excitement.

"Yeah, there's that too," Echo says with a giggle. They're all watching me, even little Jeremy.

"What?" I ask. "What is it?"

Meyer's eyebrows are drawn together like he's debating something.

"Tell me," I whisper. Whatever it is I have to know.

"Remember I explained how this isn't a dream? You must remember that, alright? Where I'm taking you, you must keep reminding yourself of that or…"

"Or what?" I ask quickly, sensing the importance behind his words.

"Or it won't mean as much." He squeezes my shoulders, almost shaking me, and says with conviction, "And I want it to mean something." He's looking at me so intensely I can't look away.

"I want to believe," I whisper, "but it's not that simple." It's true. I do want to believe in this place. Just like I wanted to believe that Meyer could fly. And that, maybe, he had feelings for me.

I reach out my hand, turning it once more to study the glow radiating from my skin. My fingers are kissed with a tinge of pink that, when held up close to Meyer, resembles the color of his lips. My eyes drop to those lips and suddenly I can't look away.

"What are you thinking about?" he asks, and I feel my eyes widen with embarrassment. "You're blushing." His hand reaches up to touch my face and I close my eyes, feeling his touch with everything I have. "You believed in magic once, why not now?"

His words brush against my lips and my eyes snap open. I shake my head. "I've never believed in magic."

"Oh yeah?" His smile shows his disbelief. "I don't believe that." His finger traces the side of my face. "And neither do you."

"But I'm in the hospital," I say out loud. "In surgery. That's real. And this place isn't real. It's the dream that I'm having, nice as it is."

"Why not, Livy? Why can't it be?"

"Places like this don't exist. Magic doesn't exist." Says the girl to the boy who can fly.

"So then it's true, you're dreaming." Meyer looks so disappointed in me I can barely stand it.

"Okay, what if I'm not," I say, backpedaling.

"Yes, Livy. What if you're not?"

Well then, what? The possibilities swim around my head like sharks, none of them are good and all of them are threatening.

"Will you stay with me? If this is only a dream, will you stay?" I whisper, and Meyer's eyes darken against the bright sky.

"The real question, Livy, is will *you* stay with me?"

"Hullo!" Jane calls from behind us. "Are you stuck? Did you forget where you were going?"

"Did you forget about us?" Echo cries.

I ignore them and so does Meyer.

I start to ask another question but Meyer stops me.

"Later," he says. "I promise I'll explain more later. But now…" His eyes take on that confident gleam of his. "It's time for us to fly."

CHAPTER TWENTY-THREE

The sun is moving sideways, following us as we make our way to the other side of Neverland. I have hold of Meyer's hand, or, rather, he has hold of mine. His grip is firm — refusing to let go — even though I feel like I'm doing this flying thing all on my own now. Occasionally when he looks over at me, his eyes are curious and a touch frustrated. I've never seen him look at me like this before. From the moment I met him he has always seemed to have everything worked out, but not now, apparently. And I'm not so sure he likes that.

I remember the first night I met him and how when he held my hand I would have followed him anywhere. Now that he's holding it again—even if it is only in a dream—I can't seem to remember why I ever wanted to let it go.

Down below us the landscape is changing. I let out a little gasp when I notice how the water is littered with mermaids. I see them all on my own now, without Meyer pointing them out to me. They look just how I would imagine they would: their hair is long, nearly as long as their tail, and of every possible shade of color. They flip around in the water, occasionally waving up at us as we pass. I wave back, wishing I could swim with them. But Meyer isn't letting go of my hand anytime soon. There is a purpose to his grip.

"Sometimes I swim with them," says Jane, who is now flying next to me. Her arms are stretched wide as she flies. She does it so effortlessly I'm jealous. She doesn't kick out her legs the way I do, thinking I need to propel myself across the sky. She glides the way Meyer glides. There is grace in flying when you do it just right. It is as though she is calmly falling in a forward motion.

"The mermaids are friendly, you know," she continues. "Not like in the stories."

"They're lovely," I say, wishing we could stop and meet some, remembering how the mermaids were always my favorite part of every story.

To Jane's right is Jeremy. He is holding her hand and grinning from ear to ear.

"I can't believe it," he says, not to me or to Jane. It is simply what he's thinking. He glances my way and laughs, and there is nothing but wonder to be found in his eyes.

I've been told we are headed toward the Treasure Islands and for some reason this makes Jeremy shiver with excitement. He keeps clapping his hands and spinning through the air. I'm not sure how he's managed to figure out how to spin so quickly, when all I can do is fly straight. I watch in envy, wishing I wasn't still so afraid I'd fall to my death.

"Which one is yours?" he asks, flying up next to me and pointing out toward the islands.

"She doesn't have one." Jane is studying me again with that all-knowing look of hers. "Not yet."

There are so many things I don't understand about this place, but the Treasure Islands are what call to me the most. From the moment I first saw them off in the distance I've been drawn to them.

I don't know if it's the child in me wanting to explore them, or if it's something more.

"I'm not sure I understand what you mean," I tell Jeremy. "Did Meyer promise you your very own island?"

"Not Meyer," Jeremy answers. His eyebrows are drawn together with concern. "And I *do* get one. He promised."

"Who promised?" I ask, still confused.

"He said I get to make my very own island!" Jeremy is fluttering now, his arms and legs stomping about the sky. "He told me everything is better here! That I'm safe here! There's nothing to fear!"

"And are you ready?" Meyer moves up close to him, hovering just over his shoulder. "Because you can't make an island if you can't see it in your mind."

His presence is calming. To me and to Jeremy. This is a new Meyer I'm seeing. The Neverland version, I guess. Back at home he was all about adventure and taking risks, but here with Jeremy he's different. More like an adult, and less like a child.

"I can see it," Jeremy says, his eyes wide and innocent. He closes those eyes, picturing his island. He drops a few feet or so in the sky and Meyer laughs, swooping him back up again.

"Keep it close." He taps his finger to the point where Jeremy's eyebrows are drawn together. "Right here." His finger moves down and touches where Jeremy's heart is beating inside his chest. "And right here. It's almost time, I promise."

"Meyer never makes a promise unless it will come true," Echo says, flapping up behind us.

"I don't understand," I tell Meyer a minute or so later, when Jeremy is back to being happy and flying by himself. "Are you telling me each child has their own island?"

"Every last one."

"But…" I look at him, wishing I could catch up with it all. "How many more are there?"

"Did you think it was just us?" Meyer asks.

Jane says, "There are hundreds of children on Neverland." She studies me for a minute. "He really didn't explain anything, did he?"

"There wasn't time, I guess," I tell her. But when Meyer doesn't respond, I do wonder.

The closer we get to the islands the more plentiful they appear. They dust the water like lily pads on a lake. Some are grouped together, reminding me of a neighborhood block with an occasional bridge connecting them. The rest are spaced out, but still close; close enough that it would only take a short swim to reach each one.

They are all as different as toys in a toy store

"Jeremy truly gets to create his own island?" I whisper to Jane and she nods, a rare smile lighting her face.

"It is our way of welcoming him here," she tells me, and with these words I begin to love Neverland that much more.

The first island we come to is lush and green like a rainforest. I can hear birds and monkeys and all sorts of wildlife floating up from the island. I wish we could explore awhile, but we just keep flying overhead. Down near the shore a few children are playing, but they stop and look up when our shadows cast over them. Their arms stretch wide as they wave up to us and I wave back. So do Meyer and Jane. Echo lets out a loud crow, his voice so powerful it rockets across the sky. I laugh when the children crow back as if this is some accepted form of greeting.

The next few islands are decked out like pirate ships. They're all facing one another as if the battle is between a handful of different captains. There are treasure chests a-plenty spilling about their decks, and each island sports a large pirate flag flapping in the breeze. These islands are overrun with children, or should I say pirates. They're racing about deep into a day of sword fighting and treasure hunting.

"Ahoy!" Meyer calls out to them. "See here, maties."

"Ahoy!" they yell back. They aim their swords toward the sky in salute to Meyer and he salutes back.

"Spread the word!" he tells them. "Let us all meet on Sunset Hill."

"Sunset Hill!" they echo back and then they all start crowing.

"So you *do* crow on Neverland. Just like in the stories."

Meyer shrugs, his smile still in place. "We borrowed that one from the movies, actually."

"So what does it mean?"

"Nothing. It's just fun."

We are flying over a fairyland now; at least that's what it looks like from up here. I tug on Meyer's hand begging to get a closer look. He answers with a smile and we descend. Up close I realize it's not fairies that belong here but princesses. The ground is covered in pink and green spongy moss and the leaves on the trees are plated with silver and gold. In the center of a large canopied gazebo is a marble dance floor. Suddenly I'd do anything to spin in circles on that floor. I imagine the gown I would be wearing and the slippers on my feet. I don't have to be a child to see the inspiration behind this island. I've read it. Imagined it.

"It reminds me of a story," I tell Meyer. "You know, *The Twelve Dancing Princesses.*"

There's a look about him, a hesitance that wasn't there before.

"It was my sister's favorite."

We are low to the ground now, but still slightly above it. I stretch out my hand, feeling the gold-tipped leaves. They are just as I always imagined: smooth and slightly sparkly, and cool to the touch.

"I used to read it to her every night," I tell him. "Sometimes twice."

Meyer stays silent.

A flash of movement catches my eye and I turn just in time to see a little girl run down the spongy path. Her dress is gold in color. Her hair is blonde and long down her back. I swing around to the other side of Meyer. I want to see this princess. I want to see the child who has created this island. But she is running away from me, her feet moving so quickly they barely touch the ground.

And just like that I'm caught up in a memory. Jenna is waving; her feet slowly moving her forward while her wobbly smile is aimed back at me. Her first day of kindergarten is still so clear in my mind, along with the feeling of guilt that accompanied it. She was so excited to go to school. She'd even packed her very own lunch. I remember feeling anxious about getting myself to class, but my mom had been called to a last-minute meeting and couldn't drop her off, so I took her instead.

"Will you be here to pick me up, Livy?" she'd asked, a hint of worry tugging at her smile.

"Mom will be here, don't worry. Just have fun."

Sheila was standing next to me. I remember how she wouldn't stop talking. She was so excited to finally drive us to school. It was all she'd spoken of for weeks.

"Let's go, Livy!" she kept saying, to the point that it was annoying. "We don't want to be late." I rolled my eyes at her, knowing that being late was never one of her concerns. She just wanted to get out of there.

"Kindergarten really isn't my scene, you know. Let's go." She pulled at my shirt while Jenna's eyes begged me to stay.

I was so concerned about AP Chemistry and how I was probably going to be the only sophomore in the class. Sheila had begged me to take some art class with her. She was convinced AP Chemistry was social suicide, but I was thinking college, you know. Future stuff.

I wasn't focused on Jenna. Instead I was slowly inching myself away from her.

But Jenna's worries were different.

"I'm not feeling so well," she'd told me. "I feel funny."

"It's just butterflies," I'd quickly answered, brushing her off with a wave of my hand. "You'll feel better once you're in there." I dropped a kiss on top of her head, and tucked her hair back behind her ears. And she'd smiled at me, believing every word I said.

She'd walked away thinking this was the beginning of the end of her childhood. She was a big girl now. All grown up and ready for school. And I ran off to Sheila's shiny new Volkswagen, and a backseat filled with close friends who would later stop talking to me.

I've thought back on that day so many times, how my life will forever be divided by the before and the after. The way we used to live — each memory a brighter shade of color than the ones we're making now. How once we learned of Jenna's sickness it didn't feel like much living was happening at all.

I've wished many times to go back and sit in that memory a tiny bit longer. I would have stayed in class with Jenna. I would have held her hand and taken in each minute we had left before everything changed. But not since I was a child have I truly believed in magic and fairytales, and when you lose someone you love you stop believing altogether.

"Meyer," I whisper, my heartbeat suddenly quick inside my chest. I squeeze his hand, wanting his attention, but he's already watching me. His eyes are so heavy in their intensity they're shining like glass.

"What is this place?" My voice sounds shaky and faint, just like how I feel. "Who are these children?" I keep searching for the child on the path, wanting to see her face. But she is no longer there.

"Look!" Jeremy shouts. He's pointing to the hills that stretch alongside of us. "Look at them all!"

The children of Neverland are making their way toward a large hill overlooking the water. Jane is right. There are hundreds of them.

So many, in fact, that the path they travel is blurry with movement. It's difficult to make out their ages or their faces. Their clothing is colorful, that much I can see. They are dressed to match their islands. I could probably guess which child belongs where simply by their attire.

They are excited as they wave at us, each child jumping higher than the last in their need for us to see them.

"Wait!" I cry, tugging on Meyer's hand. "I want to go back to the princess island. I need to go back!"

"Livy, they're waiting," Jane tells me, pointing to the children on the hill. She shakes her head, gesturing for me to come, but I keep tugging on Meyer's hand.

"Please!" I beg him. "Just for a minute." I want to find that little girl.

But Meyer keeps flying, his fingers locked around mine. He won't look at me now instead he stares straight ahead.

Back behind us there are more children in the air. There are so many of them, they fill the sky like a flock of birds. We're all moving so quickly now, I worry what will become of us once we all converge on one another since we all seem to be heading toward the same destination. But apparently I'm the only one concerned. Meyer, Jane, Echo and even little Jeremy are all smiling.

"We're here," Meyer says, interrupting my thoughts. He squeezes my hand and then all at once we're descending down to the ground.

My feet touch sand and I'm reminded that I'm still barefoot. The sand feels wet, but not cold. The tide slaps at my feet and it's refreshing. Not like when I'm at Alki Beach and even with the sun shining I still feel a shiver when I'm in the water.

I look around, searching for something, no longer aware of the beauty around me. No longer caring. All the while Meyer is watching me.

The children close in, moving down the hill toward us through bushes and around trees. Each face lit with curiosity and a smile. They all appear so young, the oldest no older than ten or eleven. At least that's my initial impression.

I sense that they want to come even closer, but most hold themselves back. They are lined up now, at least ten children deep. It is as though they are awaiting instruction. Some wave at us shyly, while others simply grin. But all are happy. You can see it, feel it, surrounding us.

"They all live here?" I say, still in disbelief. "How did they get here?"

At first no one answers me. But then a young boy comes forward. He touches my arm lightly like he's trying to figure out if I'm real. "I was sick," he tells me, resting his hand upon my skin.

"Sick?" I spin around, feeling more movement behind me, and then I turn back to him. "You feel sick?"

The children are dropping from the sky now. Some splash in the water first, making their way up to the shore. There are so many of them. Most of them barefoot like me.

"Not anymore," he tells me. "Not since Neverland."

"Me too," a dark-haired girl chimes in. "I was sick too." She tugs on my hand and then slips her fingers through mine. "My name is Alice, and my mommy had hair just like yours. Do you know my mommy?"

I shake my head while she blinks up at me.

"I still remember her," she says, not with sadness, more matter of fact.

"You were sick?" I ask, taking in her bright brown eyes and that Neverland glow.

"Not me," a blonde boy says. He swaggers up to us with his arms crossed. "Mine was an accident. Right, Meyer?" He glances at Meyer with uncertainty before turning back to me.

"Right, CJ," Meyer answers, and CJ's expression softens.

"What are you talking about?" I ask. I turn to Meyer. "What are they talking about?"

My heart is pounding. I feel like I can't breathe. Alice squeezes my hand and I feel like I could find the answers in her eyes if I looked hard enough, but I'm not sure I'm ready.

The children are inching closer now; every last one of them wants to be heard. I turn to Meyer and even though there are at least a dozen or so kids vying for his attention, he's still got his eyes on me.

I make my way toward Meyer, bringing Alice with me. As I move through the children they smile up at me, curious about the girl who is so much older than them. They ask me questions I can't answer, like: "How did I get here?" Or, "Will I be in charge now, like Meyer?" But there's only one question on my mind.

When I'm finally in front of him I grab his arm, dragging him toward me. Once he's close, I roughly push him away.

"What is this place?" I hiss at him, not even realizing I'm hitting him until he stops my hands against his chest. He holds them there, not allowing me to have them back, even when I continue to push and pull.

"I don't understand," I cry. "What happened to me?" But he doesn't speak. The emotion behind his expression is clear.

"No! I don't believe you!" I keep pushing at him, wanting to get at the truth, but still afraid. I close my eyes. If I can't see him, I can pretend this isn't real.

Meyer is stronger than me, and eventually my shoulders drop and I collapse against him.

"They're dead, aren't they?" I whisper. "All of them, dead." My voice is soft and muted against his chest. I'm not sure he's heard me, until at last he responds.

"Yes."

I'm struggling to catch my breath, it's coming at me much too fast. I'm dead. I've died. But that can't be right. Wouldn't I know if I were dead? Wouldn't I have felt it? Feel it?

And if I'm dead… if it really is true…

I grip Meyer's sweatshirt. "Where is she?" My voice is so raw I barely recognize it. "Please," I beg, breaking down into tears. "She has to be here."

I turn around, searching the crowd of faces — pausing only on blonde hair and blue eyes. My heart is stopping and starting — there are so many of them. But I can't see her.

"Where is she? She has to be here, Meyer! Please! Tell me she's here."

I don't wait to get an answer. I take off running and the children shift out of my way as though they know what I'm looking for and want me to find it. I reach the edge of the cliff and jump off. I don't worry that I will fall. Not this time.

"Livy!" Jane calls out to me, but I ignore her.

I aim my head down the way the others do when they fly, and spread my arms out. I don't let myself marvel at how I'm flying all on my own, my only thought is getting back to that island.

It's only a little ways back, but it feels like forever. I'm struggling to keep myself afloat and once the sparkly trees are in sight I let out a sigh of relief and drop toward the ground. My landing is awkward — a wreck more like it — but I don't care. I've made it.

"Jenna!" I call out, my voice so loud in the silence it startles me. "Jenna! Are you here?" *Please be here.*

I run down the spongy path, moving toward the grand gazebo. I slip near the bottom and slide to a stop just before I hit the marble dance floor. I'm on my knees, taking in everything at once, looking in every direction.

"Jenna!" I call out again and a few birds surge from the trees, flapping off into the sky.

I plant my hands on the dance floor and surround myself with maybes. Maybe she isn't here. Maybe this really is just a dream, or worse, maybe I'm dead and in my own private hell. I push my fists against my eyes. I want to stop these tears that are falling, just for a moment, so I can think this through. If this isn't a dream and these children are dead, if I'm dead...

My heart is pounding. It nearly covers the sound of footsteps along the path.

"Livy."

The sound of my name breaks through my thoughts. I can't tell if it was inside my mind or if I heard it out loud. Then I hear it again.

"Livy?"

I open my eyes, but keep them aimed at the ground. I could be imagining it. I could be going insane.

A scuffle against the dirt catches my attention, and I shift my focus over a few inches, still staring at the ground. Two black Chuck Taylor's come into sight. They are worn around the toes, but they're familiar. I know who they belong to.

"I just thought... I figured..." My bottom lip begins to tremble and I bite down on it, holding back my emotion. "I really wanted her to be here," I whisper with my head down. I don't want Meyer to see me this way: lost, without a speck of hope.

I hear shuffling all around me, and without looking up I know the children of Neverland have followed us here. I close my eyes tight, trapping the tears that threaten to fall.

"Livy," Meyer says, and then I feel his hand against my face. "Look up."

My eyes open, albeit reluctantly, and he takes in my sadness. I watch it color his eyes. I feel like he is sharing it with me. Or, perhaps, taking it from me. He holds my gaze a moment longer before it moves off to something behind me. He reaches his hand out, summoning someone toward him, and I hold my breath.

"Everyone gets a wish when they enter Neverland," he tells me. "What is your wish, Livy?"

My wish? I get a wish?

"Close your eyes and make your wish," he tells me. When I don't do it right away, he adds, "Those are the rules."

My eyes flutter shut and all the want I have left inside of me merges together all at once. I can see her, but more importantly, I can feel her.

"Did you make your wish?" a young girl whispers.

"Yes," I choke out, squeezing my eyes shut.

"Did you wish for me, Livy?"

"Yes." I cover my mouth, holding back the emotion tearing me in two. Did Meyer hear it? Did he hear her too? I open my eyes and stare up at the girl holding Meyer's hand.

She is dressed in pink, all the way down to her toes, and I sputter out a laugh because of course she'd be in pink, what else would she be wearing. My laughter fades into a whimper and the children move further away from me. I've frightened them. They aren't used to sadness here.

She is taller now. I almost don't recognize her. Her blonde hair is long and unbound, flowing down the length of her back. The way she always wished it would be.

"Livy?" she says, unmoving for a moment. Her voice is exactly as I remember. Her face looks the same but something is different. I can't quite put my finger on what.

She runs at me, wrapping her arms around me, and I realize there is weight to her. She is real. I am not imagining this. I want to say her name. There are so many things I want to say to her right now, but I can't stop crying. I keep touching her face, her hair. She feels real, like Jenna. This would be a cruel joke if this were only a dream.

"Surprise," Echo says softly and I realize that every other child has grown quiet. Through my tears I start to laugh. It bubbles up from inside of me and once I start, I can't stop. Soon Jenna is laughing with me. She is holding my hands, gripping them tightly in her own, and I am crying all over the both of us.

"You're here," she whispers against my cheek before pulling away to look at me.

Her eyes are different. Older, I think. I'm not used to seeing her cheeks so pink and full.

"I don't understand any of this," I tell her, but I'm still laughing so she laughs with me. I pull her close and against her hair I whisper, "Please don't wake up. Please, Jenna, please don't let me wake up."

"You're not dreaming," she tells me. She's brushing the tears away from my face. But I just keep making more.

Her words should mean something to me but I'm still pleading with God or anyone to keep me in this dream.

Please don't wake up.

Please don't wake up.

I turn and look at Meyer.

Please.

Meyer is watching us. I have never seen him so happy. I want to smile back, but instead I just keep crying. Jenna is in my arms now and I can't stop touching her. I don't think I'll ever let her go.

"Why are you here? What happened to you?" Jenna asks. With her face pressed to my shoulder, I can hear the concern in her voice.

"Livy is just visiting," Meyer tells her.

"Visiting?" I ask him. What does that even mean?

"Visiting?" a child near me says. The children are circling us now. They can't quite decide what to make of us, but they're curious just the same.

"No one has ever just visited before."

"You're right," Meyer says. "Just Livy."

"But I don't understand how you got here?" Jenna glances over at Meyer, and so do I.

Meyer shrugs without making eye contact. He looks down at the ground and I find this very interesting considering he seems to know every other child's reason for being in Neverland.

"Is mom here? Or dad?" Jenna asks. "Did they come with you?"

I open my mouth to answer and then shake my head. I don't want to disappoint her. It's funny how that never goes away.

Jenna's eyes are concerned. They stand out against the backdrop of happy, smiling children. "How long—?"

"As long as she wants," Meyer answers, his gaze finally meeting mine. He nods his head once, wanting me to believe it. And I want to believe it too, especially now that Jenna's smile is back.

I run to him and throw my arms around him, nearly knocking him off his feet.

"Thank you," I whisper. "Thank you for…" I shake my head, unable to finish. My words are too raw. "I don't know who you are," I force out. "Or how you've done this—"

"You *do* know me," Meyer interrupts. He pulls away slightly, a hint of desperation in his eyes. "Don't ever say that you don't."

"Livy." The children are whispering my name, trying it on.

"Isn't that…?"

"Isn't she…?

"Sisters!"

"Jenna's sister!"

"Yes," Jenna says, still beaming at me. "She's my sister. The one I told you about."

"Where's my sister?" a little blonde girls says, tugging on Jenna's sleeve.

"I have a brother. Are brothers okay?" the boy next to her asks.

They're all around Meyer now, their questions insistent, until he has no choice but to let out a loud whistle. And then they all stop.

"Livy is my friend," he tells them, his eyes moving over me before quickly slipping away. "She's just visiting."

"Unless she decides to stay," Jane adds.

Echo crosses his arms. "That's right. Unless she decides to stay."

Meyer is quiet. He stands there towering over the children and they watch him, waiting on his next word. "This has never happened before," he tells them, all the while focused on me. "We will welcome her and show her around." His gaze intensifies and then rather quickly he looks away. "She's here to visit her sister."

With a rush of air I let out a breath. I'm not sure why I was holding it.

"But now!" he shouts. "It's time to make an island!"

"An island!" the children erupt. Some roar, some crow, but they are all cheering. They jump up and down and run around. It is a miracle no one gets hurt.

"Jeremy!" Meyer yells over the crowd. "Are you ready?"

"I am!" Jeremy yells back. He flaps his arms and shoots himself into the sky. His laughter spills over us, spreading through the crowd. He lands back on the ground in a perch. He is a fast learner, this flyer. He takes his place next to Meyer, and that Neverland glow is nearly shooting off of him.

Alice shyly approaches Jeremy. "What about you?" she asks softly, reaching for his hand. He takes it, somewhat hesitantly. "How did you get here?"

"I…" Jeremy loses some of his glow and his smile drops off. "I…I got lost," he says. He inches closer to Meyer, dragging along the little girl. "But Meyer told me everything is better now. And I believe him." He says this last part with a nod of his head and I smile because he looks just like Meyer when he does this.

"Everything is always better in Neverland," Alice says, turning in my direction.

"Yes. I believe it," I say.

She tugs on Jeremy's hand, gifting him her biggest smile. "I'm Alice. And that," she points at my sister, "that's Jenna. She's my best friend. And we live here, on the sparkly islands."

"Oh," says Jeremy.

She moves closer to him, her steps so confident. "You can come visit us if you want. We have lots of dances every day."

"Sure," Jeremy says, looking up at Meyer and then down at the ground. "But. I have to build my island first, right Meyer?"

"Right. Island first. Dancing after." Meyer winks at me, and I don't know why but I immediately feel heat rise to my cheeks. A few of the little girls around me start to giggle, nudging Jenna. But Jenna simply smiles.

"I told you he's nice," she tells me.

"You what?" I push her hair back behind her ear, the way I always did. I can't stop touching her.

"I told you, right before I came here. I told you he was nice and that you'd like him."

"I don't…" I shake my head, trying to focus on her words. She looks so serious. She looks so alive. "What are you talking about, Jenna?"

She blinks up at me, waiting, and all at once there's this feeling in my chest. I remember. I remember this conversation.

"I told you his eyes were green and that they —"

"Sparkled," I turn and glance back at Meyer.

"Like he's winking," Jenna says.

"Winking?"

"Yeah, like Santa does," Jenna explains.

"Ho ho ho!" Meyer belts out while rubbing his belly, and the children break into fits of laughter.

When I laugh Meyer winks again and Jenna claps her hands and yells, "See!"

"I do remember that." My voice is soft against the growing excitement of the children, but she still hears me. They're all swarming Meyer, their voices competing against one another, desperate for his attention.

"So you saw him too," I whisper, and she nods her head enthusiastically. "Right before you came here."

"He visited me. He sat with me in the hospital and told me a story about Neverland, just like you used to."

"But I don't understand. Does that mean…?" My chest is tightening up again. The colors around me begin to swirl. "What happened to me? Am I—?"

"You're just visiting." Jenna is holding my hand now and I'm glad for it. I need her to keep it from trembling. She looks so calm, so grown up. For a minute there she could be my mother, the way she rubs my hand and speaks softly. "You're just fine, Livy," she tells me. "You're safe."

"Safe," I repeat, feeling like Echo. *But how am I here?*

"If you're all…" I stop myself, still unable to say the word.

Jenna nods in understanding.

"Then that means…" I look to Meyer, knowing he's the only one who can clear this up for me. And he's watching me. Rather closely, actually.

"An island!" he calls out, breaking through the sudden haze around me.

"An island!" they yell back.

And then the children of Neverland are marching, lining up in rows of three and four, chanting, "an island!" as they move up to the highest point of Jenna's island.

"I knew he would bring you." Jenna is the only child who hasn't joined them yet. I look down at her, still at my side. I can't get over how mature she seems. "I asked him to keep an eye on you," she says with a giggle. The joke is hers and hers alone. "But I think he did a whole lot more than that, Livy."

CHAPTER TWENTY-FOUR

Meyer stops once he's reached the edge of the island. The children fill in around him.

"Are you coming?" he calls down to us. "You won't want to miss this, Livy."

"It really is amazing. I've seen it a hundred times before, but I still love to watch." Jenna's feet rise off the ground. She is hovering just over me. "Don't you love flying? It's my favorite part."

"Jenna," I whisper, feeling overwhelmed in this moment.

"Yes?"

With her pink satin dress flowing all around her and her long, thick hair, Jenna is part of the magic. She is a breathtaking piece of Neverland, like the mermaids or the golden sun.

I shake my head, unsure if I can say what I'm actually feeling. It's all too much.

She tilts her head slightly and her blue eyes sparkle like the water behind her. "Aren't you coming?" She tugs on my hand, nearly lifting me off the ground. "Come on, Livy. I want you to see!"

"Livy! Jenna!" Meyer is chanting.

"Livy! Jenna!" the children repeat.

I laugh, raising my face up to the sky. With a little leap I take off. I'm flying with Jenna, soaring back to the top of Sunset Hill.

"I can't believe you're here," Jenna whispers, her words floating upon the air, over to me. "I wished it the first day I got here, but Meyer said we couldn't wish for people, only things."

"I wished it too," I tell her. "I wished to be with you every day you were gone." I'm still wishing it, afraid that if I stop, she'll slip away.

The children clear a spot for us to land right next to Meyer and Jeremy. Echo and Jane move up beside me, looking strangely smug for two people so young.

"Are you ready?" Meyer asks Jeremy, even though it's obvious from his excitement that he is.

"Close your eyes," he tells him. "Tight." And Jeremy listens. I almost do too.

"Imagine it in your mind. Every color, every shape. Do you see it?"

"I see it," Jeremy whispers. He reaches his hand out as though it's so real he can almost touch it.

The children around me draw in a breath and I drag my attention away from Jeremy and gaze out over the side of Sunset Hill.

The water below us is moving. It swells and buckles and then something breaks free, surging up and out. The creature opens its mouth, letting out a cry that should terrify the children, but instead they just inch closer. Some run down the hill to get a better look, while others clap their hands and dance around. All the while Jeremy's eyes are still closed.

The creature's head swivels around, pushing its body toward the surface. And then another head emerges. And another.

"What else do you see?" Meyer whispers. His arm is wrapped around Jeremy's shoulders, their faces close.

"I see trees and birds and tall cliffs the birds can soar from."

As he speaks the words, each thing appears, thrusting up through the water, until every piece is in place, and Jeremy's island is complete.

"And dinosaurs," he whispers reverently. "Lots and lots of dinosaurs. Are they here yet?"

"Open your eyes and see for yourself," Meyer tells him, positioning him just right so that when he opens his eyes he'll have the best view.

Jeremy peeks through his fingers, slowly at first, as though he's afraid its all a big trick, and his island will forever remain inside his imagination. But then his eyes widen, and his hands drop to his sides. His mouth opens up and one word slips out. It's the same word the rest of us are thinking: "Amazing!"

"Amazing is right," Meyer laughs. "You've done a great job, Jeremy. Dinosaurs are just what Neverland needs."

"Am I the first?" he drags his eyes away from the view in front of him just long enough to glance up at Meyer.

"Hmm…" Meyer tilts his head, considering this, his thumb pressed against his bottom lip. "I wouldn't say you're the first. But it's been a while since we've had such a *variety* of dinosaurs. That's for sure."

Jeremy is beaming now, his hands rubbing together with anticipation. "Don't worry, I didn't make any theropods. Just sauropods."

"Thero-what?" Jane asks.

"Theropods," Meyer answers. "Carnivores."

"Gross," Jane says with a shudder. "Meat-eaters. That's disgusting."

Jenna scoots closer to me and I wrap my arm around her, protecting her. But when I look down at her there is nothing but excitement in her eyes. She is not afraid, only curious. "So that means they're friendly, right? Sauropods?"

"Why, of course." Meyer is gazing out over the island. "There's no fear, remember? Nothing here can harm you."

Nothing here can harm you. Nothing to fear.

These words of his rush through my memory so clearly, taking me back to an adventure-filled night at the carnival. When he turns and looks over at me his expression is dark and serious. He must remember as well.

"Most of the dinosaurs are from the Late Jurassic period," Jeremy tells us. "But I snuck in a Plateosaurus. They're my favorite."

"Jurassa-what?" Echo says, throwing up his hands in bewilderment.

"Do you know what he's talking about?" he whispers to Jenna.

"Dinosaurs?" she answers with a laugh.

Echo nudges her playfully. "That much I know."

"Dinosaurs roamed the Earth during the Triassic, Jurassic and Cretaceous periods," Meyer explains.

"Meyer knows everything," Echo tells me, grinning from ear to ear.

"Really," I say.

"You're not the only one who reads," he says with a wink.

"Go ahead," Echo continues. "Ask him anything."

"Anything?" I say.

"Anything."

"Well then." I move a bit closer to Meyer. "If I can ask anything…"

Meyer's arms are crossed, his shoulders back. When he lifts an eyebrow at me I almost laugh. He is exactly what I imagined he'd be.

"I used to dream about you," I say before I can stop myself. "I used to wonder what you'd be like if you were real."

My words knock that smug expression right off his face. His eyes widen with surprise and then blink back at me.

"I guess that's why Peter Pan was always my favorite story to read."

"Mine too," he tells me, without a trace of presumption. "But I'm not him. It's just a story."

"But you're real, aren't you? And all of this?" I sweep my hand out, gesturing toward the islands. He's so close my fingers brush against his arm before falling back to my side.

Meyer stares down at the place where I've just touched him as if he doesn't recognize his own skin. His hair has fallen across his forehead, nearly covering his left eye. I reach up to brush it back, and then stop myself. What am I thinking, touching him? He isn't mine to touch. Not like that. He belongs here with these children.

I clear my throat, and take a step away from him. He watches me do it without stopping me. There's a trace of sadness in his expression that wasn't there before.

"I have my question," I tell him, barely above a whisper. "When it's time I'll ask it, and you must promise to answer."

"I promise," he says with a nod of his head. His voice so soft, it's almost haunting.

"Is it done?" Jeremy squeals, jumping up and down. "Can I go now? Can I see it?" His enthusiasm has shattered the mood wrapped around Meyer and myself. For a moment there I'd forgotten there was anyone else around.

Jeremy lifts off into the air without waiting for an answer. He circles his island, taking it all in, and then he spins in the air with a peal of laughter.

The dinosaurs move toward him, their footsteps so heavy they shake the ground. They stretch their necks out in his direction. Their eyes and mouths are bigger than Jeremy's head, and when they breathe him in his hair flutters across his face, much to his delight. He laughs and flips upside down in the air, while the dinosaurs reach up to the trees, plucking and nipping at the leaves.

NEVERLAND | Shari Arnold

I glance over at Meyer. The sadness is gone now. His eyes are back to sparkling.

"It's smooth!" Jeremy cries out, tentatively touching the first dinosaur's neck. "And rough at the same time! Just like I always thought." He flies down the length of the dinosaur's neck to the belly. "Do you think he'd let me ride him, Meyer?"

"Maybe if you ask him," he laughs.

Jeremy flies back up so that he and the dinosaur are face to face. "If I promise not to kick my feet, will you let me ride you?"

The dinosaur's dark eyes blink back at Jeremy. I hold my breath, waiting to see what happens next.

"Do you think he'll let him, Jenna?" I'm worrying my lip, afraid to look, and yet finding it impossible to look away.

"Just watch," she answers. She takes my hand, perhaps sensing how nervous I am.

Leaning close, the dinosaur rubs his face against Jeremy's. I cover my mouth in fear. This would be the moment I would run away screaming. But Jeremy is nothing like me, apparently. He giggles and hugs the dinosaur close. I guess he has his answer.

With one long, drawn-out stretch of its neck, the dinosaur bends down to the ground anticipating Jeremy's ascent. But Jeremy flies up instead, settling himself on the dinosaur's back.

"I'm doing it!" he yells, holding onto the dinosaur's neck as it begins to move. "I'm riding him!" And that breath of air I'd been holding slips through my lips with a loud *whoosh*.

All at once the children fill the sky. They've kept their distance long enough. They circle around, watching as Jeremy begins to explore his island by dinosaurback.

"Come on!" he calls out to them. "They're friendly!" The rest of the children start to move in. Soon each dinosaur is giving a ride. Some take on more than a handful of children.

"Come on, Jane!" A small group of girls is waving at her from their perch on the dinosaurs. "Ride with us!"

Jane hesitates a moment. Her arms are crossed in front of her as she stands next to Meyer and Echo. The three of them resemble parents on the playground, excited for their children to play yet withdrawn from the experience.

"Go on," Meyer tells her, nudging her from behind. "You know you want to."

And then she's gone, joining the children as they explore the newest addition to the Treasure Islands.

"Isn't it amazing, Livy? I can't wait for you to explore mine. We'll have a dance today! In your honor, of course," Jenna says with a bow.

"Of course," I say, grinning back at her. "I can't wait."

Besides Echo, Jenna is the only child who hasn't joined in now and I worry my presence is holding her back. "What about you?" I ask. "Why aren't you down there?"

"Dinosaurs aren't my favorite," she tells me.

"Or your best?" I laugh, pulling her close.

"You're my favorite, Livy," she whispers, and all those things I've wanted to say to her since the moment I got here are unnecessary now. With those few words she's made it clear we feel the same.

I lower myself to the ground, taking Jenna with me. I pull her into my lap and she rests her head back against my chest in that place where her head always fit best. While the dinosaurs roam Jeremy's island I begin to believe in it all. In Neverland.

We sit like this a while, talking softly to each other, but mostly staying silent. At some point Echo and Meyer join us on the grass, but they keep their distance. The sky is still a sunny yellow with periodic swirls of purple and pink. It reminds me of summer fruit or rainbow sherbet.

I comb my fingers through Jenna's hair and kiss her pink, full cheeks. She laughs and points out her favorite islands — the ones we can see.

"I could live in this moment forever," I tell her, and she smiles at me and squeezes my hand.

The tension builds before anything else. It feels like static electricity moving across my skin. The grass begins to shiver and then the hairs on my arms rise up. The air around me is all at once thick and heavy, making it difficult for me to catch my breath.

"Get up, Livy," Meyer says, and then he's standing over me, pulling me to my feet. "Get up! We need to go!"

"What is it?" I ask but he doesn't answer. He drags me toward the edge of the hill, and then out into the sky. His grip on my hand is so tight it's almost painful.

"Livy!" Jenna calls after me, and I twist my wrist, anxious to return to her. But Meyer refuses to let go.

When I look back she and Echo are following us. Their heads are aimed down to maximize their speed, but still they're unable to catch up.

Meyer is flying faster than ever; my hair whips around my face making it difficult to see. The wind is pushing against us. Down below, the mermaids hide under the surface of the water, a water so dark now, it mirrors the sky. I can just make out their frightened faces as they stare up at us. I'm afraid of what they see, their view of the sky is better than most.

"What is it? What's happening?" I ask Meyer, not sure he can hear me over the angry howl of the wind. He keeps flying, never looking back. But I do. And so do Jenna and Echo.

"What is it, Livy? What's happening?" she calls out to me. It terrifies me that she has to ask me this, seeing how this is her world and not mine.

"I don't know!" I shout, but I'm pretty sure my words get lost somewhere between her and me.

We keep flying, heading toward the one patch of blue in a sky burning black. And once that blue disappears Meyer stops. He pulls me up close until our faces are almost touching. His eyes are dark green now, taking on the shadowy colors of the sky.

"Do you trust me, Livy?" he whispers, and I've heard this before, but this time I know the answer.

"Yes," I tell him, nodding frantically. "Yes, Meyer. I do." I stare into his eyes, afraid to look behind me. Afraid to look anywhere else. I am out of breath, and my heart is beating wildly. For the first time since this all began I truly feel fear.

"He has no claim over you. He can't make you leave."

"Leave?" I choke out the words, staring back at the darkness swirling around us. "Who? Who wants me to leave?"

Jenna wraps her arms around me, squeezing me tight. "I don't want you to go!" she yells against my chest.

"Me neither," Meyer whispers, his fingers digging into my flesh.

Soon Echo arrives and begins circling around us. The fear coming off of him is palpable. I don't know what it is that has everyone afraid. I'm not even sure they do. But even without any answers from Meyer it is dreadfully clear.

Something threatening has entered Neverland.

CHAPTER TWENTY-FIVE

The wind is getting stronger now. It surges around us, whipping us about in the sky. Jenna slips free of me and I scream, reaching for her. But the wind is too strong to fight. It sounds like it's hissing, a large balloon deflating right next to our ears.

Meyer pulls me close, our foreheads touching. I don't know how he can keep hold of me when everything else around us is blowing away.

"Come down now, Meyer," a voice calls out. "You can't hide her from me forever."

"Don't listen," Meyer tells me, but it's too late. Those angry words are so loud they feel like they're trapped inside my chest.

"Come down," the voice booms again and I close my eyes. I don't want to see the thing that can make its voice fill the skies.

"Livy!" Jenna screams. Her arms are reaching for me as she falls. She is so terrified I forget to fear anything at all.

"Meyer! Let me go! I just need to get to her. Please!"

He still has hold of my hand. For a moment I don't think he's going to let go. I glance back, catching his indecision, and then he lets us drop.

Our fall is slow and heavy. The closer we get to the ground the tighter his grip on my hand feels. We land near the field of gold, where I first entered Neverland. We are far away from the Treasure Islands, as far as you can get without actually leaving this place, and yet once we've landed the children begin to join us. They drop to the ground with hesitance. They've braved the wind for us, leaving behind the safety of the islands, and I'm not sure how I feel about that.

"What is it?" Jane asks, landing just opposite me. She's holding onto Jenna but once she sees me, she lets go.

Jenna runs straight at me, crying out my name. "I don't understand! Nothing like this has ever happened before!"

I hate those words. They make me feel responsible. Did I bring something with me? Did I drag along some unseen darkness?

I take her in my arms wanting to protect her, but I'm still unsure what I need to protect her from. The air seems to crack, splintering upon my skin. It should feel painful, this electricity, but instead it makes me more alert. More on guard.

And all at once he's here, the one responsible for this nightmarish energy. He walks toward us through the tall grass. With his long black coat and his black hair, he is the darkest thing here. The colors react around him, straining against his mood. The trees, flowers and grass shrink away from him, and then bounce back once he's passed.

"James," Jenna whispers, coming out from behind my back. "What are you doing here?" She wipes at her cheeks, her smile a bit wobbly. But she is no longer afraid.

"James?" I stare at the man in front of me with disbelief. He's the monster? He's the reason Meyer was running away? Why is he here? And how did Jenna recognize my substitute tutor?

Meyer won't look at me. He's locked on to our newest arrival. His jaw is tense, his hands in fists at his sides. He is nearly trembling with fury.

The children rise from their fearful crouch. Their backs straightening as they resist the tension in the air. They're not afraid of him, just a little unsure.

James comes to a stop a few feet away, and when he opens his arms some children run to him, hugging him close. They reach up, touching his face. To them he is a friend it seems. Someone they haven't seen in a while.

"You don't belong here," Meyer says, his voice stern. "You should go."

"I'm afraid you've mistaken me for someone who takes orders," James drawls, while his eyes strike against Meyer.

"Well, hello there, Livy," he says once he notices me. His smile is soft upon me, but there's still an edge to his expression. "So this is where you've been hiding."

I stare back at James, not quite sure of his place in all this. That foreboding feeling swells around him, but that shouldn't come as a surprise. It's how I usually feel around James.

"Livy?" Jenna says, turning her concerned expression on me. "You know him?" That flash of panic is back, and then her bottom lip begins to tremble. "How do you know him?"

"He's my tutor," I tell her, feeling like the only one not in on the secret. "I don't understand."

"Yes," James says. "And as your tutor, it's my responsibility to let you know you've broken the rules. I'm here to take you back." He's smiling now, his regular charming self. But I don't trust him.

I guess all that darkness and wind was just for dramatic effect because the sky is lightening up — the blue more prevalent than the black — although there is still tension in the air. That has yet to clear.

"No!" Jenna cries.

"She's not leaving," says Meyer.

"We don't want Livy to leave!" The children join in. "Can't she visit a little longer?"

James is just about to answer when one little boy says, "Can *I* have a visitor? Can my sister visit?"

"And my sister?"

"My brother would come, I'm sure of it!"

"I want my mom to visit! I miss her! And my dad!"

One by one, they start crying. Their sadness spills over the meadow as the sky begins to darken once again.

"I think I'd rather just go back," a little girl says, moving up close to me. "Do you think you could take me with you when you go?"

"I'm…" I look to Meyer for help and the wave of sadness coming off him nearly crushes me.

"Enough!" James yells, and the children all stop at once. They cower away from him. Some rush to hide behind Meyer or Jane.

James clears his throat and starts again. "Listen to me. There are no visitors in Neverland." He glares at Meyer, his message loud and clear. "Livy has to go."

"But she just got here!" Jenna stands in front of me, my own little guardian angel. She reaches for James' hand, squeezing it tight. "Please don't take her from me. She's my sister."

"You know the rules, Jenna." His gaze is soft upon her. It nearly kills me. "She doesn't belong here. You know this." He kneels down in front of her and touches her face. It's everything I can do to keep from slapping his hand away. I don't like him touching her. Not at all.

"Would you want this for her?" he goes on. "Would you want Livy to miss out unnecessarily? She has more life left back home. She doesn't belong here." He glances up and his next words pin me to my spot. "She's too old for this place."

Too old? I look around at the children and then down into my own sister's face. There is youthfulness here, that's for sure, but more importantly there is innocence. The innocence that comes with hope. These children all lost something to get here. They lost their futures. Every last one. "I don't understand," I say. "Any of this." My throat is tight. I'm so overwhelmed by everything that has happened I'm not sure whether to cry or scream. "So you two know each other?" I look to Meyer for answers but he's too busy glaring at James to notice.

James stands up, towering over us all. "I'm sure he hasn't bothered to explain any of it, have you, Meyer?"

"We've been busy," he says through gritted teeth. "I was going to—"

"Were you?" James smirks. "Which part, I wonder. Were you going to explain how Livy's parents are, at this very moment, holding her hands, and begging her to hang on? Or how her little friend, Jilly, is undergoing surgery? She's been crying for days, worrying about Livy and how she won't wake up."

"Jilly?" Jenna chokes out. She reaches for me, gripping me tightly. "Livy, what's happened to Jilly?" Her bottom lip begins to tremble and then she's crying into my side.

"Is she okay?" I ask James. "Is she well enough for surgery?" I don't question how he would know this or how he's come to relay these messages to me. I just need to know that Jilly is going to be alright.

"You're dying, Livy." James' eyes flash at me. "Don't you think you should be more concerned about *your* wellbeing right now."

"I'm…what?"

Jenna's soft weeping comes to a sudden stop. She looks up at me, her eyes wet and frozen with fear. Her every emotion so clear in front of me, I can almost breathe it in.

"You're in a coma," James continues. "You had a reaction to the anesthesia they used during your surgery. Your body tried to reject it. You had a seizure. You've slipped into a coma."

"So I'm asleep then?" Neverland begins to fade, the bright colors begin to dull and appear hazy. "So I *am* dreaming."

"You're not dreaming!" Meyer shouts. "This is not a dream. None of this is!" He closes the distance between us in a few steps, and grabs hold of my shoulders. "How can you still believe that's even a possibility, after everything you've seen and felt?" His eyes search mine. They are desperate, and wild. I can almost see the words he's not saying. It's like he's begging me to stay here. He wants me to stay. But he won't say it. At least, not in front of James.

"That's true," James chimes in, glaring at him. "But you're not supposed to be here." He lowers his voice so that only Meyer and I can hear. "She's not yours to keep."

"If I'm not dreaming, but I'm asleep…" I shake my head and take a step back. Meyer's hands drop from my shoulders, but the look in his eyes tells me he hasn't quite let go. Not yet.

"You can't exist in both worlds," James tells me. "If you choose to stay then you can never return to the life you knew." He pauses a moment. "Or you can choose to go back."

Back? Back to what? The way it was before? Life without Jenna? Where I roamed my quiet little world alone and sad. Back to how it was before? Before Meyer?

"What if I don't want to go?" I whisper. "What if I want to stay?"

Jenna tightens her hold around me. "Is that really what you want, Livy? Do you want to stay?"

Yes! Maybe? I don't know!

The tears are sliding down my face, but I can't stop them. Nor can I stop these thoughts from racing through my mind. What if I *do* want to stay? Is that so horrible? Would I be an awful person for abandoning my family and my friends? Especially when I know exactly what they'll feel once I'm gone. How terrible of me to do that to them, right? Especially to my parents. How could they handle losing *both* of their children?

I start to shake. It's like my body is shutting down. Am I really thinking about this? Strangely it was better when I thought I might be dead. I mean, sure, I didn't allow myself to think about it, but it was there. All the time. But now… knowing the choice is mine, knowing I can go back…

It should change things. It should change how I'm feeling. And even with all of this racing through my mind I don't think I can leave this place. Not yet. I'm not ready.

"If you want to stay, you stay." Meyer crosses his arms in front of his chest as though it's that easy. There's a look of superiority about him now.

"Oh come on." James rolls his eyes. "You don't have that kind of authority. In fact after this stunt you may have finally crossed that ever-moving line of yours."

The children gasp as they turn back to Meyer. They've been following our exchange rather closely. They're not quite sure what's happening, but I'm sure they've grasped that something *is* happening. Something big.

"What do you mean?" Jane asks. She's been silent up to this point, watching James as though at any moment she might need to take off running. "You can't mean—"

"That he's finished? That he might no longer reside over Neverland? I most certainly do mean that. You've been breaking rules long enough, Meyer. Sooner or later you're going to be replaced."

"There is no replacing me," he scoffs. "I've been here longer than the stories have been told. For centuries."

"Numbers mean nothing, neither does time, in the grand scheme of things." James shrugs his shoulders as if it's all so insignificant. As if we all are. "We can always find another guardian."

"But not now," Meyer says evenly.

"Not *yet*," James answers, with a cross of his own arms.

"Well then." Meyer strolls over to me, looking quite pleased with himself. "Now that everything is decided, let's be off. We have a lot to do today."

"She's coming with me," James says, stepping in front of him.

"You heard her. She doesn't want to go." Meyer takes an aggressive stance, bringing them face-to-face. They are nearly the same height, I notice. Although, Meyer does appear taller, glowering in the face of James.

Everything falls silent in Neverland, even the grass stops swaying. Meyer turns and smiles back at me, his eyes almost pleading. "Do you, Livy?"

"I... I." I don't know what I want. I know I don't want to leave Jenna. I can't even bare the thought. But in all the time I've been here, I haven't worried or even thought about Jilly or my family, not until now.

"Who are you?" I say, staring up at James. "Why did you come to my house and pretend to be my tutor? What was that all about?"

"He's death," Meyer says, just like that.

"Death?" That tightness moves back into my chest. I feel like I'm suffocating.

"Stop calling me Death," James growls, pushing away from him. "It's not true, first of all. And it frightens the children."

I look around and find he's right. They do look frightened. Like they've finally figured it out. James is the one who brought them here. I let out a gasp that startles Jenna. Her fingers dig into my skin when her grip on my waist tightens.

"So that night in Sammy's room…?" I turn, searching the crowd of faces. Is Sammy here? Did James take him away from his family?

"He's alright," James says, reading my thoughts. "For now."

"For now? For now?" My voice is high-pitched and slightly crazed, but I can't help it. "So that's what you do? You go around collecting kids? You're the thing they fear at night?"

"It's not like I'm some kind of grim reaper." James brushes his hands down the length of his coat. "You two are making me out to be the bad guy. And I'm not the bad guy. Like Meyer, I'm simply the messenger."

"The messenger of death." Meyer shoves his hands in his front pockets as if he's bored with this conversation, but I doubt that's the case. If anything he's nervous. We're getting closer to the truth now. And for some reason Meyer hates the truth as much as he hates James. Which is a lot, apparently.

"So then…" I turn to Meyer and that snide smirk he's wearing falls off. "What does that make you?"

"He's the guardian of Neverland," Echo tells me. "The guardian of lost souls."

"Lost souls," I repeat. "So… You're not there when… You don't come for them when…" Jeez, Livy! Just say the words, already! I take a deep breath and try again. "When they die?"

"No." Meyer points his finger at James. "That's his job. I'm not even supposed to leave this place."

"Funny thing," James drawls. "That's never stopped you before. Listen, Livy." He moves toward me and I stand my ground. "You should know your friend Sheila has been by. She visits you every day. And so do the children in the hospital."

Every day? How long have I been gone?

"Only a few are allowed to come," he continues. "Not Jilly, of course. She's still too weak. We won't know for a few days how she's recuperating, that is *if* her surgery works out." James has moved to

257

stand at my side now. With Meyer on the other and Jenna in between, that suffocating feeling reaches up and takes hold of my throat.

"So they did the surgery," I manage to get out. "Did they get my bone marrow?"

"They got enough."

"And Jilly gets her surgery?" A wave of guilt rushes over me. I should be there for her. She's probably so scared.

"It's going on now." James drops his head low, staring at his hands. He is a picture of concern. "She isn't having an easy go of it, but she's hanging in there."

I snap my mouth shut, wanting to ask more questions, but holding back. I know what he's doing. He wants me to feel them at home. He wants me to feel something other than what I feel here.

"Livy?" Jenna's eyes are searching mine and I wonder what she sees. Does she read my hesitance? My fear? Does she know how much I want to stay with her even though the thought of everyone mourning me back home nearly destroys me?

"You have until dawn to make your decision," James tells me. He rests his hand against my face. His touch is warm, far warmer than I expected. "Dawn and no longer, Livy. Don't doubt me on that."

"Dramatic much?" I squeak out. My chest is so tight, I can't breathe.

"Well I could just force you to make your decision now." He raises an eyebrow at me, those clear gray eyes of his breaking through my hesitation. "If ever there was a time to make a selfish decision, now's the time, Livy. No one expects you to play the martyr here. Least of all me."

"I'm not…" I shake off his intensity and glare back. "I'm no martyr."

"Then choose to live," he whispers, brushing his hand along the side of my face. "Choose to continue on."

The clouds gather up around us and then break away, displaying the most amazing rainbow I've ever seen.

"I love the theatrics here," he tells me, laying it on thick with his most charismatic grin. And then he's gone. No warning. No wave goodbye. Just, poof! No more James.

"It's about time," Echo says. "That guy gives me the creeps."

"That's an understatement," Meyer mutters.

"He only triggers a memory," Jane says, still staring at the spot where James just was. "He makes me think of home."

CHAPTER TWENTY-SIX

The sky is turning orange now, the color of afternoon. The trees and leaves take on a fall-like glow and I realize how each day on Neverland leads you through the change of seasons. Morning is spring; noon becomes summer; and afternoon is obviously fall. All that's left to discover today is nighttime, which will surely look like winter.

Meyer stretches his arms up like he's rising from a catnap, not an altercation with the angel of death. I wish I could do the same, but I'm too tense to stretch. Too confused to simply move on.

The children begin to take to the sky. Now that the drama has passed they're anxious to get back to playing.

Jenna has hold of my hand still, but her grip is easing. When Jane catches her eye she moves away from me. With James gone she must feel the threat has passed. She doesn't appear overly concerned about the decision I have to make. She must think I've already made it. Strange thing is, I think I have. I don't want to leave her here, not when I've only just found her. And I don't want to leave these children either. Or Neverland. Or Meyer.

I don't want to go back.

I make my way over to Meyer and he holds his stance as though he knew this moment was coming.

"I deserve an explanation."

"Yes," he says. We stare at each other a moment longer and then he rubs the back of his neck. "I told you I would explain."

"So…" I say, when he still doesn't speak. "I'm not supposed to be here, huh?"

His lashes lower, hiding his every emotion from me. "It's not like I had it planned. It was a surprise to me too, you know."

"No. I don't know."

He glances up and then looks away. "I didn't plan this, Livy. I couldn't just leave you there. I couldn't…" He stops. His lips flatten out into a hard line, a sign he has nothing more to say about that.

"And you and James? I take it you *do* know each other?"

Meyer's lips twitch. "Yeah, about that."

"I'm listening."

"He and I don't exactly see things the same way."

"No?"

Meyer's eyes narrow. "No."

"Is he really a tutor? I mean, I know he's isn't *just* a tutor, but why did he pretend to be?"

"I guess he was keeping an eye on me."

"On you," I say. "Not me, but you."

"Mostly me," he answers, looking away. He shifts a bit under my stare and then faces me directly. "I've never really taken such an interest in someone from your world before. I guess he wanted to keep tabs on the situation."

"The situation?" I whisper.

"Yes," he says softly.

"So… I'm the *situation*?"

"Yes," he says with a smile.

And just like that I'm blushing.

"So then," I begin, clearing my throat. "What makes you different from James?"

"I'm *very* different from him." He folds his arms, one eyebrow raised.

I hesitate a moment. "I don't understand any of this." I gesture around me and then let my hand drop back to my side. "Are you … What are you?"

"I'm just like you, Livy." Meyer throws his hands up in the air. "How can you ask that?"

But he most certainly is not. Isn't that obvious by now? I can't move between worlds. I can't fly.

"No you're not. How could you be?" I reach out, holding my hand just shy of his chest. "How is it I could feel you, you know… before. When you're not…" I trail off while my hand continues to linger.

"I *am* real." Meyer takes my hand and presses it against his chest to show me the truth behind his words, but I'm pretty sure neither of us anticipates the heat that immediately rips through us. Meyer's grip on my hand tightens and I feel that familiar stirring in my chest.

"And James?" I whisper, forcing my breathing to slow down. "How can the two of you move back and forth between this place and mine?"

Meyer flinches at the word mine, but it's the truth. It's the only place I can call home.

"We are different from the rest of them. They had their chance at life."

"And you didn't?"

Meyer simply shakes his head.

"Does that mean you aren't dead like the rest of them? Like…" *Jenna.*

"It's always been this way," Meyer explains. "I never chose this life. It just is. Just like you never chose to be you and Jane never chose to be Jane." He shrugs as though there's my answer. But it's not enough. I'm slowly working out this new information in my head. I like that he's not dead. A lot. But it still doesn't make sense.

"I'm the guardian of Neverland," he continues. "I'm here to keep them safe. To make them happy once they've lost everything." His eyes flitter over the sky and then fall upon me.

"James is right," he says begrudgingly. "I'm not supposed to leave here. I'm not supposed to move between the worlds the way I do."

"You weren't supposed to meet me," I whisper.

Meyer doesn't answer my question. For once he doesn't have to. It's clear what he's done.

Leaving Neverland was an adventure, while bringing me here was a risk.

The afternoon sun is warm and heavy on my back. And Meyer's green eyes fill me with a whole different kind of warmth. The intensity behind his gaze holds me in place even though we're no longer touching.

"Thank you," I whisper. "Thank you for bringing me to Jenna."

Meyer nods his head but stays silent.

"You broke the rules." I force out a laugh. "I mean, obviously."

He doesn't even crack a smile.

"Why did you do it?"

The silence stretches on a bit long — to the point that I feel awkward — and then just when I think he isn't going to answer, he whispers, "Are you going to stay?" I can see how much this question cost him. His gaze is hooded in vulnerability.

I close my eyes, desperate to give in to this heaviness between us. It would be so easy just to give in. That string between us is back, pulling at me, pulling at him, threading us together.

"Meyer," I sigh, with my eyes still closed. I don't need to see him to know that he's here. He surrounds me.

"Stay," he whispers, and I feel that word like a shudder.

"So, um. Sorry to interrupt," says a voice.

Meyer and I immediately break apart and my eyes snap open.

"I'm sorry," Jane says, but she's smiling. She doesn't look sorry. She looks a bit embarrassed, but not sorry.

"You're needed in the field," she tells Meyer.

"Right," he says, still looking at me.

"So, like, probably, right now," she continues.

Meyer doesn't react for a moment, just continues to study me, and then he gives me one of his heartbreaking smiles before jogging off.

"Jeremy was asking for him," Jane explains once he's gone.

"Of course."

"He's having a bit of trouble adjusting."

"Right." Aren't we all?

"Jenna's with him," Jane explains and I'm immediately horrified. For a second there I'd completely forgotten about Jenna. "Don't worry," she says, picking up on my panic. "She's okay. She helps out a lot. Especially with the newbies."

"That's great." I nod my head as though it doesn't hurt me to hear this. I should be happy for her. I should be grateful. I shouldn't have a sick feeling in the pit of my stomach.

Jenna has moved on.

Something heavy tugs at my chest. Something deep and empty. I feel a pull, almost like I'm being led backwards, and I stumble a few steps before I catch my footing.

"You alright?" Jane asks, her eyes narrowing upon my face.

"I'm fine," I tell her, but she doesn't look away.

When it happens again, this time I lock my knees up, and hold my feet in place. A wave of longing rushes over me, filled with images of my parents. My mom is smiling at me, she seems so far away. I can just make out her voice; it sounds like she's singing, but that can't be right. She doesn't sing. At least I don't remember her ever singing before. Then she fades out and my father appears. He is holding onto my hands as we slide along the ice. He's smiling, his nose red from the cold. I feel a tug on my hands and then he falls out of sight when he slips and goes down on the ice. He's laughing so hard, he makes me laugh and soon we're both on the ice. I remember this day. I remember it so vividly. It was my first time ice skating, and his as well, I believe.

Suddenly Jane is in front of me, her concerned expression snapping me out of my memory.

"You felt it, didn't you?" she asks me. "You felt them calling you back."

"What?" I place my hand over my heart, feeling it race inside my chest. "You scared me. I must have been stuck there for a moment."

"You weren't stuck. You were having a memory."

"How—"

"That's how it works whenever you're called back. Was it someone you care about? Was it your parents or your friends?"

"My parents," I say in a whisper, still not understanding how she could know any of this, and really not wanting to talk about it. At all. I glance over at Jenna and watch as she laughs with Jeremy. She doesn't even notice us and I'm grateful for that. I don't want her to know what I'm feeling.

"I used to get them," Jane tells me. "It's like something's pulling at you, right? Like they have a rope tied around your waist and they're tugging you backwards?"

When I don't answer she moves closer and her voice drops a little.

"For me it was my nana. She was the only one who took care of me. My parents weren't into the whole parenting thing. So I moved in with her. She was sick, but she still took care of me. She used to make this cinnamon bread on my birthday. When I first got here I could smell it everywhere I went. It was like she was trying to lure me back with the scent."

I stare down at Jane in horror and she just shrugs her shoulders, perhaps shrugging off the memory, but the effect of it is still clear in her eyes.

"I used to think maybe she was making it and bringing it to the hospital with her, that's why I could smell it. But then it stopped one day. Just went away. It was there one moment, like I was breathing it in everywhere I went, and the next it was gone."

"What happened to you?" I ask, barely getting the words out. I keep forgetting how every last one of these children has a reason for being here. And while those reasons aren't happy in the slightest, I get the feeling Jane's is worse by far.

"I don't know, exactly." Jane stares off at something in the meadow, but her eyes are glazed over, unfocused. "I don't remember all of it. I know that I was walking home from my friend's house. I know that it was close to dinnertime and that my nana had called to tell me to come home. I remember I had run most of the way, but then I got tired and I slowed down." Her breathing sounds heavy, like she's living the memory. Or perhaps, reenacting it.

"Jane, don't." I feel as out of breath as she sounds. All at once I'm afraid to hear the end of this story. "You don't have to tell me—"

"It's okay," she says, her voice shaky. "It helps to talk about it. At least, that's what James says. Nothing can harm me now. Not here. Not in Neverland." She wraps her arms around herself. For this part of the story she needs protection. I inch closer, afraid to startle her, but she doesn't notice me. She's lost in her memory.

"He looked familiar. That's why I went to him." Her eyes take on a distant look and I want to drag her back from where she is. I want to make it so that she never has to visit that place again.

"I don't remember what happened after that. I know I was in the hospital for a while. I know I held on longer than they expected. And then James showed up and told me everything was better now and that I would be safe. Forever. I just had to let go." She turns back to me, and her hands drop down to her sides. The worst of it is over.

I release a breath, wishing I could just scream. It's not fair, this place. None of these children's stories are fair. I turn back to the meadow, watching as Jeremy and Jenna sit close. Jenna's hand is resting on Jeremy's shoulder. She is comforting him.

Sure this place is beautiful and peaceful, chockfull of everything they could possibly imagine, but all that overcompensation is not quite enough to make up for the loss—at least not all of the time. It's not home. How can they not feel lost without their parents and friends? Or their sisters and brothers and everything that made them feel safe and loved before this? Why do they have to be here? Why couldn't they have more time?

"It's okay if you want to go back, Livy. I would go if I could." Jane snaps me back from my brewing anger.

"I'm so sorry, Jane," I say, not knowing what else to say or do. I want to hug her, desperately. I want to tell her that never should have happened to her and how it's not how a childhood should end. But mostly I just wish she'd made it back to her nana's house.

"Not everything is great where we came from," she tells me. "I'm sure you know that already." She's still staring out over the tall grass, and in this heavy afternoon light, with that lost look upon her face, she looks more like a child than I've ever seen her look. "I just miss everything else, you know."

We are silent for a moment. I have so much to say, but nothing feels right. I miss everything else too. I miss my parents. I miss Sheila. It feels wrong that I've been brought to this place, that I've been given a glimpse into where my sister is and what it feels like to be near her again when I know that I don't belong here. I get it. I'm too old. I'm not a child anymore. There must be a different place for people like me. Not this place of wonder, perhaps a more grownup Neverland, but just as safe.

What I hate is that I have to choose. It would be so much easier if I were like Jane, and I didn't have to make a decision. To know there's no going back and to make the best of it. But then again easy isn't what Jane's feeling now. If what she's telling me is right and my family is calling me back, I have a choice, and Jane never did. I can't even imagine how it must have been for Jane to feel her nana so close, and yet never be able to reach back to her.

"It might go away if you decide to stay," she tells me. "You might stop feeling that pull, or you might not. It's hard to know for sure. I've heard it goes away completely once you move on and accept it. But since I'm still here I can't actually tell you if that's true."

"Move on? What do you mean, move on?"

"This is only meant to be a temporary stop." Jane glances over at Jenna. "We get to decide how long we stay, but we're all supposed to move on eventually."

"I don't understand," I say, feeling a bit panicky all at once. "Where do you go from here?"

"I don't know," Jane says. "Someplace else, someplace different. No one talks about it, really. Not James. Not Meyer. I don't know how much Meyer actually knows about it, since he's really only in charge of Neverland. I get the feeling James knows, but he won't tell us. He says it's not something we should worry about until we're ready."

"Ready? Ready for what?"

"To move on," Jane says, even though those words still mean nothing to me.

"But what does that mean?" I say with frustration. "What does *move on* actually mean?" This is all too much. Here I was just beginning to wrap my head around Neverland, knowing it was a safe place. That Jenna would be here, even if I weren't. But now I come to find out that she could disappear from here too?

"Where else is there to go?" I ask Jane, desperate for any insight.

"I don't know! How would I know? I haven't done it before."

"Well, what do you think it means then?"

Jane's expression tightens as though she has an idea but she's not sure she wants to share it with me. But then she does. And it hurts my heart to hear.

"I think it means to grow up."

CHAPTER TWENTY-SEVEN

Grow up.

Those two little words add to my heaviness. They settle on my chest and nearly choke me. I remember the night I said them to Meyer, how angry I was, but mostly afraid I'd lost my best friend.

Grow up. The way Jane says it makes it seem like such a horrible thing but maybe the horrible part of it is that they'd be doing the growing here and not with the ones who deserve to see it happen. Like their family. Like me. Maybe that's why her words make me feel like this, like all the hope I had is gone. Neverland may seem like a beautiful place with its unlimited supply of wishes, but are wishes enough when you can't share them with the ones you love?

I stare across the field at Jenna, watching as she laughs at something Jeremy is telling her. And then it hits me. Jenna's going to move on from here. She's going to leave. Again.

That pull I felt before nearly knocks me back a few steps and Jane grabs hold of my arm, steadying me.

"Are you alright?" she asks me. But it's not Jane's face that swims before me, it's my mother's.

"I promise," she tells me. "I promise if you wake up, Livy, I'll be a better mom. I'll be fun again and I won't leave you alone as much. I promise, Livy. I promise you. We can go to that store you like and we'll take a trip. Just you and me."

"Livy?" Jane says to me.

"Livy. Please wake up!"

"Livy, are you alright?" Jane has hold of my shoulders. She shakes me a bit and I take a breath, just now realizing I've been holding it.

"No. I don't think so." The second the words leave my mouth Meyer looks up and the smile on his face drops off completely.

My feet begin to move, slowly at first until my momentum increases and I'm nearly charging toward Meyer. I can feel the anger rising to the surface. I am my own little black cloud. I stop directly in front of Meyer and he takes a deep breath, but he doesn't say anything.

"I have a wish," I tell him.

Jenna and Jeremy look up, drawn by my voice. Jenna smiles at me, climbing to her feet, but then something in my expression must worry her because she freezes and doesn't come any closer.

"I can wish for anything, right? That's what you do here?"

Meyer's mouth tightens and he nods his head. The look in his eyes is as dark as my mood.

"Well then," I cross my arms against my chest. "I want Jenna to come with me. That's my wish. I want to hold her hand when James comes for me tomorrow and I want her to go with me."

"Livy—"

"No. Don't say it." I look to Jane to help me out but she's back to gazing off over the meadow as though we aren't having one of the most intense conversations of my life. "I can wish for anything here, right? And it's your job to get it for me. Well, that's what I want, Meyer. I want my sister. And I want the two of us to leave together."

271

"There are rules—"

"Rules for wishing?" I cut him off. "Now that doesn't seem fair, and everything is fair in Neverland, right?"

Meyer nods his head, and looks down. His hair has fallen across his forehead, blocking his eyes — and his true feelings — from sight.

"I don't want anything else," I say, holding back my tears. "Nothing at all. I never have."

"You have to know, Livy. I would do it, I would give you anything, if I could." He's still staring down at the ground, doing everything he can to avoid looking at me.

"Well, that's what I want." That panicky feeling rises up, making it difficult to speak. "I want her," I choke out. "She's mine, Meyer. She doesn't belong here."

Meyer's eyes snap up at this, piercing through me with a vibrant mix of anger and sorrow. "And why not?" He grips my arm, pulling me up close so that our faces are mere inches apart. "At least she's happy here. These children, they have everything they need. Everything they can imagine."

"Not everything," I whisper. "She doesn't have me."

Meyer stares at me for a minute, his eyes searching mine. "Well that's your choice, now isn't it?" His hand drops from my arm, nearly pushing me away.

"You could make a memory." Jenna stands apart from us, but nevertheless she's still following the conversation. "Something you could leave here, you know that would remind me of you when—"

"No, Jenna," I choke out, running to her. "No more wishes! Why can't you just come with me?" I turn to Meyer, pleading to him with everything I have. "He could make it happen, I know it! He just has to try!"

"No he can't," Jenna says, staring up at me with wide eyes. "That's not how it works!"

"But how do you know? Maybe he's never tried it before! Maybe if he talks to James, I could get a little more time or maybe Jenna could...?" I can hear the desperation in my voice. I can see it reflected in the other children's eyes around me. But I can't stop it. I can't stop wishing.

"Livy," Jenna says, shaking her head. "Don't." Her little chin starts to tremble and then just like that she lifts it defiantly. I am in awe of her strength. I am humbled by it.

"So, you've made your decision then, have you?" Meyer's arms are crossed, his expression drawn and angry. "You'll be leaving in the morning?"

"I didn't say that!" I wrap my arms around my waist, nearly folding in on myself. "I just..." I shake my head, feeling my last ounce of hope slip away.

"Never forever," Meyer says with a touch of sorrow. "Everybody leaves sooner or later."

I lift my head at this, sensing there's more to his statement than what he's willing to share.

"It's the way of Neverland," he tells me, his words so quick, so flippant. "Everybody eventually moves on."

I stare at him, strangely drawn to this vulnerable side of Meyer.

"See, Livy," he says, lifting an eyebrow at my reaction. "We're really not that different. Shocking, isn't it?" He rubs the back of his neck and stares off over the meadow. "The thing is, they *choose* to leave me." He gestures around us, "With all of this, they choose to move on."

Meyer takes to the sky leaving us all staring after him.

"You can't take me with you," Jenna says, clutching my hand. "You need to understand that."

"I do," I tell her, wrapping her in a tight hug, even though I don't really. After all that I've experienced in the last few weeks it shouldn't seem that far-fetched, should it?

"Well that was interesting," Jane says, startling me. I'd forgotten she was still here.

"I'm sorry," I whisper to Jenna. "I didn't mean for that to upset you."

"It didn't upset me, Livy," she says, but I know that's not true. I can see it in her eyes.

"If anyone's upset, it's Meyer," she explains.

"He's just mad at me," I tell her, gesturing at the empty sky.

"I wouldn't say mad exactly," Jenna says. "He didn't seem mad, just…"

"Afraid," Jane pipes up. "He seemed afraid."

I turn to Jane. "Why would he be afraid?"

She is staring off at the place where Meyer was a moment before. For a moment I wonder if she even heard me.

"Jane?"

"He's not like us," she says, gesturing to herself and Jenna. "He has a choice."

"What choice?"

"Whether or not to live."

When we realize Meyer isn't coming back for us, Jenna and I decide to move on to her island. She shows me her room with more closets than any young girl could need, each filled to the brim with dancing clothes. And each dress a different shade of pink or purple. I smile at her and touch her hair, reminding myself that she's real, but I find it's difficult to concentrate. I keep wondering where Meyer is, and why he ran away so quickly. There's a strange feeling in my stomach, as though the emptiness I usually carry around has expanded. Being with Jenna should ease that emptiness, but for some reason I feel worse. I keep biting my nails — which I never do — and I feel like I'm crawling out of my skin.

Jenna takes my hand as she leads me to Alice's island and then points out the differences between Alice's version of *The Twelve Dancing Princesses* and hers.

"Alice thought the trees should be covered in gemstones," she explains, whereas Jenna held true to the original story version.

I sit on the sand near the shore, pulling her down next to me. Staring into Jenna's bright blue eyes is the only time I feel peace. She is my own little form of meditation.

"Jilly still asks me to read her that story," I say, and once I speak Jilly's name I instantly feel a pang of guilt. She must be so frightened not knowing what's happened to me, especially with so much else to worry about.

"It's not her favorite, you know," Jenna tells me as we sit with our feet in the water. She keeps lining up rocks, watching as her little wall gets knocked down each time the water laps the shore. "She only picks it because she thinks it's your favorite. Her favorite is *Rapunzel*."

"She has me read it because it's your favorite," I say, knocking shoulders, and she knocks right back, nearly pushing me to the sand.

"It's really not, though," Jenna says, turning back to her rocks. "It really just reminds me of you."

When I fall silent, she looks up at me and the wisdom in her eyes is startling. She's no longer my little sister, she's moved beyond that.

"It's okay if you want to go back, Livy. Believe me when I say, I think you should."

There are no words for me in this moment. Jenna has always been wise beyond her years, I guess childhood leukemia will do that to you. But this is too much for me now. To have my sister encourage me to choose life, when she was never given the choice.

"I haven't decided," I tell her drawing my finger in the sand. "I really wish I had more time."

"I don't know how long I'll be here, you know," she says when I don't continue. "They talk about moving on and I think that I might like that."

"Moving on?" These words continue to generate panic. "What do you know of moving on, Jenna? What have they told you?"

"Not a lot. Mostly they don't talk about it. But there was this girl when I first got here. You would have liked her, Livy. She was a lot of fun, used to dance with us, and come to our tea parties." Jenna watches as the tide washes away her rock wall. This time when the tide moves out she doesn't attempt to rebuild it.

"She told me she was ready and then the next day she was gone."

I look off toward the water, avoiding Jenna's eyes. I don't want her to see how upsetting this is to me. I don't know how to explain that if I leave Neverland it would be incredibly helpful knowing she was here. Forever. How knowing she was here — visualizing her here — would make it easier for me to go back. It's the not knowing that's terrifying to me.

"I miss her," she tells me. "And I think I'm ready."

"You're ready?" I glance around quickly, wondering if this is the moment I will lose my sister again. Convinced that I can't do it.

"Soon," she tells me, as she gets back to stacking her rocks. "Not yet, but soon."

We stay like this a little bit longer, neither of us talking while our silence holds meaning. I'm not ready to leave my sister yet. I don't think I'll ever be. But it's pretty clear she's trying to get me to let go.

CHAPTER TWENTY-EIGHT

The sun has turned a softer shade of pink. The sky is a grayish-blue when Jenna sits up and asks me if I'd like to speak with the mermaids.

"I write them letters, sometimes. They always respond, especially when I invite them to our parties."

"How do you write them letters?" I ask, completely intrigued. "How do they read them without getting the paper soaking wet?"

Jenna bursts out with laughter. "They aren't on paper, silly!" Her eyes are bright as she giggles. For a second she's my little sister again.

"I write them messages in the foam, see?" She leans over, dragging her finger in the sea foam.

"Dear Mermaids," she spells out. "If you could help me..."

"What are you asking them?" I'm completely caught up in this method of communication, but mostly I want to keep our conversation light. "How about if we ask them to come for a visit?"

"We could do that," Jenna says, turning her back to me so that I can no longer see her words. "There's actually something important I need them to do for me."

"What is it?" I say, wanting to peek over her shoulder but holding back.

"You'll see."

A couple minutes later it isn't the mermaids who arrive, but Meyer. His aura isn't nearly as fierce as the last time I saw him, but there's a wariness still present behind his eyes. I hate that seeing him gives me this heady thrill, that the emptiness I felt before doesn't seem as suffocating. I tell myself I was simply worried about him, nervous that I'd hurt his feelings. But the truth is I like being near him.

"You rang," he drawls, his smile resting upon Jenna, while his eyes avoid me.

"Yes, thank you," she says, giving him a low curtsy.

Meyer lets out a laugh and that wariness slowly fades. He is so relaxed around the children. And so restless with me.

"I have a request," she tells him, reaching for his hand. And he gives it to her, pulling her in to his side as though it's the most natural thing in the world. All at once I feel a spark of jealousy watching them, a flash of pain that he can do this whenever he wants. That he can float back and forth between the real world and Neverland. That he can see Jenna, touch Jenna, whenever he wants. Why can't that be me? If given a choice that is what I'd wish for. I'd want to be Meyer. I want his freedom, his connection to both places. But I'm pretty sure that's not an option for me.

"Whatever my lady wishes," he says, ruffling her hair. "Your wish is mine to give."

I glance up, catching his eyes and he quickly looks away.

"Alright." Jenna shifts her feet in the sand, hesitating a moment and then she pushes her words out with a rush of air. "I want Livy to tell the bedtime story tonight." Her smile is a bit wobbly as though she's afraid she wont get this wish, that something more will be taken from her.

"Bedtime story?" I say, stalling. Meyer is tapping his finger to his lips, pondering his response, and even though I doubt he would begrudge her this, I don't want her to worry unnecessarily. "You have a bedtime here?" It doesn't really make sense to me, seeing as they don't have to eat or drink in Neverland. Why would they need to sleep?

"The children find it comforting to continue the ritual of sleep," he tells me. "And because it never truly gets dark in Neverland they don't fear the night the way they do in your world." His words aren't meant to be hurtful, or maybe they are, it's impossible to tell from his expression. He's so closed off to me, so shuttered. I might as well not be here.

"Meyer is usually the one who tells the story at night," Jenna explains. "If he's gone then Jane or Echo does it." She smiles up at him, tugging on his hand. "Oh, Meyer! I know! Tell her about the man who caught you once. Tell her what happened!"

Meyer smiles, absorbing her excitement, and then he turns to me. I suck in a breath, reacting to his beauty. I would miss that smile if it were to leave me. I would miss all him, really.

"It was nothing," he says with a shrug, but I can see from the gleam in his eyes that this can't be true. "I was visiting a hospital one day, telling this young boy there a story, just like you do, Livy." This last part he says while finally meeting my eyes and I feel those words stir up something inside my chest.

"I didn't notice the man in the doorway," he continues. "He was so quiet, just listening."

"Tell her what story you were telling!" Jenna pipes up, nearly ready to spill it herself.

Meyer laughs. "I'm getting there, I'm getting there." He reaches out and fluffs her hair. She grins up at him with a look of adoration and I can't really blame her. Meyer is quite amazing when he's ablaze like this. It makes it rather difficult to look away.

"I was telling the young boy about Neverland, going into detail about the Treasure Islands and the mermaids, you know, really selling it to him."

"Right," I say, a bit breathless.

"Well the man stopped me mid-story. Had a bunch of questions, you see. I set him straight on a few things, gave him the name of the place." Meyer smiles, looking quite pleased with himself. "He asked me if I would mind if he shared it a bit, perhaps change a few things so as to hold true to the mystery. He told me I resembled a young chap he knew." Meyer laughs over this. "I love the word chap. Used it a few times myself."

"Tell her the rest, Meyer!" Jenna says, jumping up and down.

Meyer looks at me, his smile charmingly lopsided.

"Well? What is it?" I ask, smiling back.

"He told me the chap's name was Peter."

I stare at him, waiting for more, and then it hits me. "You're kidding me," I say with a laugh. "This is a joke, right?"

"No, Livy! It's true! Tell her, Meyer!"

Meyer gives me his most mischievous smile. "I told you. There's an element of truth in every story."

"Huh," I say, lost in thought. I can see it in my head: Meyer in a hospital somewhere, telling stories. I wonder if it really is the truth. But why would he make it up? It's a fun story, nonetheless.

"I think it's a perfect idea, Jenna. Having Livy tell the story tonight," Meyer says into my silence.

When I glance up at him his eyes soften upon me.

"That is, if Livy is up to it?"

"Livy?" Jenna says, flashing me a hopeful look. She places her hand on my arm and I look down at it, noticing how it's still small, how *she's* still small, even though it is very clear to me she is no longer a child of six.

"Of course," I tell her. "I'd love to." But I sense there is more to this request; the tightness in my throat is sign enough. She's asked this of him for a reason — one last hurrah for me, I fear. When her eyes flit away, hiding from mine, I know I'm right.

When darkness does fall on Neverland it takes its time and doesn't commit entirely. It's more like dusk that lasts for hours. The sky is a pale blue, the trees and ground are covered with long stretches of faint shadows. It's winter in the late afternoon. It's a soothing palette. With its blue tinged with gray and the wispy stretch of pink atop the mountains, I can see why the children choose to rest at this time. There is no fear to be had in the color of a Neverland evening. Only the promise of countless wishes come morning.

We are all gathered on Sunset Hill again. The children are nestled together near the bottom of the hill while I'm at the top. Jenna is with me, taking her usual place at my side when story time draws near. Alice sits right next to her.

Down in the crowd Jeremy is sitting next to Echo while Jane is fully immersed in a conversation with about ten or twelve little girls. She towers over them. From up here she could be their older sister. And even at this distance you can tell how much they adore her.

The noise of the crowd drifts up to me and I wonder how I'll ever be heard, but then Meyer lets out a shrill whistle and the crowd pitters off into silence. He hasn't spoken a word to me since we left Jenna's island. He has kept his distance, which is fine. It's easier to ignore him when he's ignoring me. But it's times like now, when he hangs back, his arms crossed as he leans against a lone tree, that are more difficult. Because I know he's watching me, his eyes narrowed in the twilight. I can feel his curiosity without having to look at him. But even more than that I can feel his intensity. It weaves its way around me, a web of his own making. The part I find most difficult is that I'm not so sure I want to be set free.

"The floor is yours," he tells me when I finally glance his way. His posture is relaxed and casual; his gaze is anything but.

"Well," I say into the hush of the crowd. "Does anyone have any requests?"

The children are silent for a moment and then they begin to shift about with excitement. They lean toward me, their hands popping up into the air, each one wanting my complete attention. I don't know all their names so I just point. Soon the noise in the field is deafening as each child begins to call out their suggestions all at once.

"The Little Mermaid!"

"The Frog Prince!"

"Captain Jack!"

"We heard Captain Jack last night! And I'm tired of stories about pirates!"

"But Captain Jack is my favorite and it's my turn to pick. Echo said so."

"Echo told me it was my turn!" cries another child and Echo shrugs as though he doesn't remember either of these conversations.

"Alright everyone, quiet down." My voice is too soft to be heard, but I can't bring myself to yell over them.

They continue to shout out their requests while Meyer just smirks from his lounge near the tree. There'll be no help from him, I see. Not when he can sit back and watch me struggle.

"Hold up!" I yell, my voice stretching out over theirs. And just like that they stop. It's like I've muted them.

I look to Jenna for backup. I'm not sure why this is so uncomfortable for me. It's not like I've never done this before. I can get a crowd to settle down and I can definitely tell a story, but I'm so terribly nervous all of a sudden I can't even think straight. Could it be the number of children who are listening? Can't say I've ever performed to a crowd of this size before. Or maybe it's that one pair of eyes watching me from the sidelines. Back at the hospital, once I noticed he was listening from the doorway I was always so aware of him I would stumble over my words.

"You should pick your favorite," Jenna tells me, her voice low enough so that only I can hear. "You can't please everybody, you know."

And she's right. I can't please everybody. That's for sure. Truth is, this moment is for Jenna and nobody else. If I'm going to try to please someone, it will be her.

"Alright," I say under my breath. "I can do this."

Jenna smiles at me encouragingly, and Alice reaches over and squeezes my hand. They just want to hear a story tonight. No big deal. It's what every child wants before they slip off to sleep. One last adventure.

I clear my throat and take a deep breath. "Tonight I'll be telling the story of the Twelve Dancing Princesses," I begin, and as if they are one the children all sit back to listen.

"There was a king who had twelve beautiful daughters." The words fall from my lips easy enough. I could tell this story in my sleep.

Jenna slides up closer to me, her excitement a temperature that keeps me warm. She and Alice are spellbound. They're the reason I love to tell stories. It doesn't matter how often they've heard it, or that they already know what will happen next. A story is a story. It takes you away from what you're doing and how you're living right then, and whisks you away into someone else's world.

But now, looking at Jenna, I want more than just a story. I want these children to be the characters, to become a part of this last adventure. I wish it, completely. The energy of this desire moves along my skin and fills my chest. The colors of Neverland start to seem a bit brighter. The children don't notice the change. They're too caught up in my words. When we get to the part where the soldier is about to follow the king's daughters to their dance I pause a moment and ask everyone to close their eyes. Once they've done this —Jenna and Alice included — I glance over at Meyer, needing his help with this next part of the story.

What I see when I look at him flutters my stomach. He's watching me so closely, his eyes dark and intense, tinted with pride and something more. I see it, but mostly I feel it, surging toward me.

"Will you help me?" I whisper, knowing he will hear me. This story won't be the same without a location change, and I know just where we should move it. Hopefully he's on the same page.

When the children open their eyes they're no longer on Sunset Hill awaiting the end of their bedtime story. Rather, we've all arrived in Jenna and Alice's wonderland. The gold-and-silver tipped trees sparkle all around us so the entire island twinkles in the twilight. Each child is dressed as a prince or princess, from the crowns on their heads to the dancing slippers on their feet.

The children gasp in awe and wonder. Their reaction surprises me considering these children are so accustomed to wishes. But I guess it isn't everyday you find yourself completely swept up into a story. This is not the average day in Neverland.

"Thank you, Livy," Jenna whispers, close at my side. "It's like I'm seeing it for the first time again." But with every child present and dressed for a ball she's never seen it look like this before.

"May I have this dance?" Echo says, bowing low at the waist in front of Jenna. He holds out his hand to her and she giggles when she takes it. Her eyes light up under the Neverland sky. She's never looked happier.

"Um… yeah, me too," Jeremy says, shuffling his feet. With Echo's encouragement he bows low to Alice, but it's more of a stumble than a bow. Alice doesn't seem to mind. She clasps his hands, beaming, and just like that we've got ourselves a dance.

The children fill the pavilion and when that fills up, they spill out into the meadow. The music seems like it's coming from everywhere at once. I'm pretty sure the mermaids are the ones supplying it, but I can't figure out how. There are at least a dozen of them lounging along the shore, half in, half out of the water. They appear to be enjoying themselves, even though it seems a shame they can't dance along with us.

"This is quite the bedtime story," Meyer says from behind me. He's hanging back in the shadows, watching like I am, as the children spin and laugh on the dance floor.

"A story is always better when you fully immerse yourself in it."

"I can see that." He takes in my pale silver dress — the dress I always imagined I'd wear each time I told this story. It has blue flowers stitched along the waist and bust line, and it sparkles when I swish the skirt, which I do a few times before I can stop myself. I lift it at my ankles to find my dancing shoes are silver as well. They're so light and comfortable, I barely know I'm wearing them.

When I look up Meyer is beside me. "Well, then, Livy. How about a dance?"

"A dance?" I stare down at his outstretched hand.

Meyer's the only one not dressed for the occasion, and yet he doesn't look out of place. He smiles at me, his face as confident as ever, and something catches deep inside my chest. "I promise I'll be your tallest partner."

I laugh at this and take his hand, allowing myself to be led onto the dance floor.

When the children notice us their eyes light up and they close in around us. Near the edge of the dance floor I catch Jenna watching. She gives me a knowing smile and I roll my eyes, feeling like the younger sister for the first time.

"Alright, the lot of you," Meyer calls out to the children. "Give us some room."

Which of course they do. It's amazing how they listen to him. They giggle and smile, some shoving each other in their haste to get back to what they were doing. But for the most part they move away. Our dancing space isn't large, but it's enough. Once a slow song begins we don't need a lot of room. With Meyer's arms around me I feel no need to move at all.

"It's a great story," Meyer says. "It's always been one of my favorites." One of his hands is at my waist while his other holds my hand out to the side.

I can't decide whether to keep my hand on his shoulder or place it lower on his arm. The shoulder feels more intimate, even though there's still some distance between us, and intimate feels risky tonight. "Let me guess, you've always wished to be a princess?" I tease.

Meyer's laugh is rich and deep. I feel it down to my toes. "I wanted to be the soldier, of course. I wanted to figure out the secret before anyone else and then report them back to the king."

"That sounds about right. All about the adventure."

Meyer laughs and spins me suddenly. My hand slides down his back a bit, holding onto him, but once we stop I quickly move it back to his shoulder. "Would you have married one of the king's daughters?" I ask him, breathless.

"I'm not sure." He takes his hand from my waist and positions my wayward hand against the back of his neck. The movement draws us closer together, dangerously so. When his hand returns to my waist he holds it there for a moment and then slides it to the middle of my back, pulling me closer still. Our noses are nearly touching now. "I've never really been into princesses," he says, and I miss a step.

I look down at my sparkly ball gown and try my best to sound unaffected. "Not into princesses, huh?" But I am affected. His casual attitude bothers me more than I'm willing to admit. I try to pull back a bit — needing some distance between his offhand remark and my hurt feelings — but his fingers dig into my skin holding me in place.

"Yeah," he says, his eyes locked on mine. "I much prefer pirate queens."

Oh.

OH.

"Well… um. Kay." I drop my gaze to his chest. It's safer down here. I just hope he can't see that I'm blushing. When I sneak a peek back up at him he's smiling, laughing at my obvious embarrassment.

I roll my eyes and slap his shoulder, and he quickly recaptures my hand, gripping it tightly in his own.

"I owe you an apology," he says suddenly, and I look up, giving him my complete attention. "I shouldn't have raced off like that. I shouldn't have abandoned you."

"Oh. Well. Thank you." I clear my throat and drop my eyes. I can't hold his gaze long, it's too distracting. "I'm sorry if I upset you."

Meyer shrugs his shoulders and an edge slips into his smile. "This is Neverland," he says. "Can't stay sad for long."

We dance a bit more without talking — either this is the longest song in the history of songs or the songs are moving seamlessly into one another.

"What about you, Livy?" Meyer suddenly asks.

"What *about* me?" I whisper.

"It is my role as the guardian of Neverland to make sure that everyone is happy here." Meyer reaches up to tuck a stray piece of hair behind my ear. "What would make you happy, Livy?"

We're still dancing close — my hand on his neck, his hand on my back — so there's no escape from his question, or this moment.

Stalling, I look around at the children dancing. Another slow song begins and I glance toward the mermaids. They're watching us, their chins resting in their hands, their eyes starry under the twinkling lights.

"Traitorous mermaids," I mumble under my breath.

"What's that?"

"Oh, nothing. I was just…" I look up, meeting his questioning gaze, and then all at once it hits me. This is my last chance. We're drawing painfully close to the end of my bedtime story. Soon morning will come… along with James.

"You know what I want," I tell him and he tilts his head inquisitively. The music keeps playing around us, but it sounds as though it's getting further and further away. "It's the same thing you want. The same thing you're looking for."

"And what is that?"

I take a breath, wishing I were fearless and maybe a little less of a fool. "You want the promise of something real," I whisper. "You want to be so important to someone that they'll want to be with you forever."

Meyer is silent. He doesn't deny it, which is something I guess. His eyes are guarded, his head down.

"You don't have to answer, you know," I tell him challengingly. "I know it's the truth. I know it because I feel it too. Always."

"What does it matter? You're leaving in the morning."

"I haven't made my decision— "

He cuts me off with a harsh laugh. "You will. Nothing lasts forever."

For a moment we just stand there, staring at each other. Neither of us wants to say too much, even though I feel as though I already have. Here I am putting myself out there when I could easily lose everything come morning. That empty feeling sinks down deep into my chest. Somehow it has followed me here.

Meyer goes to leave again but then he turns back. "You should finish your story soon. The children need their rest." His voice is soft, spoken down to the ground.

I nod my head, hating that our dance is over.

"I don't understand how they can sleep here. I'm not even tired." I laugh it off, wishing this moment wasn't so awkward, wishing I knew what was going on inside his head.

"Good." Meyer looks up and, in that moment every emotion he feels is laid out for me. He pulls me close, his eyes holding my gaze. "Neither am I."

CHAPTER TWENTY-NINE

Jenna and Alice sleep together under the stars. Their beds are perched high in the trees so that they can stare out over Neverland until they feel the need to go to sleep. They still wear their ball gowns and cling to their crowns against their chests, looking like two little fairies nestled together in a fairyland. I am the only one of the three of us who doesn't fit in this picture. With my jeans and sweater back on, I've hijacked their fantasy.

"It was a beautiful story," Alice tells me, snuggling close to Jenna. "My favorite part was the dance, of course." She giggles, touching the smooth silk of her pink ball gown. "I hope we can do it again tomorrow."

I smile down at her, holding back my sadness. Tomorrow is a word I'd love to forget. It used to mean more of the same, but now it means the end of everything.

"We will dance again," Jenna tells Alice, holding onto my hand. "If we believe in it, it never ends. Right, Livy?" She holds my gaze, communicating something I can't read. But I nod anyway.

How can I leave her? How is it even possible? When I think about tomorrow I feel as if I'm choking. Like someone has their hands around my throat, squeezing so tight I will suffocate. It isn't fair that James has forced me to make a decision. I shouldn't have to choose.

"Sleep well," I tell them, kissing them both on their soft cheeks. When I hug Jenna close I hold on a bit longer, whispering promises of returning back to her side.

It doesn't take long before they drift off to sleep. All I had to do was whisper "goodnight," and their eyes fluttered shut, their breathing slow and steady. I lay on my back next to Jenna, wishing I could sleep here always, wondering if it's possible to stay. There are moments when the pull from the ones back home is faint — like when I was dancing with Meyer — and it can be ignored. But I worry about the day they'll stop and like Jane I'll realize they've given up on me, believing I've given up on them. There is no easy choice here. Stay or go, I'm sacrificing a crucial part of myself.

The sky is littered with sparkling stars that blur together when my eyes well up. I don't know how long night lasts in Neverland, but I'm sure of one thing: morning will come too soon.

I decide to take a walk and explore Jenna's island on my own. But it isn't long before my steps are matched and Meyer appears. We walk for a while in silence. He's giving me space while staying at my side. And I like that he's here with me. Too much, I think.

He holds the silver and gold-tipped branches up over my head so that I can pass and I thank him, but that's all that is said. Our silence is louder than the soft splash of the tide. It nearly deafens me. But neither of us dares to break it.

When we reach the edge of Jenna's island we stop and stare out over the water. I sense he's battling with something, and I'd love to know what it is, but I'm afraid to ask. I worry that what he has to say will only make my choice that much harder. And yet I still want to hear it.

We stay like this awhile longer — staring out at something, but not really seeing anything too clearly. Then, finally, Meyer turns to me.

"Will you come with me, Livy? There's something I'd like to show you."

I don't give him an answer, I simply take his hand when he offers it. I feel limp, and pliable. My hope is that if I stay like this I can't be broken.

We lift off into the sky, moving slowly. We fly quite a distance before we finally begin to drop toward the ground. Nothing around me looks familiar. This is a part of Neverland I've yet to see. There's a large forest directly below us. Straight ahead of the forest is a tall mountain.

"What is this place?" I ask, but he doesn't answer.

For a moment I wonder if he's going to try to keep me here. Hide me from James and the depressing sunrise. A tiny flutter of hope rises inside my chest but then it's gone before it can build into something more. If James found me the first time, he will find me again.

Up the tall mountain we climb, Meyer pretty much dragging me. I figure we're going clear over the top, but I'm wrong. As we get closer I notice that carved into the side of the mountain is a dwelling made up of open caves. Does he live here? Is this where Meyer calls home? As we draw closer I notice how clusters of fireflies light all the rooms, giving the space a candlelit glow. There are no outside walls or windows, no barriers to keep from falling down the side of the mountain, which may seem slightly off-putting to anyone other than Meyer, but it does provide him with the most amazing view. We alight in the center of what could only be called the main room. There are a few comfortable chairs around and a small table near the back, but what stands out to me the most are all the bookshelves lining the walls, each stacked high with books clear up to the ceiling.

"Isn't it amazing?" Meyer asks, gesturing out toward the view. His eyes are shimmering for the first time since the dance. He stands so sure of himself as he gazes out over all of Neverland.

I inch closer to the edge of the cliff, still slightly intimidated by the idea of heights, even though I've spent the last 24 hours defying gravity. I can see the Treasure Islands and then over to the west is the meadow where James appeared. I can even make out the Waiting Room, the place I caught my first glimpse of this world.

"Amazing is a good word," I tell him, smiling for the first time since he's joined me tonight. "You're very lucky, you know."

Meyer glances my way and then moves further into the room. "How about a tour, yeah?" He stops in the center of the room and looks around. He appears dazed for a second and then shrugs it off with a smile. I get the impression he's never done this before. "So this is, well, this is... this room."

"Your reading room, I take it?" I say, looking around at all of the bookshelves.

"Why would you think that?" he says completely serious, gesturing for me to follow to the next open room, but when I catch his eye he smiles.

In the narrow path between the two rooms the light is dim but I can make out countless drawings covering the rock wall. I inch closer, taking in each picture, noticing the different mediums. Some are sketched with charcoal, while others are painted with brush or fingertip. They are beautiful, these pictures, but they all seem so sad. The pictures are of families, moms and dads or just a mom or an older brother. Some include pets. Most include siblings. They're all taped together, hanging on the rock wall in this dimly lit hallway.

"The children make those for me," Meyer says from just behind me. "I need a bigger place so that I can put them all up. Right now I have this system where I change them every other day." He shrugs his shoulders. "It works for them. It works for me."

"There are so many," I say, noticing how every last inch of rock is covered.

"My favorites are in here." He takes my arm, leading me down the long hallway and on to the next room. But I don't think I can stomach anymore. I don't want to think about these children's families. That must be why Meyer keeps them in the hallway, and not somewhere with better light.

"The children don't actually come here," he explains once we're in the next room. "So they don't know which ones are my favorites. I wouldn't want to hurt their feeling, you know?"

"No. Never that," I say, not entirely listening. I'm too distracted by Meyer's living quarters.

The room we're in now must be where he sleeps. It is the larger of the two and has a long couch of some sort pushed up against the far wall, with a bookshelf on either side. There's a desk with a light peering over the top, right near the edge of the cliff. It reminds me of my father's drafting table. It is covered with bits of charcoal and a stack of drawings that Meyer flips over once he notices me looking their way.

"So you draw?" I say, wishing I could see his work, but assuming he'll say no if I ask.

"A little."

"But you didn't do these?" I point to the far wall where the countless pictures are taped to the rock.

"Those are gifts from the children," he tells me, and I move closer to inspect them.

"I can see why they're your favorites." I'm studying a watercolor of Meyer holding hands with a young dark-haired girl. The girl resembles a more youthful version of Jane. Whoever drew her made her so much shorter than Meyer, although the illustrated version of Jane and the real Jane share the same scowl. I move on to a crayon depiction of Meyer and two young boys dressed as pirates. They're standing with their arms linked, each carrying a sword.

I go from picture to picture. Each one depicts a happy memory of Neverland that specifically includes Meyer — until I come upon the very last one. It is larger than the others and behind glass. It resides in a prime spot directly above Meyer's drawing desk, singled out from the rest. The people in the painting are portrayed as colorful and happy, but because I recognize the location I know they're not.

"Who did this?" I whisper, staring at the girl in the picture, who is shown reading a story. She is surrounded by at least a dozen children, some resting in beds while others sit around her. I recognize each and every last one.

"Jenna gave that to me," he tells me from across the room. "It was the first picture she made for me, right after she arrived in Neverland."

I stare at the painting, not sure I can drag my eyes away. "I remember that day," I say out loud. "I was reading—"

"*Sleeping Beauty*," Meyer interrupts. "Yes, I know."

"How do you—?"

"I asked her. When she gave it to me."

He moves up next to me, but I don't turn around. "There's Jilly," I say, pointing at the girl sitting next to Jenna.

"And Sammy's the one with the bear." Meyer points out the children, naming each one as though he knows them, and I get a panicky feeling, worrying that he just might.

"This painting is my favorite one of all," he tells me, sliding his finger along the gold frame. "It's how I like to think of you."

I turn to him suddenly. "Me?"

"Why, of course. You're the reason I come to the hospital."

"But I thought…"

"That I was just out looking to steal a child or two away?" He smiles and looks down, but there's a trace of sadness in his smile.

"I figured that's why you were there. For the children, I mean."

"Sometimes it is. I like to prep them a bit." He scowls up at the picture. "He doesn't do it the way I'd do it."

James. But the name goes unspoken.

"And how is that?" I ask. "How would you do it?"

Meyer is somber. "I would give them more time."

I stare up at him, shocked.

"It's true. I would. No one knows better than I how hard it is for them to say goodbye." He turns away from me, his arms crossed. "Goodbyes aren't easy on anybody."

"So why do you come to the hospital?"

Meyer looks back at me, his eyes hooded in the evening light. "You tell a good story, Livy. You make it better for them there." He rubs the back of his neck. "Truth is, you're the only thing of interest I've found in your world."

For a second I hold his gaze, wanting to hear more. His words are like precious objects, so significant and important to me that I weigh each one.

But it also weakens me, these moments. Stirs something I can't really have. And with morning closing in I'm already aware of the cant's in my life. I'm afraid to hope for something more I can't have.

I move toward the bookshelves and let my fingers trace the spines of the books. The covers appear old, or maybe they've just been handled too often. One book stands out to me and I slide it from its place near the top of the shelf. It is bound in blue and gold, but familiar. "*Moby Dick*?" I say. "I guess I could have called that."

"What do you mean?" he asks, watching me from across the room.

"You seem the type to enjoy the classics."

"It's a story isn't it?"

"Yeah," I say, drawing out the word.

"Well." He smiles, giving a little shrug. "I like all stories."

I look at him a moment longer, studying him so closely he cocks his head in question.

"Which ones are your favorites, I wonder. I know you like adventures, the stories that have the most danger, of course. With a mystery on the side."

His smile grows wider, waiting for me to finish.

"I just wonder…" I stop, fearing that what I'm about to say will change the lighthearted mood between us.

"Yes?"

"You promised me an answer, you know? When I first got here, and Jeremy was making his island, you promised I could ask anything and you would answer."

Meyer's eyes narrow on me. But he doesn't deny it. "Have you got it then, your question?"

"I do."

"Well? What is it?" His arms are still crossed, his tone abrupt. When I don't answer right away he forces out a small smile of encouragement, but he's not fooling me. I can read his hesitance from where I stand.

"Do you ever wish you could live your own adventure? You know, something that doesn't come from a wish?"

I fully expect him to claim how he has adventures every day, every minute. But he says nothing.

"Do you ever think about what the children leave behind, the feeling that draws them back? Don't you wonder what that would be like? To miss something, to love something, so completely?"

Meyer stays silent, unmoving.

"Those pictures in your hallway, they're all portraits of the children's families."

297

His mouth thins out into a straight line. "Do you think I don't know that?"

"Is that why you keep them in the dark? So you're not reminded each and every day?"

Meyer glares at me, his eyes flashing. I worry he'll storm off again. I gauge the distance between us, wondering if I'd have enough time to stop him.

I take a small step closer. "You told me nothing lasts forever." I point back toward the hallway. "If that's not forever then what is it? The love those children feel for their families hasn't disappeared. When they saw me they hoped for their brothers or sisters to visit. Their families are first in their thoughts when they arrive here, and they're still first, months and years later."

"You don't know that—"

"Yes I do!" I point back toward the hallway again, to where my proof lies in the smiles of their loved ones. "They are lost, these children. You can't tell me those pictures stop once they've been here a while. You can't tell me they forget about them, because I won't believe you. I *don't* believe you."

"I don't think of them as being lost," he tells me, and there is such sadness in his tone. "To me they're just passing through. It is my job to protect them."

I take a few steps closer to him, wanting to shield him from the loss he must feel when these children leave. But I can't. Not yet. I'm still desperate to get through to him.

"I know you love them, Meyer. I know you feel more than anyone." My hands are trembling. I press them together, but it doesn't help. "I understand that everything you do is for them, to make them happy. Honestly, I keep wishing I could be you. That I could stay in this place but also visit my world, my family. But I can't. That would be too easy."

The word easy has him angry again. His arms drop to his sides, his fists clenched.

"And I'm right, you know. This is easy for you. You get to avoid the pain of life at the expense of only witnessing other people's happiness." I take a breath, hating what I'm doing, but unable to stop. "You say you fill your days with adventure, but your adventures are make-believe. They're just pretend." I take another step closer to Meyer, willing him not to run away. "A real adventure involves life and risk. What have you ever truly risked, Meyer?"

Meyer's expression is so severe, I can't read his thoughts. But he can't hide that flicker of hurt in his eyes. It's so clear and sharp as though I physically wounded him with my words; I'll remember it always.

"So answer me," I whisper. "If you could wish anything, if you were given the chance to be like me, would you take it?"

He pushes his answer out with so much force I flinch. "No."

I take a step closer, holding back the tears that are threatening to drown me. "Are you sure about that? Are you sure you wouldn't give all of this up for a chance at something real?"

He's silent for a moment, just staring at me as I inch closer.

"No," he whispers, his eyes wary, watching me. "No."

We are so close now, but not touching. "Pain or suffering?" I ask and his flinch is unmistakable.

"Go on, Meyer. It's your turn. Choose."

His shoulders straighten, his fists still clenched at his side. "Alright, suffering," he says, just as I knew he would.

I hold back my smile, willing my body to keep it together. I'm trembling so badly I'm afraid he'll notice it. I'm sure he already has.

"I dare you," I say slowly, taking one last moment to draw from my strength. "I dare you. To kiss me."

Meyer's eyes widen with surprise, and then zero in on me. "You what?" he breaths out.

"You heard me," I say with a lift of my chin. "I dare you to— "

"Yes, alright. I know." His gaze darkens on mine, holding me to my spot. But I'm not going anywhere. Not now.

"Is that what you want, Livy? A kiss?"

I nod my head, thinking, it's a start, but I'm also very aware that I'm gambling here. I want him to feel the possibility of something more, to want something he can't have. If he's felt anything close to what I have felt for him leading up to this moment, this dare will pay off. For both of us, I hope.

"Alright." His hand reaches up, brushing my hair back, and then it settles along the side of my neck. And it's not fair how immediate my reaction is. I feel a burst of warmth rush through me, followed by a jolt of nervousness. He takes that last step, closing the distance that separates us. His body is pressed to mine now. Nearly everywhere.

I know I should close my eyes, but I don't want to. I want to see him in every moment of this kiss. I want proof that he feels what I feel. I don't trust him to be honest with me.

Meyer leans down and then stops so that our mouths are just shy of each other. I start to tremble, anticipating his next move.

"I wonder," he whispers against my lips, "if this plan of yours is going to backfire on you." His breath is warm, mixing with mine. "Or if maybe I'll be the one to lose something tonight." When I don't say anything and instead drop my eyes to his lips, he smiles at me, slow and deliberate.

I raise my eyes to his, taking in his challenge and issuing one of my own. "Or perhaps I'll win this last game for the both of us. Did you ever think of that?"

Meyer's smile widens — that glint of determination ever present in his eyes — and then he pulls me in and kisses me. At first it feels as though he's punishing me for this dare. His kiss is almost painful in its forcefulness. There's a battle to be won here tonight, and it's clear to me he intends, as always, to be the victor.

I match him, kissing him back with everything I have and more, willing him to feel something. Believing it's impossible for him to not. I know there's something in the way he looks at me. There's an energy that moves between us. If he won't admit it to me or even himself, I'll make him feel it. And what he does with that is up to him.

Meyer's kiss gentles for a moment, and I worry he's going to pull away, that we're done and I've lost this game.

But he doesn't pull away. Instead his hands move into my hair, drawing me in until we're so close there's nowhere left for me to go. His mouth is warm against mine but even more than that, it is insistent. His fingertips move up my neck and then slowly travel along my jawline as though he's tracing me. I feel as if that spot, where his finger and thumb grip my chin, is no longer mine, but his.

His hand moves to my hip, his thumb sliding along the waistline of my jeans, and I sigh when his touch reaches my bare skin. He nudges my lips apart, seeking something deeper, and when I give it to him his fingers dig into me in response. My legs tremble beneath me and I worry I no longer have the strength to hold myself up. I've never been kissed like this, like I'm needed, desperately.

"Stay," he whispers against my lips. "Don't go back, Livy. Stay."

My chest tightens as though I am dying. I suck in a breath, but it's not enough. My eyes well up, wanting to say yes, wishing with all that I have that I could.

"Come with me," I whisper against his lips.

I open my eyes, realizing for the first time I've closed them. And Meyer does the same. We stare at each other, still touching, but no longer moving. Just breathing each other in. Then it hits me — what I've done — what I've asked him to do.

Now would be the time for him to tell me how he feels. Right now, this instant.

"Meyer?" My voice is soft between us but he jumps.

His eyes go wide and he pushes me away, grasping for some distance between us. He holds his hands up as though holding me off. He is a wild animal, cornered in a cage. All I can do is watch helplessly as he shuts down completely. His expression is wiped clean, a blank canvas. He is back to the closed-off Meyer, the mysterious Meyer.

"You should return to Jenna now. You wouldn't want her to wake up and find you're gone."

"I— What?" I reach for him, but he brushes me off.

"You know you're way back."

And then he's gone.

I stand there, frozen, thinking he'll come back. Hoping. But he never returns.

CHAPTER THIRTY

I am awake in an instant. I don't know how long I've slept. I don't actually remember closing my eyes. I'd made a conscious decision once I returned to Jenna that I was going to stay awake, just to watch her sleep. But I guess sleep does come to Neverland, even when you're no longer a child.

I'm not sure what has awakened me. The sky is only slightly brighter and Jenna and Alice are still asleep. And then I hear it. Footsteps. Someone is walking toward us on the path.

"Well, isn't this sweet," a voice says, and I freeze.

"Look at you, watching over her like you can protect her from me." The voice is clear now, and so close.

James.

"It truly is sweet, Meyer," he says, "and a little sad, actually. But just because you're guarding over her doesn't mean she'll stay."

I sit up slowly, not wanting to wake the girls. But my gasp of surprise stirs them anyway. Meyer is perched near us in the tree. His knees are drawn up, his head resting back. He appears so relaxed he could be he's sleeping, but then he blinks at me. He is definitely awake.

"Come down, little children," James calls out. "Don't make me come up there."

"How long?" I whisper, staring at Meyer. "How long have you been here?"

He doesn't answer at first, just holds my gaze.

"Maybe you were right," he says finally. He doesn't shift from his position in the tree, nor does he acknowledge James.

"About what?" I whisper.

James is getting closer; his footsteps crunch directly below us.

"Everything," Meyer chokes out.

"Livy?" Jenna sits up, looking a bit startled.

"It's okay, Jenna. Go back to sleep." I reach back and pat her hand, but I can't bring myself to look away from Meyer.

What does he mean, *everything*? What is he saying?

"But I thought I heard James…" Jenna shifts toward me, rubbing her eyes. She looks so young right now with her princess dress and her sleep-rumpled hair. I brush her hair back behind her ear and she smiles at me. She is so beautiful.

"You don't have to leave," Meyer says, moving closer to us in the tree. "You could stay here, Livy. I don't want you to—"

"Come down!" James' bellow startles Alice awake and she sits up with a cry.

"It's alright, Alice," Jenna says, rubbing her back. "It's morning now. Time to wake up."

Morning. I look around, recognizing the blue-green sky. I've seen this sky before. It was just yesterday.

"I told you I would be back," James says, and I jump. He's joined us in the tree now. With his long black coat and his dark features, he is the raven, stirring up trouble in a tree filled with fairies. "It's a tad bit crowded up here, don't you think? Why don't we all return to the ground." He flashes his charming smile at us and Alice's whimpering tapers off. But now that she's stopped I wish I could start. I don't want to leave the tree. Leaving the tree is definitely not a good idea. I don't want it to be morning.

Jenna is the first to listen to James. She pulls her blankets back and rises to her feet. Alice follows soon after.

Meyer is standing up in the tree now and when he catches my eye he holds out his hand and helps me to my feet.

"I mean it, Livy. You don't—"

"She can hear all you have to say… on the ground!"

James leans close and whispers something in Meyer's ear, and whatever it is it doesn't sit well with Meyer. He glares at him, but James is unaffected. James gives him a little shove and then waits for us to exit the tree.

"Right, then," James says once we're all back on the ground. He turns to me; his smile is ever so casual. "What have you decided?"

Decided? Have I decided? I grip my hands together in front of me. I thought I'd made a decision. I was pretty sure I knew what the right thing was to do. But now? Now I'm not so sure anymore. Actually, I'm pretty confident I don't know. Kissing Meyer changed everything.

I look to Alice who's staring at me, obviously terrified, and still slightly confused from being startled awake. She doesn't know whether or not to let herself feel fear. It hovers near her mouth, trembling in her forced smile. She keeps trying to push it back as though it's not something she's familiar with. She looks so brave, braver than me.

And there's Meyer. He's standing just apart from us with his arms crossed, and his eyes watchful. He's not saying anything. And I really wish he would say something. Why isn't he telling me what he wanted to tell me in the tree? If he really feels something for me why isn't he fighting for me like I've been fighting for Jenna? Or like I've been fighting for him? Is it because of James? I keep sending pleading glances his way, wishing he would help me out here, while his expression grows ever darker.

And then there's Jenna. She's holding my hand, gazing up at me with such serenity. Does she think I'm going to stay? Does she think there's no fear of losing me again? Whatever she thinks, she is at peace, and I wish she would share that with me. Right now.

"Livy?" James taps his finger on the large black watch strapped to his wrist. I've never noticed this watch before. How does it even work here? "It's time to decide."

"Well. See," I stall, clearing my throat and then taking a few deep breaths. "I was hoping you could give me another day or two, you know, to really make my decision. We've been so busy here, and I haven't had a chance to—"

"No. No more time. It's time to decide." He leans toward me, leaving no room for misunderstanding. "Now."

"But—"

"Now, Livy."

I hate James. I hate him more than anything I've ever hated. And I will always hate him. I glare at him, but he only smiles back.

"Livy?" Jenna tugs on my hand but I ignore it. I can't look at her now while I'm completely consumed by hate. I don't want her to see his effect on me.

"It's just one day," I plead. "One day isn't going to—"

"No." James snaps the word out so fast it feels like an assault. "And it's not just one day. While you've been lollygagging here in Neverland you've already missed an entire week of life."

"What?" I take a step back, dragging Jenna with me. "A week? That's not possible!"

"Are you telling me I'm wrong?"

Alice chooses this moment to burst into tears, and Jenna runs to comfort her. I guess she finally figured out whether or not to be afraid.

"I don't understand what's happening," she mumbles into Jenna's arms. "I don't like this."

"Livy." James has moved closer to me. He rests a hand on my shoulder and I pull away. "This is it," he tells me. "This is your second chance. Do you understand what I'm telling you? Nobody gets a second chance to say goodbye."

"Goodbye?" I can barely breathe now. I keep thinking about how a week has passed and how worried my parents must be. And Sheila. And Jilly. "Goodbye?"

"You never got to tell her. Now you can, Livy. Take this opportunity. Live your own life."

Goodbye?

I peek around James, searching for Meyer, and he's still where I last saw him, standing to the side as though not a part of this. He looks up, sensing my distress. His eyes are dark, his jaw tense. For a second his expression softens, and then he looks away.

"Livy?" The voice comes out of nowhere. It stirs the leaves on the trees and then with a force I'm not expecting, it rushes right through me, nearly nocking me back. "Livy?"

"What? Who is that?"

James moves closer, blocking everyone else out. "What is it?" he asks me. "What did you hear?"

"I don't—"

"Livy?"

"There it is again!" I push James away, searching for the voice. But it's just us: Alice, Jenna, Meyer, James and myself. Everyone else is still sleeping.

"You must decide," James tells me. "Now."

"No." I move away from him, hating how I can't see Jenna. "I'm not ready."

"Livy!"

"What?" I spin around, shouting into the cool-colored sky. "What do you want? Who are you?"

"Livy?" Jenna approaches me slowly, her eyes all at once afraid. "What is it? What's wrong?"

"It's nothing," I say looking around. "I just—"

"Livy!"

"What?!" I throw my hands out wide, spinning around. "How is no one else hearing that?"

Everyone is staring at me now like I'm crazy, and maybe I am. Meyer uncrosses his arms and takes a step toward me, but James steps between us, blocking him from view.

"This is it. Decide now or I make the decision."

"What? You can't do that!" I try to push away from him, desperate to get to Jenna, but he has hold of my arm and he won't let go.

"I can and I will," he tells me. "But it would be so much better — better for you, Livy — if you made this decision on your own."

"But I can't," I choke out, my voice nearly inaudible. "Can't you see that? Can't you understand how difficult—" I stop, unable to say anything more. I look to Meyer to help me. There has to be a way he can get me more time. His body is so tense now, as though some invisible force is holding him back. And in his eyes, well, he just looks broken.

"She's going," Jenna calls out. She's still standing near Alice, nearly holding the young girl on her feet.

"You need to go, Livy," she says, her eyes pleading with me. "It's not right that you're here. You know that. I know that." Her smile is so strong it nearly breaks me.

"No, Jenna. I don't know that." My tears are falling now. I have nothing more to keep inside. They're all that's left of me.

"It was never your time. It's not fair that you stay. Not to mom and dad. Not to you."

"But I can't leave you!" I push past James and run to her, and then I hear it again.

"Livy! Please wake up. Wake up, Livy!"

I nearly fall to the ground, holding my hands over my ears as the voice pounds against my head.

"STOP IT! PLEASE!"

Jenna is in front of me now. She takes my hands in hers, holding them to her heart. "Just say goodbye."

"No!" I pull my hands free, gripping her face, kissing her cheeks. I can't tell if she's crying or if I'm just crying all over her. But both of us are covered in tears. "No, Jenna. I don't want to. I don't want to leave you here!"

"It's time for you to go," she says. "It's time for you to live. Please do it."

"But I want you to come! Why can't you just come?"

"Because she can't, Livy," James says.

I glare at James, hating him with everything I have.

Jenna turns me back so that I'm facing her, and with her little hands against my face she holds me there, her forehead resting against mine. "Can you see me, Livy?"

"Yes," I say. *Always.*

She holds my face tight, her eyes in my eyes. "You can do this. Just say goodbye."

"I can't, though. I don't want to."

"You can. I know you can."

I try to shake my head at her, unable to say anything more, but she's holding me so tightly I can't move at all.

"Goodbye, Livy. I love you. *Always.*"

"No! Wait!" I try to grip her to me, tighter. But she's fading away. "Wait!" I call out. "Wait, Jenna!" Her eyes flutter back in sight, blue like my mother's. "I love you," I whisper. "I love you, Jenna."

And because I've never been able to say the word, I just think it. Imagine it. One word that is nearly impossible to say.

Goodbye.

PART THREE

For to have faith is to have wings.
— J.M. Barrie
Peter Pan in Kensington Gardens

CHAPTER THIRTY-ONE

There is a beeping sound somewhere near me. It fades in and then fades out. I latch onto it, pulling myself up from the heaviness that's burying me, but I still can't figure out where it's coming from. There are distinct voices now. They sound far away and then close. I wish I could see where I am, but it's too dark here. My eyes open and then immediately close. Why is it so bright? It's blinding. And what is that terrible beeping noise?

I open my eyes slower this time and focus on the face staring back at me.

"Livy?

My mother is in my room. She's leaning over my bed, her eyes so wide they nearly take up her entire face.

"Livy? Can you hear me?"

"Of course I can hear you," I say, but it doesn't sound like me, more like a really old, chain-smoking version of me.

"Livy!" she cries, gripping my hand so hard it hurts. "I was so afraid! They told us… I wasn't sure how you would be if you woke up. I mean, *when* you woke up." She's talking so quickly I can only make out half of what she's saying.

"What is this place?" I ask her. Just now noticing I'm not in my room. "Where am I?"

"You're in the Seattle Children's Hospital, Livy," a new voice tells me.

Standing on the other side of my bed is a man in green scrubs. He looks too young to be a doctor. Is he my nurse?

"My name is Dr. Garrett. I'm the chief neurologist here at Children's. I've been watching over you while you took your rest." He smiles at me as though this is funny. But I don't get the joke.

"Wait." I turn back to my mom, who's still holding my hand, smiling at me while tears run down her face. "Wait." I say again. "I'm in the hospital?"

I notice now that there's an IV needle in the top of my left hand and a bunch of wire thingies strapped to my chest. Images of Jilly flash into my mind. Words like, "donor," "bone marrow," "surgery" all surface at once as everything comes back to me.

Right. I'm at the hospital.

"How's Jilly?" I ask. "Is she next?" Wait. That can't be right. She's already had her surgery, hasn't she? And how do I know that?

"Livy." Dr. Garrett sits on the side of bed, looking serious. "There was a complication during your surgery. You reacted badly to the anesthesia they gave you and suffered a complex seizure."

"Right. I know this part," I say and they both look at me so intently I realize I've said something wrong. "But what about Jilly?"

"Jilly?" Dr. Garrett says.

"Do you remember, Livy?" my mother says at the same time. She turns to my doctor and asks, "Would she have any recollection of what happened?"

"I guess it's possible. She could have felt the reaction. Most people feel a seizure coming on, but she was heavily anesthetized at the time." He turns to me then, studying me as though I am under a microscope. "Do you remember anything?"

Do I remember? Flashes of color blur my vision for a moment and then I feel wetness slip down my cheeks. Do I remember? I remember an ever-changing sky and the Treasure Islands. I remember Echo and Jane and Alice. I can see it all, feel it so close, like I've just awoken from a dream. I close my eyes, wishing I could return to it. And for a moment I think I have. The memory is so strong I can see it. But then my mom touches my hand, drawing me back, and it disappears.

"Are you alright, Livy?" she asks. "Dr. Garrett, is she's alright?"

I immediately respond to the worry in my mother's voice and open my eyes. Both my mom and the doctor are leaning close, just staring at me. My mother looks terrified, which I don't like because even at Jenna's worst she never looked like this. And Dr. Garrett looks a bit alarmed himself.

"I think she could do with some rest," he says. "There are a few tests I need to do first, but I believe she'll be just fine."

My mom smiles at this. She's not used to hearing those words.

"Fine," she says, not completely convinced, but choosing to believe it nonetheless. "I like the sound of that. May I stay here? While you do your tests?" Her words are phrased as questions, but you can tell by her expression she's not going anywhere.

"Of course," he says. "That shouldn't be a problem."

The questions and tests that follow never seem to end. Finally, after countless doctors have evaluated me Dr. Garrett announces once again that I'm fine.

"You worried us for a while there, kid," he says, rising from the side of my bed. "We weren't sure if you were going to return to us."

My mother laughs this off, but I can tell by the bags under her eyes what he's said isn't that far off from the truth.

I am heavy with guilt when I look at my mother's smiling face. *I almost stayed. I nearly stayed away.*

"If you need anything, just push that button and your nurse will appear."

"Yes. Alexis," my mom says. "She's wonderful. So attentive. And so are the rest of the nurses who work this floor."

Dr. Garrett smiles at this and after one last check of my vital signs, he leaves.

My mom is fluttering about the room now. Straightening the flowers near the window and pushing the chairs back against the wall. I watch her, wishing she would just sit still, but that wouldn't be like my mother at all. When she runs out of things to straighten she pulls my blankets up, tucking me in tighter. It's about a thousand degrees in my room, but I let her do it anyway. I even smile in thanks.

"I want you to tell me about Jilly," I say, once she's returned to her seat. She's pulled it up close next to my bed. But once she's heard my request, it's as though she wishes she were across the room. "Mom," I say again, when she won't look at me. "How is she? Is she okay?"

"I don't know, actually," she tells me. "I haven't been up there."

"Why not?" I push against my mattress, wanting to sit up.

"Let me help you," she says, hurrying to my side. "Maybe you should just lie back, you know, until you've had your rest."

"I want to see her. I want to see Jilly."

"Well that's just not possible right now, Livy. You heard Dr. Garrett. You need to rest. You've been through quite an ordeal."

An ordeal. Is that what I've been through?

"You had a seizure, Livy." Her hands stop and press down against me on the bed. "Do you understand how serious that is? You were in a coma!"

"I know, but—"

"A coma, Livy! Do you know how frightened we've been?" The panic is back, draining my mom's face of color. "I didn't know what

316

to do. I didn't know how to help you." She's crying again, big salty tears that go unnoticed down her face. "Don't do that again," she chokes out, her voice raspy.

I stare back at her completely speechless. I want to fight her on this, but I do feel tired. My head feels heavy and my eyes as well. I rest my head back against the pillows and a look of relief settles into her features.

"Will you check on her?" I ask, my voice faint. "Please, mom? I need to know how she's doing."

For a moment I think she's about to refuse, but then she nods her head and smiles at me.

"I can do that, Livy. While you're sleeping I'll slip up there and check on her, alright?"

"Yes," I say, already giving in to my exhaustion. "Thank you."

She leaves the room, closing the door behind her and I wait a solid ten seconds, making sure she's really gone. And she is gone. All of them, gone. Jenna, Meyer, Alice, Jane. Gone. I close my eyes and let the tears fall. And when I fall asleep this time, I don't dream.

CHAPTER THIRTY-TWO

The sound of a door closing startles me awake. It's much darker in my room now. I can't tell if it's nighttime or not because the curtains are all drawn. I wonder if my mom has been back. If she's seen Jilly or heard how she's doing. I don't know how long I've been asleep.

Something stirs near the back corner of my room. I can barely make out a figure sitting up in a chair. The bathroom light is on, but the door is almost closed, leaving only a sliver of light in my room. The shadow stirs again and this time I make out a familiar shape.

"Daddy?" I whisper, and the shadow springs up from the chair.

"Livy," he says, moving toward me with caution. "Your mother said you were awake, but I didn't want to disturb you."

I smile at him, wishing I could see him better, but it's so dark in this room.

"If you're still tired I can—"

"No, I'm not." I sit up a bit and then reach for the button on my bed that moves me all on its own. The noise is loud in my quiet room and it catches us both off guard.

My father hovers near my bed, he doesn't sit on the side the way Dr. Garrett did.

"Do you want to…?" I point to his chair near the back of the wall and he hurries over to it, dragging it to the side of my bed.

Once he's situated he just stares at me, and then neither of us say anything for a really long time. If it weren't so quiet out in the hallway I wouldn't have noticed when he starts to cry. He does it so silently.

There is nothing worse than seeing a parent cry, especially when you know you're the cause of it. My throat feels tight and I worry that we'll both be crying soon, even though I'm not sure why it is we're even doing it.

"I'm sorry, Daddy," I say, needing to break the silence, not realizing that saying the word sorry is like opening the floodgates. I should be happy that he's here, outside of our apartment. I should be grateful he doesn't have a real reason to cry this time. But it's true, I am sorry. I'm sorry I almost gave up on him. I almost left him here with *two* daughters to mourn. And I don't think I'll ever stop feeling guilty for that.

He leans his elbows on my bed and grips my hand with both of his hands. He kisses my hand and rubs it against his face. "I thought…" He stops and shakes his head, refusing to say the rest of the words. "I'm glad you're okay, Livy."

"Me too," I whisper, and then realize it's true. I want to be here. *I want to live.*

My mother chooses this moment to enter the room and once she sees that I'm awake and I have a visitor, she flips on the light, nearly blinding my poor, emotional father and me.

Once I've adjusted to the light I finally get a good look at him. His eyes are swollen and red, which is expected considering he's crying, but he looks so much older somehow, weakened by the events of the last year. His hair has gone gray around his ears and his skin is so pale he looks unwell. He no longer resembles the dad of my memories, the dad who called me back from Neverland.

"I'm sorry," I say again — I feel as though I've done this to him. My voice is so soft I'm not sure he's even heard me, but then he squeezes my hand, his grip solid and strong. In his eyes I can make out a flicker of something. It could be a glimmer of hope, and a glimmer is better than nothing.

"Livy! How are you feeling? How long have you been awake?" My mother bustles over to us and sits alongside my father's chair. It's been a while since I've seen them this close to each other, let alone in the same room. For a moment I don't answer her, I just take it in.

Finally I say, "I... I don't know? A few minutes or something?"

"Dr. Garrett wants you to stay here for a few days. He just wants to make sure everything's okay."

"Is everything okay?" my father asks, his voice slightly elevated.

"Everything's fine! You know how they are here." Her voice drops off when she realizes what she's said. Yes, both my parents *do* know how they are here. And being here again is the last place either of them wants to be.

"You don't have to stay," I say, feeling the guilt settle heavy and thick inside my stomach. "I'm fine. Just pick me up—"

"Don't even think about it, Livy," my mom says. "I've been here every night. I'm not leaving here without you."

"You've been here? In the hospital?"

"We both have," my father says. He's staring at me, confused by my confusion. "Where else would we be?"

"But..." I stop myself before I say what we're all thinking: this is where Jenna died. Why would you want to stay *here*? "But with the election?" I say instead. I'm still not entirely sure how many days I was away, but I'm pretty sure the election is close, if not over.

My parents exchange a look and then my mother gets to her feet with a sudden need to fix my blankets. Again.

"Don't worry about any of that, Livy. Now, are you hungry? Have they given you anything to eat?"

"I'm not." I look around noticing how I'm no longer attached to an IV and wires that were stuck to my chest earlier are now missing. How long was I asleep? Or better yet, how tired was I? How did I miss them removing a large needle from the top of my hand?

Something occurs to me and I grab my mom when she flutters nearby. "Did you see Jilly? How is she?"

My mom tries to distract me by fixing my pillows, but I grab her hand. There's not much pillow fixing she can do with just one. "She's recovering. They should know more in a couple of days," she tells me, avoiding my eyes.

"But did you see her? Did she look okay?" There's something she's not telling me, I can feel it.

"I didn't see her—"

"Well go back then! I need to know how she is!"

"She's in the PICU, Livy. Only family is allowed in. You know that."

The PICU. The Pediatric Intensive Care Unit. This isn't the first time Jilly's been down there. It shouldn't surprise me that she's there. But it terrifies me.

"It's alright," my mom says, for the first time meeting my eyes. "It's going to be okay. I know it."

I nod my head, wanting to believe her. "I need to see her."

"In a few days, maybe. Once they release you and she's up to visitors. Maybe then, alright?

I nod my head again. No, it's not alright. But it's all I have right now.

My mother smiles at me, walking backward toward the door. "So, if you're feeling up to it, I thought maybe you'd like another visitor."

Sheila bursts into the room as though she's been listening at the door.

"You bitch!" she yells. "I can't believe you messed with me like that!"

My mother's face is priceless. It's like she doesn't know whether to be surprised, horrified or furious. She settles on disgusted, but when she catches my eye she pins on a smile. I guess she's willing to endure anything if it means I'm happy. And I love her for that. I owe her big time, that's for sure.

The sight of Sheila brings a rare hint of a smile to my dad's face. He's always liked Sheila. Whenever he used to drive us places he always loved how she knew all the words, and sang along, to his music. But he hasn't seen her in months.

"Hey dad," she says, giving him a hug as though it was just yesterday we were all riding in the car together.

My father has already recovered from her loud entry into our conversation. Unlike my mother.

"Hey kid," he says, rustling her hair.

Sheila acts like this is no big deal, this new and halfway social version of my father. But when she turns to me, her eyes widen, giving me a look that clearly says, *holy shit!*

"Hey," I say, smiling back at her. I don't want to make too big a deal about it. For all I know, once I'm back home he'll be safe behind his office door, blaring Simon & Garfunkel.

My parents leave us alone for a while, claiming hunger. But I know they just want to give me some space. Even though I'm hesitant to see my father leave, I know that if my mother stays too much longer that fake smile she's forcing on Sheila will eventually snap her face in two.

"So you're alive," Sheila says once they're gone. "How's that feel?"

"Oh, you know. The usual and stuff. Don't tell me you missed me?"

Sheila rolls her eyes and then throws herself on top of me, squeezing me so tight I squeal.

"Oh, shit!" she says and surges back. "Did I hurt you? Are you like, injured or something?"

"No," I say, laughing. "I'm not injured. Just human." I rub my stomach — where her very bony elbow probably left a mark — all the while smiling right back at her. I didn't realize how much I missed her. For the first time since I woke up I feel a flutter of anticipation in my chest, like I'm excited about something.

"I hate you, you know. I hate you for making me feel like that." She glares at me before slowly moving closer to give me another hug. "Don't ever do that to me again, okay?"

"Okay," I say, scooting over so that she can lie next to me on the bed.

"Promise?"

"Promise."

"Alright, then," she says, bumping her shoulder against mine. "You can still be my friend."

"Good to know," I say, bumping back. "Now *you* have to promise."

"Promise what?"

"You have to promise not to go falling off any more rocks."

Sheila has pulled out her cell phone and I watch as she changes her Facebook status update to: *She's alive!!!!!*

Once she hits enter she turns to me, her expression curious. "What are you talking about, fool?"

"You know. That night… when you almost drowned?" I roll my eyes at her attempt to play it off.

323

"Yeah, right," she says, glancing back down at her phone. When I don't say anything more she looks up. "Seriously, Livy. What are you talking about?"

I shift on the bed so that I can see her more clearly. "You know what night I'm talking about. The party? The cliff diving? You, me, Grant and Meyer?"

"Who?" Sheila has a look of panic about her now. Her color is pale under the hospital lights. "What are you—" And then she stops and bursts out laughing. "You suck!" she says, slapping my shoulder. "I can't believe you got me like that. You totally had me freaked out for a minute there."

"Got you like what?" I ask, still confused.

"Yeah, yeah. I get it. You playing all dumb and weird like there's something wrong with your brain. Funny, ha ha, Livy. But I don't want to play anymore. Its not funny." She frowns at me, letting me know she's serious, and then her focus is back on her phone.

"Sheila." Now I'm starting to freak out. "I'm not playing anything. You fell off that rock." I look at her more closely. Is she the one who's playing me? Or worse, is something seriously wrong with her?

"I've never fallen off a rock — let alone cliff dived — in my entire life! Now knock it off Livy before I hit that nurse button and tell them you're afraid to go to the bathroom on your own and you need a catheter."

I stare at Sheila, waiting for her to yell "just kidding!" or, "you're such a sucker," or something more Sheila-like, but she just stares right back. She's serious. She's really not messing with me.

"And who's this Meyer kid?" she says, glancing back down at her phone. "Is this someone I'm supposed to know?"

"What?" I choke out, but luckily she's too distracted by an incoming text to see the expression of horror on my face. By the time she does finally glance back up, I've got myself back together.

"So who is he? Someone you met here? While you were sleeping, and scaring us all shitless?"

I am too confused to speak. My brain is frantically trying to put things together.

"No," I say, pasting on a smile. "Nevermind. Just messing with you."

Sheila leaves a little while later once my parents return. She promises to come visit me tomorrow, and mentions how she hopes I'll be allowed to go home soon. I nod and smile, pretending I'm not totally freaking out inside. Apparently she buys it because she leaves and doesn't ask me what's wrong.

My nurse checks in to help me to the bathroom — no catheter for me. Later she brings me chocolate pudding and applesauce (which my dad eats once I've convinced him I'm not hungry).

My eyes grow heavy soon after, but I'm too upset to sleep. I can't seem to work out the details. I keep seeing Sheila's confused expression and hearing the words, "Who's Meyer?" None of it makes sense. And when I asked my mother if Sheila spent any time in the hospital last month she immediately called the doctor in who shines a light into my eyes and asks a bunch of questions to make sure that I'm not completely insane. A part of me wonders whether I *do* have brain damage — did something actually happen to my brain during the seizure? Wouldn't the doctor know that? It's not like they haven't done enough tests. The only rational conclusion I can come to is that Neverland really *was* a dream.

But then how do I explain the depth of my memories? How do I explain the ache I feel when I think of it? How do I explain Meyer?

CHAPTER THIRTY-THREE

It takes another two days before both Dr. Garrett and Dr. Lerner determine that neither my brain nor my body is needed further. After many more tests they finally make it official and tell me I'm allowed to go home. Dr. Lerner tells me that because of my week-long sleep, I won't have to worry about any sort of recovery due to the bone marrow surgery. He says to take it easy just in case, and Dr. Garrett agrees. Luckily my mom isn't present to hear this bit of news otherwise I'd probably be confined to my bed for the rest of the year.

I've stopped asking questions about the events leading up to my surgery. After overhearing a conversation between my mom and Sheila, I realized it was better to work the mystery out on my own. I mean, yeah, it's great to see them coming together over something, but I'd rather it didn't involve questions regarding my sanity.

I drop by the PICU on my way out but Jilly's visitation level is still listed as family-only, so the only thing I can do is leave a message for her grandma. It's killing me that I'm not in there with her, but at the very least I want Jilly to know that I'm okay.

My parents help me climb into the car like I'm an invalid, and I let them because I do feel somewhat wobbly. Now that we're on our way home they appear nervous, as though they're afraid that once we're all back to the apartment things will just return to how they were before I slipped into a coma. Truth is, so am I.

"So, how's the election coming?" I ask when the silence in the car becomes unbearable. I'm scrolling through my phone, searching again and again through all of my saved numbers, but I can't seem to find any that belong to Meyer's friends. How is that possible? I saved them all. I know for a fact I didn't delete them. And yet they're nowhere, not even in my call log.

"Well, that's the thing," my mother begins, shifting in her seat so that she can look back at me. "I dropped out, Livy."

I nearly drop my phone. "What?" I reach over and carefully place my phone on the seat next to me. "You did what?"

"I dropped out," she says with a smile, like she's telling me about a new shade of paint she wants to try in the bathroom.

"But… how is that even possible? The election was only a few days away."

"Yes, it was," she says spinning back around in her seat. "And because I dropped out, the spot automatically went to Curtis."

Curtis Brunning is the man who lost to my mother last time, but was determined to win it this year.

"But…wait…I mean, but it's Curtis!" I can't even count how many times my mother has rolled her eyes after saying Curtis's name. I wonder if that's why she turned around, so that I wouldn't see how much saying his name affects her. "Are you really okay with that?"

"I'm very okay with it, Livy. I'm more than okay with it."

"O-kay." My heart suddenly feels heavy. I can't tell if it's guilt weighing it down or remorse. "But why?"

"Believe me, I'm actually enjoying my time off. Government jobs are so draining. It took your seizure— well, it took me a while to realize this, but now that I have, I'm very happy with my decision."

My mother spins around in her seat to smile at me again, and I want to believe her. I really do, but it's about as believable as a boy who can fly.

"One of my favorite things to do when I was younger was cloud gazing," she continues. "Your father and I used to go to the park. He would sketch the buildings around us and I would stare up at the sky, and daydream."

I stare at my mom, not quite seeing this version of her in my head. I've never known my mom to not be busy. I honestly can't imagine her sitting still for longer than a minute or two, especially in the grass. She'd get her clothes dirty.

"Once you came along I was too afraid to take my eyes off you and cloud gazing became something of the past."

"So you dropped out of the election to cloud gaze?" I'm sorry. I'm just not buying it.

"In a way," she says, all mysterious-like. "I guess I just want the option."

"Well," I say, waiting for more, but not getting it. "If you're sure…I mean, you can always—"

"I'm very sure." She reaches back and squeezes my hand. Once she's spun back around in her seat, I watch her fingers tap tap tap against her knee.

I open my mouth to argue a bit more and then close it with a *snap*. With my father out of the house and my mother rethinking her life, it feels wrong to be the one to pop this shiny bubble around us. I don't know how long my mom can stay not busy, but I guess some time off can't hurt her.

Our apartment looks the same: clean to the point of appearing barely lived in. We all step off the elevator as though there's a monster lurking somewhere inside.

"I changed your sheets and washed them," my mother says once we're in the kitchen.

"Thanks," I say, hovering near the hall.

To get to my room I have to pass Jenna's. I wait for my mom and dad to move on to their opposite sides of the apartment, but they don't. They're still together in the kitchen when I make my way down the hall. I stop for a moment outside Jenna's door and listen as they talk in muted voices. Maybe worrying about me is a reminder that they still have some things in common. Or maybe my slipping into a coma reminded them that I still exist.

After a brief moment of hesitation I slowly open Jenna's bedroom door. I don't know what I expect to find in here, but it's all still the same: pink walls, pink bedspread with pink and purple pillows. Our homemade version of heaven still hangs from her ceiling; the marshmallows are also still pink. I move to her bed and sit down, noticing how it still smells like Jenna in here. Strawberries and bubblegum, her favorites.

I've thought of this moment since this morning when I knew I would definitely be coming home today. I imagined myself sitting here, looking at all her things. I truly believed I'd feel different. I'd hoped to feel peaceful. Now that I know where she is, and that she's more than fine, I really believed I'd be more okay with her being gone.

But I'm not. Now that I've said my goodbye she feels even further away than before.

Back in my room I lie down on my bed and think about all that has happened since the last time I was home. But mostly I think about Meyer. I don't understand how Sheila could forget him or how I could lose all those phone numbers. It's as though he doesn't exist. Or never existed.

Is it possible I really did just dream it all? Was I so out of mind with worry for Jilly that I imagined a boy in the stairwell? A boy who

329

could fly? Could Neverland be a drug and coma-induced dream? I know if I tried to tell anyone about it they would have me back in the hospital, perhaps even in the psych ward. They would think it was some kind of hallucination or side effect of the seizure.

But what about Meyer? Could all of it have been a dream?

I close my eyes and remember Neverland. I focus on the details and the colors, allowing myself to feel everything I felt when I was there: the happiness of the children, the joy at seeing Jenna again. With my eyes closed I think about Meyer and the kiss we shared. I can almost feel his touch, firm and then frenzied. I let myself remember how I felt just before I left and the sadness washes over me. It's just not possible that I imagined it. The feelings are too intense — too real — to be a dream.

I open my eyes and stare out the window at the Space Needle. It is hovering above us all, half in and half out of very diluted sunlight as the rainy mist of Seattle attempts to cover it completely.

At some point my mother comes in and checks on me. It's well past late afternoon, and I pretend to be sleeping. I'm too wrapped up in my thoughts to chat with anyone. I just want to be alone.

When she leaves, she closes my door, and that's when I notice it. Jenna's painting. It's hanging on the back of my door, like it's always been there — its own little hiding place from everyone but me.

I sit up and blink at it a few times, convinced that it's a flashback of some sort. That I'm imagining it. And then I get up off my bed, and cross my room to touch it.

How did it get here? Did Meyer send it? Did he deliver it himself?

My fingertips brush against the cool glass protecting the painting, and then slide over the rough texture of the gold frame that holds it all in place. It is real. It feels real. And somehow, it's mine now. Meyer has not only given me a part of Jenna, something that meant a lot to him, but he's given me the answer to all the questions

I've been struggling with since I got back. Neverland is real. It wasn't just a dream, I was there. I did spend time with Jenna and the other children. And I did meet a boy who could fly.

I sit on my floor and stare up at the picture. I'm so overwhelmed by the sight of it I feel as though I'm floating.

About an hour later I get up and open my closet. I flip through my clothes until I find it: Meyer's dark green sweatshirt. I slip it on over my head. It still smells like him. Like fall.

I curl up on my bed, making sure that I can see Jenna's painting. I don't close my eyes, I don't need to, Meyer's face is more than a memory to me. What does he mean by giving me this gift? What did he mean when he said back in Neverland that I might be right about everything? What didn't he tell me? I wish I could have had just a few more minutes in Neverland. Even though those few minutes would never have been enough.

"Thank you," I say out loud, hoping that he can hear me. "Thank you for this." And of course there is no reply. He's not here. I may never even see him again. But he's thought of me, and sent me something of his to share. A bit of proof that everything I feel is real. A reminder of Jenna. Where she is, and how she is now. A simple reminder of the things I love.

Around dinnertime I get a text from Jilly's grandma. She's finally been given my message and she wants me to know she's cleared me to visit.

Come now, she writes me. *As soon as you can.* And I don't even bother to respond. I just leave.

I make it to the hospital in record time but it still feels like a lifetime has passed before I arrive on the second floor. Jilly's grandma is waiting for me at the nurse's station. Her hair is tied back at her neck and she looks like she hasn't slept in weeks.

"She's sleeping right now," she tells me, "but you should go in. She's been asking for you."

"How is she? How did the surgery go?" I'm holding her hand while we hurry down the hallway. I'm not sure why we're rushing, but we are.

"It went very well at first," she says, and then her eyes well up.

No.

No. No. No. NO.

"And she was recovering great. That's what they kept telling me."

We stop outside room 2332 and Jilly's grandma clutches my hands in hers.

"It was just yesterday that everything began to change." Her eyes spill over and she completely breaks down. Her sobs are heavy, like she's been holding them back, waiting for someone to share them with. "She looks so pale, my Jilly. Like she's some other child."

No.

I shake my head, not believing anything she's telling me. This wasn't supposed to be how it happened. She was supposed to get better. She was supposed to be okay. She promised, just like I promised. Before I went away.

"I need to see her!" I pull my hands free of hers and hurry to open the door.

"I'll give you some time," she calls after me. "But, Livy!"

"What?" My hand is on the door handle when I turn back around.

"She may not…" Her bottom lip begins to tremble and then she forces in a deep breath, digging deep for the last of her strength. "She may…

Be awake? Know I'm here? I keep myself from yelling at her to say what she needs to say and let me go, already.

"… not remember you." And then she turns from me, moving back down the hallway.

I open the door slowly, my breathing so loud and heavy in my head and chest I feel like I'm thunder entering a church. The divider screen is pulled back, keeping the rest of the room concealed from anyone passing by in the hallway. I close the door softly behind me and then force myself to move beyond the screen.

There's a man sitting on the side of Jilly's bed, blocking her from my view. For a second I hesitate, wondering if this is some member of Jilly's family I don't know, someone here to say goodbye. But then he shifts slightly and I suck in a breath.

"What are you doing here?" I hiss at him. "Get away from her!"

James turns to me, his expression so serious and calm, I want to smack it right off.

"You can't do this! Not to her! She was doing great! They told me." I hurry toward the bed and pull at him, yanking at his arm, desperate to get him away from her. "You can't do this. I won't let you. You can't take her!"

"Livy."

James isn't moving anywhere. He's like a big solid wall that seems more permanent the more I push at it.

"Please, not her. Anyone but her." My tears are spilling down my face, soaking the collar of my sweater. "I hate you for this! Please. Just leave her alone!"

"Livy." James reaches up. His hand brushes against my cheek, turning my face so that I see Jilly for the first time. "Look at her," he says.

A guttural cry escapes from me. I cover my mouth, holding back the emotion that threatens to follow. Jilly is lying on her back. She's so still, her eyes open. She is looking at me, but not really seeing anything. She's practically already gone. I collapse against the bed, and James reaches for me, holding me up. She looks so pale. Her grandma was right. She does look like someone else's child. But she's still Jilly. I can see it in her eyes.

"Is she…?" I can't bring myself to say the word. I just keep staring at her. It appears she's staring back. And then she blinks at me. Once. Then twice.

I whimper out loud, covering my mouth.

"Livy?" Her little voice is so faint. I lean closer and touch her face. "Livy," she says again. "You came back." She smiles at me, her eyes brightening in the dark room. "He told me you would."

"Jilly," I cry, not caring if I frighten her. I can't keep it in any longer. Not when a minute ago I thought she was dead. Not when she's now smiling at me.

"I missed you," she tells me, reaching for my hand. "But he told me you'd come back. He promised."

I glance back at James, waiting for an explanation, but he's gone. It's just Jilly and me now.

"Who?" I ask her. "Who told you I'd be back?" I'm wiping my tears away, but they're happy tears. I don't actually mind if they stick around. "Who are you talking about, Jilly?"

"You know who," she says, smiling as though it's a secret. "He told me you'd know."

"Was it…?" I turn and take in the rest of the room, afraid that James could be lurking in the shadows. "Was it the man who was just here? The man who just visited you?"

"What man?" she asks me with a hint of a frown. "There's no man. Just you."

"No, I mean, he was just here. He was sitting on the edge of your bed."

Jilly stares at me a second longer and then she shakes her head. "He's not a man, he's a boy." She giggles, her entire face lighting up. "And he has the most beautiful green eyes."

I lean closer, squeezing her hand. My tears have stopped now. Her words have driven them away. "What did he say to you, Jilly? What did he tell you?"

She must sense how important my questions are, how important her answer is to me. She thinks about it for a moment and then with a rather serious expression she says, "He told me not to fall asleep. That I had to keep my eyes open." Jilly sits up a bit, her movements shaky but determined. "And I stayed awake, Livy. I promise I did."

"You did great," I tell her, grinning. "You did better than great. You're amazing."

Jilly's grandma comes in at this moment and stares down at her granddaughter not quite believing what she's seeing. Jilly calls her name and reaches a hand out to her. There is much crying from Jilly's grandmother and even more from some of the nurses when they enter the room and find that Jilly is now sitting up in her bed. They flutter around her, checking her vital signs. To them there is no explanation for this sudden change. As the minutes slip by, bringing more color to her cheeks, they just stare at her, disbelieving.

No one notices when I sneak out. They're too astounded by the little girl who can't stop smiling. I run toward the stairwell, hoping Meyer will be waiting there. I have to see him, but instead I just find James.

He's waiting for me at the end of the hallway with his long black coat slung over his arm. And I know then. I know Meyer isn't here anymore. I know in that moment I'm not meant to see him today.

"Thank you," I say to James. "I don't understand... but thank you. I really thought—"

"I know what you thought," he says quickly. "That much was obvious."

I look down, feeling bad now for the things I yelled at him and the punching and flailing as well. "I'm sorry I—"

"There's no need to apologize, Livy. Or thank me." He leans against the wall.

"Well, I… Thank you… I mean." I stop myself. There are so many things I want to ask him, but I just settle with, "Why?"

"Why did I save her?" When I nod he shrugs it off and stares back down the hallway. "Sometimes the world needs a miracle. Hope, I find, can go a long way."

He tilts his head at me and smiles, and I can't stop myself, I reach up and wrap my arms around him, needing to share the things I'm feeling, but am unable to say. The strangest part about it is he hugs me back. Being held by James feels comfortable. And safe. I think about the things he tried to teach me when he was my tutor, how he wanted me to believe that nothing is lost forever. It's strange how I fought his words so passionately only to force them on Meyer a short time later.

Once we've pulled away he puts on his coat like he's getting ready to leave.

I have so many questions for him. I want to know how things are with Jenna. Has she decided to move on yet? Will she soon? And what does that mean, exactly?

"What is it, Livy? What is it you want to ask me?" James asks, seemingly reading my mind.

"What now?" I say. "What do we do now?" Does he go back to being my tutor? Do I go on pretending that what happened didn't actually happen? That Meyer was never a part of my world?

"You're not supposed to know everything, Livy," he tells me, flashing me one of his charismatic smiles. "You're just supposed to keep trying."

CHAPTER THIRTY-FOUR

When James walks away I figure that's the last time I'll see him, and I'm pretty sure of it until he shows up in my lobby a few months later. He's waiting for me when I get home from school. Just sitting in one of the lobby chairs with his legs crossed, like he's any other normal person, waiting to meet someone.

"I thought we could grab some ice cream," he tells me. "Since it's such a nice day today." He points out the window where spring is just becoming reacquainted with Seattle. Up until the moment I recognized James I was feeling lighthearted myself, but not now. Now I worry he has some dark reason for visiting me. He is death, after all.

"It's just ice cream," he says, reading my hesitation. "And before you ask, yes, you're mom knows I'm here. She was very happy to see me again." He takes in my sudden panic and quickly reassures me, "And, no, I didn't kill your mother. She's fine, Livy. You're both fine. I just want to chat."

"Chat?" I ask, not completely convinced.

"And eat ice cream," he says with a smile. "My treat."

"Well, then. If you're buying…" I give him a half teasing look, "And you're not here to, you know, throw me in front of a moving bus, then I guess it's fine" I point to the door and gesture for him to follow me out.

We don't speak much on our way to Molly's. Once or twice I almost ask him about Meyer, but then I stop myself. After the last time I saw James I spent quite a few days trying to track down Meyer's friends, but I never had any luck. Eventually I just stopped trying. I figure if he wants to see me he will. And until that happens — even though I don't like it — I'm forced to move on. He promised me once that he wouldn't leave without saying goodbye, and there's a part of me still holding him to that promise. I stare at Jenna's picture every night before I fall asleep. It's now the one thing I have to look at before I close my eyes. And it isn't Jenna I think of when I study it, I think of him. When I think of Jenna I imagine her in a pink dress sleeping under a Neverland sky. And it doesn't tear me in two any longer. Not like it used to.

James orders strawberry ice cream, which is such a happy flavor I can't help but laugh.
"It's always been my favorite," he tells me a bit defensively. "What about you? Still ordering Bubble Gum Jenna?"

"Actually, I prefer Mint Chocolate Chip," I tell him and the girl behind the counter.

James raises an eyebrow and takes a bite of his ice cream, not entirely convinced.

"It's not as sweet," I say with a shrug. "And theirs is really good here."

Once we're seated he asks me what's new and I tell him how I'm back in school now and how I've taken up ice skating. It was quite a surprise for my father, actually, when, just after Jilly had recovered and was soon to be released, I came racing into his office and demanded he take me ice skating. And Jilly as well. I made him promise we'd go as soon as she was up for it, and he kept his promise about a week later. Now he takes us every week, staying for our lesson, and then we all stop to get hot chocolate on the way home. I suspect the hot chocolate is Jilly's favorite part. And my father's as well. Not the ice skating.

"I'm in the beginner's class," I tell James, grimacing at the floor. "And, yeah, I'm the oldest kid in the class, but I don't care because it's something I've always wanted to do."

"I think that's great," James says smiling at me from across the table. "Who knows, maybe you won't break your arm."

When I look up at him with alarm, he laughs, and I kick him under the table.

After his laughter has died down we both turn back to our ice cream. There are still a hundred things I'd love to ask him, but I hold myself back. I'm not afraid of him any longer. I still feel that energy about him, but it doesn't frighten me the way it used to.

"How is she?" I ask when I can't hold it in any longer. "Is she still—?"

"She's where she needs to be." James finishes his ice cream and stands up. I take it that's all he's willing to give me, but it's not enough.

"Is she… does she still remember me?"

James stands by the open door, waiting for me, and once I'm through it he whispers his reply. "There isn't anything I can tell you that you don't already know."

I glare up at him, hating these puzzles of his, and he simply smiles back.

"There's someone I'd like you to meet," he tells me as we're leaving Molly Moon's. He leads me though the park just a street or two away and it's so nice out, I don't mind the detour. With the sun finally shining after three straight months of rain, the park is crowded today. There are children on the swings; their laughter spills over the grass toward us, and it makes me think of Jenna. A few kids are playing Frisbee and we take the long way around them to get across the grass.

"Here we are," James says as we approach a smattering of trees, and I glance up, searching for this mysterious person he's dragged me to meet.

There's a young man sitting against a tree, his knees are up as he sketches into a sketchbook. His face is turned away from me as he focuses on his work and I don't recognize him at first. But then he glances up and I come to a complete stop.

James touches his hand to my arm. "He won't remember you," he says. "He doesn't remember anything."

"What?" I force out, feeling as though my chest might explode. For the last few months I've been searching in shadows for any possible glimpse of Meyer. And to have James lead me up to him so nonchalantly is more than I can handle right now.

"I plan to introduce you, Livy. It's why I've brought you here." He gestures to the small distance between us and gives me an exaggerated roll of the eyes. "But I can't do that, can I, if you don't move forward."

"I don't understand. What do you mean he doesn't remember anything?" I keep staring at him, still not believing he's here. I'd almost convinced myself I'd never see him again.

"He was given options and he made his choice."

"Choice?" I pull my eyes away from Meyer and gaze up at James in confusion. "What choice?"

"To come here, Livy. To live as you do. He's always had the option. He just never seemed that interested in it."

"You mean he…?"

"Yes, he left Neverland. He gave it up for a chance at a real life."

"Oh." Wow. "So that means…?"

"He doesn't remember anything from his time before. There are rules. He won't remember you. He won't remember any of it."

No. It's not possible.

I gaze back at the boy under the tree. He is watching us curiously, but he hasn't moved from his spot.

"What about Neverland?" I whisper, without taking my eyes off Meyer.

"What *about* Neverland?"

I spin toward him, nearly knocking him over. "What about the children? Who's watching them? How—"

James rests his hand on my arm in an attempt to calm me down. "There has always been someone willing to take the role." He pauses for a moment and then adds, "And she's doing a great job so far."

I stare up at James, unable to comprehend all of this. He just blinks back.

"He did ask that your memory of him not be erased," he tells me.

"What?" My voice is barely a whisper.

"He asked me to let you keep your memories when you returned. He wanted you to have the freedom to remember. He hoped you would not forget."

"I didn't forget," I say, my eyes returning to Meyer.

"No. I can see that." James shifts his feet impatiently. "So may I begin the introduction then?"

"Yes. Sure." I'm not really listening, I'm too busy trying to wrap my head around all of this. Meyer left Neverland. And he doesn't remember me.

James takes a step forward but when he notices I'm not following he turns back.

"I figured he never wanted to see me again. I've believed all this time that he wanted nothing to do with me."

"Well, I'm sure that's not true," James says with an impatient sigh.

"What? Why?"

"He's here, isn't he?"

I continue to stare over at Meyer, still not quite believing. Yes. He is here.

"I imagine you had a lot to do with his decision to leave Neverland," James tells me. "Can't imagine what else it could have been."

Was it really me? I flash back to that last morning in Neverland and the word, "everything." That word has haunted me these last few months. Still does.

"So?" James gestures to the path. "Are we doing this or what? Perhaps you'd rather not. It is your choice, Livy."

"Yes," I say. "We are definitely doing this."

Meyer is still watching as we make our way across the lawn toward him. He puts his sketchbook down, making sure to close the book, and then he gets to his feet.

"This is Livy, one of my previous students," James says to Meyer. I smile up at him, still a bit shaky. "This is Meyer," James continues. "He attends my drawing class."

"You're a student?" I ask, reaching out to shake Meyer's hand. When he touches me I feel a surge of energy, a warmth stronger than my memories. At least that hasn't changed. I can't take my eyes off of him.

"Yes," he says, his voice so familiar. "At UDUB."

"Oh." I smile. "So you're in college."

"Yes." Meyer smiles back.

I realize I've been staring at him quite blatantly and I quickly look away. "So you draw then?"

"Yes."

"Like I said," James says, looking at me rather pointedly, "he's in my drawing class."

"Right." What is wrong with me? Meyer must think I'm a complete idiot! And this is going to be his first impression of me? Wonderful.

"Well, it's nice to meet you, Meyer," I say, doing my best to sound relaxed.

"It's nice to meet you too, Livy." There's a gleam in his eyes and I take that as a good sign. Perhaps he's figured out I'm not completely hopeless, just entertaining.

We stand there a bit longer, just staring at each other— and grinning — until James finally says, "Alright then. We should be off." He nods at Meyer and tells him how he's looking forward to seeing more of his work in class, and then he takes my arm and leads me away.

"See you later," I call back over my shoulder, not entirely committed to leaving, but nonetheless being dragged away.

Meyer lifts a hand in a wave. He is still watching as we leave.

"I can't believe it," I mutter to myself. "How long has he been here? When did he start school?" I turn and look up at James. "You teach art now?"

"He's been here about a month or so." He lifts an eyebrow, studying me closely. "He's quite partial to this park. Comes here every day to sketch. Even the rainy days." He points at the gazebo near the children's playground. "He sits in there when it gets too rainy. Just in case you're curious."

"So he's been here over a month and you're just telling me now?" I slap James across the shoulder and he stares down at my hand, obviously displeased.

"There were other things on my mind, you know. I'm actually quite busy."

"Right." I look away sheepishly. I guess following my life isn't the only thing he has going on.

"And you had some things you needed to work out as well," he adds, bumping my shoulder the way Sheila always does. He stops for a minute, turning so that we're face to face. "I must say, I'm rather pleased with how this has all worked out." He turns back to the path, his hands in his pockets. "Rather pleased indeed."

The next day is Saturday. I wake up long before anyone else is awake in my house, long before I should be up. But I can't help it. I have plans. I eat breakfast and clean the kitchen, even though it doesn't need it. I don't know what time Meyer usually gets to the park, but on a beautiful Saturday like today I'm hoping it will be on the early side. My plan is to arrive around lunchtime; I've even packed a light lunch. And I'll wait all day if I have to. I can't wait to see him again.

I hold my breath as I near the park and then let it out in one loud poof of air. He's back in his same spot, sitting by the tree. My steps are unhurried as I approach him. The nervousness I feel could fuel my mom's car for a month. It took me all night to come up with this plan, but now that I'm here I'm second-guessing it.

I have it in my head that he'll notice me before I make it over to him. I'm hoping he'll smile and ask me to sit down. But the closer I get the less likely my fantasy will come true. He's concentrating so completely on his drawing he doesn't even notice me. I stand there for a minute, studying his face. His hair looks a bit longer than it was in Neverland. It hangs over his right eye, hiding his brilliant green eyes from me completely. He reaches up and brushes his hair back, and for the first time I get a good look at his drawing. The girl on the sketchbook is so meticulously drawn and detailed she almost looks real. Like a black-and-white photograph. Her eyes are wide and expressive, her smile a perfect depiction of happiness. I stare at her not quite believing what I'm seeing. The girl he sketches looks just like me. Meyer has drawn me. Even down to the dusting of freckles along the bridge of my nose.

"I've been working on this for a while," he says, making me jump. "A few weeks now actually." He glances up, his eyes sparkling. "I didn't know her name until yesterday."

"Livy," I say stupidly. "My name is Livy."

"I know," he says, smiling. "I remember."

"So you've been sketching me? Even before we met?"

"Strange, right?" Meyer says.

"Yes." Strange.

"It gets stranger. This isn't my only one. I have more at home." He glances back down at the sketch, as do I, both of us staring at the girl who is so familiar. "Would you like to see them one day?"

"Yes," I answer immediately. "I'd love that."

I stare at him a minute longer until his smile widens and I realize I'm doing it again, staring at him like a fool.

"I didn't think I'd see you today, Livy," he says, looking at me expectantly.

"I...um... I thought..." I slide my hands into my front pockets. "Since it's such a nice day out." I quit my rambling and start again. "Do you swim?"

"Do I swim?"

"Um...yeah? There's this place where a lot of kids go. The warm springs, so the water is warm. I thought you might like it."

"And this place... is it near here?"

"Yes. It's just a short drive, actually." I point back to where my car is parked near the sidewalk. "I can drive us. If you want?"

Meyer smiles up at me, but doesn't make any motion to leave. What am I thinking? He doesn't remember me. To him I'm some strange girl he met yesterday! Why would he want to go somewhere with me?

"I mean, you don't have to. I just thought—"

"Because it's so nice out and all... Yes. You said."

"Right." I look down at the ground, anywhere but into his laughing eyes.

He closes his book with a snap and I jump again.

"Alright then. Let's do it." He climbs to his feet and I back up a few steps, giving him space. But he just moves closer. "I don't have a swimming suit, though? Do you?"

"No, but you kind of don't need one, you know? Nobody really swims, they just jump."

Meyer looks at me like he doesn't get it, so I continue: "You see, there's this big rock you jump off, into the water, and then when you're done there's a place where you can get warm and dry off." I'm talking with my hands now, not really making much sense. But I can't stop myself.

"Oh, I see." His eyes are narrowed while he contemplates what I've just told him. "Have you jumped from this rock before?"

"No. I usually just watch." I shake my head. "Never tried it myself."

"And this is something you want to do?"

"Well, I thought it might be fun... that you might think it might be fun."

"To jump off a big rock?" he asks, studying me closely.

"Um...yeah?" Crap. Maybe I didn't think this all the way through. I figured this would be something Meyer would want to do. At least the Meyer I knew would, but who knows? Maybe this new version of Meyer doesn't live for adventure the way the old one did. Maybe now that he's not invincible he won't want to risk his life at every turn.

He's still studying me, trying to work something out. I can't tell whether or not he believes I really want to cliff dive so I flash him an encouraging smile and say, "Cliff diving, yay!"

"How about this," he says. "How about we go check out this rock and see what it's all about, and if we decide it's something we both want to do then we go from there. Does that sound good?" His eyes are sparkling, his mouth tipped up in a smile. At this moment I'm just so happy he wants to keep spending time with me I don't really care what we do.

"Alright. I like this new plan," I say, smiling back.

Meyer gathers his stuff and follows me to my car. The ride isn't long, but in that short amount of time I learn that he's living in Seattle, near UDUB. He doesn't know what he wants to major in yet, but he really enjoys art. Oh, and creative writing. He was living with his uncle (his parents both died a long time ago, and he doesn't really remember them much) and then a few months ago James showed up. He told him he was a close friend of his father's and invited him to check out Seattle and later convinced him to stay and go to school here. He has no plans to leave anytime soon. He wants to graduate school before he thinks of doing anything else. And he likes it here. He says it feels right.

I smile at this, thinking about how it feels right to me as well. And how I owe James a big thank-you hug the next time I see him, which hopefully won't be until I'm old and gray.

I like asking Meyer questions, mostly because he answers them. He even asks me things as well. He wants to know what my plans are after high school. He asks about my friends and my family. He seems strangely interested in the time I spend at the hospital, even asks if I'd mind him coming along one day.

I decide that new Meyer is amazing actually. Especially when he keeps glancing over at me and smiling.

And when we do get to the rock and find it's not that big of a rock and not that big of a drop, we both decide to do it. To jump. Meyer takes my hand and squeezes it tight and on the count of three we close our eyes and step off the rock together. The water is freezing

— who the hell told me it was a warm spring? But we don't care. We climb back up on the rock, and we do it again. And it doesn't feel like such a big risk. Not with Meyer.

It feels like living.

Acknowledgements

Without J. M. Barrie's imagination I never woul— e spent most of my life thinking about a boy who could fly. I also p— vould have been reminded, at the age of twenty, that magic does — when I stumbled upon his Peter Pan sculpture in Kensington Garden—

Thank you.

This story has traveled with me for a — and because of that there are many people to thank.

To the amazing Jessica Spotswo— ose insightful edits helped encourage and strengthen the stor— y heart.

Again a big THANK YOU t— nael Weaver who is always willing to make sure my words make sen— Your patience with me is immeasurable.

To the Binders who sh— love of all things YA — thank you for sharing your experience, — n and encouragement. And thanks for allowing me to be a par— ar secret world. =)

To Tracy Bangh— o reads and listens and never gives up.

To Emily Lieb— believing in me. Thanks for the check-ins. They mean more than— I ever say.

A giganti— NK YOU to my family. Thanks for talking about characters w— t in my imagination and believing, as much as I do, that they can f—

Th— u to my mom. I will always be grateful for your strength and your — anks for always being my biggest fan.

— eering section is much louder with you on board, Lynne and — venstein, and I can't thank you enough for that.

— o Michelle, thanks for traveling to Kensington Gardens with me and — ing while I stared in wonder at the one character that has stayed with me — e longest. We need more adventures like that one. =)

And the biggest thank you goes to my amazing husband, Jason. Even though we still fight about the ending, words can not express how much it means to me that you care enough to shake your head and storm off. =) Love you bunches and punches.

51317637R00220

Made in the USA
San Bernardino, CA
20 July 2017